Amazing. *Noble Imposter* is a book that was nearly impossible to put down. The characters are lovable and believable, the dialogue real, and the story original. I would recommend this to anyone looking for a really good book to read.

Kira Thomas, Age 13

Amanda L. Davis has done it again. I was pleasantly surprised by *Precisely Terminated* and couldn't wait to get my hands on this one. She has crafted a unique story that grabs your attention so you cannot turn the pages fast enough. *Noble Imposter* has definitely bumped its way to the top of my list of favorite books.

Tucker Clement, Age 14

Wonderful! I wasn't expecting to enjoy this book as much as I did, but *Noble Imposter* captured my full attention from the very beginning. The plot is excellently written and very captivating, and the characters and details are described beautifully. I didn't want to put it down! Amanda L. Davis has done a fantastic job so far with the Cantral Chronicles trilogy. This is one story I will never forget.

Nicole White, Age 17

Noble Imposter was even better than *Precisely Terminated*. The plot was brilliant, and it kept me guessing and turning pages through the entire book. The characters are realistic, and this book has a message of hope, something rare in dystopian novels. I can't wait for the third book!

Gabe, Age 14

Davis has done an expert job in crafting a sequel to go beyond the reader's expectations and to deliver on what she promised at the end of *Precisely Terminated*. *Noble Imposter* is an excellent work with a tension-filled plotline, an admirable and persuasive main character, and excellent writing to fluidly move the reader along in the story. Davis has well-earned her spot on my shelf with this work. Readers won't be disappointed.

Josiah DeGraaf, Age 15

Amazing! *Noble Imposter* grabs your attention from the very first page and pulls you right into the story, making you feel like you're actually there! Monica is the kind of character with whom you can relate, and the book is exciting enough to keep you eagerly turning the pages. Overall, I had only one problem with this book: I didn't want it to end!

Sarah Pennington, Age 14

Full of adventure and suspense, *Noble Imposter* will hold your attention until the very last page. Hold on tight, with Davis' clear writing, and realistic characters, you're in for a fantastic ride from the very first page. Amanda L. Davis is pure genius.

Janae Schiele, Age 18

BOOK TWO

THE **CENTRAL** CHRONICLES

NOBLE IMPOSTER

SLAVE TRANSPORT

NOBLE IMPOSTER
THE CANTRAL CHRONICLES® BOOK 2
Copyright © 2012 by Amanda L. Davis
Published by Living Ink Books, an imprint of
AMG Publishers, Inc.
6815 Shallowford Rd.
Chattanooga, Tennessee 37421

This is a work of fiction. Names, characters, places, and incidents either are the product of the author's imagination or are used fictitiously. Any resemblance to actual persons, either living or dead, events, or locales is entirely coincidental.

First Printing—June 2012

Print edition	ISBN 13: 978-0-89957-897-2
EPUB edition	ISBN 13: 978-1-61715-391-4
Mobi edition	ISBN 13: 978-1-61715-392-1
ePDF edition	ISBN 13: 978-1-61715-393-8

THE CANTRAL CHRONICLES® is a trademark of AMG Publishers

Cover layout and design by Daryle Beam at BrightBoy Design, Inc., Chattanooga, TN
Interior design and typesetting by Adept Content Solutions LLC, Urbana, IL
Edited by Susie Davis, Sharon Neal, and Rick Steele

Printed in the United States of America
17 16 15 14 13 12 –V– 6 5 4 3 2 1

The Cantral Chronicles series
by Amanda L. Davis:
Precisely Terminated
Noble Imposter

CHAPTER I

Simon sat in his desk chair as he peered at Monica over a handful of papers. "When you first meet a couple at a formal gathering, what do you do?"

Sitting in a straight-backed chair and facing Simon, Monica licked her lips. "Curtsy to the lady first, then to the gentleman. I wait for the host to introduce us and for the lady to speak to me before I say anything."

"Correct." His brow bending, Simon began shooting out questions with barely a pause in between. "What is your maternal grandmother's name?"

"Eunice."

"Your paternal great-grandfather?"

"Maxwell."

"Your great-uncle, father to your mother's sister?"

"Dante."

"What is your favorite fruit?"

"Blackberries."

"How many years have passed since Cantral outlawed personal communications using wireless technology?"

"One hundred and seven. That's when the messenger system began."

Simon scowled. "I didn't ask you about the messenger system."

"I know but—"

"No buts. Maintain etiquette. The Nobles think it's impertinent to answer questions that haven't been asked. Amelia knows this, so you need to know it."

Monica nodded. "Okay. Sorry."

He showed her one of the sheets of paper. "You have ten seconds to study this map."

She squinted at the diagram of rooms and hallways on the hand-drawn map. The labels were scrawled in Simon's usual scribbles.

Simon snatched the page back. "What room is next to the library?"

"A study room."

"Which directions would you go to get from the study to the main entrance?"

"Northwest from the study. Turn north into the hall until I get to the main hall. Turn east and keep going until I reach the main entrance."

"Correct." His scowl eased. "Amelia, what is the programming language you invented for your own use?"

"Um …" Monica searched her brain. The computer questions were always the hardest. Studying for them was so confusing. Nothing made much sense. "Anagram?"

Simon threw the papers on the floor, scattering them. "Too slow!"

"But Simon, I—"

"I said no buts!" He shot to his feet and kicked a page. "You can't be Amelia if you don't immediately know the answer to such a simple question! The computer questions would be the easiest for her to answer."

"Of course." Monica looked down at her wrist where a wrist-band should be. What time was it? She hadn't had a band since she lost her last one, and Simon had disposed of his and Alfred's bands as well.

"We're not done yet, if that's what you're wondering."

Monica jerked to attention. "I wasn't. I was wondering when you would give me the dictionary like you promised."

"So you say." Simon waved a bony finger at her. "You're going to regret not studying harder when someone asks your new identity about the inner workings of a computer or where to sit at a banquet." He rummaged in a desk drawer and withdrew a thin booklet. "But here it is."

She snatched the book from his hand. "Thank you!"

"I really shouldn't give it to you," he muttered. "You don't seem at all repentant for your lack of study."

"Thanks for being so understanding." Flipping through the pages of words in Old Cillineese, she smiled. "Once Amelia is pardoned by the Council, I'll be able to go where I want. And don't worry; we still have plenty of time before I have to take Amelia's place."

"No, we really don't." Simon sat at his desk and shuffled his papers before sliding them into a yellow folder. "I received news a few hours ago that Amelia has taken a turn for the worse. They're not sure she will live through the night."

The dictionary slipped from Monica's hands, but she caught it, keeping it from hitting the ground. "But I thought you said they predicted she would have at least another week!"

"Apparently they were wrong." Simon handed her the folder, staring at her over the top of his steel-rimmed glasses. "Would I lie to you?"

She took the folder, tucked the booklet inside, and met his gaze. "Probably."

"I take offense." Simon removed his glasses and started cleaning them with the hem of his wrinkled black shirt. "This role is extremely important. You can't just act like Amelia. You must *be* Amelia."

"Yes, I know." Monica placed the folder on the desk. He wasn't really angry. He never got angry with her anymore. Their brush with death two weeks ago had calmed him down more than he would ever admit.

"Now." Simon slid his glasses back into place. "Sit." He pointed at the armchair pulled close to the other side of the desk.

Sliding into the leather chair, she asked, "So that's what has you in this mood? The early identity takeover?" She put her hands on the desk, showing her scarred left palm and thinly bandaged right hand. "It won't be a problem. My hands are mostly healed now, and I can walk out in the open and everything."

"Not quite 'and everything.'" Simon shook his head. "Your knowledge of computer circuitry is completely lacking, and your tutors will be baffled at your newfound stupidity. It doesn't help that we can't find Amelia's computer or notes. It's probable they were taken with her to Cantral, but her nurse told me she can't find them anywhere. They might have been lost on the way. You will want to think of some excuses for the Council."

"Okay." Monica fingered the folder Simon had laid on the desk. "At least I have these study sheets you made for me, and Amelia won't be doing any computer work for a while, even after she is suddenly better."

"The only reason the Council of Eight cut that deal with Gerald is because of Amelia's knowledge. If you don't perform, they might nullify it, and then you would be in a real fix."

The library door swung open. Simon pushed back from the desk. "What took you so long?"

Monica twisted around in her chair. A short boy with a pointed nose, carrying three plates, walked around the desk to Simon's side. He handed one plate to the old librarian, gave another to Monica, and kept the third for himself.

"Thank you, Alfred." Monica placed the plate on the desk's edge.

"You're welcome." He sat on the floor nearby and began eating a brown mash, scooping up bites with his fingers.

Simon sniffed the goo on his plate. "What *is* this, Alfred? Garden mud?"

"Something called potatoes. They're really not bad."

"Well there's no time for it." Simon shoved his plate away. "We must get Monica on her way to Cantral before Amelia dies."

"She has to go now?" Alfred looked up from his food. "You said—"

"I've explained it once to Monica already; I won't explain it again." Simon reached into his shirt pocket and withdrew a brown paper package. He unfolded the top and sprinkled some white powder onto Monica's food. "Eat quickly. Alfred and I have a few last-minute things to do before you depart."

She pulled her plate away. "What did you put on it?"

"The Nobles add this spice to their food to keep slaves from eating it." Simon pulled her plate from her hands and dumped more of the powder onto her meal. "It creates terrible stomach cramps in someone who hasn't eaten it all his life."

Monica stared at her ruined dinner. "I know about the spice. Alyssa . . ." She touched the necklace that hung around her neck, half of a medallion, torn during her journey to the Cillineese computers. "Alyssa told me about it." She sat back in her seat. "You said we had to leave. If I have cramps, I can't travel very well."

"These will be the worst of the cramps. You can get over them while Alfred and I run an errand or two." Simon marched to the door. "We'll be back in a few minutes. Eat."

Alfred sighed and wiped his fingers on his black pants before jumping to his feet and following Simon out of the room.

Monica sighed and pulled her plate close. Taking her spoon in one hand, she grimaced. Eating such foreign food was difficult in the first place, but making herself swallow something she knew would put her in agony would be almost impossible. She regripped the spoon and brought a bite of potatoes to her lips. Simon was right; she had to get used to the spice, and it would be better if she didn't have to explain stomach ailments to a doctor. They would have enough questions already because of her scarred, bandaged hands. She downed the bite in one swallow. As the potatoes hit her stomach, the food turned sour, and her belly ached. She forced another bite before plunking her spoon down.

Her stomach in knots, she slid off her chair and held her hands close. Stabs of pain shot through her, as if the food she had eaten were trying to claw through her abdomen.

She rolled onto her back and squeezed her eyes shut. The spice worked more quickly than she thought it would. If only she could concentrate on something other than the cramps. Maybe her fellow slaves. After all, she was doing this for them. If she didn't get used to the Nobles' food, she could never fit in with Amelia's identity, and everything would be lost. Cillineese might be free for a while, but Cantral would overtake it once again. A few cramps were nothing compared to the freedom of millions. If Cantral fell, so would the Council of Eight's grasp on the rest of the world. There would be no more terminated cities.

Slowly, the invisible grip on her stomach loosened, allowing her to sit up. Her arms and legs shook, and sweat poured down her limbs. After wiping a stray strand of hair from her eyes, she crawled to her feet and crept to one of the leather chairs near the desk. Sinking into the cushions, she sighed. Her arms and legs still shook, but the quakes lessened with every passing minute. She curled up in the center of the chair and rested her head on the arm. Her breathing evened out, and she fell asleep.

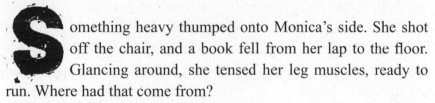

CHAPTER 2

Something heavy thumped onto Monica's side. She shot off the chair, and a book fell from her lap to the floor. Glancing around, she tensed her leg muscles, ready to run. Where had that come from?

"I thought so." Simon walked up and retrieved the book. "Still have those survival instincts embedded in you, in spite of your efforts to hide them."

Monica rubbed her eyes. "A normal person would just tap me on the shoulder or something."

"You definitely need to work on your Noble act, but there's no more time." Simon shuffled to his desk, set the book to the side, and sorted through an open file folder. "Now you must go to Cantral. Amelia has only hours left if Tresa's estimations are correct."

"Tresa?"

"Amelia's nurse."

"Good to know." Monica let the words sink in. Only hours left. This plan had been an exercise in theory, but now that the first step was about to begin, her legs trembled at the thought. "How do I get to Cantral?"

"The usual route. It's evening, so all the messengers will be heading back to their dorms. You shouldn't have any problem getting in."

"Great." Monica extended her bandaged hand. "My bandages are getting kind of old. Should I change them before I go?"

"Tresa can take care of that for you." Simon piled more papers into the folder and handed it to Monica. "Your notes on etiquette and decorum. Make sure you study these, but don't let anyone but Tresa see them. She's on our side, but I don't know the other Seen there."

Monica took the folder and tucked it under her arm. "And my mother's diary?"

Rolling his eyes, Simon dug into an open desk drawer and withdrew the thin book. "I was hoping you would forget about that. You won't have much time for translating while living Amelia's life. You'll be expected to mingle with the other Noble youth."

"I know. You've lectured me about that." She rattled off the sentence Simon had drilled into her a thousand times. "The north wing councilman, Aaron Markus, is the most important in the Eight, and his relatives are always sending their children to stay in Cantral for the educational opportunities." She placed the book into the folder with the papers and dictionary. "But if you wanted me to forget about the translation, you shouldn't have given me the dictionary."

"Don't be impertinent." Simon handed her a small metal cage containing a brown rat. "Don't forget Vinnie. With all those silly tricks Alfred taught him, he might prove useful. Besides, you'd better take him with you, unless you want me to eat him."

"You would never." She pressed Vinnie's cage to her chest. "Amelia's seventeen years old, so won't her chip be the old style?"

"Yes, it should be, but we can't be certain. Those years were a transition period." Simon headed out the door. "We might have trouble getting the tunnel access open, so we will leave now."

"Can I say good-bye to Alfred?" Monica tramped after Simon into the hallway leading to the main staircase. "I don't know when I'll see him again."

"No time. No time. He's sending messages around the city for me." Simon quickened his pace. "We don't know when Amelia will perish, and you need to be there when she does." He stopped beside an empty spot on the wall. The carved boards here appeared darker, as if something had stood in front of them for many years. "I think this is where Alfred said he found an access door."

Monica placed Vinnie on the floor and knelt. She pushed on the wall, and a knee-high door opened. "He was right, but you don't know the slave walls well. You could get terribly lost on the way back."

"I won't get lost. I've been down here before—directing guards." Simon's shoe nudged her bare foot. "Hurry up. We haven't got all afternoon. Someone wasted time by sleeping."

Shoving Vinnie's cage through first, Monica crawled into the opening and rose to her feet in the slave tunnel. The thought of going back to her old life raised a shiver, but taking over for Amelia would be even more frightening, more difficult.

Simon closed the panel behind her and took the lead, marching through the dark hall as if he had lived in it his entire life. A lone light illuminated the cramped corridor. It flickered, as if struggling to stay on.

"How do you know where to go?" Hugging Vinnie's cage close, Monica followed Simon while keeping the papers out of the rat's reach.

"I was born with an excellent sense of direction. Don't worry; I never get lost."

She stepped under the pool of light, and her next footfall brought her out of it again, allowing the hazy surroundings to envelop her in shadows. Another light flickered farther ahead. Eerie quiet filled the long corridor, broken only by their echoing footsteps.

No wall slaves whispered in the corridors, going about their duties, creeping around like mice, fearful of the computers that controlled them all. They lived outside the palace, taken in by the peasants of the vast city of Cillineese, adjusting to normal life. Though the city's borders kept them confined—they were free.

Simon turned right into a corridor, and they took a flight of stairs down to the dirt-floored messenger tunnels. She ran her hand along a wall, disturbing a spider web that stretched to the ceiling, one of many that hung over the once well-traveled passage. Now abandoned, no messengers would come pelting down the paths with courier tubes to be delivered.

"Don't dawdle," Simon called from farther down the corridor. The dirt ceilings and floors absorbed the sounds, muffling his words.

Monica quickened her pace and jogged to Simon's side. "I don't know how to get to Cantral's north wing."

"You'll find your way eventually. You can ask the wall slaves there for directions. I certainly don't know." Simon cleared a hanging spider web with a wave of his hand, sending the resident spider running. "You'll need to be more careful than ever before with your identity. The Nobles are questioning the circumstances surrounding your reported death, so suspicions that you might be alive are swirling. They think the Cillineese computers might have been fed a virus that shut them down, but the security teams can't get in to investigate, because the peasants have figured out how to keep the dome raised, and they won't lower it enough for anyone to get through. They're at a stalemate for now, but who knows how long that will last? Some diplomat from Eursia is there stirring up trouble as well."

Monica nodded. "That must make the Eight furious. Their own domes are working against them."

"Indeed it does."

They turned another corner and stopped in front of a sheet of metal barricading the tunnel. Raised lumps marred the surface, as if someone had been banging on the door from the other side. A light above the door flashed green, yellow, and red, cycling through the colors as if it couldn't make up its mind.

Simon pointed at a mud-caked, metal wheel embedded in the wall beside the door, shoulder high and as big around as a pumpkin. "This will be tricky. These emergency access wheels have been buried for some time. One of our guards discovered them just a few days ago. They don't turn very easily."

Monica placed Vinnie and the papers on the tunnel floor. "Is there one on the Cantral side?"

"How should I know?" Simon snapped. "I've never been there." He touched one of the raised marks on the metal. "The guard who discovered it should be here now. This new system will never work if people don't learn to cooperate better."

Monica gripped the cold metal wheel. It pressed against her palms, sending shivers of pain through her right hand. The injuries she had sustained two weeks ago had healed somewhat, but the slightest exertion could tear the wounds open again.

Simon's hands joined hers, holding the wheel next to her pale fingers. "On the count of three, put all your weight into it." Simon glanced at her. "Not that you have much, but it'll have to do."

Nodding, Monica readied herself for the pain that was sure to come. She braced her arms and gripped hard.

"One . . . two . . . three!"

Monica pulled down on the wheel with both hands. The door groaned. Dust fell from the cracks at the edges, and the metal started sliding upwards.

"I think we've got it!" Grunting, Simon inched his hands forward, pulling the wheel in a counter-clockwise motion.

She copied his actions, and the door continued its ascent. When the metal slab rose to a foot above the ground, Simon looped an arm around the wheel, holding it in place.

"Slide your things under now. We won't get it much higher."

Monica shoved Vinnie's cage and the papers through the opening with her foot. Her hands ached where they had gripped the wheel.

Simon forced the door up another inch. Sweat beaded on his wrinkled forehead. "Quick, get under there. Find a messenger to give you directions, but don't trust anyone except Tresa. Remember all your lessons!"

Monica nodded. "Thank you for everything, Simon." She ducked, slid beneath the door, and scrambled to her feet just in time to see the metal slide shut.

"Good luck." Simon's voice came through muffled. "Never lose faith."

Monica gathered Vinnie and the folder into her arms. She nodded though he couldn't see her. "I won't. Good-bye."

She squared her shoulders and glanced around. The lights overhead buzzed angrily, a reminder that she now walked on paths monitored by the Cantral computers. Not having a chip made her invisible to their gaze, but there were millions of others under their watchful eyes who weren't as fortunate.

Running a hand across the clay wall, she shook her head. No sign of any wheel. Maybe there was one only on the Cillineese side. But . . .

She knocked a knuckle against the hard surface. If there were one here, it would be buried. She scurried down the path. And it would stay that way, if she could help it. If a security team made it into Cillineese, it would spell disaster for everyone inside.

Her steady breathing seemed deafening in the musty, empty tunnel. She continued without slowing. There would be no messengers to ask where to go. They had no reason to come this way now that Cillineese was closed off from Cantral. Perhaps she would meet one in a side tunnel. They still needed to use part of this path to reach cities beyond Cillineese.

A tune came to mind, a song her adoptive mother sometimes sang to her late at night to calm her nightmares. But her mother would no longer sing—both her birth parents and adoptive parents had been swept away years ago by simple commands from the computers. Only recently had she learned anything about her birth mother, Rose, from the diary left to Simon. Before that, she didn't know a thing about the woman who gave her life. The diary held so many secrets locked away in a dead language, but Simon's dictionary would be the key.

Vinnie reached through his bars and tugged on the pages in the folder, pulling Monica from her grief-filled thoughts. She stopped and unlatched his cage and placed him on her shoulder. He grabbed a handful of her hair, his whiskers tickling her ear. Setting the cage under her arm, Monica started down the tunnel again.

Another passage intersected with hers, interrupting her path. She glanced left, then right. A messenger would come by soon. With Cillineese out of the trading route, New Kale was the most prominent city-state in Cantral, and the closest, and the Nobles were sure to be sending many messages.

Vinnie's nose nuzzled her neck. She patted his head and sighed. This could be a long wait. The rat nibbled at her fingers.

"Don't do that, or you'll go back into your cage." She drew her fingers away. "I didn't get to eat much either. That spice stuff is strong. I think it could kill you if you tried it."

Licking her lips, she looked both ways down the tunnel once more. The pain from the spice had gone, but every stab still lingered in her memory.

Pounding footsteps echoed down the tunnel. Monica tightened

her grip on the cage and papers, and Vinnie hid behind her neck, covering himself with her hair.

A tall, thin man raced up the side passage. A leather bag flopped at his hip, but he kept his gaze straight ahead.

Monica took a step forward. Did he see her? She sidled into the passage in the middle of the runner's path.

The man's eyes widened, and he skidded to a halt. "Who are you? What are you doing all the way out here?"

She pursed her lips. *Don't trust anyone except Tresa.* Simon's warning still rang clear, but she had to get directions. "I'm just passing through. I need to get to Cantral's north wing. Can you point me that way?"

Nodding, he glanced up and down the passage. "Yeah, go right here toward Cantral, and take the first left fork you come to. I know it's in that direction, but not exactly where. You'll have to ask someone else." He winced and started running again. "I'm late!"

"Thank you." Monica jogged down the tunnel. There was no telling how much longer Amelia would live. Was it possible to make it to Cantral before she died? If not, the plans would be ruined.

CHAPTER 3

The north wing of Cantral. Monica planted her feet beside the steel door blocking her entrance to the Cantral palace. After running for a few miles, she had finally made it.

She plucked Vinnie from her shoulder and laid him back inside his cage despite his squeaks of protest. "Sorry, but this could be a rough ride. I don't want you to get hurt." She latched his cage and tucked it under her arm.

After double-checking the papers, she crouched beside the door, ready to spring. If a messenger or a delivery boy came through, she would have just seconds to leap through the opening. If only she could have gone to the west wing instead. Any friends from her past would have gladly helped her.

The door slid into the ceiling, revealing a skinny, dirt-smudged little boy on the other side. He clutched a wheeled metal cart tightly with both hands.

Monica leaped forward, jumped onto the top of the cart, and slid off to the other side of the tunnel. The boy gaped at her, and the door banged shut.

"What do you think you're doing?" The boy released the cart and stepped toward her. "Now I'll have to open the door again, and I'll be in trouble."

"I didn't mean for you to get in trouble." Monica backed away from him, heading deeper into the tunnel toward the north wing. "But I'm in a hurry."

The boy narrowed his eyes. "You shouldn't be down here any-way. I should report you. Girls aren't allowed in the tunnels."

"I know." Monica tightened her grip on Vinnie's cage. Would he report her being out of bounds? In the east and west wings of Cantral, the wall slaves avoided the Nobles and Seen as much as possible, but what if the north wing was different?

The boy turned back to his cart. "I don't have time for this." He placed his palm on the door, and it slid open again. As soon as he pushed his cart to the other side, the door slammed shut, and a red light blinked on above the sheet of metal.

As Monica crept down the narrowing hall, the dirt floor smoothed out, and the walls became wooden planks instead of packed clay. After walking a hundred feet more, she came to a solid wood floor. It extended only a few yards before ending at a metal door.

She tiptoed up to the door. A red light shimmered above it, indi-cating she could go no farther. Buzzing lights overhead illuminated a narrow staircase to her right, revealing the smooth, foot-worn planks of the wall slaves' passages.

Tensing her muscles, she started to climb the beaten boards. Thousands of feet had tramped this area before, those of slaves carrying out the Nobles' wishes.

The walls seemed to creep up on her, closing in. She kept glancing at the boards, double-checking to make sure they didn't really move. Weeks ago a passage like this would have felt like home, safe and secure, but now it threatened to swallow her.

She reached a landing, and a second passage opened to her left.

Placing a hand on the wall, she peered down the poorly lit hallway. Chest-high panels—closed accesses to the Nobles' rooms—lined both walls, separated by a few feet of space. Could one of them be Amelia's? Would she have to check every one to find out? All of the wall slaves would be about their duties; maybe someone would provide directions.

After putting Vinnie's cage and the papers down, Monica crept past them and peered into the view port of the first panel on the left. The metal grate allowed a peek into the room on the other side—a parlor with lounge chairs and couches.

A woman knelt on the floor just inside, scrubbing the wood planks with a black bristle brush. Her drab gray dress clung to her stick-thin legs where water had sloshed from a bucket next to her.

Monica tapped on the wood. The woman jerked and glanced around the room. Her arms quivered as she placed her brush in the bucket and rose to her feet. She stared at an archway leading into another hall and backed toward the hidden exit.

Monica pushed on the panel, and it swung open easily. She crawled into the parlor and jumped to her feet.

The slave woman stared at her. "Who're you?"

"No one important." Monica glanced at the open panel. It was a good thing she had left Vinnie behind. He would raise more questions. "I need to get to Miss Amelia's room, the Noble who transferred from Cillineese recently. Do you know where it is?"

Nodding, the woman frowned. "Yes, but I already cleaned that room this morning. No one's scheduled there until tomorrow. Why do you need *me* to tell you?"

"Just tell me, and I'll be on my way." Monica waved a hand dismissively. "If I get in trouble, then it's on my head, not yours. I don't even know your chip number, so I can't tell them who told me even if they asked."

The woman nodded again. "All right, but don't say I didn't warn you. It's just two rooms down from here."

Monica breathed a sigh of relief. "Thank you." She ducked back through the panel. After fetching Vinnie and the papers, she rushed past the parlor farther down the tunnel. She crept by one more room before stopping at a view port. If the woman's instructions were correct, this would be Amelia's.

She placed Vinnie's cage on the wood floor with the papers just out of his reach. Switching the view port's slats open, she leaned close. A four-poster bed dominated one side of the room—the usual furnishings in a Noble's suite, but the hangings and lavish decorations were missing.

White paint gleamed on the walls, and in addition to the bed, a chair, dresser, nightstand, and cot stood in the room, their dark woods making a stark contrast with the white walls.

Monica pressed her face against the slats, but if a person occupied the giant bed, he or she was out of sight. She shoved the access panel inward and crawled through the opening.

"What are you doing?" A woman's sharp voice cut through the stillness.

Monica lurched back toward the wall. "Nothing!"

A tall, thin woman stormed to Monica's side and yanked her from the opening. "Who are you?"

"No one important." Monica tried to pull away, but the woman's bony fingers dug into her forearm, pressing against her old wounds.

"Amelia cannot be disturbed! Wall slaves are scheduled here only once a day. One has already been here." The woman released Monica's arm. She glared, her gray eyes flashing menacingly. "You're not from around here. I know the wall slaves who work this area, and you are not one of them."

"I know Amelia's not doing well." Monica watched the woman carefully. This had to be Amelia's nurse, Tresa, the one who spoke to Simon, so she could be trusted, couldn't she? "Does the name Simon mean anything to you?"

Tresa's eyes narrowed, and she gave a short, quick nod. "I know who you are now." She rushed to the door and flipped a metal latch, locking it. "I'm sorry for being so abrupt."

"It's all right." Monica sighed. Finally, someone she could trust and talk to. "Simon said Amelia isn't doing well."

"No." Tresa crossed to the large bed. "In fact, she's dead."

Monica froze. "Dead?"

"She stopped breathing a few moments ago." Tresa pulled a packet of wrapped linen from her dress pocket. "I went to get the surgical tools for . . ."

"Right." Monica nodded. A pang of grief tugged at her heart. This was her cousin, a girl who barely had a chance at life, a sick child who was stuck in the middle of a political battle, and now she was dead. Was there anything after that for her?

Monica's thoughts drifted to her mother's journal. The pages spoke of holy words and of faith, but did Amelia know them any better than Monica did? With a father like Master Gerald, how could she?

"Are you all right?" Tresa placed a hand on Monica's shoulder. "We need to get that chip out now."

Monica stared at her. "But it's supposed to be an older chip—"

"Supposed to be, yes, but it might be a newer one. We can't risk it dying." Tresa slid a hand behind Amelia's neck. "We have to work quickly."

CHAPTER 4

A beep sounded from a thin, gold wristband on Amelia's lifeless wrist.

Monica flinched and looked at Tresa. "What's that for?"

"I'm not sure." Tresa slipped the wristband over Amelia's curled fingers and held the small blue LED screen close. Her face turned white, and she handed Monica the wristband. "The doctor is coming to check on her."

Monica stared at the tiny black words marching across the screen as she buckled the band in place. *Doctor Checkup in One and a Half Hours.*

Tresa pulled the sheet off the bed, exposing Amelia's bare feet. "There's little time to waste." She rolled the dead girl onto her stomach with one quick shove. "I need your help, and we'll have to work quickly."

Swallowing, Monica nodded. Tresa expected her to help with the chip extraction? She had never performed one before and had seen it done only once, and that was enough to last a lifetime.

Tresa snatched up her packet from the nightstand. She unfolded the linen wrapping on Amelia's back, revealing two surgical knives, a pair of scissors, and an unfamiliar instrument.

"What do you want me to do?" Monica grimaced as the words escaped her lips. Could she bring herself to cut into her dead cousin's neck? Was the plan worth all of this? She sighed. Of course it was. There were thousands—millions—depending on her.

"Just help me find the chip as quickly as possible." Tresa selected a knife and sliced into the pale skin at Amelia's hairline.

The tissue peeled easily away beneath the blade, revealing muscles and bone. Blood oozed between Tresa's fingers and trickled to the sheet below. Her mouth tightened into a straight line as she lengthened the cut into the dead girl's hair.

Monica's stomach churned. It wasn't as if she hadn't seen blood before, but this was different. She had known this girl. She was part of her family.

"I think I see where they drilled into the bone." Tresa pointed with a bloody finger to a spot in the exposed skull. The bone had grown in a circle of ripples, about half the size of a fingertip, a scar from the surgery Amelia had at age five like every other Noble child at the time. Tresa grabbed another instrument and sawed at the spot. More blood flowed beneath her fingers.

Gulping, Monica nodded. "Yes. I see it."

Tresa nodded at the table by the bed. "Get the spare knife and cut away more of the skin around the scar so I have more room to work."

Monica took the knife from the nightstand and did as Tresa instructed. As more sticky, warm blood coated her hands and knife, her mouth dried out.

"I think I got it." Tresa reached into the small hole she had dug in Amelia's skull and withdrew a fingernail-sized piece of metal. She placed her bloody knife on the table and handed the chip to Monica. "We still have a lot of work to do. Don't freeze up on me now."

"I'll try not to." Monica wiped the chip off on the hem of her dress. The shiny gray piece of metal felt so light and insignificant in her palm. This little bit of metal with all the information stored in it could give her access to so many things that could help the slaves' council.

Tresa handed her a glass vial tied at the end of a piece of string. "You can use this to secure it around your neck. I heard that's how you usually carry a chip."

"Right." Monica popped the chip into the vial and screwed its metal top into place. "What do we do with Amelia?" She tied the string around her neck, allowing the chip to rest beside her half-circle medallion.

"You'll take her to a tunnel and bury her—unless you think taking the body to the furnaces is a better idea. It will be difficult to navigate her through the air ducts, though I hear you've had some experience with the ducts." Tresa wrapped the bedsheets around Amelia, covering the girl completely, though blood seeped through the white fabric, creating a circular stain over her hidden neck.

"I don't want to go through the ducts ever again." Monica glanced at a grate in the wall near the bed. The metal vent hid the opening to the ducts that twisted all through the palace walls, eventually ending in the furnace below. Just thinking about them raised memories of the dark journey weeks ago—the journey that had stolen part of her finger but saved many lives.

Tresa finished bundling all the bedclothes around Amelia's body and knotted them at the top. "If you can carry her into the messenger tunnels, you won't have to use the ducts, but it would be best if you do it unseen. The wall slaves don't spread rumors outside their walls very often, but whispers have been floating out recently. The Nobles are on edge. Delegates are here from other sections of the world discussing what you did in Cillineese."

Monica nodded. "I can take her tonight between shifts, but I don't know any of the messengers here, so it will be difficult to get into the tunnels." She looked at her dirty, bare feet. Simon had said not to trust anyone. The messengers could have contact with the Nobles if they chose to. "How do I know who I can talk to?"

"It will be difficult." Tresa wiped her hands on the sheets, leaving bloody prints behind. "Since neither of us knows any messengers well, perhaps you could bury her yourself or take her to someone you do know."

"That would mean dragging her all the way to the east wing!" Monica bit her bottom lip. She would have to bury Amelia somewhere deep in the messenger tunnels where no one would find her.

Tresa began cleaning the knives. "I am only here to help you. It's up to you to make the decisions. I know nothing about getting around the wall slaves' tunnels. But if you don't dispose of her body soon, the doctor will find out about you and kill us both."

Shivers ran down Monica's spine. She checked the wristband. *Doctor's Arrival – 1 hour 10 minutes.* The body had to be disposed of now, not later, and she would have to bury it herself.

Tresa tucked the packet of knives into her pocket and crossed her arms over her chest. "Well?"

"I'll take her to the tunnels now and bury her." Monica pulled the chip from around her neck and held it tightly in her hand. "I haven't had one of these in a while. I'm used to the newer chips. The chip will be fine staying here by itself, right?"

Tresa nodded and held out her hand. "Only if Simon's suppositions are correct. He thinks this type of chip can't tell if its owner is dead, but we don't want to take any chances. That's why we had to do the surgery right away. We already talked about this."

"Sorry. I was flustered." Monica crept to the wall slaves' access, passing Tresa's outstretched hand. "I'll leave it with my friend, just in case Simon's wrong."

Tresa stiffened. "Someone else is here? Why didn't you tell me?"

"I didn't think you would care." Monica opened the access

panel and pulled Vinnie's cage from the passage. "He's not much trouble, and he helps me get places I need to go."

"You have a rat?" Tresa's voice sounded strained. "Do all wall slaves have pets?"

"He's not really a pet." Monica lifted Vinnie and tied the string around his neck. He had worn chips like this before, keeping them alive in her place.

Patting his head, she put him back in the cage. "You know the drill." She retrieved the papers she had left in the passage and carried them and the cage to the bedside. After shoving both beneath the bed, she stood. "And no, the other wall slaves don't keep pets around. It's not worth it to feed them."

"I agree with them." Tresa shuddered. "Vile creatures. Simon has a fondness for them. I never understood it."

Monica nodded and looked at Amelia's shrouded body. Now that the chip had been removed, there was nothing to stop her from continuing with the grisly task ahead. She gritted her teeth and hooked her arms under the corpse. As she pulled the bundle off the bed, it bent in the middle.

Tresa slid her arms under the burden from the other side. "I'll help you get her into the walls."

After they lowered Amelia's body to the floor, Monica pushed on the hidden panel. It sprang open, revealing a dark passage. She scooted inside, pulling the body after her. Tresa shoved the dead girl the rest of the way into the opening, leaving a dark smear on the wood floor.

Monica gripped a handful of the sheet and tugged Amelia farther into the wall.

"Hurry. You need to be back in time to prepare to see the doctor." Tresa closed the panel.

The passageway dimmed, and only the small overhead lights illuminated the way to the main stairs. She adjusted her hold on Amelia's body and tugged it through the hall. As she guided it down the stairs, the dead weight seemed to grow heavier. Her arms ached and quivered. The body probably weighed about as much as she did. Amelia's sickness had left her almost as thin as Monica herself.

As Monica eased Amelia down the stairs, the girl's covered feet banged on the steps, making thumping noises. Monica grimaced. There was no way she could stop the noise without help, and who would help her? The north wing wall slaves knew nothing about her, and the Council of Eight would search the walls at a moment's notice if the chip-less girl rumors started again. Even after assuming Amelia's identity, she wouldn't be safe from probing questions and computer scans.

She trekked down the stairs at a steady pace, the beat drummed out by Amelia's heels on the floorboards. In minutes Monica reached the steel door separating her from the messenger tunnels. The wood floor beneath her feet raised fresh thoughts about the dirt and digging that waited on the other side.

Shoving Amelia's body against the wall, she sighed. How was she going to get through? She would have to get help from a delivery boy with a cart, but would he let her through without question?

Whispers floated down the stairs along with the sound of soft footsteps. Monica tensed. Someone could come this way at any moment.

Seconds later, a towheaded boy trotted down the steps, half a meal bar clutched in one hand. He took a bite from it as he jumped off the last stair. His eyes met Monica's, and he stopped dead in his tracks. "Who are you?"

"No one important." Monica shrugged. Maybe if she acted nonchalant about the situation the boy wouldn't question her too much. But the wall slaves were so jumpy, it was hard to tell what they would do. "I need to get into the messenger tunnels. Can you help me?"

"Why should I help you?" The boy's gaze traveled to Amelia's wrapped body. "You should be able to get in by yourself."

Monica folded her arms over her chest and firmed her voice. "Because I won't let you pass if you don't, and then you'll be late."

The boy glanced over his shoulder. "Okay. Fine."

"Thank you." Her muscles relaxed, and she sighed heavily.

"Just 'cause you're bigger than me. I wouldn't help you otherwise." He glared at her. "Get your stuff and let's go."

Monica grabbed hold of the sheet and rolled the bundle into her arms. She would have to move quickly through the doorway, and dragging Amelia through probably wouldn't work.

The boy inched past her and palmed the door. It slid into the ceiling, and he stepped into the revealed passage. Monica staggered after him, Amelia's weight heavy in her arms. A breeze whipped by her legs, and the edge of the door brushed her heels as it slammed shut.

She jerked away. Amelia's body tumbled to the floor, and the dead girl's arm came free from the wrappings.

The boy gaped at the pale limb protruding from the sheet. "Is . . . is that a body?" He pointed at the lifeless form.

Monica tucked the cold arm back into the sheets, her heart racing. "It's none of your concern."

He touched his wristband. "If it gets me in trouble it is. Only the furnace men handle bodies."

"It won't get you in trouble if you leave and don't ever mention it to anybody," Monica hissed. Why wouldn't he just go? Wall slaves were usually more timid. If someone had confronted her like this a few weeks ago, she would have darted off in an instant.

He narrowed his eyes, glanced over his shoulder again, then looked back at her. "All right, but you'll have to find a way back in yourself." He ran farther into the tunnel and turned down one of the side passages.

Monica scooped the body back into her arms and tromped after him. He was right. She would have to find another way in. Maybe someone else would let her through, but convincing him to do so might be more difficult. A small boy could be bullied, but a messenger wouldn't be so easily cowed. Even though the boy had been compliant, he might still report her.

She squared her aching shoulders. But who said this would be easy? The hardest part was yet to come. The Nobles had to be fooled, and the computers had to be broken, tasks that would require much more pain and suffering than the little turmoil she bore now. But it was for the good of everyone. The boy would thank her in the end.

CHAPTER 5

Monica laid Amelia's body on a section of packed clay deep in the maze of messenger tunnels. An overhead light buzzed noisily. Damp, motionless air pressed around her, smelling of must and mold. She glanced around the empty tunnel. There had to be something to help her penetrate this hard floor. The smooth dirt walls were interrupted only by support beams every five feet or so, and more beams held up the clay in the ceiling. Glowing white lights protected by glass globes shone from every beam.

She stood on tiptoes and tried to reach a light's glass covering, but her fingers didn't even come close to touching it. Sighing, she surveyed the tunnel again. Digging a hole big enough to hold a body using just her bare hands would take too long. The light fixture was a good option, but how could she reach it?

Gripping a wall support beam with one hand, she planted a foot on the wall, two feet above the ground. She braced her weight on her foot, lifting herself. Pain riddled the fingers clamped around the wood post, but she held on, stretching her other hand toward the light.

Her bandaged fingers brushed the hot surface of the glass, but the cloths protected her skin. Her other hand began slipping from the support beam. Splinters dug into her fingertips.

She reached for the fixture again and clamped down on the globe. With a quick tug, two screws popped loose, and she brought the glass into her hand and hugged it to her chest. Releasing the beam, she jumped to the ground.

The heat from the glass radiated through the bandage, forcing her to set the globe on the ground. She wiggled her fingers, flexing the sore muscles beneath the cloths. Maybe Tresa would help her dress it with fresh cloths. Digging would certainly get the wrappings even dirtier, but that didn't matter right now. She had to get the body buried before a messenger came by and started asking questions.

Grabbing hold of the light fixture again, she brushed the tunnel floor with a foot. Maybe there would be a spot where the dirt wouldn't be so tightly packed. Her foot stirred some loose dirt right next to the wall, where few messengers had trodden.

She knelt at the spot and dug the now-cool glass into the ground, using the edge of the globe to penetrate the loose clay.

Every scoop with her makeshift-trowel deepened the hole in the tunnel floor. It seemed like she had been digging for half an hour, but the grave was still too shallow, not even four inches deep. Monica gritted her teeth and threw herself into her work. The dirt flew from the globe onto the knee-high pile. Her hands ached where they clutched the smooth glass, and her severed finger throbbed with every swing of the globe.

When the hole seemed deep enough, she plunked the light fixture on the ground and stepped into the hole. The sides came up to her calves, and she touched the edges of the hole. Just barely wide enough for the body.

Nodding to herself, she clambered out of the trench. It would have to do—a poor grave for the daughter of the ruler of Cillineese, but there was nothing else to grace the tomb. No marker would indicate the girl's resting place. Soon her burial site would be forgotten, lost in the winding maze of tunnels.

Monica knelt beside Amelia and rolled her body into the grave. The dead girl's wrapped corpse thumped softly on the hole's dirt floor. Monica wiped a stray piece of hair from her own face, pushing it behind one ear.

"I'm sorry it had to be this way." She scooped up a handful of dirt and sprinkled it onto Amelia's burial wrappings, covering some of the bloodstains. "I wish we could have known each other better. We could have been friends if our fathers had chosen differently."

She pushed more dirt into the hole. Sometimes the yearning for a better life was overpowering, but she had been chosen to suffer for others. She would try to make her parents proud, though they could no longer be with her. Would they approve of all this deception?

Almost all the dirt fit back into the hole, but a small mound remained behind, even after she tamped the grave site down with her feet. She kicked at the dirt, scattering it farther into the tunnel. Maybe that would help disguise the disturbed area. Fortunately, no messenger would have time to stop and investigate, even if he did notice the uneven floor.

She dusted the dirt-caked light fixture with the hem of her dress. There was no way she could return it to its place. Getting it down had been hard enough. She smoothed out a few more rough spots in the floor with the ball of her foot.

She tucked the globe under her arm and walked in the direction she had come. After traveling a few yards from the burial site, she threw the globe to the ground, and it shattered into a dozen pieces. Anyone who saw the fixture would probably guess it had fallen and a messenger had kicked it in his hurry.

After taking a few more steps away, she looked at the site from an angle. The grave was almost invisible. Nodding to herself, she crossed her arms over her chest and continued walking down the tunnel toward Cantral. Her job here was done. Now she had to return to the north wing and take Amelia's place in the world, an imposter among Nobles.

Her wristband beeped and vibrated, a sharp reminder of Tresa's warning to hurry back. The small screen lit up, and digital words floated across the surface. *Doctor will arrive in ten minutes.* The message repeated twice before the screen dimmed and turned off once more.

She willed herself into a fast jog, forcing each foot in front of the other. Her legs felt stiff and sore from crouching in a hole for so long, and her arms complained of the same aches. As she ran, all the turns she had taken to reach the desolate tunnel came to mind. The memory drills Simon had required were coming in handy now, though when he had said she would need to memorize things after seeing or hearing them only once, he probably didn't have tunnel mazes in mind.

Thoughts of Amelia returned, but she pushed them away. There wasn't time to mourn now. There was too much at stake. If the doctor arrived before she did, all their plans would be discovered.

Monica picked up her pace, tearing through the tunnels at top speed. She couldn't let Tresa die. There had been enough deaths in Cillineese. But even if she reached Amelia's room before the doctor did, she still had to get cleaned up and have her bandages changed.

In moments Monica reached the steel door barring the way to the north wing. Pounding to a halt, she gasped for breath. She bent over and rested her hands on her knees. Blackness swam at the corners of her vision, but it lessened with every breath. The weeks of resting and reading in Cillineese had decreased her stamina, but years of running stairs and racing through the wall passages kept her strong, despite the break.

Placing a palm against the door, she sighed. Now the waiting.

She should be used to it but time pressed her patience. What if no one came to open the door? She couldn't force it like she and Simon had done in Cillineese; the computer controls and emergency controls on the inside kept it tightly closed. Only because the Cillineese computers were shut down were they able to use the wheel to force up the other door.

She checked her wristband. *4:00 p.m.* Maybe a delivery boy would be by soon with the supplies for tomorrow's meal bars. She would have to wait.

Just as she slid to the floor, the door creaked open. She stopped halfway down, planting a palm on the ground to keep herself from falling. As stabbing pains shot through her hand, she jumped to her feet.

A scrawny boy stood at the other side of the door. He marched through without a sideways glance, as if he didn't even see her.

She dove and rolled beneath the closing metal. The metal slammed on her skirt hem, pinning her to the floor. Her wristband vibrated. She crawled to her knees, but her skirt wouldn't pull free. Leaning against the door, she tugged on the fabric. It stayed firmly in place despite her frantic pulls.

The wristband beeped again. She glanced at its illuminated face. *Doctor will arrive in five minutes.* Panic rose in her throat. What if she couldn't make it? What would Tresa say? Amelia was too ill to get out of bed, so she couldn't have wandered off somewhere.

She jerked at the fabric again, but her fingers slipped on the material. A few of the scabs on her right hand ripped open and drops of blood dotted her dirt-stained bandages. As she regripped the skirt, her heart thumped wildly in her chest. With a final tug, it tore free from the door's grip. Monica tumbled back, then leaped to her feet. Her head pounded from the adrenaline rush. She ran down the tunnel and up the stairs, retracing her path to Amelia's old room. After checking the view port, she darted in.

"What took you so long?" Tresa rushed to her side, a basin of soapy water hugged close to her chest. "Didn't you see the message? He'll be here at any moment!"

Monica nodded and shucked the bandages from her hand, revealing the raw wounds. "I'm sorry. My dress caught in the door, and I couldn't get free."

Tresa pushed Monica to a sitting position and scrubbed the dirt from her arms with a rough cloth. "You're a mess. I'll need to find a change of clothes for you, too."

As the sodden cloth ripped away Monica's scabs, revealing pink healing skin, pain lanced her arms. She whimpered. "I know. I'm sorry."

Tossing her the rag, Tresa stood. "Wash your face while I look for suitable clothing. Hurry up!"

Monica dipped the cloth in the warm suds and wiped it across her face. Brown water trickled into the metal basin. She washed her face once more before dropping the rag.

Tresa handed her a cotton nightgown. "Quickly. He could be here any second." She snatched the basin up. "We'll have to clean you more thoroughly later."

Monica unfastened the buttons on the back of her dress and pulled it over her head. After tossing the torn black garment to the floor, she picked up the white nightdress and slipped it on over her tight gray shorts and camisole. She scurried to the bed and climbed between the sheets.

As she settled into the feather mattress, shivers ran down her spine. Just over an hour ago Amelia rested here taking her last breaths before they dug the chip from her skull. Now the soft, freshly changed sheets caressed Monica's skin, a reminder of the Noble lifestyle she had to assume. Wall slaves never had luxuries like these, but life as a wall slave was over. She would either succeed, resulting in freedom for everyone, or the Nobles would expose her, resulting in one former wall slave's execution in the blink of an eye.

Tresa retrieved the discarded dress and stuffed it under Monica's bed near Vinnie's hidden cage. "That will have to do." She tucked the covers tightly around Monica's arms and gave them a final pat. "I noticed your wounds earlier. Try not to let the doctor see them. There will be too many questions."

Footsteps echoed in the outside corridor. The doorknob turned and creaked.

"He's coming." Tresa backed away from Monica's bed. "Remember, you're dying. Act like it."

CHAPTER 6

The door swung open, and a tall, thin young man wearing a white coat entered. He snapped the door closed behind him and marched up to the bed. Monica closed her eyes, but reopened them a slit, just enough to see.

Nodding at Tresa, he said, "How's the patient? Any better?"

Tresa's gaze stayed locked on the floor. "Yes sir. She's been doing much better. Speaking to me even."

"Really?" The man bent over Monica, blocking her view of Tresa. "The others didn't think she would recover. They laughed at my predictions. They think students don't know anything." He touched her forehead with a cold hand. "She looks healthier. Has she been eating?" He leaned back, his brow furrowing. "She looks . . . different."

"Yes sir, she has been eating." Tresa stood beside him now. "She looks the same to me, sir."

The man pressed a cold metal object on her brow. Something beeped low and long, then shut off. "No more fever, though she's still·

a bit flushed. I think she might have turned a corner. Amazing!" He shook his head, as if he didn't believe it. "My medication worked!"

Monica's heart raced, pulsing in her throat. She had to fight to keep from swallowing audibly. Wasn't he done yet? He should just leave.

"Really, sir?" Tresa asked.

He put a finger to his chin. "I'll have to include this case in my final report. It might be the boost I need to graduate." He smiled, barely showing straight, white teeth. "A case all the others had given up on, yet I held out. And see now—she's cured! And Aaron said that this was a foolish degree for someone in my position."

"Sir?" Tresa spoke up.

The man turned his back to Monica. "Yes, what is it?"

"You think it was your medicine?" Tresa's voice shook. "That took away the disease?"

"Yes, that's what I just said, you silly Seen." The man walked to the other side of the room, his hands now in his coat's roomy pockets. "Call me when she wakes up. I'd like to speak to her. Get her bathed and dressed if it doesn't fatigue her too much." He exited the room, closing the door with a soft click.

Tresa let out a long sigh. "Well, that's that."

Monica sat up and rubbed her forehead where the cold metal had made contact. What had he put on her?

"I agree with Master Aric that you definitely need to bathe. We'll take care of that and talk some more before calling him. We don't want him to think you woke up too quickly." Tresa pulled Monica's covers off.

She slid from the bed and checked underneath. Vinnie stared back at her, Amelia's chip still tied to him. Good. "He barely even noticed anything different about me. Amelia and I look alike, but we aren't . . . weren't identical."

"As a general rule, Nobles aren't very observant of people they think aren't as important as they are. Amelia was a prisoner of war, and Master Aric was distracted by your recovery." Tresa crossed the room in a few strides to a door on the opposite wall. "I'm sure when he comes back he'll want to do a more thorough exam."

"What kind of exam?" Monica tiptoed after Tresa. Where was she going, anyway? That door didn't lead to the hallway, did it?

"Just feeling for muscle tone, monitoring input and output, and taking some blood for tests. He had me draw her blood every few days. He didn't come to check in on her very often. He had me send reports to him." Tresa pushed open the door. "Here's your bathroom. I expect you know how to use the tub. I'm sure you've cleaned many of them."

"Taking blood?" Monica looked down at her hands. Drops of blood had seeped out of some of the raw spots, but most had healed enough to resist Tresa's scrubbing. "How does he do that?"

"He'll stick a needle in your arm and draw out blood." Tresa circled Monica and poked her in the back, pushing her toward the door. "Now hurry up. You can fill your own bath. You might be Amelia out among the Nobles now, but you're still a wall slave to me. You don't need to get a big head."

"That's fine with me. I'm used to taking care of myself." Monica stepped into the room and closed the door behind her. As her feet registered the cold tile beneath, shivers ran from her toes to her head.

The bright lights in the bathroom reflected off the shiny white tile, creating a stark contrast to the dimly lit bedroom. Blinking, Monica put a hand on the countertop and slid it along the glossy porcelain surface to a deep sink in the center of the counter.

She crossed the bathroom in four steps, and her knees touched the side of a shiny white tub, which rested on two pairs of gold-clawed feet.

After switching the water faucet on, she sat back on her heels. It seemed silly, filling up a tub for one person. A slave would never think of having a bath to herself. When she lived in the west wing, she had bathed with all the other female wall slaves in an underground, spring-fed pool. This was certainly a step up from that. What would Maisy think of her now? Would her childhood friend feel she was just like the other Nobles? Taking advantage of the wealth and ordering the wall slaves around? She could pretend to be Amelia for the rest of her life and never consider the wall slaves again.

Monica stuck a hand in the half-full tub and swirled it around. But she wouldn't do that. She was in this until the end. The slaves would be free if she had anything to do with it. She just had to convince the Council of Eight that Amelia was innocent of the destruction of the Cillineese computers so she could be free to find a way to the Cantral computers.

She stripped off her clothes and laid her medallion necklace and wristband on the bundle before stepping into the steaming hot water. The clear liquid almost scalded her skin, but it felt good after such a long time with no bath. When she was in Cillineese, it had been difficult to get enough water to drink, let alone bathe, with all the electricity in the palace struggling to stay on. Simon had made Alfred and her trek into the village to fetch their water. Sometimes they convinced him to let them fill their buckets in the bathing pool beneath the palace, but he almost always told them that the path was too dangerous with the residual gas lurking in the lower passages.

The dirt on her limbs washed away in minutes, and she scrubbed her hair with scented shampoo from a bottle beside the tub. After rinsing out all the suds, she settled low in the luxurious water and took in the lovely scent. Lingering here for a while wouldn't hurt anyone, would it?

A knock on the door jolted her out of her reverie. She clambered out of the tub and grabbed one of the fluffy towels off a rod over a toilet. "Yes?"

"Are you almost done?" Tresa's voice came through the thick

door, annoyed and tense. "I need to send a report to Master Aric soon, and I still have to bandage your arm. Are you having trouble with the tub?"

"I'm done. Just a minute." Monica quickly toweled off. "I didn't have any trouble." She slipped Amelia's nightdress back on.

After using the toilet, she snatched up her necklace and wristband and crept from the steamy bathroom. The chilly air from the bedroom swept over her, sending shivers from the roots of her wet hair down to her bare toes.

Tresa waited at the door, her arms crossed over her chest. "Well, you certainly look more presentable now. I suppose I'll have to do something about your hair. It looks like your rat made a nest in it." Tresa grabbed Monica's wrist and punched a few buttons. "Master Aric should return soon, now that I told him you're awake."

Monica pulled her hand away and touched her shoulder-length hair. "I won't have to cut my hair, will I?"

"No." Tresa rummaged through the top drawer of the dresser. "I can braid it for you. Since you've been ill, no one will expect much from you. Your family is still in shame, anyway. You won't want to draw attention to yourself." She brought a bundle of white bandages, a pair of scissors, and white tape to the bed. "Come here so I can take care of your arms. I don't know how we're going to explain that finger to Master Aric. It's not likely he won't notice."

Monica scurried to Tresa's side and held out her arms. "I'm sorry. Trust me, I'm not happy about it, either. It doesn't hurt much anymore, but it makes holding a pencil difficult. I had to keep taking breaks from my classes with Simon. The bandages didn't help any, either."

"I'm sure." Tresa cut the bandages into thin strips and began expertly wrapping the gauzy material around Monica's right fingers, down her wrist, and to her elbow. "Maybe we could say you hurt yourself in the bathroom. You could have fallen since you're unsteady on your feet after being in bed so long."

"I don't think that would work. He'd want to know where the fingertip went. I'll just have to hope he doesn't notice, and if he does, I'll make something up as I go."

Tresa taped the bandage in place. "If you think you can. Fine." She turned Monica's left arm over and examined the scars on her palm. "I don't think this one needs a new wrapping. It would draw more attention to the wounds, and it's healed enough."

"Okay." Monica examined the strips covering her arm. They felt snug, but not constricting, and these were clean, unlike the last wrapping she had created from rags in Cillineese.

"Back into bed with you." Motioning toward the four-poster, Tresa guided Monica to the bed's side. "No telling how long it will take for Master Aric to arrive. It might be hours, but it could be minutes."

Monica crawled between the sheets once more. The cool fabric no longer felt inviting on her warm skin. What would Aric do in the coming examination? Who ever heard of drawing blood from someone on purpose? Her blood should stay inside her. When she had injured herself in Cillineese, it had taken three days to even be able to walk without swaying, and she still had dizzy spells once in a while. She pulled the cushy, floral comforter up close to her neck. "Does it hurt? I mean, when he takes blood?"

"I think it hurts, but I know others don't agree. I've never had it taken from my arm, only from my fingers." Tresa tucked the covers around Monica's legs once more. "Haven't you ever had your blood drawn before?"

Memories of past injuries sent tingling sensations up Monica's arms. "Not by a doctor, but I lost a lot when I got hurt."

Tresa unfolded a wooden seat that had been leaning against the wall and placed it beside the bed. Lowering herself into the creaky chair, she let out a long sigh. "But you're old enough to have the monthly blood tests. All the slave women get them." She held out her thin fingers. "Just a pricked finger once a month for various tests." She folded her hands on her lap. "How did you avoid them?"

Monica shrugged and laid her head back on the pillow. It felt so silly to rest here talking to this Seen woman. In a few minutes she would be interrogated by a probing Noble doctor who was probably stuck up and cared only about himself. What if the Council of Eight decided to have Amelia killed even after all this trouble? Could she get away in time?

"Then don't answer me." Tresa folded her hands in her lap. "I suspect now that you're a Noble you're going to start acting like one and threaten to punish me at any moment." She sighed. "This was supposed to be a dead-end job anyway. I was happy to have it instead of being demoted. Once Simon contacted me about you coming, I thought things would change."

"I'm sorry." Monica clenched a fistful of sheets in her unbandaged hand. "I don't really know how I avoided it. I guess I switched chips so often I never had a chip that was due to be tested. Sometimes I even had a man's chip."

"I suppose that makes sense." Tresa folded her arms across her chest and stared at the far wall. "I've heard about you switching chips. The rumors aren't rampant here in the north wing yet, but transfers are whispering about a chip-less slave and the fall of the Cillineese computers."

The wristband on Monica's left arm beeped loudly. She turned it and read the small blue screen. The words *Doctor Arriving Momentarily* flashed. Pushing her hand beneath the covers once more, she shivered. All the talk had been a welcome distraction, but now the dread of Aric's visit crept back into her heart. The real danger was about to begin.

CHAPTER 7

"How is the patient now, Tresa?" Aric strode into the room without bothering to knock.

Tresa leaped from her seat, and the chair banged to the floor. She hastily set it upright again. "Oh, Master Aric, she's all right, though nervous about having tests done."

Aric shut the door behind him. He held up a small black leather bag. "There's nothing to be afraid of, Amelia. It doesn't hurt."

Pushing on the mattress, Monica struggled to sit up. Her arms shook beneath her. Would this man realize now that she wasn't Amelia? That she was too healthy and looked different?

"Don't try to get up." Aric dropped his bag on the bed and pressed Monica's shoulders gently back to the mattress. "I don't want you exerting yourself. There will be plenty of time for physical therapy, once you're fully recovered."

Sighing, she looked away from his green-eyed stare. If she kept their gazes locked, he'd see her nervousness. Water from her still-wet hair seeped into the back of her nightdress, raising a shiver.

He opened his bag. "Are you cold? Your fever has broken, but you could have residual chills." He glared at Tresa. "You should have dried her hair. She needs to be kept warm, especially since they don't heat this part of the palace well."

"I'm sorry, sir." Tresa bowed her head.

Monica let out a long sigh and relaxed against the pillows. "I'm not cold. I feel much better than I did before. I don't think I need an exam."

Aric smiled. "Of course you need an exam. You might not realize it, but you just left death's doorstep. You were delirious for such a long time, I'm sure you don't recall my visits."

"I don't." Monica stared at the wall behind Aric, focusing on the grainy, stucco-textured surface. At least she wouldn't have to recall anything said in the days before Amelia died.

Aric dug into his bag and pulled out a long tube with a piece of cloth on one end and a rubber ball on the other. "That's to be expected. It's nothing to worry about." He fumbled with the piece of cloth at the end of the tube. "I need to put this on your arm."

She stiffened her arms under the sheets. Amelia probably knew what this was. "Oh. Okay."

"You were unconscious almost every time I did this before. Don't worry. It's only a sphygmomanometer. It takes your blood pressure. It won't hurt, but it's necessary to make sure you're healthy." He said the words like an adult might speak to a young child.

Monica glanced at Tresa who gave a quick, short nod.

"Right. My doctors in Cillineese used them." Monica tugged her left arm out from under the covers and held it out.

"Of course. I just wanted to be sure you knew what I was doing. You seem nervous." He slid the cloth band up her bare arm all the way to her shoulder. After securing it tightly with a strap, he squeezed the ball at the end of the tube a few times. "Most people are when it comes time to see a doctor." He smiled. "I never understood the fear, myself."

"I'll be fine." Monica licked her lips. Pressure built up around her arm, pinching her skin and bearing down on her muscles. She frowned at the black constrictor. How was it supposed to tell the pressure her blood was under? It was the one putting pressure on her.

Aric pushed a cold metal disk onto her arm. Tubes extended from the disk to his ears.

She frowned at the contraption. What was that for?

He pulled the device away and unwrapped the band from her arm before touching her wrist with two fingers and glancing at his wristband.

Monica fought the urge to pull away. "What are you doing now?"

"Just taking your pulse." A small smile grew at the corners of his mouth. "You're rather jumpy, aren't you?"

"Sort of." Monica kept an eye on his cold fingertips pressing against her wrist's pasty white skin and crisscrossing scars. She licked her lips. So far he hadn't noticed the scars, or if he had, he hadn't said anything about them.

"Your heart rate is slightly elevated, but that's expected after such a stressful experience." He withdrew his fingers and slid the cloth band from her arm. "Your blood pressure is a little low, but it's within the normal range." After stowing the cloth band in his bag, he retrieved a pad of paper and a pencil and jotted down some notes. "So far, you are surprisingly healthy, Amelia. I told some of the other students about your recovery, but they thought I was joking."

Monica pulled her arm close to her body again. The cold pressing of Aric's fingers lingered on her wrist, as if they were still there, threatening to clamp down and drag her in front of the Council of Eight. "Do you think I'll be allowed out soon?" She stole another glance at Tresa. Should she mention Amelia's family? Would the Noble girl be worried about them at all?

The Seen nurse stared blankly back at her.

"I don't know." Aric continued scribbling away at his notepad. "I'll have to consult with the senior doctors after your tests come back." He plopped his pad on the bed and withdrew a wooden box from his bag. "This is probably the part you've been dreading." He unbuckled two silver clips on the box's side and lifted the lid. It swung open on two hinges and smacked against the box back. Lifting a glass vial from a plastic tray filled with identical tubes, he nodded at her. "I'll need your arm again for this."

"Okay."

He withdrew a plastic cylinder from another pocket in the box along with white fluffy balls and a small bottle of clear liquid. When he had laid all the items out in the box's lid, she extended her arm toward him, her lips pursed.

After wetting the white ball with the liquid from the bottle, he swabbed it over the skin in the crook of her arm. A smell like the cleanser the wall slaves sometimes used wafted up her nose, and the spot on her arm turned cold. She sniffed and turned her head away.

Aric held her wrist tightly. A sharp jab stuck her arm. She tried to pull back, but Aric's firm grip held her in place.

She glanced back at the spot. A plastic needle and tube extended from her arm into one of the glass containers he had selected. When the tube filled with her blood, Aric replaced it with another empty vial. He did this five more times.

"How many are you going to take?" She frowned as another tube of blood emptied from her vein.

He snatched away the needle and pressed another white ball to her arm. "That's all." After placing a sticky bandage over the puncture, he gathered up his supplies and carefully laid the vials full of blood back in their places in the box. "Last time I did that, you weren't even awake."

"Oh." Monica brought her arm close to her face and examined

the bandage more carefully. The plastic substance on the outside felt nothing like the sticky underside that adhered to her skin, keeping the white ball in place.

Aric paused his packing and stared at her. "What happened to your arm?"

She hugged it close to herself, still careful to keep her right arm beneath the blankets. "What do you mean? You just stuck it with a needle, that's what happened."

Tresa coughed.

Monica forced herself to relax and drooped her shoulders, trying to look as subservient as possible. "What's wrong with my arm?"

He held his hand out toward her. "May I look at it again?"

Extending her arm toward him, Monica kept his wristband in the corner of her eye. If he tried to report her, she'd be ready to run.

Aric grasped her arm below her wristband. "What did you do to yourself?" Pointing at the mesh of scars on her palm and wrist, he shook his head. "It looks like you used a cheese grater on your hand."

"That happened a while ago. It was an accident." She forced a laugh. "I'm fine. You said yourself that I'm healthy now."

"I'm just wondering why I didn't notice the scars before." Aric released her hand and closed his black bag. "None of the senior doctors did, either." He frowned. "Of course, we were rather concerned about getting that surgery done." He opened his bag again. "Which reminds me, I should check the incision."

Fear rushed through Monica's heart. Incision? She had no scar from any surgery. Why hadn't Tresa mentioned Amelia having surgery?

Rushing forward, Tresa put a hand out toward him. "But sir!" She placed the hand on Monica's shoulder. "It was two weeks ago, and I checked it this morning, and she's been through so much, especially after being up for the first time in weeks. If she's exerted, she might relapse."

Monica shot a look of thanks to Tresa, but her heart still pounded wildly.

Aric's brow wrinkled as he picked up his bag once more. "I suppose I can check it later. It looked fine last time." He started for the door. "Once her tests come back she'll be free to mingle with the others, but it will take a day or two. Plenty of time for her to recover and gain strength."

"Thank you, Master Aric." Tresa rushed forward and opened the door for him. "When can we expect you to return?"

"Maybe this evening. The doctors will want to see this miracle." He nodded to Monica. "It's good to see you better, Amelia. I hope you continue to improve."

Monica forced a smile. "Thank you, sir."

Tresa closed the door and slid the lock into place. Leaning against the wood, she breathed a long sigh. "That was close."

"Definitely." Monica sat up. "I was expecting him to question me a lot more and wonder if I really am Amelia . . ."

"Why should he?" Tresa crossed her arms over her chest. "To him, it's impossible for you to be anyone but Amelia."

Monica nodded. The Nobles considered it impossible for anyone to escape their system. If the Nobles thought their system to be perfect, why should Aric worry about her identity? "So Amelia had surgery?" She crawled out of bed and tugged Vinnie's cage from beneath.

"Yes. I forgot in the rush. I should have remembered, but there's nothing we can do about it now."

"I guess not." Monica untied Amelia's chip from Vinnie's back and fastened it around her neck. "What was the surgery for?"

"To remove a growth from her leg. It was killing her, spreading a disease through her body, and none of the treatments the doctors were giving her helped."

Vinnie crawled up Monica's arm and perched on her shoulder. She set the cage on the night table with her mother's diary resting on top. "How are we going to keep them from looking at my leg, then? We can't fake an incision well enough to fool a doctor."

"There are other options." Tresa put a hand over her pocket where she had stowed the surgical instruments.

Monica sat on the bed. Other options? "You don't mean . . ."

"We could actually cut your leg. I saw Amelia's wound often enough to be able to copy the incision."

Drawing her legs up onto the bed, Monica stared at her. Cut her leg on purpose? Was this woman insane? "You're not a doctor. You could sever a tendon or something. I wouldn't be able to walk again, and besides, the wound would be fresh. Amelia's was two weeks old."

"I wouldn't need to make it deep, just enough to fool them." She shrugged. "It's up to you. I've already helped make an excuse. I don't know if he'll believe me again, and if I speak out of turn too many times, I'll be demoted." Tresa yanked the linen bundle from her pocket and dropped it on the bed. "I risked at least a scolding, but if you're found out, you'll be killed. I think a small cut on the leg is negligible compared to our freedom, don't you?"

Monica's calf muscle tingled. "When you put it that way . . ." She rubbed her exposed lower leg with a hand. The idea was crazy, but it could work, couldn't it? It was important that she look as much like Amelia as possible. No matter how much pain this cut would bring, it was better than death. She still had so much to do. The slaves of Cantral needed her. Her mission was far from over, and she couldn't let a small incision stop her—not after what she had been through in Cillineese.

Firming her lips, she nodded at Tresa. "I'll do it."

# CHAPTER 8

onica lifted Vinnie from her shoulder and plunked him in the cage beside Amelia's bed. "If you think you can recreate it accurately and stitch it up again, I'll let you make the cut."

Tresa unwrapped the surgical equipment from its binding. "Then we should proceed as quickly as possible."

"Great." Monica blew a long sigh. "The only thing is, how are we going to explain why it's so . . . fresh?"

"Simple." Tresa selected a knife from the pile. "You tore the wound open again by walking too much too soon. I didn't think it was urgent enough to warrant a call to the doctors and sutured it myself. I used to work in the Nobles' infirmary, so the doctors shouldn't question it." She disappeared into the bathroom, but her voice came out clearly. "I just need to sterilize this scalpel so I can get to work." The sound of running water issued from the small room, and a cabinet door opened, then closed.

Monica tucked her feet under her and moved her mother's diary out of Vinnie's reach. She held it close to her chest, rubbing the coarse yellow binding with a thumb. There was no time to work on the translation now, but just holding it brought a sense of comfort, as if her mother's words were seeping through the pages into her heart. Her mother never knew what her daughter would go through, but she wrote about the possibilities in these pages—the work that was being done and how she expected her daughter to carry on their mission, no matter the pain it would bring.

Tresa entered the room again, holding the knife and a small bag, a white towel over one arm. "Are you ready?"

"As ready as I'll ever be." Monica let her legs dangle off the side of the bed. "Which leg was it?"

"The right, on the back of her calf." Tresa placed the knife on a tray by the bed and withdrew a curved needle and a spool of shiny black thread from the bag. "Let's get this over with." She laid the towel on the bed, protecting the sheets, and motioned toward it. "Lie on your stomach."

Monica placed the diary on the bed beside her and did as Tresa asked, her head pounding. She folded her arms on the pillow and rested her chin on her wrists. Would the coming pain compare at all to the pounding she had received in the river in Cillineese? Most of that was a distant blur now. Clinking noises sounded from the table beside her. She inhaled sharply. "Just do it quickly, please."

"I suggest biting the pillow. This could hurt a lot." Tresa spoke in a soothing tone, but the words felt like an uncaring jab. "I promise to do it as quickly as possible, but if I rush too much I could cut deeper than I mean to."

Biting into the pillowcase, Monica closed her eyes. The smooth cloth coated her tongue and made her want to gag, but she bit down harder until her teeth ached.

Tresa pushed Monica's nightgown up to her knees and placed a hand on her calf. Something wet and cold rubbed against her skin, and the odor of cleanser bit the air. A second later a sharp blade cut into her skin. Pain flared around the incision and shot up her leg.

She released a muffled cry through her clenched teeth. The slicing sensation ran around her leg, farther and farther. How long was this wound?

Tears welled in Monica's eyes, but she blinked them back. If she flinched, Tresa's hand could slip and bring more pain.

"I'm almost done." Tresa's tight voice barely reached Monica's ears. "I need to stitch it now."

Monica released the pillow and nodded before burying her head in her arms. A quick jab stuck her in the leg next to the burning cut. It struck again and again as Tresa pulled the wound closed with the needle and thread.

A last quick jerk tugged at Monica's skin, and a snip sounded. "All right." Tresa sighed. "I'm done."

The burning sensation continued as Monica rolled onto her back. She pulled her knees up, keeping her newly mended calf from touching anything. As the pain grew, more tears filled her eyes, and she brushed them away with her sleeve.

Tresa wiped her hands on a cloth. "You did well. I was expecting more noise. The pain will get worse, but they'll give you antibiotics, so you won't have to worry about infection. I didn't go very deep. It should heal quickly."

Monica turned her leg to the side and looked at the cut. The raw wound began six inches above her heel and curled around to her shin, running across her calf muscle. She blew a long breath and it hissed through her clenched teeth. "Thanks. I hope this works."

"It should." Tresa wiped her knife on the cloth. "The Noble doctors weren't at all concerned about Amelia. If it weren't for Aric being so worried about her case, she wouldn't have had the surgery at all and probably would have died unattended. Apparently there's a connection between her family and his." She packed the medical supplies into the bag. "In spite of the promises to Amelia's father, the doctors aren't very attentive." After setting it to the side, she pulled the bloody towel from the bed and walked into the bathroom, reemerging with a clean one. She wrapped it around Monica's leg. "Keep this in place for an hour, at least. We don't want your leg bleeding everywhere."

"Okay." Monica gripped the edges of the towel. "I thought Amelia knew a lot about computers so the Council wanted to keep her alive. Simon and I have been basing all our plans around that." Her leg pulsed with warmth as she tightened her grip on the towel. The pain would probably get worse as time went on, but for now it was starting to dissipate.

"The Council seemed to think so, but the doctors and the Eight don't always communicate very well. There are other things going on right now that are more important to the Eight than a young girl who works on illegal computer programs." Tresa walked to the other end of the room. "Amelia was quite adept at programming and creating computer chips, though, if what I've heard is true." She dropped the bag of supplies on the counter just inside the bathroom door. "They say the talent runs in the family."

"I wish I had some of that talent." A bit of blood dotted the side of the towel near Monica's fingers. "When can I get out of this room?"

"Supposedly the doctors preferred to keep you confined, to keep you safe." Tresa pulled her folding chair out again and resumed her seat, shifting as she settled. "I warn you, sitting here every day all day will get very boring."

Monica set her feet on the white wooly rug beside the bed and stood, putting weight on just her left leg, while making sure the towel stayed in place. "Maybe you have to stay here all day, but I can sneak out. I'm sure there are things I need to be doing. Simon will want to know I got here safely."

Tresa shook her head. "He wouldn't want you to go back to Cillineese, and we have no way to send a message at the moment. Our main contact was transferred just a few hours after you arrived. Besides." She pointed at the bed. "You need to lie down. Do not try putting any weight on that leg, or I'll be forced to sedate you."

"Fine." Who did this woman think she was, being so bossy? But she was probably right. As Monica brushed her right foot across the carpet, her toes tingled. The movement fired a shot of pain up her leg. She gasped and sat back down. "This cut had better fool those doctors, or I'm in trouble." Curling up on the bed, she rested against the carved headboard. "What do you do all day?"

Tresa sat back in her chair. "I was stuck here for over two weeks watching Amelia, making sure she was still alive—taking care of her basic needs—and that's what I'm supposed to do still." Closing her eyes, she breathed a long sigh. "There's little we can do until the doctors declare you well."

Monica grabbed her mother's diary from the bed. "I wish we had a better plan. I hate feeling useless. There are so many people who need my help."

"What you're doing now will help them in the long run." Tresa opened her eyes. "We have lived in suffering this long; we can stand a few more weeks or months or however long it takes. As long as there is hope we can hold on to, we can wait."

The pain in Monica's calf lessened to a dull ache. She stretched her legs keeping the makeshift bandage in place. Tresa was right, they could wait, but the wall slaves' pain stabbed more fiercely than any physical pain, the pain she had tried to grow numb to. Every time a memory of her friends' bondage returned, or when the sounds of the inhabitants of Cillineese rejoicing at being set free came to mind, their sufferings pealed in her heart with a fresh throb. If only she could free the people of Cantral as quickly—but now that she would work right under the Eights' noses, it would be even more difficult to slip by unnoticed. In Amelia's shoes, she would be dancing hand in hand with the enemy, trying to charm them in a dead girl's guise.

Still sitting, Tresa shuffled her polished black shoes across the rug and sighed loudly. "Monica?" She looked down at her hands. "How is everyone in Cillineese? I mean, how many dead are there?

We Seen have tried to find out, but none of the Nobles are saying, and . . ." She bit her lip.

Monica shivered and pulled one of her blankets around her shoulders. There had been so much death—no one was sure they had even found all the bodies. "They didn't have an official count when I left. Simon was trying to get everything organized." She studied Tresa's expression, tense and sad. Something more than curiosity lay behind her question. "Do you have loved ones there?"

"I think so." A corner of Tresa's mouth quivered, as if she were trying to hide a smile. "They were there last I heard, anyway. It's so hard to keep in touch, you know. The Nobles never consider that we slaves would like to talk to our relatives after we're transferred."

"I know what you mean. My mother was transferred to the fields years ago. I didn't get to say good-bye, and I never heard from her again." Monica sighed. "But maybe I can tell you about your relatives. I didn't know many people, but perhaps I met one of them."

"Your mother?" Tresa sat up in her chair. "But you're a Noble. Your mother couldn't have been transferred to the fields."

A fresh stab of pain slashed up Monica's leg. "No." She gritted her teeth. "That's not what I meant. I meant my adoptive mother. She and my adoptive father took care of me my first four years after . . . Cillineese was terminated the first time." Her stomach turned as memories resurfaced—all the deaths in her family. "But that's in the past." She turned to her side to get a better look at Tresa. "What were your relatives' names? The ones that got transferred."

"I was the one who was transferred," Tresa said. "They took me away from my family, and I was never even told why. I didn't do anything wrong."

"I'm sure you didn't." Monica fingered the edge of the quilt. Most of the slaves who got transferred never did anything wrong. The Nobles were always shifting the slaves around, bringing in new workers and sending out the old. No one knew why, but the slaves often came up with their own speculations. Maybe the Nobles liked to keep the slaves off balance, to quell any threats of rebellion that even the fear of the chips couldn't reach.

Tresa sniffed, but her eyes were dry. "What kind of person takes a mother away from her children? Or sends a father away from his family? I haven't seen my sons in almost a year, and I can never hope to again." She glanced at the door. "You'd better bring this empire down soon, or I might just do it myself."

Monica followed Tresa's gaze to the carved door blocking the room's exit. "Just don't let them hear you say any of that. You'll be out in the fields or dead before you can blink."

"I know, but don't worry. No one can hear us here. We're in the north wing's farthest corner, tucked out of sight and out of mind." Tresa stood, crossed the room to the dresser, and pulled open the middle drawer. She withdrew a sock, a ball of yarn, and a needle. "I just wish they would send me back to Cillineese, but now that the computers are shut down, I'm sure there's no hope any slave will ever come or go from there again. I'll never hear any news about my sons. They're probably both dead."

Monica sat up straighter. Certainly she could bring some comfort to this grieving woman. "What are their names? If we could get a message to Simon, maybe he could find out something for us."

Tresa waved a hand. "No, no. It's too risky."

"Aren't the messengers around here trustworthy? We can send Simon a note through one of them, or I could do it when I'm well."

"You won't have time once you're well, and while some of the messengers are trustworthy, it's too difficult for them to get near the Cillineese tunnels for something of such little importance. Our main messenger was transferred. I told you that." As Tresa returned to her seat, she scuffed her feet across the floor. "There're thousands of other people who want to know about their family members just as I do, and I'm no more important than them." She threaded her needle with the yarn. "I'll just have to pray that my Alfred and Jonas stay safe. Perhaps the Lord will heed me this time."

"Alfred?" Monica sat up straighter. "I know an Alfred!"

"You do?" The ball of yarn fell from Tresa's hand and rolled under the bed. "Tell me what he looks like!"

Monica provided the best description she could, his dark curly hair, and pointed nose—just like Tresa's—his easygoing temperament—his love for animals, especially Vinnie, and the way he liked to teach the rat tricks. Alfred was certainly unique and easy to identify.

Tears glistened in Tresa's eyes. "Simon said he would look after him for me, but with so many transfers and all the uncertainty, I couldn't be sure he would be able to. I've been so worried about him!" She lifted her brow high. "How is he?"

Monica tried to explain the situation, but it was so hard to make someone from the outside understand. It might look difficult and hopeless from Tresa's point of view, but the people of Cillineese were happy despite their struggles. Alfred loved his job helping Simon, and he was better treated than he ever had been.

Tresa sat back in the chair with a thump, making the wood creak. "I can only hope that's true." She closed her eyes. "You should get some rest before Aric comes back with the other doctors. It will be a long day tomorrow if they decide you're allowed out with the others."

Monica nodded and sank into her pillows. "You're right." She started to turn to her other side, but the pain in her leg kept her in place. Hugging the diary close to her chest, memories of her mother's words filtered in, words she had read so many times, they were now permanently etched in her memory.

My dear Sierra, I hope someday you will read this journal. By the time you are old enough to understand these words, you will likely have already experienced much suffering, and I weep even now for the heartaches, bruises, and tears our plans will almost surely bring upon you. Tyrants will never voluntarily loosen their iron grip. Resistance only makes them tighten their choke hold and crush those who threaten their power. Yet, since they will scan the skies for attacking eagles, perhaps a quiet mouse will be able to sneak past their defenses and penetrate their power structure.

She focused on her throbbing leg. Suffering. Yes, it was horrible, but it also served as a poignant reminder. The other slaves still suffered far worse tortures, and as long as pain pulsed through her leg, it would be a badge of courage, a stimulant to continue this mission no matter how much persecution those tyrants could deliver.

CHAPTER 9

Why did her leg hurt so much? And since when was her bed in the cold Seen dorm so warm and comfortable? A soft blanket hugged her shoulders and wrapped snuggly around her arms.

As the movement brushed her right leg against the mattress, a jolt shot through her. Gasping, she sat up and pushed the sheets away.

A hazy light from an open door lit the room. She leaned over and examined the lengthy incision along her calf. Bits of black dotted her skin near the cut. Dried blood?

Resting against the headboard, she closed her eyes once more. Of course. That was it. She was in the north wing of the Cantral palace. Tresa had cut her leg so she could look more like Amelia.

She glanced around the room. "Tresa?"

Tresa sat up on her cot, her eyes scrunched closed. "What?"

"Did the doctors come?"

Metal squeaked against metal as Tresa got up from bed. "You slept through their visit. They wouldn't let me wake you." She shuffled over to Monica and held out the vial with Amelia's chip inside. "I took this off and held onto it while the doctors were here. I didn't want to risk them finding it."

"Thanks." Monica took the vial and tied the cord around her neck. She touched the screen on her wristband. It lit up, showing *6:00 a.m.* "How could I have slept so long?" Her stomach rumbled, a reminder that she hadn't eaten since yesterday. "I've never slept this much at one time before."

"It's almost time to get up, anyway." Tresa crossed the room and opened the bathroom door more fully, letting in more light. "I think the doctors gave you a sedative. They didn't tell me what it was, but they injected you with something. I protested, but . . ." She turned her head so the light from the bathroom shone on her cheek, illuminating a shadow of a bruise.

Monica winced. "They shouldn't have done that."

"It's nothing." Tresa shrugged.

Gulping in a big breath, Monica swung her legs over the side of the bed. She would have to fight through the pain. When her heels rested on the bed's sideboard, she released the breath in a long sigh. "What *did* they say? Obviously, my tests must have come back normal. Am I allowed out now?"

Tresa snapped on the overhead light. "Too many questions at once." She rubbed her eyes. "Fortunately for us, your blood type was the same as Amelia's. We forgot to take that into consideration, but it turned out all right." She walked to Monica's bedside. "And no, you're not allowed out yet. The therapy Aric mentioned is scheduled for this evening. You're allowed out in two days, and after that, they expect you to socialize with the others your age who live here."

Monica gulped. Of course getting to know these people had always been part of the plan, but would she ever be able to be friends with Nobles? It would all be pretense. If they knew she was really a wall slave, they would think of her as dirt and wouldn't even flinch at the thought of terminating her.

"Don't worry." Tresa crouched beside the bed. "It won't be too difficult. The others will want to know all about you, and Aric is sure to have encouraged them to welcome you warmly. I think he views you as a trophy, a tribute to his accomplishments." As she reached beneath the bed, her voice grew muffled. "It's pathetic. His treatments failed, and he doesn't even know it."

"Telling them all about me will be the difficult part." Monica leaned over the bedside. "And I don't really know Aric. Besides, he isn't my age, is he? He's a doctor."

Tresa reemerged from under the bed, a pair of crutches pressed to her chest. "I believe he is nineteen. He's a student doctor, not an actual doctor. Your illness was part of his graduation project." She handed the crutches to Monica. "You can practice using them while I go get our breakfasts." As Tresa walked to the door, she pointed at the bed. "I put your rat under the bed before the doctors arrived last night. We can take care of him when I get back." She exited the room but left the door ajar. Her footsteps echoed outside as if she were walking down a long corridor.

Resting her hands on the horizontal bars halfway down the crutches, Monica let her right foot touch the ground, slowly adding weight. Hot flashes of pain skittered up and down her leg, emanating from the wound. With a sigh, she took all her weight off her injured leg. It would be a while until she could use it again.

Now was a perfect time to work on her translation. The yellow booklet rested on the night table, a small piece of paper protruding from its pages.

She pushed herself onto the bed and propped the crutches against the wall.

Leaning forward, she slid a hand along the back of her calf, feeling the tight black stitches closing the wound. Dried blood flaked off and fluttered to the sheets, marring the white fabric with black flecks. The wound felt hot and tight.

Scratching sounded from beneath the bed. She smiled and

picked up her mother's journal. Vinnie didn't appreciate being ignored for so long. Monica tugged the loose page from the journal and scanned Simon's scribbling. Key words from the Old Cillineese language were translated into Cantral—words that would occur in many sentences, helping her figure out the others. She flipped open the journal to reveal another loose leaf tucked among the bound pages of her mother's flowing script. This page had Simon's more careful, spidery writing scrawled across it—a translation of her mother's earliest journal entry.

She squinted at the first page of the journal, the words in Old Cillineese. They seemed to float on the crisp page, words that provided no mental picture. Though the letters were the same as Cantral's alphabet, the order made no sense.

Simon's two pages contained only about a hundred translated words, not nearly enough to decipher the journal. Maybe the north wing library had books that could help. Simon had taught her all about library shelving, so it should be easy to locate something in Old Cillineese if it existed.

She pursed her lips and scanned her mother's entry. One of the words on the page jumped out—*Sierra*. That was her name—the one her birth parents gave her—but no one ever used it and barely anyone even knew it. Sierra was supposed to be dead, killed in Cillineese's termination twelve years ago.

Footsteps sounded outside the bedroom door. Monica stuffed all the papers back inside the journal and shoved the booklet under her pillow. There would be time for translation work after she found a dictionary.

The doorknob turned. Tresa pushed the door open with a foot and entered the room with a sideways shuffle, carrying a silver tray laden with dishes of food. She closed the door with a heel and set the tray on the end of Monica's bed. "So you didn't get up?"

Glancing at the crutches, Monica shook her head. "It hurt to move."

"You might as well get used to it." Tresa slid the tray to Monica's side of the bed. "It will hurt for the next few days."

Monica pulled the meal tray onto her lap, careful not to overturn the glass tumbler full of orange liquid. She pointed at a bowl filled with steaming white globs and black specks. "What's that?"

"Oatmeal with blackberries and brown sugar." Tresa laughed. "Haven't you ever seen oatmeal before? I've heard it tastes good."

A silver spoon rested beside the bowl. Monica picked it up between her thumb and forefinger and plunked it in the gooey substance. Blackberries. Amelia's favorite. "I guess so. I've seen lots of food on the Nobles' tables, but I don't know the names of all of it. I only know the ones I overheard through the walls." She glanced at the panel leading to the wall slaves' hallways. "Speaking of which, there's no one in there, right?"

Tresa shook her head. "There's no one scheduled to be in this section. Don't worry. I wouldn't have let you blather about our plans if there were." She crossed her arms. "Now eat. You need to get some weight on those bones."

Digging out a spoonful, Monica wrinkled her nose. "This isn't going to be pleasant." She took a big bite of the thick oatmeal. The flavors exploded in her mouth—sweet, spicy, and bland all wrapped together with unidentifiable flavors. The sticky meal took some effort to swallow, but after forcing herself to eat half of it, she placed the spoon back on the tray. "How do the Nobles eat this stuff? It's way too strong."

"The Noble children love it, actually. It's considered healthful as well." Tresa shrugged. "You couldn't pay me to eat Noble food. It might smell appetizing, but meal bars are the only food I'll eat. They don't have any foreign spices in them."

A churning sensation rolled Monica's stomach. "I forgot about the spice." She lay against her pillows. "Simon gave me some for the first time yesterday. It made me really sick."

"Nonsense. You'll be fine." Tresa pointed at a cup of orange liquid. "Now drink your juice. That's good for you, too—full of vitamins."

A stabbing pain jolted Monica's stomach. Would the attack be as bad as last time? "I don't think I can handle that. Whatever it is."

Tresa held out two large white pills. "Orange juice. You need to drink something when you swallow these."

"I can tell it's orange."

"Oranges are what it's made out of. They're a type of fruit." Tresa dumped the pills into Monica's hand. "These are to help keep infection out of your leg." Withdrawing a third pill from her pocket, she said, "And this one is to make sure your illness doesn't come back, but I think it might be best to . . . misplace it."

After popping the chalky pills into her mouth, Monica took a swig of the juice and almost spat it out again. The tangy sweetness was so overwhelming, she could barely keep it in her mouth.

"Swallow it quickly before the pills dissolve." Tresa took the cup from her.

After forcing them down, Monica held the tray up to Tresa. "Here. I couldn't eat another bite even if I wanted to."

Tresa steadied the tray in her arms and nodded. "I understand. I've witnessed the aftereffects many times when Seen children sneaked Noble food. I've never tried it myself." She set the tray on the dresser.

More nausea and cramps attacked. Closing her eyes, Monica blew out a long breath. At least Simon wasn't there to throw things at her if she fell asleep. Monica bit her lip. Her stomach seemed to be trying to tie itself in a knot. Maybe getting up and moving around would relieve the cramps.

Rustling noises came from the other end of the room where Tresa worked. A drawer opened and closed. "Amelia's clothes should fit you. You're around the same size, I think, and you're both skinny. I hope you'll get used to the food and put some weight on."

Monica groaned at the thought of food. If only Tresa would be quiet.

A hand touched Monica's shoulder. "I'm sorry you're in pain, but you'll get used to the spice eventually."

Monica nodded. "At least it will be a couple of days before I have to meet the other Nobles."

***

"Today's the day, Miss Amelia," Tresa called.

Monica opened her eyes and sat up in bed. "I know."

"How's this?" Tresa held out a light blue dress with silver beading on the bodice. "I think it will look good on you." The blue material shimmered as if it were running water.

Monica slid off the bed, reached out, and stroked the fabric. When she set her right foot down, a stab of pain shot through her leg. She grimaced. The wound had healed some in two days, but it still hurt quite a bit.

"Put it on." Tresa laid the dress on the bed. "I'll go get your breakfast." As she headed for the door, she called. "Don't try to walk without your crutches!"

Monica waited until the door closed before grabbing the crutches and hopping to the bathroom. Even after bathing each night, the feeling of dirt never seemed to go away, bringing back a reminder of Amelia's burial.

She scrubbed her arms and hands with hot water and foamy white soap. As the bandage on her arm peeled away, the scalding water reddened her skin and made her pink scars stand out. She changed quickly and laid her nightgown on the counter.

The bedroom door opened and closed.

Monica grabbed her crutches and peered out. A small girl in a Seen uniform tiptoed across the bedroom. She opened each dresser drawer and peered inside before closing it. The girl's black ponytail swished back and forth as she sneaked about, checking all the drawers and cabinets in the room.

Monica's stomach lurched. What should she do? Stop her?

The bedroom door opened again. Tresa walked in, a tray of food in her hands. Her gaze immediately locked on the little girl. The girl bolted for the exit.

Tresa dropped the tray and grabbed the girl by the collar. The dishes scattered, and food flew across the floor. "Shora! What are you doing in here?" She shook Shora, making her head wag. "Your assignment isn't anywhere near this room. No one's is."

Shora choked. "Please, Aunt Tresa, let me go!"

Tresa stopped shaking her but kept a hold on her dress. "Not until you tell me why you're here. I could report you."

"Please, don't do that!" Shora's eyes widened. "I was told to come here and look around. I couldn't disobey an order! He'd have me terminated!"

Monica bit her lip. Should she interfere?

"Fine." Tresa released Shora, and she fell to the floor. "Tell them you didn't find anything, and don't you dare come sneaking around again. You could upset the patient."

Rubbing her neck, Shora climbed to her feet, tears welling in her eyes. "Yes, Aunt Tresa. But I made sure no one was here before I came in, and how am I supposed to say no to a Noble? I can't!"

Tresa glanced at the bathroom door, meeting Monica's gaze. "Well, then just come here and tell them you didn't see anything. Or that we were here." She turned and looked around. "Who told you to come?"

"I can't tell you." Shora's lips pressed together in a thin line.

"Fine." Tresa steered the girl toward the door. "Don't tell me, but I'll speak to your mother tonight, and you'll regret not telling. I have a right to know who's spying on me."

Shora ran for the exit. "He's not spying on you, Aunt Tresa; he's spying on Miss Amelia, and I can't tell!"

After Shora darted through the door, Tresa slammed it shut. Putting her fingers to her temples, she called, "You can come out now . . . Amelia."

Gripping her crutches tightly, Monica hopped out of the bathroom. "I didn't know what to do when she came in here."

Tresa flipped the door's latch. "You could have ordered her out. You are a Noble, you know." She put her hands on her hips. "I don't know what she was thinking. It was dangerous to come in here, even if she couldn't see you."

"She seemed scared to me." Monica leaned against the wall. Her leg ached so much. She twisted around to see the back of her calf. The dress's hem didn't hide the wound or the bruises that accented the ugly black stitches.

"She's a good actress, that one. She'll find her way into every kind of trouble when she's older. Wants to be a Noble someday." Tresa shook her head. "Hasn't sunk in yet that that's impossible." She turned to the dresser and pulled open a drawer. "I see she's been looking in here."

"She was. I saw her." Monica edged closer to the dresser. "But maybe she could be more than a Seen sometime. Isn't that what we're fighting for?"

"Of course." Tresa pulled a pair of white socks from the drawer and sighed. "But I don't want to give anyone false hopes. I'd rather not encourage her thinking. It will only bring her sorrow." She handed Monica the socks. "I don't want her to go through that."

"No, I guess not." She gripped the knitted material tightly. Of course not. No one should have to go through so much suffering. There had been enough suffering already.

She touched the pendant necklace hidden beneath her dress. She wouldn't ask anyone else to help. Too many people had given up their lives for her, and for a cause they believed in.

Monica leaned against the bed and pulled her socks on. She

would just have to go with what little she knew. Tresa said not to trust, but many others had told her differently.

When she looked up, Tresa stood right in front of her, a pair of white boots in hand. "I hope these fit."

As Monica took them, she studied Tresa's thin face. The dark lashes shrouding her gray eyes gave her a sad expression, magnified by the barely visible bruise on her cheek. Frown lines dominated her skin, but some remnants of smiles from long ago remained by her lips. Was this sad Seen someone she could count on? Monica forced her own smile. "Thank you."

Monica slid the boots onto her feet, but the long laces confused her fingers. Tresa knelt and tied the laces for her.

"Thank you again." Heat crept into Monica's cheeks. "I guess I've never really tied shoes before. These are my first pair that I can remember."

"There's no need to be ashamed. I know wall slaves don't have shoes." Tresa picked up a hairbrush from the night table. "Brush your hair and then we need to go." She shook her head and crouched by the mess of food scattered across the floor. "I'll clean this up when we get back. I'll get you more food once we get to the library."

"There's no need. I wasn't hungry anyway." Monica ran the brush through her tangled hair until it lay smooth, then tossed the brush on the bed. "I can't understand how Nobles eat so much."

Tresa nodded at the door. "Let's go."

"Wait." Monica grabbed the journal from under her pillow. "I'd like to keep this with me."

"I suppose you'd like to take the rat, too?" Sighing, Tresa retrieved a shoulder bag from the dresser drawer.

Monica held the journal out. "No, I think he'll be okay here, but he'll need some food and water soon."

"Don't worry. I'll give him water when I get back." Tresa slid the diary into the bag. "Now let's go. We're late."

Monica crutched her way to the door, her boots making clacking noises with every hop.

"Remember." Holding the door open, Tresa whispered, "Out here you're Amelia and Amelia only. You're a Noble. Act like one."

CHAPTER 10

"How far is the library?" As Monica and Tresa climbed into the upper levels of the north wing, the rubber bottoms of Monica's crutches squeaked each time they gripped another wooden stair.

Tresa walked beside Monica, her head bowed. "Only another flight of stairs and then a hall, Miss Amelia." She touched the brown strap of the bag on her shoulder. "We might come across someone else soon. These are the more traveled parts of this wing."

As Monica heaved herself onto the landing, her limbs quivered. Sweat beaded on her arm beneath her bandage, despite the cool air trapped in the stone walkways. Two weeks of being idle had cost her a lot of strength, but her mangled arms had needed the rest. At least her leg had stopped hurting for the moment, though a cold and clammy feeling now crept across her skin. Two days of being secluded in Amelia's bedroom hadn't helped any, either.

"We're almost there. Then you can rest." Tresa spoke with a soothing tone, completely unlike her normal voice.

Biting her lip, Monica tried to keep a straight face. Of course

Tresa had to act differently in public. She was a Seen speaking to her Noble master. Monica followed Tresa down a long, narrow hall. They were both actors now, hiding their true roles and gambling with their lives. As they approached a pair of double doors, Monica's heart raced. Would she ever be able to just live—no longer pretending to be someone else? She touched her dress where the vial containing Amelia's chip lay hidden. There was still a job to do.

Tresa waited for her at the door. When Monica stood by her side, Tresa whispered, "Remember, you're their equal, even if your family is in disgrace." She draped the bag over Monica's shoulder. "Just don't say anything stupid." She swung open the door, revealing a well-lit library, and stepped behind Monica.

Shivers ran down Monica's spine, but she forced herself out onto the wooden floor and across the floral-patterned runner leading to a large, circular desk in the room's center. Tresa closed the door behind her with a loud click.

A girl sat cross-legged on a swivel chair inside the desk's circle, a large book held open on her lap. A pair of black glasses perched on the end of her nose, a reminder of Simon's lenses and his beady-eyed stares.

Monica glanced around the room, but there was no sign of another person. The ceiling-high bookshelves cast shadows in the rows upon rows of books. There must have been at least twice as many aisles as in the Cillineese library.

She crept toward the girl as quietly as she could with the clunky crutches. The girl spun her chair around in circles with one hand while using her other to skim through the pages of her book.

"May I help you?" The girl kept her chair turning even as she spoke, not looking up from her book.

"Yes." Monica tried to make eye contact with the girl, but the constant motion made it impossible. "I'm supposed to meet some people."

The girl closed her book and hopped off the still-spinning chair. "I don't know you." She placed the book on the desk. "Some new distant relative come to try to butter up dear old Uncle Aaron, I suppose?" Her gaze traveled up and down before resting on the crutches. "It doesn't work, so you might as well go back home. I've been here half my life, and he doesn't even know it."

"Actually, no." Monica turned her head away from the girl's prying stare. How would Amelia respond? "I was brought here for medical attention and . . . other reasons." Would this girl know who Amelia was? Maybe Cillineese's fall wasn't common knowledge among the younger Nobles. The older wall slaves often hid information from the children. The Nobles probably did the same.

"I see. I can tell you've been ill." The girl pushed up a section of the desk and stepped out of the wooden circle. "I'm Regina. Who're you?"

Monica's mouth automatically started to form an *M*, but she bit back the letter just in time. "Ah . . . Amelia." She nodded. "I'm from Cillineese."

"Cillineese?" Regina's eyes widened. "I heard someone was coming from there. I wasn't sure who or when, though. The adults don't include us in their 'top-secret' discussions." A smile spread slowly across her face. "Not that that stops me." She played with a strand of black hair that had come loose from her ponytail. "If you ever need to know anything, just ask me. I can get you any information."

"Really?" Monica's voice came out as a squeak. Regina couldn't really know everything, right? Otherwise she would know all about Amelia's death, and no one could know that. She was probably overstating.

"Really."

Monica swallowed hard. "Do you know where I'm supposed to go?"

Waving an arm at the door, Regina said, "Wherever you want.

All the others are in anterooms or in the aisles, studying whatever they're supposed to."

"So you guys don't study together? Tresa said . . ." Monica stopped. It would be okay for Amelia not to know this, right? She had had her own tutor in Cillineese, and there were only a few other children in that palace.

"Nope." Regina picked a white speck from the sleeve of her navy shirt. "Who's Tresa? I don't think I've met her. Did she transfer from Cillineese, too?"

"She's a Seen." Monica's gaze trailed to Regina's dark, tailored shirt and pants. Monica frowned. Wasn't Regina a Noble? Otherwise, why would she be talking with such authority? Then why was she wearing an outfit so closely resembling a Seen's? And if she was a Seen, she would know Tresa. "Why are you wearing a Seen uniform?"

Shrugging, Regina pushed up the desk partition and entered the circle again. "A few reasons. But it's not exactly their uniform. I had a hard enough time convincing the Council to allow me to wear this. They wouldn't let me wear the real thing." She rested her hands on the desktop. "Anyway. What's your major? I can help you find the books you need. Unless." She nodded at Monica's shoulder bag. "You brought your own."

Monica glanced at the bag. "No. I didn't bring my own to study." She looked down at her thin hands clutching the crutches. What was it that Amelia studied? She knew this. Simon had drilled it into her, and she had even read a little about it, but now when she needed the information most, it slipped away.

"Everything here is categorized through a decimal system. It used to be alphabetized, but I cleared that out a while ago. It was hard to find things that way." Regina climbed back into her seat, tucking her feet beneath her. "I guess you can find your own books if you're not going to tell me what you study." She shrugged. "Some kids like to keep it secret until after their exams. I understand. My own brother is extremely secretive about his graduation project."

Monica regripped her crutches. Would this girl ever be quiet? "I'll try to find some on my own, thanks." She turned to an aisle on her left. "Where's the librarian?"

"That'd be me." Snatching her book up from the desk, Regina pointed at herself. "The Seen librarian got demoted ages ago. She was too uppity."

"Oh." Monica turned to the left and crutched into one of the dim aisles. This situation was definitely unexpected. She had imagined a roomful of students bent over their work. Simon had described classroom settings that way.

She paused in front of a stack of books piled in the middle of the walkway. Who ever heard of a child running a library? There had to be a Seen helper somewhere. Maybe Regina just didn't want to admit it.

Microchips. The word popped into Monica's mind without warning. Of course. That was Amelia's expertise. *It runs in the family.* Tresa had said those words in Amelia's room a little while ago. That was the whole reason she was here. She shook her head. How could she be so stupid?

Monica hopped around the stack of books in the center of the aisle and continued down the row. Her father had been good with computers. Otherwise he would never have figured out how to write those notes about the Cillineese control center, but how would that help her? She was a wall slave, if not in name, then certainly in knowledge. She didn't know a thing about computers, while Amelia had been studying them during her entire education.

Pausing in front of a shelf, Monica leaned heavily on her crutches. Her leg ached from disuse, and hot pain shook her shoulders and arms. These crutches were more work than anticipated. Even the exercises the therapist had made her do over the past couple of days hadn't prepared her for this.

She pushed a lock of hair from her eyes and squinted at the titles lining the shelf in front of her. Bound in leather covers and lettered with peeling gold, the volumes appeared old, so these couldn't be about microchips, could they? If only it were brighter in here. At least in Cillineese each bookshelf had its own set of lights. Regina probably couldn't keep up with all the maintenance by herself.

A quick tug on a book brought it down into her arms, along with a few dust particles. She stood on one foot and rested her crutches against the shelf on the other side of the aisle.

Light shone from behind. She dropped the book and whirled around, placing her right foot on the ground. Pain shot through her leg and brought her to the floor. Biting back a cry, she pulled her knees up to her chin. The pain would soon pass.

She forced herself to look at the lights shining from the bookcase that the crutches leaned against. A dozen tiny bluish lights illumined each level of shelves, making it easy to read the titles in their neat rows. *Sugar Cane and Its Uses*, *Harvests in the South*, and other titles swam in front of her eyes as she tried to focus on anything but her leg.

When the pain receded, Monica hoisted herself to her feet, using the crutches for support. The lights blinked off. She touched the shelf with a finger, pressing against the smooth grain. The lights turned on again. She withdrew her hand, and the aisle slowly dimmed.

She reached down and picked up the book she had dropped and put it back in its place. This section seemed to contain books about farming and foods, so microchips would probably be in another section. Tapping the shelf one last time, she shook her head as the lights flashed on then off. It was silly to be startled so easily by such a little thing. Simon was right. She was still too jumpy.

A twinge pulled her attention to her calf. Half a dozen red specks dotted the back of the white sock that hid her wound. She grimaced but turned and hopped down the aisle. Maybe no one would notice. And if they did, what would it matter? She could explain it away easily. Only the doctors would care.

She soon found the aisle with books about computers and made her way down the row. A quick tap on a shelf illuminated the titles. After traveling the length of one aisle, she finally arrived at some books that looked promising.

Thumbing through one thick volume's pages revealed a vast array of diagrams and sketches from early versions of computers and their inner workings. The text beneath the diagrams was easy enough to read, but the words spoke of motherboards, circuitry, and lists of unfamiliar parts.

One paragraph explained in depth about theories on cloning a chip's programming. Monica slid the book back into place. What in the world was cloning, anyway? Did Amelia actually know all of this stuff?

She glanced around the aisle. Regina was probably still sitting at her desk. Monica pulled Amelia's chip out from under her dress and let it dangle in front of her, but the cord caught on the medallion necklace. After untangling the leather cords, she turned the chip's vial over in her palm. The chip did sort of look like the drawings in the book. Thin, raised lines crisscrossed the chip's surface, and embossed bumps dotted the metal wherever a line ended.

The glass warmed her fingers, but the chip gave no other indication that it was communicating with a giant machine beneath the palace. She stuffed the necklace back under her collar. She had to push the computer room from her mind, but how? She was surrounded by tomes that spoke of the machines and the chips that held people captive, chips she knew nothing about. Yet when Amelia was called before the Council of Eight, the Noble girl's years of study and knowledge were expected to come with her, years of knowledge Monica had only days to learn. There was no telling when the Council would call her, and when they did, she had to be ready. The slaves' freedom depended on it.

She shoved the thoughts away. Worrying about it wouldn't do any good. After selecting two books on microchips and sliding them into her bag, she crutched out of the aisle, the book bag thumping against her thigh. Maybe the library would have a dictionary, and she could work on the diary translation. Perhaps it would have some information that would provide help in the coming days. After making some headway on the diary she would try to decipher some of the words in the computer books.

She sighed. Cloning? Microchips? It might as well have been written in Old Cillineese. Amelia's world was just as foreign. Using crutches to walk in her shoes never seemed more appropriate than it did now.

CHAPTER II

"Here you go." Regina lay on her stomach in front of a waist-high shelf piled with thick dictionaries. "I think I got it now." She reached her arms inside the shelf, pushing them into the recess all the way up to her elbows.

Leaning on her crutches, Monica peered down at Regina. The Noble didn't bat an eye when asked for a Cillineese-to-Cantral dictionary. Not having to answer questions was a relief.

Regina yanked a book from the shelf. Crawling to her knees, she let out a long breath. "I hope that's the right one. It's hard to see down there." She sat cross-legged and pulled the four-inch-thick tome into her lap. After flipping through a few pages, she shook her head. "No, this isn't Cillineese. I think it's New Kale's original language, which is similar to Old Cillineese, but not at all like New Cillineese." She slammed it shut. "Your grasp of our language seems pretty good to me, though. You don't even have an accent, so I wouldn't worry about not having a dictionary."

"Oh." Monica's face grew warm. Regina thought she wanted the dictionary to learn Cantral better. "I guess you're right. I won't worry."

"Okay then." Regina started to slide the dictionary back in place.

Monica dropped one of her crutches. "Wait!"

The crutch hit Regina's head with a thump. "Ow!" She grabbed it and threw it to the side. "What was that for?"

"I'm sorry." Monica stooped and picked up the dictionary with her free hand. "It was an accident."

Regina retrieved the crutch, rubbing the top of her head with one hand. "Here." She thrust the crutch at Monica. "If you wanted to keep it, you could have just said so. No need to attack me."

Sliding the dictionary into her bag, Monica grimaced. Did Regina not believe her? "Sorry. It really was an accident." She fastened the bag's clasp and took the crutch back.

"So you said." Regina scuffed her shoes on the floor on her way back to the desk. "Why do you want that, anyway? It won't help you."

The bag weighed Monica's shoulder down, but she followed Regina as quickly as she could. "You said it was close to the Cillineese language, right?" She winced. Too many questions would arouse suspicion.

Regina hopped over the desk's top. "That's right." She slid into her chair. "Which is why it won't be helpful to you. Old Cillineese isn't at all like New Cillineese. The languages are totally different. It'll just confuse you."

Monica nodded. She needed to say something to throw Regina off track. What would Amelia be interested in? "I know, but it is a piece of my history, right? Learning from the past can be very valuable."

Leaning back in her seat, Regina examined her short, grubby fingernails. "I suppose." She sat up suddenly. "Oh! Your uncle was the ruler of Cillineese before Gerald, right?" She bounced up and down in her chair. "Of course. You're a history major, aren't you?" She laughed. "I have it all figured out now. I would have thought you would have done your city's history first, though, and moved on. You're almost ready to graduate, right? I doubt the examiners will accept a history on Cillineese as your thesis project, considering your relationship with the past rulers—especially now."

"I guess they wouldn't." Monica shrugged. Was Amelia almost ready to graduate? It didn't really matter. If Regina wanted to believe she was a historian—that was all right. "But it's good to know something about my own history. Ge—my father never talks about his brother or anyone or anything else from his past."

A smile played at the corner of Regina's mouth. "Oh, I see. Forbidden information. Of course you're interested."

"Um. Right." Monica raised her eyebrows. This girl was full of crazy ideas, but at least she wasn't on the right track. "I guess I'll get to work."

Regina sat up straighter in her chair. "That dictionary won't be much help without something to translate. There's a whole section on Cillineese history. Want me to show it to you?" She patted a book on her desk. "I do love a good adventure, and while defying teachers isn't anything like slaying dragons, it's about as exciting as it gets around here, so I'll be happy to help you."

Monica took a step back and fumbled with her crutches. "No, thanks. I'll find it myself, thanks, and I'm not defying the teachers. No one has said I can't do this project."

"All right." Letting out a long sigh, Regina crossed her arms over her chest. "I'll just work on my own, then."

Monica hopped away from the desk, choosing a random aisle to disappear into. If only Regina knew how much trouble this "adventure" would cause if the teachers found out.

Monica turned down a second row. At least she had kept her cool. In fact, the conversation felt almost natural, as if she really were Amelia and not just pretending to be. Maybe this wouldn't be so hard after all. If she could just forget about playing the role and act natural, she might survive. Simon would be proud if he could see her now . . . Maybe.

A third row led into an open area. The walls curved around, and a large window on one wall allowed light to stream in, illuminating eight bookshelves that followed the wall's curve, four on either side of the window.

Adorning the top of each shelf stood a solitary brass letter. Monica crutched to the bookshelf to the right of the window where a large *C* glittered proudly. She scanned the shelf, but all the books had names like *Cantral – A.D. 2650 – A.D. 2675* and *Cantral – A.D. 2675 – A.D. 2700*. All the other titles bore the same words with different dates ranging all the way up to the present year, 2870.

These books weren't what she was searching for, but maybe a history book would come in handy if Regina came snooping. At the opposite side of the window, another shelf with a *C* held dozens of books. Monica started to make her way over to them. Maybe those would be the Cillineese history books.

As she neared the window and its seat, her leg began to ache again. She gritted her teeth and eased onto the tan cushion beneath the glass panels. Resting her crutches against the wall, she let out a long sigh. This wound had better heal quickly. Crutches made it hard to sneak around. At least the stomach cramps had faded, and they weren't as bad as last time. Maybe it wouldn't take as long to get used to the food as Simon thought.

She turned to look out the window, but a foggy sheen covered the glass, making it impossible to see through, though light filtered in easily. A beep sounded on her wristband. She glanced at the blue face. Text edged across the surface. *Meeting with the Council of Eight – Five Minutes.*

A tremor of fear ran through her. A meeting now?

"There you are!" Tresa scurried into the room, her face white.

"I was looking all over for you, Miss Amelia." When she reached Monica's side, she leaned over and hissed in her ear, "The Council has called for you to appear before them."

"I know." Monica's voice came out as a squeak. "But I'm not prepared!" What would they ask, and how would she answer?

Tresa took Monica's book bag. "We can't keep them waiting." She slung the strap over her shoulder. "Let's go. There's no telling what they'll do if you're late."

As she followed Tresa out of the library, tremors ran along her arms and legs. Of course there was no telling what the Council would do. She was already in their bad graces. Anything might change their minds about letting her live, and with her leg in the condition it was, she wouldn't be able to escape if they did try to kill her.

Tresa continued walking ahead of Monica, her black shoes making barely any noise on the rug. She kept glancing over her shoulder. "Come on. It's both our heads if we keep them waiting too long."

Monica forced herself to move her crutches more quickly, hopping along behind Tresa. "I'm trying, but these things are heavy." The crutches' feet squeaked every time they hit the floor.

Sighing, Tresa slowed her pace. "It's not too far away from here, but I can get you a wheelchair if you think you need it."

"I can make it a little farther." Monica hurried along after Tresa. Quiet whispers floated from the walls along with the soft rustling of fabric and footfalls. The wide hallway almost swallowed the sounds, but her trained ears still caught the subtle noises. The wall slaves must be busy at their work, ready at any time to clean up a Noble's mess.

"Unfortunately, they have the library tucked away in a pretty remote part of this wing." Tresa's words sounded tense. "I wish they had told me about this meeting earlier."

They entered an oval-shaped room with a pair of double doors on the opposite side. Spaced evenly around the room, eight white pillars rose to the dome ceiling. At the base of each pillar, a white statue sat on a carved granite throne. Four doors stood to the left and two to the right of the double doors, each between two pillars.

"I really hate this part." Tresa stopped in front of a pair of double doors. "I will go in first, but I'll be right back." She gripped one of the gold knobs with a white shaking hand. "If they decide we're on time and don't terminate me."

She knocked on the white and gold door before pressing her wristband against the surface. When a small beeping noise emanated from somewhere in the room, Tresa pushed the door open just enough to slip through.

Monica clutched her crutches tightly. The Council had to let Tresa live. She tried to get them there on time. It wasn't her fault they were late. The Council gave them such short notice—but they would never take the blame themselves. Nobles always found someone else to take their fall.

Monica's whole body tensed. She had to be prepared to face these men—the eight monsters who ordered people's deaths every day. To them, she was Amelia, a girl who by rights should have been terminated almost a month ago. They wanted to grill a disguised girl for information she didn't have. Her whole family manipulated computers brilliantly. Everyone except for her. She would never be able to answer their questions or perform any tasks.

There would be no escape from these Nobles, no way to run. Simon's training would work. It had to! Just survive this interview and everything would be all right for a while. Gaining the Council's trust was the only way to get access to the computers.

When the door opened again, Tresa sidled through. "Ready?"

A lump formed in Monica's throat, but she forced a nod.

Tresa motioned to the door. "Let's go, let's go. They've waited long enough."

Monica repositioned the crutches under her arms. Every drop of blood drained from her head down into her toes.

"You should be fine—they don't seem too upset." Tresa squeezed Monica's shoulder. "I can't go in with you. You have to do this on your own, but you should be used to that by now."

Her throat tightening, Monica nodded and limped into the room. She wasn't really alone, not according to her mother.

The door closed behind her with an almost inaudible click.

CHAPTER 12

onica stopped just inside the Council's meeting room. The Council had called her to come before them, but what did they want?

"Come in, Amelia. We have other audiences to attend to today, so be quick about it." The deep, resonant voice echoed loudly across the low ceiling and dark, wood paneling, which seemed to contradict the grandeur of the room just outside the double doors.

Monica forced her crutches and legs forward three steps, her knees shaking. Eight carved desks formed a semicircle across the other side of the room, surrounding her. One desk sat in the room's center with four flanking it to the right and three to the left. A man lounged in a cushioned throne behind each of the eight desks except one, where a woman sat at the edge of her chair, her face pale.

Monica's gaze traveled to the middle of the room and locked on the man at the center desk. As he stared back, a shiver ran through her. His gray eyes bored into hers, forcing her to look at the ground again. She studied her white boots, memorizing the marks that already scuffed the toes. That man had to be Aaron Markus, the north wing Council member. No other man would be placed at the center in the Council room.

What should she say? She couldn't say anything if they didn't ask a question, could she? But maybe they expected her to speak anyway and would terminate her if she didn't. Nobles were impossible to read!

"Welcome to Cantral, Amelia." Aaron spoke with the same deep voice that greeted her earlier.

Monica jerked her head up. Welcome? Tresa acted like they would kill at the drop of a hat, and now they welcome her?

Aaron spoke again. "I apologize for not calling for you to come earlier. An uncle should not ignore his niece, but we couldn't risk spreading any contagion."

A short gasp escaped Monica's lips before she could stifle it. Another uncle? How many brothers did her father have? And the north member of the Eight, too—why had no one told her?

Aaron's brow twitched, but he kept speaking. "Now that you're here, however . . ." He clasped his hands on his desk. "We can discuss the project you were working on before you took sick. The Council finds the rumors of your skills most interesting."

The woman sitting in the last seat to Aaron's right nodded, as did a man sitting in the seat beside her.

Dryness returned to Monica's mouth. What project had Amelia been working on? She and Simon had never found anything in their searches of Amelia's rooms. Whatever her cousin had been trying to create, she had hidden it well, despite the rumors that leaked out.

Monica cleared her throat. "I'm sorry, sir. I have recovered, it's true, but . . ." The crutches dug into her underarms. But what? "But I'm afraid it will be some time before I remember all the details and am able to report them. I was sick for so long, and when I was taken from Cillineese, my Seen and my tablet and notes were supposed to come on another transport, but it never arrived." Sweat formed on her palms. Think, Monica! "I'm hoping it will be found soon. Shipments don't stay lost forever." That would stall Council for a while. Whatever Amelia had been studying, she had wanted to keep away from the Council for a reason.

"You sent your notes on a different transport and didn't keep them with you?" Aaron sat back in his chair and shot a quick glance at the man to his left in the east chair before looking at her. "Yet you knew we spared your life for the sole reason of receiving this information from you. If you don't have it . . ." He raised his hands, palms up. "Then we have no use for you. We'll have to send the orders for Cillineese's termination once again and take you back to your family. Your pardon is only in place if you bring your programs forward."

She shifted in place. Maybe that worked too well. Of course they couldn't really send her back to Cillineese, they couldn't even get in, but Amelia wouldn't know that. She had been sick the entire time. All she was supposed to know was that the termination had been called off because of the knowledge she could offer.

"Or," the woman to Aaron's right spoke, "we could give her more time, Aaron. She has just recovered from a serious illness. If she were given—"

"Felicia!" Aaron stood, almost knocking his chair over. "Need I remind you that you were absent from the meeting that resulted in Amelia being brought here, and therefore the southwest has no say in this matter? You are here now only as part of protocol. I and the others will decide her fate."

Felicia looked down and away, frowning.

Turning back to Monica, Aaron said, "We will send a priority alert for the transport drivers to be on the lookout for this . . . missing shipment. You will return to your room and wait for our decision, but be prepared to receive a command for your termination. If you're the religious type, I suggest praying."

Monica felt the blood draining from her face until she was certain her complexion matched Felicia's. "I'm sure I'll remember soon enough, sir. Please, I—" A buzzing vibrated against her chest where Amelia's chip dangled.

Aaron held a finger poised over his gold wristband. "Amelia, I suggest you leave now."

She put a hand to the back of her head before edging toward the door, her ribs still tingling.

The Council members whispered among themselves, except Aaron Markus who stared her down.

As Monica's shoulders touched the door, it swung open and a pair of hands gripped her. She stumbled out, her crutches tangling with her legs. The door closed silently.

Tresa handed Monica her book bag. "Let's go. You can tell me about it when we get to your room."

They passed through the halls silently, Monica glancing at the murals, embroideries, and paintings that graced the walls leading to her room. Soon she might have to go back to Cillineese with Amelia's dead chip and tell Simon how she had failed. At least she would be able to look for Amelia's project again and make sure the Council never got a hold of it. But how would she let Simon know she was coming? She wouldn't be able to get in if he didn't open the door with the wheel. The Cantral security team had been trying for weeks to get into Cillineese with no success. None of their tactics seemed to be able to force the doors open, despite the many days of banging and knocking on the various access points.

Tresa stopped at the top of a long flight of stairs. "We could go back to the library, if you'd like, so you can get to know the other children and eat lunch with them."

Scrunching her nose, Monica shook her head. "I don't think I'll be here much longer, so there's no need." She inched down the stairs. "*Uncle* Aaron sent me to my room."

"Uncle?" Tresa trotted past her and walked down the stairs backwards just in front of her.

"Apparently. I thought you would know that." Monica paused her descent. "What are you doing?"

Tresa backed down two more stairs. "Making sure you don't tumble headfirst. You don't look very steady on those."

"I'm fine." Monica sped up her pace, the crutches thumping loudly on the wood stairs. "So why didn't you know that Aaron's my uncle?"

"I'm new at this sneaking around." Tresa lowered her voice. "Before a year ago, I minded my own business and never got in any trouble. I didn't pay attention to anything except my duties, and I was a perfect Seen with the best jobs." She stomped on the last step. "Now look at me—taking care of a girl destined for termination. Because I started getting nosey. But not about Master Aaron's extended family. There was no need."

"Not that it really matters. My father doesn't have a very good record so far when it comes to brothers. Aaron isn't someone I want to get to know."

Tresa led the way down a hall to the left. "It's best to get on his good side. I'm guessing that didn't happen in this meeting."

"No." Monica sighed. "He was calm enough in the beginning, but then the southwest Councilwoman spoke up, and he acted like she had suggested terminating him."

A smirk grew on Tresa's lips. "Now that's a relationship I do know. She's his younger sister by about ten years."

"So my dad has a sister I don't know about, too?" Monica's crutches caught on a black and gold runner on the wood floor.

Tresa grabbed Monica's arms and steadied her. "Careful." She released her tight hold. "I suppose so. He might have been lying. Have you thought about that?"

"Yes, I suppose." She sighed and trudged after Tresa, keeping her gaze on the ground. Why couldn't Simon have gone over that part of the family instead of those distant relatives? He had insisted on spending most of their study time on protocol, but when it came time to remember those rules, they had all fluttered away like the butterflies in the garden. At least if she was in her room when Aaron ordered her terminated she could probably get away. She could take Vinnie and run to Cillineese, get Simon to let her back in, and find another way to shut down the computers. The computer room doors were guarded, and there was no other way in, not even any accessible air ducts, but maybe with more time she could figure something out.

Tresa stopped and opened a door. "We're here."

Monica crutched into the room and plunked herself onto the bed. The muscles in her arms felt like jelly as she leaned the crutches against the wall. "I guess I'm not as strong as I used to be." She managed a breathy laugh. "Just a few weeks ago I—"

"Just a few weeks ago you were on your deathbed." Tresa jerked her head at something to Monica's right. "It's a miracle you're doing as well as you are."

Whirling around, Monica gulped. Who was there? Did the Council's messenger arrive before they did?

Regina sat perched cross-legged on the chair by Monica's dresser. "There you are. I was about to give up and go back to the library."

Monica's gaze darted to the hidden wall panel. She gripped the bedspread with one hand. "H-hello, Regina."

"Hi." Regina stared at Tresa. "Are you sticking around?"

Tresa backed against the door. "I can leave if you would like, Miss."

"I hate it when Seen hover, don't you?" Regina bounced across the room and jumped onto the bed. "Since you were asking about Cillineese stuff, I went and looked into some genealogy and all that."

Monica scooted farther onto the bed and leaned her back against the headboard. "Oh." She stretched her right leg out on the bed. The muscles seemed to tighten around the stitches as if they were about to pop out of the seam. "Thanks for doing that."

Creeping forward, Tresa spoke in a whisper, "May I take off your shoes, Miss, and then go fetch your lunch?"

"Um." Monica shifted in place and glanced at her shoes. It was so strange for Tresa to talk to her like that, but with Regina here, Tresa had to act subservient or risk getting demoted. "Sure. That's fine. Thank you, Tresa."

Tresa's nimble fingers made short work of untying the boots before she backed out of the room, giving a quick head bow as she left.

"At least she's gone now." Regina settled herself at the foot of the bed. "So I discovered we're related. I mean. I knew we were." She laughed. "What Noble isn't related in some way? But I was actually able to track ours. Most people aren't able to find their relatives so easily."

Monica nodded and placed her book bag on the floor. "I know. Aaron Markus is my uncle and yours. You said he was your uncle when we were in the library."

"Yeah, but he's more mine than yours." Regina leaned against a bedpost. "Aaron's married to Melody, you know, so he's only your uncle by marriage. He's my dad's youngest brother, so I'm actually a blood relative." She crossed her arms. "Not that it makes any difference. I never see him."

Wrinkling her brow, Monica gave another nod. Who was Melody? Her father's sister, maybe? It probably wasn't safe to ask. Regina seemed to like to hear herself talk, and that probably meant she spread stories to every other Noble in her circle of friends.

Gossiping wall slaves often found their meal bars stolen and their water pails missing, penalties imposed by those who hated wagging tongues. Yet the rumors and lies still spread through the wall dorms. The older women never let little things like a missing meal get in the way of spreading a story of someone's misfortune. She had often been the subject of their tales, and every one had stung, though she knew how silly and untrue they were.

"Are you listening to me?" Regina's sharp voice cut into Monica's thoughts, scraping her from those bittersweet memories of a simpler life.

"Yes." Monica blinked. "Miss" had almost slipped out automatically. The habits she had picked up as a Seen were proving difficult to stamp out.

Regina's dark eyes drilled into Monica with an accusing stare. "All right. It looked like you had zoned out. I would think you'd be interested in this, since you're a historian."

"I am interested!" Monica let the last comment slide, though it pricked at the back of her mind. Should she go on letting Regina believe she was a historian when she really wasn't? As soon as the thought entered her head, she had to hold back a laugh. What was she doing at this very moment but pretending to be Amelia?

"Good. I can find a family tree if you want. The library has one for every wing of Cantral. They're very interesting. I considered bringing them with me, but then I figured you might not even be here, so I didn't bother."

Picking at the bed cover, Monica nodded. Thoughts about the lies still swam around in her head, but Regina's talking made it too hard to focus on them.

A soft knock sounded at the door, a welcome distraction from Regina's chatter.

"Come in!" Monica breathed a sigh of relief. Tresa would certainly make Regina leave. She would say her patient needed rest.

The door creaked open, and a middle-aged Seen woman stepped in. She held a message tube clutched in both hands, her fingertips white. Tiptoeing to the bed, she held it out. "This is for you, Miss. From the Council. They said you were to read it right away and that you must send a reply."

"From the Council?" Regina clambered off the bed and held her hand out for the tube.

The Seen woman drew back. "I'm sorry, but it's for Miss Amelia.

I can't give it to you." She circled around Regina, never taking her eyes off of her as she handed the tube to Monica.

The slick metal cylinder felt cold and heavy. Monica pulled it close. "Thank you." The words barely made it past the lump in her throat. This was it. This tube would reveal her fate. Would she stay and try to free the Cantral slaves by being Amelia? Or would she be terminated? The Seen stepped away from the bed, her hands clasped in front of her, her gaze on the ground. She backed against the wall and stood as still as a statue, as if waiting for a command to come alive again.

Regina tapped her foot. "Aren't you going to read it?"

Hugging it close, Monica summoned her courage. "I'd rather read it alone if you don't mind."

A scowl drew Regina's eyebrows together. "Fine." She crossed her arms. "I'll see you in the library after lunch then. I can still help you with your project if you're interested." She stomped out of the room and slammed the door behind her.

Monica slumped her shoulders. At least Regina had listened. Monica glanced at the Seen woman who hadn't seemed to move a muscle the entire time. "Do you have to stay?"

The woman flinched, as if surprised that Monica had spoken to her. She raised her head and nodded once. "I'm sorry, Miss, but I've been told to wait for your reply."

"It's not your fault." Monica popped one end of the tube off and shook a rolled piece of paper into her hand. *Please let this be good news.*

After replacing the cap, she spread the paper flat on her lap. The bandage on her right hand rustled against the smooth paper.

A flowing script was scrawled across the page after the day's date and an official heading.

The Council of Eight has come to the decision that Amelia, a Noble, Citizen of Cillineese, Chip #61894101, will retain refugee status until the Council rescinds said status. All charges of treason against the Council have been waived in exchange for information pertinent to the case against Cillineese and valuable knowledge in computer programming. Information must be provided within seven days of January 17, 2870.

All of the above statuses and verdicts will be null and void if 61894101 refuses stated terms. Penalty for violation of these terms will result in the immediate termination of the subject and her father and sister. The Council is unanimous in this decision, and no appeals will be allowed.

Monica rolled the paper back up and clenched it tightly in a fist. Unanimous? Aaron Markus couldn't have been in agreement, could he? Not with the way he had been talking when she left—but what if everyone else overruled him? Could they do that? The north was supposed to have the most power, but maybe those rumors were false.

She held the cylinder out to the Seen. "Thank you. Tell them I agree and will be trying to remember despite my illness."

When the Seen left and closed the door, Monica lifted her chip and clutched it. Seven days. Was it possible? Who could tell? She had to agree or lose this opportunity forever. What else could she have done?

CHAPTER 13

When Tresa returned with the lunch tray, Monica's stomach had tied itself into knots with worry.

Tresa set the metal tray on the bed. "You don't look well."

"I feel a little sick." Monica shook her head, pulling her knees up to her chin. "But the Council said I can stay."

A smile broke Tresa's usual dour expression. "That's good!" She pushed the tray closer. "Isn't it?"

Monica shrugged. "Well, not the sick part, but yes, though I'm only allowed to live if I tell them what secret project Amelia was working on. Unfortunately, I have no idea what that was. Simon and I searched her rooms, but we never found anything except regular schoolwork. From the looks of her papers, she hadn't even chosen a major yet, which we know isn't true." She managed a weak smile. "At least the Council doesn't know anything yet, either. But if I keep stalling, they'll trust me even less, and I'll never get to travel freely."

"You'll figure it out somehow." Tresa gestured at the book bag on the floor by the bed. "Once you read some books on the subject, you'll know what to do. Computer genius is in your blood."

"You've said that before, but everyone else in my family has had the best education." Monica slid off the bed, careful not to put any weight on her injured leg. "Even with the help Simon gave me, I'm not very good at reading, and I know nothing about computers except that pulling out their wires makes them stop working."

Tresa handed her the bag. "Then you'd better get reading."

The bag weighed down Monica's hand. "I will." She slung it onto the bed where it landed with a thump, shaking the meal tray. "My life depends on it."

"You could eat while you read." Tresa righted a tipped salt-shaker. "You need to eat something when you take the medicine for your leg." She reached into her pocket and handed Monica two white pills wrapped in plastic. "They might make you sick if you take them on an empty stomach."

Monica popped the pills from their wrapper. "I'm not sure I can eat much, but I'll try." She selected a soft brown roll next to a plate full of colorful vegetables.

"Good. You're skin and bones. Even Amelia wasn't as thin as you are. I'm glad Master Aric and the other doctors were too distracted to weigh you, or we would have had even more explaining to do."

After swallowing the pills, Monica took a sip from a glass full of amber liquid. It tasted sweet but not at all like the orange juice from that morning. Why did the Nobles insist on drinking these weird liquids? Wasn't water good enough for them? At least this stuff helped get the pills down.

She repositioned herself on the bed, careful not to tip any of the dishes on the tray. "I'll eat as much as I can. I'll try to read, too."

Monica tore into the roll with her teeth as she pulled one of the thick books from her bag. She flipped through the first few pages— law codes for printed books and the obligatory brief history of the Council, including why they were so generous and benevolent.

She had read all that nauseating propaganda before when Simon pointed it out, and that was enough to last a lifetime.

After wading through the literary trash, she found an introduction to computer chips. She pored over the text, sounding out the unfamiliar words, just as her adoptive father had taught. The surrounding world seemed to disappear as the different codes and numbers filtered in and created a new world. Examples of programs and some of the simple, first-generation computer chips stirred the world into a dizzying whirlpool, but several more reads settled it down. It was actually beginning to make sense.

Hours passed. Monica's ticking wristband barely pecked through the book's mesmerizing hold. Her back and neck grew stiff as she leaned over her book, but mere discomfort couldn't draw her eyes away from the pages. This information meant life or death. Seven days. That wasn't much time.

More hours flew by until the pages, the words, and the surge of information blurred together and went black.

A moment later Tresa tapped her on the shoulder.

Monica blinked open her eyes and sat up. She lay slumped to the side, her head pillowed on her arms. "I fell asleep?" The book lay closed beside her, and the meal tray had disappeared.

"For quite some time now." Tresa set the book on the nightstand. "I would have taken this earlier, but you were holding it too tightly. I'm not surprised you slept after reading for so long. Regina came by and asked where you were."

Stiffness settled into Monica's knees and hips as she scooted off the bed. "I forgot all about that. She wanted to show me a family tree."

"A family tree? Why?"

"We're related, apparently." Monica grabbed her book bag and crutches. "I'm still not sure how, though." She glanced at her wristband—7:06 p.m. Time to clean up if the Nobles had had an early dinner. Clean up? She brushed away the thoughts. Amelia was a Noble; she didn't clean. That was the wall slaves' job.

"Of course," Tresa said. "Most of the more important Noble families are related in some way, even if it is distantly or by marriage." She shook her head. "Family trees . . . It must be nice to know who you're related to."

"Don't the computers keep track of those things?"

"No. I even gathered the courage to ask once." Tresa circled the bed and started straightening the pillows, as if she always needed to be doing something. "They only keep track of chip numbers, not names or faces. If you don't keep track of your own family, you're out of luck."

"So you don't know your family?"

"I know my sons." Tresa's tone grew bitter. "But now they might not even remember me as they grow and become men without a mother or father."

"I'm sorry," Monica whispered. What would it be like to have family out there whom she loved but would never see again? Never to know if they lived or died, married, grew old, had children. At least when her parents were killed she knew what happened to them. Even her adoptive mother who was forced to work in the fields had to be dead by now.

Tresa shrugged, though her hands were clenched. "It can't be helped."

Monica shook her head. Of course it could be helped. If the Nobles stopped their cruel regime and shut down the computers, then no one would have to be without a family, but the power-hungry beasts would never relinquish their stranglehold. She gripped her crutches and made her way to the door. Time to play with fire. Relationships had to be maintained. She couldn't afford to lose the friendship of the one Noble who would talk to her—if her talks with Regina could even be called a friendship.

"Where are you going?" Tresa hurried to the door. "It's getting late, and you never really ate anything."

"I need to find Regina and apologize for not meeting her earlier."

Nodding, Tresa took a step back. "Then if you don't mind, I won't accompany you."

Monica reached for the door, then stopped. "Why not?"

"I believe Miss Regina would prefer I not come." Tresa crossed her arms over her chest. "She doesn't like Seen. I thought you noticed." She opened the door. "But don't worry—I'll bring you something to eat soon."

"You're really determined to feed me, aren't you?" Monica grinned. "I'd be happier if you could find a meal bar for me."

"I'm sorry, but that's impossible." Tresa ushered her through the doorway. "And you know it."

"Yes, I know." Monica crutched down the hall toward the library. "Please take care of Vinnie for me! He's been ignored all day."

The door closed behind her, shutting out the little light the lamps in the room had allowed into the hall. She hopped up the stairs and through the passages to the library. The halls were empty during this journey, just like the last trip. All the other students must have already gone to their rooms or were still in the library. As she reached for the large brass doorknob, she gulped. Would there be other people her age inside? Or would it be empty like last time? She had to go in and see Regina, but what if she was mad and didn't want to talk?

She turned the cold handle and pushed the door inward. A low buzzing chatter filled the room. Regina sat cross-legged on top of her desk, peering down at three small children. She held an open book out to them, pointing at a colorful picture on one page. A group of four older girls huddled in an aisle, chatting among themselves.

Regina met Monica's gaze for a second before looking down again, but she smiled as she continued to read.

Glancing back and forth, Monica crept into the room as quietly as she could, though her crutches squeaked loudly. The group in the aisle looked at her but quickly turned away again.

After closing her book, Regina slid off the desk. She handed the book to a little girl sitting in front of her, and the little girl scurried off into an aisle of shelves.

Regina waved to the two boys still sitting and crossed the room to Monica's side. "There you are. I wondered where you had wandered off to. Your Seen said you were still recovering and needed your rest, but I wasn't sure if I should believe her or not. You never know with them."

Nodding, Monica fought to keep a straight face. *My Seen?* "I was rather tired. And Tresa's right. I'm still recovering." The wound in her leg cramped, sending a pang through her muscle, as if to agree. "I'm sorry I didn't come earlier."

"Oh, that's all right." Regina gestured to the children. "I have all these distant relations to keep me company." She put a hand on Monica's shoulder. "Speaking of distant relatives, how about we go look at those trees now? I have them spread out in the Eight room."

She steered Monica into the room with the large window and the eight bookshelves with the large gold letters. Monica barely kept her crutches moving fast enough to keep up with Regina's pushing hand.

Eight yellowing pieces of paper the size of a child lay spread out over the area rug. A breeze from small panel windows beside the larger window rippled through the pages, teasing the corners and threatening to lift the papers into the air.

The breeze picked up and whipped Monica's loose hair into her face. She closed her eyes for a second, relishing the gentle touch. She had been outside so few times that any hint of the world beyond these stone walls was a welcome treat. Simon had rarely allowed her out of the library to work on her studies, and before the fall of Cillineese, she had ventured out only one time that she could remember.

"Just a minute." Regina dashed across the room and started turning a small crank that controlled the window. As it creaked back into position, the wind died down until only the normal, drafty feeling of the palace remained. Regina flipped a small latch into place. "All right. Now they won't get blown all over. I just had the windows open to allow a breeze in here. It gets so stuffy."

Monica nodded. Stuffy? Regina had probably never experienced "stuffy" in her life. She had never slept in a dorm room with fifty other people with enough beds for only thirty. She had never sweltered in the heat of the laundry room while scrubbing clothes, or climbed through old ductwork filled with cobwebs and who knows what else. Maybe if the Nobles had a chance to experience wall slave conditions for themselves, they would make changes, but no one would ever convince them to do that.

She scanned the pages covering the rug. No, the only way the Nobles would listen was if the computers and their system were pulled out from under them and they were forced to change. And there was only one way for that change to happen. It was up to her to bring them down.

CHAPTER 14

Regina circled around the pages of family trees lying on the floor in a compass-shaped pattern, each page acting as one of the points, from north to south as well as the intermediate directions. "Which one do you want to look at first?"

Shrugging, Monica pointed a crutch at the page in the east position. "How about that one?"

"Ah, the east wing." Regina stopped her circling and stared. "Hey, where are your shoes?"

A tremor ran through Monica's body. She glanced down at her feet, clad only in stockings. What a wall slave she was. How could she forget to put her shoes on? Nobles always wore shoes. "I . . ." Heat crept into her cheeks. "I guess I forgot to put them back on in my hurry to get here."

Regina shot her a quizzical look. "I don't see how you could be in *that* big of a hurry, but okay." She settled to the floor in front of the east wing page, resuming her usual cross-legged position. "The east wing isn't a very exciting one. There's not much to it. Lots of only children, and Dristan Allen doesn't even have an heir. Why'd you pick this one?"

"I just picked it at random." Monica eased herself down onto the area rug, still careful not to put any weight on her leg. "Which do you think is the most interesting?" At least Regina had dropped the shoe discussion easily enough. Maybe it was a good thing she hopped from one topic to another so quickly.

Rolling her eyes, Regina said, "The north, of course."

Monica laid her crutches on the ground and set her book bag on top of them. "I guess it is pretty nice here."

"Of course it's pretty nice. It's more than pretty nice." Regina grabbed the north wing paper and pulled it closer. "It's the most important place in the world, Amelia. They're going to make it nice." She pointed at the family tree. "But it's not the building that's important. It's the people who live here."

"I haven't met many of them." Monica touched a dog-eared corner of the east tree. The north wasn't the most important place to some. "It must be interesting to have lived here your whole life and to know everyone."

"I suppose it would be." Pointing at a section of the north tree, Regina shrugged. "Here's my mom, Veronica. She's actually from the southeast wing. You can tell because her name is in mauve. All the trees are color coded."

"So the southeast is mauve?" Monica reached out and touched the gold words on the north tree. "And north is gold."

"Of course." Regina drew the southeast tree's paper over to her side, covering the east. "Southeast isn't a very important wing, but my mother managed to marry well anyway. You can't get a better match than to the heir to the north."

Monica wrinkled her brow. "The heir to the north? I thought Aaron Markus was . . ."

"No, no, not Aaron." Regina sighed and changed her voice to the tone mothers often used when talking to young children. "Rian, my father, was the heir, but he died, so Aaron got the job as the north wing ruler until Aric is old enough to take over."

"Aric?" Monica took the north family tree and found Rian's name on the chart almost at the bottom of the page, the dates of his birth and death printed clearly beneath his name. A line descended from between his name and Veronica's to two other names. *Aric* and *Regina*. "He's your brother?"

Nodding, Regina said, "Unfortunately. He's a real pain. He's so perfect. He's lived here his whole life. Mother wouldn't let me come until I was eight. She doesn't trust me like she does him."

"I think it would be nice to have a brother." Monica traced her finger over to Aaron's name and spotted his wife. *Melody*. That's who Regina had mentioned before.

"I'm sure having a sister would be much nicer, but then we wouldn't get to live here." Regina crossed her arms over her chest. "He's always too busy with his doctor work to pay any attention to me."

Monica reached for her book bag and drew it close. It would be nice to have a family at all.

"Don't you like having a sister?"

Hugging her bag, Monica shrugged. What could she say? She didn't even really know Audrey. "I guess so. She's a lot younger than I am."

"Oh. I didn't notice." Regina jumped to her feet and ran to the *C* shelf. She withdrew a tall, thin book and scurried back to Monica's side. "Here are the outlying city-state families. I found it when I was looking for the Cantral trees yesterday." She flipped open the red cover to the first page. "That's how I knew we were related. Here's Cillineese's."

Black lines crisscrossed along the yellowed page, forming connections from name to name. Darker, less-faded lines made up the segment near the page's bottom. Monica quickly located Joel's name. Two other people flanked him, one on either side—Melody and Gerald, his older sister and younger brother.

"See?" Regina jabbed a finger at Melody's name where another line indicated she had married Aaron Markus of north Cantral. "She's my aunt and your aunt. So we are related."

"Yes, but only by marriage. I don't think that really counts." Monica rubbed the soft fabric of her book bag. There was so much more to this family story than these trees could tell, but when would she be able to look deeper into this mystery? Whenever she was alone she had to study computers. The Council would expect an answer soon. There would be no time for translating, even if she were able to figure out the dictionary by herself. She quickly searched for her mother's name and found it, exactly where it should be, next to her father's. *Brenna Rose.*

Wrinkling her brow, Monica mouthed the name. *Brenna?* She knew the Rose part but had never heard Brenna.

Regina drew the book into her lap and tapped Joel's name. "I wonder what he did that was so bad they ordered the termination?" She slid her fingertip along the page until it came to rest on Gerald's name. "And then it happened again." Glancing at Monica, she said, "What is with your family?" Regina grinned as she pushed Monica's shoulder. "You're not going to get me in trouble, too, are you?"

"I don't plan on it." Monica gripped her bag more tightly. "I'm already in enough trouble myself." She bit her bottom lip. How much could she tell? She was already taking a chance by trying to make friends. Simon said not to trust anyone. Did trying to have friends break that command? He would want her to stay focused on her mission. He already thought she wasted too must time thinking about the journal.

Regina put the book down and murmured something.

Shaking herself from her thoughts, Monica looked up. "What?"

"You weren't listening again?" Regina stood and put her hands on her hips. "You sure stare into space a lot. I said you're not really a history or genealogy major, are you?"

Monica sighed. At least now she didn't have to figure out whether or not to continue the charade. "No, I'm not."

"I knew it. You would have been much more interested if you were."

"I am interested!" Monica grabbed her crutches and hoisted herself to her feet. "I do want to know more. It's just that I'm kind of distracted right now. I have a lot of other things to think about."

Picking up Monica's book bag, Regina said, "Sure. I understand. Your father and sister are still stuck in Cillineese."

Monica nodded. "Yes." She held a hand out for the bag. "Here, I'll take that."

"I can carry it for you. I'm sure it's no fun dealing with it and the crutches." Regina slung the bag over her shoulder. "Do you want to go back to your room?" She hugged the family tree book to her chest. "Or I could introduce you to the others! That'd be more fun. No offense, but your room is kind of gloomy and boring."

A tremor of fear ran through Monica's chest, but she shrugged her shoulders, trying to appear uncaring, though her fingers itched to snatch the bag back. "I'd ra—"

"Great! Let's go." Regina bounced ahead, the book bag dangling at her side.

Monica followed as fast as she could on the crutches. They clunked loudly despite the area rug cushioning their falls.

Stopping in front of the group of four girls in one of the aisles, Regina gestured to Monica. "Hey guys. This is Amelia. She's from Cillineese."

Monica slowed to a hobbling walk. She nodded to the group, studying them carefully—three brown-haired girls and one blonde, all four over a head taller than she would ever be, thanks to her malnourished childhood.

A wailing noise ripped through the room. Monica jerked around. Where was it coming from?

Regina glanced at her wristband. "Ugh. I forgot it was almost time for one."

The wailing continued, almost drowning out Regina's words.

"What is that?" Monica covered her ears with her hands.

"It's the weekly fire alarm test." Regina sighed and looked down at her wristband. It beeped, its screen flashing red. The siren stopped a second later, and her wristband silenced.

Monica gripped her crutch handles again. How awful.

One of the girls in the group stepped forward, just enough to be distanced from the others. "Sorry about that. It's just a test. Like Regina said, it happens every week. We're used to it." She extended a hand and flashed a straight white smile. "Welcome. I'm Lillian. It's nice to see someone from another city. We don't have many visitors. At least not many we get to meet."

After fumbling with the crutches, Monica shook Lillian's hand. "Thank you." When Lillian stepped back, Monica drew her hand to her side and gripped her crutches tightly. "So it was just a test? There's no fire?"

"No, of course not." Lillian smiled. "If there were a fire, we would have to evacuate."

"Oh, I see." Monica frowned. She had never heard of anything like that in the other wings, but the north wing probably had more security and safety measures.

"And I'm Brenna." The girl with blonde hair and wide gray eyes spoke. She twirled the end of her thin braid between her fingers.

"Brenna?" The name came out before Monica could stop it. That was her mother's name. Was it a common one?

The girl nodded. "Have we met before? Did you come with your father to one of the yearly meetings?"

"I . . . I . . ." Monica scrambled to think of something to say. Had Amelia ever come before? What if she said no, and then Brenna remembered that she had? "I'm not sure."

One of the other girls laughed. "Surely you would remember

coming to Cantral." She pushed Regina's shoulder. "Regina, where did you find this sickly country bumpkin? Out in the southern prairies? And what's with the bandages?" She nodded at Monica's wrapped hand.

Regina scowled. "Shut up, Julienne. At least she has manners, unlike some people I know."

Heat rose to Monica's cheeks.

Julienne flushed. "I see Aric's patient has a new protector. I'll be sure to tell him. Maybe he won't spend so much time obsessing over his miracle case. Come on, Brenna." She pointed at the last, unnamed girl. "Be sure to bring that book bag back to my room when you're done with it, Wren." She swept out of the room.

"It was nice to meet you, Amelia." Brenna scurried after Julienne, her head bowed. The library door closed behind them with a bang.

Wren made a scoffing noise in her throat.

Regina clenched her fists. "Great comeback, Julienne. You're so clever." She rolled her eyes. "I hate it when she tries to be smart. I wish Uncle Aaron would get rid of her."

"The papers have already all been drawn up, and everything's programmed." Wren stooped and picked up a black bag from the bookshelf. "She's not going anywhere."

Lillian nodded, her gaze mournful. "Regina, you'll probably be next, you know. Sixteen is plenty old enough to—"

"Don't even go there, Lil." Regina put her hands out in a defensive gesture. "Uncle Aaron wouldn't dare."

Monica looked from Lillian to Regina and back to Lillian. Did they even remember she was here?

Dusting off the book bag, Wren said, "The Council has many more important things to be thinking about right now, anyway." She shot a pointed look at Monica. "Like what to do with rebellious cities and their citizens."

Regina linked an arm with Monica, despite the crutch getting in the way. "It's not Amelia's fault her family's a bunch of upstarts. Besides, she's perfectly normal."

Wren crossed her arms over her chest. "What do you think, Lil?"

Shaking her head, Lillian backed away. "I'm just here to get an education and go home. I'm not interested in politics. Don't drag me into this. You'll be fighting for weeks."

"We will not!" Regina and Wren snapped.

Monica pulled her arm from Regina's grip. "I must admit I feel like a bumpkin right now. I don't know what you guys are talking about." She repositioned her crutches. "And don't believe everything the Council tells you, Wren."

"Those are some pretty bold words for a girl whose life hangs in the balance." Wren narrowed her eyes. "I've heard they've only given you a week to live."

Monica's breath caught in her throat. So other people knew about the deadline. What could that mean?

"You're making that up." Regina glared. "I would have heard about it. Aric would have told me."

"Think again." Wren jabbed Regina's shoulder with a finger. "You've been so caught up with your books lately, you have no idea what's going on outside your little library. You'd better watch it." Her voice rang with sarcasm. "Your reputation as palace gossip might be slipping. There's a lot you don't know. The dignitaries from Eursia are particularly full of interesting news."

Lillian stepped between the two. "Come on, guys, no need to show your inner witches to Amelia just yet." She turned to Monica. "They really don't hate each other that much."

"Yes, we do." Regina stuck her nose in the air. "My cousin is intolerable. She needs to go back to the south wing where she belongs."

Wren stamped her foot. "I let Julienne push me around enough, Regina. I don't need you doing it, too. You know I'd go home if I could." She stalked out of the room, slamming the door behind her.

Regina looked at the floor. "Sorry about that, Amelia." She sighed. "Things have been going on recently that are kind of stressful. She's wrong, anyway. I do know about the Eursians. Everyone is stressing about that more than anything."

"That's putting it mildly." Lillian shook her head. "But don't worry about it, Regina. It'll blow over soon enough." She headed for the exit. "I'll talk to Wren and see if I can smooth things out."

"Thanks." After Lillian left and closed the door, Regina rubbed the strap of the book bag. "So . . . that went well."

Monica stared at the closed doors, sure her eyes were as wide as dinner plates. "I really don't know what just happened." She reached for her bag. "But unfortunately, Wren is right about one thing. The Council isn't happy with me."

Drawing away, Regina held the bag from Monica's reach. "And I want to know why. You're being really mysterious. First you let me go on thinking you're a historian, and then you're summoned by the Council who I never even get to see, and I'm related to half of them, and now Wren says you're up for termination in a week." She pointed at Monica's leg. "Your injury can't be bad enough for that, and they let you come here for medical help even though by law, you're supposed to be dead." She cocked her head to one side. "So what did you do to make the Council so mad at you? I know it's not hard, but still . . . from what I've heard about you, you must have some real talent for them to let you live."

Monica stepped away from the tirade. She had to say something, anything to make this girl satisfied so she would stop badgering her. "They want some information. I told them I don't remember much, since I was so sick. Ask your brother; he can tell you how ill I was."

"I know." Regina rolled her eyes. "He was going over his patient's files for weeks. I've never seen him so obsessed with a case before. It's not like he even needs this degree. Not if he would register the credits he already has for programming."

Breathing a sigh of relief, Monica reached for her bag once again. "I'm kind of tired, so I think I'll go back to my room now."

Regina drew away, once more out of Monica's reach. "I don't think so. You're trying to distract me again." She put a protective arm around the bag. "You're not getting this until you tell me what information they want." Sliding a hand into the opening, she said, "Or . . . I could just look for myself."

"No!" The word echoed off the bookshelves. Monica clamped her hand over her mouth. "I mean." She regripped her crutch. "It's private research. Like you said earlier. I want it to be a secret."

Pouting, Regina handed the bag back. "Fine. There are rules I'm willing to break, but that's not one of them."

Monica snatched the bag and slung it over her shoulder. As it thumped against her side, a feeling of peace washed over her. Whatever Noble rule it was, it was definitely one she appreciated. "Thank you."

"Can't you at least give me a hint?" Regina's pout disappeared. "Or else I'll find someone else to do my snooping for me. That isn't against the rules."

"I . . ." Monica's leg started to throb. It would be better to just tell Regina than to have her snoop and find out more than she should, wouldn't it? What if she discovered the diary? With the Seen girl snooping around earlier, there was no doubt Regina could find someone to do her dirty work. "I'm studying computers."

"That's a rather broad topic." Regina leaned forward, her eyes pleading. "Can't you give me any more details than that? There are plenty of people who study computers. Even the techs who build the chips 'study computers,' and they don't know anything."

Monica inched toward the door. The problem was she didn't know more than that herself. "I really can't say."

"All right. Fine." Regina walked ahead and held the door open. "But I'm going to ask you questions all the time, you know. You'll get so sick of me, you'll tell me eventually."

"I think I'm more stubborn than you might realize." Though her arms ached, Monica crutched through the doorway at a fast clip. "I really don't remember much. I wasn't lying to the Council."

After closing the door, Regina skipped after her. "Aric can help with that. He has some sort of drug that enhances memory." She tromped down the stairs in front of Monica. "Are you sure you don't want me to take your bag for you?"

"Yes, I'm sure." Monica followed Regina down the steps as slowly as possible. A memory-enhancing drug? What if Aaron told Aric to use it on her? Of course it wouldn't help her remember anything about computers, but it might dredge up past events that were best forgotten.

CHAPTER 15

When Monica finally collapsed onto her bed, she lay against her pillows, her limbs feeling like dead weight. Everywhere her fingers had gripped the crutches ached. She let out a low groan.

"It serves you right for being gone so long." Tresa leaned the crutches against the wall. "I thought you were just going to go look at something and come back." She folded down the bedclothes beside Monica. "Now get under the covers and go to sleep or I'll give you a sleeping pill."

Monica groaned again and rolled over. Tucking her throbbing legs beneath the cool sheets, she let out a long sigh. "I'm sorry, Tresa. I didn't think I had been gone that long, and Regina kept talking. I thought it would be good to make friends. Especially with Regina."

"Is that because you think it will further the plan?" Tresa picked up a dark blue mug from the night table. "Or because you want friends and are losing sight of your goals?"

"I am not losing sight of my goals!" Monica sat up straight. How could Tresa even think that? "I studied for hours today, and if I don't interact with the others, I'll never get to know the ins and outs of the north wing. The Nobles need to trust me."

Handing the mug to Monica, Tresa shook her head. "I'm not sure you're being careful enough. Don't get too comfortable with them. They might act like your friends, but they're not."

"I know." Monica took the smooth, warm mug and sniffed at the steaming liquid. It smelled sour and left a bitter taste in her mouth though she hadn't lifted it to her lips. "What is this?"

"A mixture of tea and herbs. Aric prescribed it. He said it will help stave off infection." Tresa set her hands on her hips. "Drink it."

Monica put the cup to her lips and forced a sip of the hot liquid down her throat. The sour taste curled her tongue. "That's awful." Shuddering, she shoved the cup back onto the nightstand. "Something that tastes that bad can't be good for me. Not even spoiled meal bars are that terrible."

"If your leg gets an infection it will make our job much harder than it already is." Tresa glared at Monica. "Aric ordered it, so you'll drink it. Don't turn into a whiny Noble on me now."

"But I am a Noble." Monica smiled sweetly, trying to make herself look as innocent as possible. "I might as well act like one. You and Simon keep telling me that I need more practice." She took the cup from the table, held her nose, and downed the mug's vile contents. Plugging her nose muted the taste, but the liquid still made her want to gag.

Taking the cup, Tresa nodded. "That's better. Now go to sleep. I won't have you sneaking around and getting into mischief."

Monica pulled the covers up to her chin. The bitter taste of the tea coated her tongue, and her eyelids felt like someone had tied weights to them. "Tresa, you're acting like you care." She struggled to stay awake a little longer. "I thought you didn't like Nobles."

"I don't." Tresa put the mug on the dresser and picked up Monica's book bag from where it hung on the back of a chair. "But

I'm still not sure what you are yet." She wrapped the bag's strap around the body, bundling it into a tidy pile. "Sometimes you act like a Noble and then other times you're a wall slave."

Monica reached for the bag. Sometimes she didn't even know who she was.

Handing the bag to her, Tresa shrugged. "I've yet to make up my mind about you. Time will tell if you're worth the risk everyone's taking." She pointed at the bag. "Keep that close, maybe even under your pillow. I don't want anyone sneaking in here and finding whatever it is."

Monica hugged the bag. Tresa was right; time would tell. "What do you mean whatever this is?"

"You're obviously worried about someone finding it. You haven't let it out of your sight except when you saw the Council. It must be important."

Tucking the bag under her pillow, Monica breathed a long sigh. What could she tell Tresa? Nothing? If word of the journal got out and it fell into the wrong hands, all their plans would be discovered, and the Council would have her killed. Tresa would probably die as well.

Monica rested her hand on her pillow. This little book held a world of secrets in its pages. Maybe it should be destroyed without anyone ever knowing all that it contained. A shudder ran through her. No. She couldn't destroy it, the only link she had to her past. Her mother wanted her to have it—she said so in the first entry. What knowledge had she transcribed on those pages for her unborn child to read when the time came? If the journal were to be destroyed, there would be no way to find out.

"If you don't want to tell me what it is, I understand." Tresa's voice broke the heavy silence. "I know you're used to not telling anyone anything, but you can trust me." She sat down at the foot of the bed. "My sons often confided in me when we were still together. I know their problems are nothing like yours, but maybe I can help."

Monica pressed her cheek into her pillow. Tresa's assuring words were soothing, and the urge to trust her raised a heartache. She reached under her nightdress and pulled out the ripped medallion that always hung around her neck. The thin metal piece swept memories of another woman to mind, someone who had tried to gain her trust. *Alyssa.* And she had paid for it with her life.

Squeezing the medallion tightly in her bandaged hand, Monica shook her head. "I can't." Shaking her head again, she whispered, "Everyone who has helped me so far has died. I don't want you to get killed, Tresa. I can take care of this myself." Sleep tugged at her, but doubts tugged harder. The words in the diary had said she could trust others, and they had proved that, but could she risk their lives just to make her own easier? And what of the unseen Holy One her mother mentioned in her writings? How could she trust in someone she knew nothing about? She snuggled deeper into her pillows. "I just wish this could be over."

"And I wish I could tell you that it will be, but I'm afraid the end is nowhere in sight." Tresa crept to the other side of the room. "I'll wake you up early if you'd like, so you can work on your studies."

"Thank you."

Tresa touched the wall, and the lights in the ceiling grew darker and darker until the whole room was buried in a blanket of black.

Closing her eyes, Monica let sleep come, no longer fighting the pull into darkness. As she slipped into oblivion, she tucked her hand under her pillow, gripping the corner of her book bag.

***

"You're sure she's asleep?" A whisper penetrated Monica's foggy mind.

"How many times do I have to tell you that?" Tresa's sharp voice was barely audible.

"I don't want her waking up and finding me here. I could get terminated."

Monica tried to shake the haze away, but she couldn't open her eyes or move her head. What was happening? Who was Tresa talking to?

"She'll be asleep for hours." Tresa took on an irritated tone. "Now tell me what your plans were."

"I can't. They'll find out." The whisper sounded feminine.

"They'll know you were here again anyway, so you might as well talk."

"No one will check unless something goes wrong. I wanted to make sure you weren't mad."

Monica struggled again to sit up. Who was Tresa talking to? The girl who had sneaked in earlier?

Tresa sighed. "Of course I'm mad, but not at you. It's not your fault."

"Can I stay here with you? Momma's out again, and the others are so m—"

"No, I'm sorry, but you need to go back to your dorm. I don't want the computers taking more notice of you."

"But what about—"

Tresa made a soft shushing noise. "I'll try to come see you tomorrow." Silence reigned for a few seconds before Tresa spoke again. "I just wish you would tell me who made you do it."

"I can't."

"No one will ever know, honey." Tresa's voice trembled. "You know I'll try to keep you safe."

Monica's arms and head felt like lead weights. What had Tresa really put in that tea? Was she plotting something? The other voice was Shora's, wasn't it?

"You can't promise that. You can't stop them from demoting

me. No one can. There's already talk about Momma being transferred, and you know what would happen then."

Wrenching herself from sleep's grip, Monica sat up and forced
her eyes open. "Tresa?"

A dim light shone in from the hallway through the open door.
Tresa stood there, her hand on a small girl's shoulder—the girl who
had sneaked into the room earlier.

Shora's eyes widened, and she leaped away from Tresa. "You
said she was asleep! You promised."

Grasping Shora's wrist, Tresa shook her head. "She was asleep.
Stay a moment. She won't hurt you!"

Shora crumbled to the floor and put her head on her knees, one
arm still held in Tresa's grip. Quiet, muffled sobs came from the
girl's covered face.

"Shora, really!" Tresa hauled the girl to her feet. "I apologize
for disturbing you, Miss Amelia. You can go back to sleep."

Rubbing her eyes, Monica tried to shake away the dizzy feeling
that clouded her brain. She was Amelia, wasn't she? For a moment
she had forgotten. Nothing was making any sense. "What is she
doing here? What did you give me to drink?"

"I told you, Miss. Just something to help aid the healing
process."

A sullen look drew the corners of Shora's mouth down, but she
now stood. Tresa grabbed her shoulder and shook her. "Behave. I
thought you didn't want to be demoted."

Tears sprang to Shora's eyes. "No, I don't," she whimpered.
"But you lied to me. You said she was asleep."

"Shora?" Monica forced herself to concentrate. "Don't worry,
I won't demote you. I understand you wanted to see your aunt."

"Thank you, Miss." Shora hid behind Tresa.

Tresa stepped away from her. "You're much too old for that,
Shora. You're acting like a toddler."

Hanging her head, Shora clasped her hands behind her back,

taking on the submissive posture all proper Seen displayed in front of their Noble masters.

A pounding resounded in Monica's head, demanding she go back to sleep. "We'll talk about this more in the morning, Tresa. Whatever you gave me is making it too hard to concentrate."

"Yes, Miss." Tresa copied Shora's bowed head and posture before leading the girl from the room.

When the door closed, Monica lay down and shut her eyes, trying to will the headache away. A tune came to mind as she pushed herself deeper into her pillow. The melody capered along and then slowed to a dirge's pace before speeding up again. No words joined the notes, but the song became clearer. What was the name of it?

She grasped at the memory. The notes slipped away, as if teasing her mind. She clutched her hands into fists, trying to make the song stay, but the melody disappeared. What was the song from?

She opened her eyes, but the drug in the tea took over, forcing her back into the fog and into sleep.

***

The pounding in Monica's head thrummed in a steady rhythm. It beat against her skull, awakening her. Her eyelids seemed to be glued shut, but she forced them open.

Rubbing her eyes, she sat up and scanned the room. What had happened last night, anyway? Someone had been in her room. She scratched her head. Everything was so fuzzy.

Tresa lay on her cot near the door, a thin sheet spread over her curled form. She breathed steadily—probably still asleep.

Monica swung her legs over the side of the bed and rested her feet on the floor. Was it morning yet? She blinked. Tresa would be up by now if it were morning, wouldn't she?

She looked at her wristband. When she brushed the monitor with a finger, it lit up with a pale blue light, illuminating the time—

6:37 a.m. Then it was morning, but too early to be going anywhere. Only wall slaves would be up at this hour.

Caressing the gold links of her wristband, Monica wrinkled her brow. What were the wall slaves up to right now? Were they on the same schedule as the east and west slaves? Would they be crawling out of their beds, swallowing their meal bars, and marching to work? Or were they already up and in the passages, scampering from task to task?

Memories of the dim, wood-paneled passages came to mind along with faces of comrades she would probably never see again. She brushed them away. Her head still hurt, and these memories wouldn't help her cause. They would only take her back to troubles she couldn't change.

She lay back down and stared at the blank ceiling. No cobwebs clung to the corners, and not a speck of dirt marred the white surface. Thanks to the wall slaves' labors, nothing was amiss in the entire room.

Monica gritted her teeth. An unfamiliar woman's face came to the front of her memories. Her mind wouldn't settle down and let her rest. Why were these images resurfacing now? She needed to sleep, to recover from her leg wound, and to prepare for her next meeting with the Council. The past wouldn't help her with that.

Rolling onto her side, she closed her eyes, but the woman stayed—a face even Nobles would call beautiful.

The woman's dark brown hair became clear, the last reminder she needed to realize who this was. *Momma.* But not her adoptive mother—Brenna Rose, her birth mother, someone whose features she had forgotten long ago. Her face shone clearly now. Her brown eyes reflected deep pain, but they also filled with joy when she looked at her daughter.

Tears came to Monica's eyes. How could she have forgotten her own momma? True, she was only four when snatched from

Rose's arms, but why couldn't she have forced herself to keep these images close to heart as she grew?

"Are you all right?" A hand touched her shoulder.

Monica shot up to a sitting position, wiping her eyes. "I'm fine."

"Are you sure?" Tresa stood by the bed, one hand still outstretched. "I thought I heard—"

"I'll be fine." Monica's headache came back in full force. She put her hands on the sides of her head. "But whatever you gave me last night is giving me a terrible headache."

Nodding, Tresa sat on the edge of the bed. "I meant to talk to you about that. I'm sorry I woke you. I know how it must have looked, having Shora in here with me after she was sneaking around earlier."

"Yes." Monica folded her hands in her lap. "I thought maybe you had put something in my drink so you could . . . I don't know."

"I would never betray you to the Nobles, Monica," Tresa whispered. "They're our enemies. They took me from my sons. I told you that. Shora came here to talk to me. I hoped she would tell me who sent her."

"Then what was in the tea?" She put a hand to her head again. The aching subsided a little but still pulsed in the back of her skull. "I have a terrible headache. I don't think I've had one this bad since I bashed my head on the stairs in Cillineese."

"I told you—just some herbs to help heal your leg. Master Aric prescribed it." Tresa crossed her arms. "Don't you believe me?"

"Yes, I do." Monica slid off the bed and grabbed her crutches. "Some memories I haven't recalled in years are flooding back, that's all, and along with this headache, it just makes me wonder what else was in that stuff."

Tresa stood. "Where are you going?"

"To the bathroom." Monica hopped across the room. "I'm going to get ready and go to the library so I can ask Regina more questions. I don't think herbs were the only thing in that tea." She entered the bathroom and closed the door. What if Aric had slipped the memory drug into the drink without telling Tresa? Certainly she wouldn't lie about it if he had. Monica shook her head. Tresa had proven herself trustworthy too many times for that. If Aric was tampering with the tea, then it was without Tresa's knowledge.

CHAPTER 16

Monica dragged her crutches up the final step and onto the landing. She breathed a long sigh and started toward the library. Tresa had tried to make her eat breakfast again, but she had given most of the oatmeal to Vinnie. The spice didn't seem to bother him at all, and it was either feed him or release him back into the walls.

Monica's arms still felt watery from the previous day's excursions, but she had to ask Regina about Aric's medicine. At least her headache had gone away.

She stopped at the library doors and adjusted her book bag's strap. What was she going to say, anyway? Regina might not even be here yet. It was only 8:00 a.m. Most Nobles slept late, didn't they?

Monica sighed. Tresa had tried to convince her to wait a bit longer, even insisting on changing the bandage on her leg and removing the old wraps from her hand.

Twisting her hand palm up, Monica examined the scars criss-crossing her pale skin. The red, puckered slash marks made patterns from heel to fingertips, testaments to her journey through the Cillineese computer room—a journey she hoped no one but Simon and Alfred would ever know about.

The door swung open, and Regina stepped out, almost running into Monica.

Monica stumbled backward. "I'm sorry."

Stifling a yawn, Regina looked down the hall. "What are you doing here? Is it time for the review already?" She glanced at her wristband. "You're early."

"I . . . I was looking for you."

"For me?" Regina's eyes opened wider, and she stood straighter. "Really?" Her expression dimming, she drew back a step. "Why?"

Monica shrugged. "I wanted to ask you about something you said yesterday."

Regina shut the library doors and motioned down the hall. "Well, I need to go to my room and get cleaned up before the review, so you'll have to come with me if you want to talk." She started down the hall, tying her bedraggled hair back in a ponytail as she went. "You coming or not?"

"Um, okay." Monica hobbled after Regina.

Regina called over her shoulder, "Don't worry, it's not far. I had them move me to a room closer to the library. I didn't like being in the upper section." She stopped in front of a plain, dark door halfway down the hall. "Besides, the bedrooms in this wing are empty most of the year, so it's nice to be by myself."

"Empty?" Monica's book bag slapped her side, throwing off her balance. Hadn't Tresa said this part of the palace had people in it? She had been cautious about talking out in the open in these halls before, but maybe she was just being careful. Monica adjusted the heavy strap so that the bag rested on her hip.

"There are the meeting rooms and schoolrooms of course." Regina twisted the door's porcelain knob and stepped into darkness. "Usually Uncle Aaron uses this part of the wing for visitors.

It gets crowded during the annual gathering." She put her hand on a plastic panel, and soft white lights blinked on across each wall near the ceiling, illuminating every corner of the room.

She beckoned to Monica. "Come on in."

Monica inched past her into the brightly lit room. Blue paint had been spread on the walls, a different shade on each, and a bed, not much larger than Tresa's cot, stood tucked in one corner, the white sheets showing no signs anyone had slept there that night.

Closing the door, Regina motioned at the bed. "You can sit there if you want. I'm sorry I don't have any chairs." She scampered forward and straightened a precarious pile of books in the middle of the floor. Other similar stacks lay scattered across the room.

"Thank you." Monica smiled. Simon would have a fit if he saw this. He would never let Regina into a library again, facing demotion rather than letting someone terrorize a precious book.

"I have to look presentable for the inspection." Regina dug through the top drawer in a mahogany dresser. Navy blue shirts and pants flew from the drawer and landed in a growing pile. "Aaron gets annoyed when he sees me in this outfit. He thinks it looks slavish, but—" She slammed the drawer shut and opened the one below it. "Where are my other clothes?" Shoving the second drawer closed, she glanced around the room. "Bree better not have stuffed them somewhere hard to find."

Monica's arms started to ache again, but she stayed put. "What inspection are you talking about?"

Regina stepped across the room to stand right in front of Monica, a bundle of clothing piled in her arms. "What do you mean *what* inspection?"

"I don't know what you're talking about." Monica gulped. Was she supposed to know? Did she just break some rule by asking? Amelia had been sick for weeks. She wouldn't know what this rule was, would she?

"Oh." Regina deposited her armload onto the pile of clothes

she had removed from the dresser. "Once every quarter Aaron comes and inspects everyone's progress in their studies. It's the only way he ever acknowledges that we're here." She shrugged. "And if we're not up to his standards, he sends us packing to wherever we came from."

Regina opened a hidden sliding door, revealing a closet of brightly colored dresses. "But he can't send you back, can he?" Monica asked. "Aric's your brother, and he's the next ruler for the north."

"Uncle Aaron can do anything he wants." Shoving some dresses to the side, Regina stepped farther into her closet, her voice growing muffled. "So I have to make sure he doesn't get upset at me. And Aric doesn't care if I'm here or not anyway, so having him as my brother really doesn't matter."

Nodding, Monica leaned forward to try to get a better look into the closet. "You said something about Aric's work yesterday, about some memory drug."

Regina crawled back out of the closet. "Yes, I did." She brushed a stray hair out of her eyes. "It's his newest project. It's still in the experimental stages, though. They're not testing it on humans yet, as far as I know. Just on mice in their mazes." Putting her hands on her hips, she muttered. "I just can't find the outfit I usually wear."

"What about all those?" Monica pointed at the dresses hanging in the closet. "They look fine to me."

"You've got to be kidding." Rolling her eyes, Regina said, "Those are all outdated, and even if they did fit—they're dresses, and I don't wear those anymore." She rolled the closet door back into place, hiding all the colorful gowns. "I might be wearing something other than navy to please Uncle Aaron, but I'm not wearing a dress ever again if I can help it."

Monica looked down at her own dress, an ankle-length, dark purple gown with a tapered waist. When Tresa had selected it that morning, it seemed perfect—the fabric incredibly soft and the color so different from the grays and browns the wall slaves wore. But maybe it wasn't the right style for the north.

She shook her head. This was ridiculous. There wasn't any time to be thinking about clothes. When did her clothing ever matter before? As long as her garment kept her warm in the winter she never gave her attire a second thought. Wall slaves dreamed only of having enough clothes to keep their fingers and toes from freezing off, and here she was warm despite the winter month yet wondering if her dress was stylish.

Regina dug through another drawer in her dresser before pulling out a pair of white pants and a light blue shirt. "These will have to do."

"Can we . . ." Monica tensed her shoulders, as if to brace herself for a rebuke. "Can we talk more about the drug you mentioned? The memory one? I know you said they don't use it on humans yet, but—"

Waving her away, Regina nodded. "After I get changed. I'll be right out." She ducked into a bathroom next to the closet and closed the door with a sharp click.

Monica sat down on Regina's bed. This wasn't going anywhere. Were all Noble girls this distractible? Wren and Lillian didn't act this way yesterday, but did they behave differently after getting to know them? Monica rested the crutches against her shoulder. If only Simon were here, he could give some advice. What if she was wasting her time getting to know these people?

The sound of running water drifted from the bathroom.

Resting her chin on her hand, she blew out a long sigh. At least Regina seemed to trust her now. Perhaps she would help find a map around the north wing, a guide to the computer room. It would be easy enough to explain the need for one. Amelia would want to know her way around the palace.

Monica reached into her book bag and withdrew the computer book. She glanced at the bathroom door. Still closed.

The pages felt slick beneath her scarred fingers. She turned each page carefully, scanning all the words with barely a thought until she reached a section she hadn't read.

Glancing over the paragraphs, she shook her head. Programming codes. This wouldn't do. There was no way she could memorize these codes or even know what they meant. Besides, if Amelia's project were so secret, then it wouldn't be easily found in a computer book, would it?

After looking up, she turned to a new section. The sound of running water still echoed in the bathroom. Regina would probably be in there a few more minutes.

An asterisk marked the page by the new section's title—Program Cloning. Monica tapped the book. What did Simon say asterisks meant? Something about a notation? She glanced at the bottom of the page. Another, smaller asterisk was tucked in the corner, followed by two short sentences. *Research in this branch of science was outlawed in 2844. This section for historical purposes only.*

Her heart thumped. This might be it. Amelia could have been looking into program cloning. Whatever that was, it was illegal, and that's probably what the Council was looking for.

Monica slapped the book shut and shoved it back into the bag. At least it was something to tell the Council. They might want someone to do their illegal work for them, someone to pin the blame on. Even if it wasn't what Amelia had worked on, it would keep her chip alive for a little longer.

The sound of running water stopped. Monica eased herself off the bed and tucked her crutches back under her arms. As she put some weight on her right leg, the wound on her calf ached, despite the two pills Tresa had provided that morning. She gritted her teeth and rested all of her weight on her left foot again. If only she could walk normally she wouldn't have to worry about getting caught by the Council. She would be able to run and hide from anyone they sent after her.

The bathroom door swung open, and Regina emerged, now clad in her chosen outfit. She rubbed a white towel over her head, tousling her hair every which way. "Sorry—that took longer than I thought." Throwing the towel to the floor, she sighed. "I was getting kind of tired after staying up all night. I thought a shower might help me wake up."

"You stayed up all night?" Monica doubled-checked her book bag to make sure it hung by her side. "Why would you want to do that?"

Regina combed her fingers through her hair. "To finish a project for today's inspection and to look at those family trees some more." She drew back some of her hair and clipped a shiny metal pin in place, holding the locks securely. "I made some interesting discoveries." Glancing at her wristband, her eyes widened. "I'm going to be late!" She ran for the door, swung it open, and beckoned for Monica. "You can come if you want, but we have to get going."

"Okay, but going where, exactly?" Monica walked as quickly as her crutches would allow.

Regina closed the door behind them and led the way down the hall. "To the main classroom. I'll show you."

She scurried down the corridor and careened to the right, then left through a hallway toward the Council meeting room.

"Could you walk slower?" Sweat formed on Monica's palms as she gripped the crutches' hand rests.

Regina paused for a second, tapping her foot on the hall's dark carpet. "I'm already late. Don't worry. We're almost there—only a little farther." She started again, breaking into a jog.

Sighing, Monica quickened her pace, her crutches thumping loudly.

A few yards away, Regina stopped in front of a single door. She turned to Monica and held a finger to her lips.

Monica forced the crutches to make less noise as she hurried to Regina's side.

Inching the door open, Regina whispered, "He might be here already."

The door jolted inward, and Regina stumbled into the room.

"Indeed I am." Aaron Markus stood by the door, one hand on the knob. "Hello, Regina."

"Hello, Uncle." A smile formed on Regina's lips, though her eyebrows still wrinkled in a frown. "I'm so sorry I'm late. I was up studying last night and lost track of the time."

"You did, did you?" Aaron nodded. "Get inside."

When his gaze met Monica's, a tremor ran down her spine. She stepped back. Maybe he didn't want her here. She wasn't a real student.

"I wasn't expecting you, but you might as well join us." Aaron jerked his thumb toward the room. "Come. It's already late, and I have other things to attend to."

As Monica inched past him, a wave of dizziness hit. If she fainted, what would that tell him? That she was a coward, too afraid to face one man—the man who would decide if she lived or died. No. She had to summon courage. Too many lives depended on it to do otherwise.

CHAPTER 17

Aaron Markus closed the door behind Monica and gestured toward three empty chairs at a long table where other students were sitting. "Take a seat."

Regina led the way to the wooden table and slid into the second chair from the end.

Creeping after her, Monica glanced around the room. Seven other people sat at one side of the table, including the four girls she and Regina had spoken with yesterday, as well as Aric and two young men. They stared straight ahead, their gazes transfixed on the blank wall opposite them. Monica eased into a chair.

"Now that you're all finally here . . ." Aaron's gaze locked with Monica's again. "We can get started."

Monica sat up straighter and looked away, breaking the stare.

Papers rustled near the front of the room. "Aric," Aaron said, "why must you insist on trying my patience with paper copies of your work? This is the last time I will accept anything other than digital."

Monica looked up at her doctor sitting at the far end of the table. He wrote on a piece of paper in front of him, as if he weren't even paying attention.

"Yes sir." Aric looked up. "But I'm sure you'll be pleased with my work, in spite of the manner in which it is presented." He smirked. "After all, you requested the rush job, and I work best with pencil and paper."

Aaron's gray eyes clouded, and a scowl marred his features. "So you've moved on to the next phase?" His face calmed again, and all signs of annoyance melted away, the lines around his mouth and eyes smoothing.

"Yes sir, just as we discussed." Aric looked down at his paper again.

"We'll talk about this more in depth during your private session." Aaron drew out a flat gray tablet from his jacket pocket.

Monica watched the entire scene carefully. As fear rushed in, she stifled a gasp. What if Aaron asked her to give a report about Amelia's studies? She glanced at Regina, but she kept her eyes locked on her uncle.

Aaron tapped the tablet, and a light switched on, casting a glow over his face and tinting his skin blue. "Charvick, Shalton."

The two young men sitting by Aric spoke in unison. "Yes, Master Aaron?"

Aaron's fingers skittered across the tablet's surface. "Your work seems to be in order." He nodded. "Charvick, I will put in your request for transfer to the school."

"Thank you!" The blond boy sitting next to Aric nodded. "Thank you, sir."

"You're most welcome." Aaron smiled. "I'm sure you will perform admirably and not let this opportunity go to waste." He glanced at the tablet in his hands again. "Shalton, you have been approved for another year of study here."

Shalton nodded. "Thank you, sir."

"Yes, yes." Aaron tapped the tablet's screen. "These quarterly reviews always seem pointless to me. I could just as well tell you all how you're doing from my office."

Consulting his computer again, Aaron shook his head. "Julienne, your grades are poor, as usual. I would send you back home at once, but we all know that situation."

Monica kept her features blank, though a whirlwind of thoughts tumbled inside her head. Aaron Markus couldn't send Julienne away? But he was the most powerful man in the world.

Julienne folded her hands on the tabletop. "May I go, then?" A small smile flickered at the corner of her mouth.

"No. I'm not finished. I'll get back to you in a moment." Aaron marched forward. "I might not be able to send you away . . ." He laid the tablet on the table and looked her in the eye. "But I can certainly make your life miserable during your stay here." He stepped back again. "Of course, if your grades improve, there will be no need for that. Do I make myself clear?"

Julienne nodded, her face pale. "Yes sir."

"Excellent." He turned to Lillian, who sat shaking next to Julienne. "I really am quite reasonable, dear." Pointing at his tablet, he said, "I see this is your first review. I thought you looked new."

Lillian looked down. "Yes. I received permission just a couple of months ago, though I've visited Cantral many times. Wren"—she glanced at the girl to her left—"has been helping me get acclimated. I know my grades aren't the best, but—"

Waving as if to dismiss her, Aaron said, "They're fine." He shot a look at Julienne. "Unlike some, at least you're not failing every class. But I will expect better next quarter." He picked up his tablet again. "Julienne, you're held back a year—see, I could have sent you a message just as easily—Lillian, you're moving forward, and . . ." Tapping the handheld computer, he made a tsking noise.

"There you are, Wrenillee." He smiled. "Perfect grades, as usual. Keep that up and you might skip next quarter."

"Thank you, sir." Wren shot a smug look at Julienne.

"And Brenna," Aaron said, "below average. Remind me again why you're allowed to study here with grades like these when I have a dozen much more qualified applicants clamoring for the spot."

Brenna's face flushed red. "Well, sir—"

"There is no good reason, is there?" Aaron tapped his chin. "Your father claimed I had a debt to repay or some nonsense. All well and good while your grades were high and your father still worked for me, but now . . ." He shook his head. "I'll be submitting your report to the Council for further review, but I'd be surprised if you were even allowed to stay in the southwest wing."

Julienne snickered.

Aaron shot a freezing glare at the group. "I would send all of you away if I could. I have no use for children, no matter how close you are to legal age." He nodded at the door. "You may go. Aric, Regina, and Amelia, you will stay here."

Brenna cast a sorrowful look back at Monica and Regina. "Sorry," she mouthed.

The four girls slipped from the room, followed by Charvick and Shalton.

Sorry? Monica shuddered. Did Brenna know something Regina didn't? As soon as the door closed, Aaron stuffed his tablet back into his pocket. "I won't need this anymore. Your records, Regina, are forever ingrained into my memory." He rubbed his temples. "I doubt I could get them out of my head even if I bashed it against a wall."

"Sir?" Regina squeaked. "I thought I did well on my last tests." She held her hands in her lap, her fingers trembling. "Weren't my scores high?"

"Your tests went well, yes." He paced back and forth in front of the long table. "But everything else, completely abominable. You kept no records of study hours or any of your other assignments. You never reported to your tutor. I believe I even heard rumors that he gave up on you and took a transfer rather than work with such a stubborn student. I had no records of your whereabouts for the past month since you never recorded any studies, and I had to have your chip tracked myself." He stopped right in front of Regina. "It's a lot of work to do that, did you know? You should realize that I haven't time for this."

Regina shrank away from him. "Yes sir. I just—"

"Just like your father. He was always getting into trouble, making my father angry." He planted his hands on the table and leaned close. "You probably cheated on these tests, just like your father did, didn't you? I have no proof that you studied, so how can I think anything else? All I know is you were snooping around the palace, making mischief."

"No!" Regina shot from her seat. "Uncle, I didn't cheat! I wouldn't!" Tears welled in her eyes. "I know my father didn't have the best reputation, but I'm not like him."

Aaron folded his hands behind his back. "I have no idea if what you say is true." He shrugged. "You know what will have to happen now."

"Uncle!" Aric half rose. "I don't think that's necessary. She'll do better next time, won't you, Regina?"

"Stay where you are," Aaron snapped. "We don't want Regina setting a bad example for the new girl, now do we?"

Monica trembled under his stare. What was going on? Did he expect her to speak? Regina hadn't cheated, had she?

Aric sat down hard in his seat. "No sir. But I don't think my patient will suffer from contact with Regina."

"Please." Regina's bottom lip quivered. "Please don't send me back. I didn't cheat. I'll log my hours this time—just don't send me back."

"I decided last night." Aaron tapped his wristband. "Your

mother will be arriving to take you to New Kale this afternoon. I suggest packing your things."

"You can't send me back!" Regina banged a fist on the table. "This is my home." She shot a pleading look to her brother. "Please, Aric. You know what it's like there."

He started to rise from his seat again but stopped. "Regina, I can't."

Regina threw back her chair. It fell to the floor, clattering on the wood. "You mean you *won't*. You could do something if you wanted to! You could make him let me stay. You just don't care!"

"I do care!" Aric stood and shoved a chair out of his way.

"You never p—" Regina's eyes rolled back in her head, and she started to fall. Her head hit the side of the table with a resounding smack, and she crumpled in a heap on the floor.

Monica's jaw dropped. "Regina?"

Aaron held a finger to his wristband. "Much better. I was getting quite tired of all of that bickering."

"What did you do?" Aric scrambled over the chairs between him and Regina and gathered her into his arms. "Regina?" he whispered. "Come on, wake up." He laid her on the table, cradling her head in one hand and brushing his fingers across the growing knot on her forehead with the other. "Uncle, I don't often use my position against you, but I demand you tell me what you did to my sister."

Aaron's eyes grew narrow. "I did nothing but put her to sleep. She was working herself into a frenzy. I didn't think it healthy. She'll be perfectly fine."

"I'm her brother and her doctor. I'll decide what's healthy and what's not!"

"I only put her to sleep through her chip." Aaron shrugged.

Aric gathered her into his arms again, cradling her head against his chest. "I've never heard of putting someone to sleep with their chip, and besides that, tampering with chips is illegal."

"Not for me." Aaron waved him toward the door. "Now collect your two patients and go. I'll have my discussion with you and Amelia at a later time. Just make sure your mother takes Regina home without a fuss."

Aric's jaw tensed, and his fingers gripping Regina's shoulder turned white. "She'll get home safely." He nodded to Monica. "Let's go."

Monica picked up her crutches from under the table and hopped out of the room. She turned to close the door behind her and met Aaron's smoldering gaze. Quickly releasing the door, she gulped and hurried after Aric.

They retraced the path to Regina's room in silence. Aric seemed not to notice the weight as he hurried down the steps.

Monica struggled to keep up with his steady pace. The watery feeling in her arms from earlier was nothing compared to the ache that coursed through her limbs now, and it was still morning. She shook her head. The wall slaves said Nobles were weak and use-less; she was certainly playing her part well.

"Are you all right?" Aric paused a few steps in front of her. "It was thoughtless of me to run ahead. I'm just worried about Regina." He shifted her in his arms. "I'm not sure what he did, but as soon as I get my equipment, I'll find out."

"I'm fine." Resuming her clunking walk, Monica caught up to him. "You don't have to worry about me. I can take care of myself."

"I'm your doctor. It's my job to worry." Aric stopped in front of Regina's room. "Could you open the door?"

Monica nodded and did as he asked, letting Aric walk in first.

He settled Regina onto her bed before clearing a stack of books from beside her pillow. Unfolding a blanket that lay at the foot of her bed, he spread it across her body.

As Monica watched his swift, sure movements, she bit her lip. How nice it would be to have an older brother or a family member of any kind—someone to look after her and make sure she was safe and comfortable.

"Will you stay here while I get my bag?" Aric knelt beside the bed, still facing Regina.

Glancing over her shoulder, Monica asked, "Me?"

"Yes." He smiled. "Regina doesn't have much choice but to stay." He touched his sister's shoulder and whispered in her ear, just loud enough for Monica to hear, "Don't worry, I'll be right back, and I'll find out what he did." He trotted to the door and turned as he closed it. "Please explain the situation to my mother if she arrives before I return."

The door closed behind him before Monica could protest.

She fiddled with her wristband. The screen hadn't lit up or beeped since the fire alarm. Tapping the screen, she watched the blue light flash on and off with every fall of her finger. That noise had been terrible. Did the Nobles really put up with it going off every week?

Her wristband screen went dark again, despite her tapping. She stopped and grabbed a fistful of her skirt, twisting the fabric around in her fingers.

Regina groaned and rolled to the side, but her breathing remained even, and her eyes stayed closed.

"I don't even know what your mother looks like." Monica rested her chin on her hands. "I wonder if I'm supposed to have met her."

***

The door burst open, and Aric stomped in. He breathed heavily and wiped a hand across his red face. "Sorry. My room's rather far away."

Kneeling beside the bed, he unclipped his bag. He withdrew a handheld metallic device and punched some buttons on a silver number pad. "I'd appreciate it if you didn't tell anyone about this. It's a project I designed on my own. It's not sanctioned."

Monica leaned closer. It looked almost like a compressed version of the wand-like instruments the furnace workers used back in Cillineese. "What is it?"

"It's complicated." Aric rolled Regina onto her stomach and waved the device above the back of her head.

Monica settled onto a book stack. "Is there anything I can help with?"

"Not really." Reaching into his kit, Aric muttered, "Faulty battery pack." He pulled out a tablet similar to Aaron's, as well as a thumb-sized gray block. "That's the problem with not being sanctioned. I have to make do with thrown-out equipment." He snapped the block onto one end of the handheld device, and a green light flashed on. "I'm sure you know all about it."

"I don't know what you mean." Monica watched intently as he waved the wand over Regina's head again.

Smiling, Aric plugged one end of the wand into the tablet and pressed the top of the tablet's upper edge. "Of course you don't. What student would admit to having an unsanctioned project? Especially one in your situation."

Three dots appeared on the tablet screen, then blinked off one by one.

"Y-you know about all that?" Monica gulped. Did the girls know, too? Maybe that's why they shunned her and Regina. "It's just that Regina didn't seem to know. She said she didn't, anyway."

"Regina says a lot of things that aren't true." Aric set the tablet down and rolled his sister onto her back again. "I know everything that goes on in the north wing." His smile fell, and he pushed a lock of hair from Regina's cheek. "At least I'm supposed to. I don't know what . . ." Shaking his head, he sighed. "Never mind."

"I see." Monica grasped one of the bedposts. She tried to smile, but her muscles refused to cooperate. No one but Simon really knew all the secrets she carried. "It probably sounds silly, but you can talk to me. I'm trustworthy."

"Says the girl whose family is trying to overthrow the empire I'm supposed to inherit." Aric's eyes narrowed, though he still smiled. "If I remember my history correctly, your uncle tried the same thing."

Monica winced. Not her uncle. Her father. And now her. But it was the right thing to do. She couldn't be blinded by the grandeur the Nobles lived in. She turned and stared at the wall. She had to remember the slaves who maintained this façade for their taskmasters. They were the ones who mattered. They suffered while she took her time trying to find a way to free them. She had to remember that.

CHAPTER 18

"I didn't mean to upset you." Aric shrugged. "Diplomacy isn't my strong suit."

The tablet vibrated and emitted a beep.

Aric snatched it up. "Finally." His gaze roved up and down the screen. "There's a lot of coding here that's far from normal." He ran a finger along the side of the text, scrolling through long lines of jumbled letters and numbers.

Monica leaned forward again. Some of the strings of letters were similar to those in her book, but they zipped by too quickly to decipher. "Where is it coming from?"

"Her chip." He wiped a hand across the screen, and the coding disappeared. "I know what to do now, though it's technically illegal."

"But Aaron said she'd be fine."

As Aric typed furiously on the screen, numbers appeared. "I think he's testing me. Now please be quiet—I need to concentrate. This would be a lot easier if I had his tablet. I'm sure he has both the program to put her to sleep and to wake her up on there."

Aric's fingers blurred as he muttered under his breath. "Using a beta program. He's insane. He lied. She's not going to be fine." The code filled the tablet's screen and scrolled into the top, disappearing as he pounded out more. "She's not some wall slave. He's probably never even tested it before."

Monica's stomach twisted. Not some wall slave? Aric was just like the other Nobles. He seemed nice enough a moment ago, but now he showed his true colors. Yet, maybe it was just the stress of watching his sister in this state and trying to save her. Maybe he didn't mean it.

"I think that should do it." Aric tapped the computer one last time. "If I did it properly, it should wipe the program and reset the chip to normal." Fingers shaking, he unplugged the handheld device from the tablet. "It's dangerous, but I'm not sure how to turn his program off any other way."

Regina lay as still as ever on her bed, her breathing slow and even.

He tucked the tablet back into his bag and pulled out two palm-sized pieces of plastic attached to each other with a length of curling, rubber wire. "Hold these."

"Okay." Monica cradled the devices in her hands. "Maybe we should just ask Aaron for help. Or someone who's . . ."

"Better qualified?" Aric frowned. "Aaron won't help, and don't worry—I am qualified." He slid a hand behind Regina's back and lifted her to a sitting position. Her chin flopped to her chest. "I have all the requirements for a computer programming major. I just didn't register them into the computers. I'm not old enough to officially have two degrees yet." He rested Regina's head against his shoulder. "And I'd rather be a doctor."

Holding her shoulder with one hand, he poised the handheld computer over her neck. "Are you ready?"

Monica widened her eyes. "No! I don't even know what you're doing, or what I'm holding!"

"Defibrillator paddles. I don't think I'll need them." Aric closed his eyes for a second. "You don't have to do anything. Just hold them out and be ready for me to grab them. It's a worst-case scenario precaution. You won't have to do a thing."

"That's not very reassuring." Monica held a disk in each hand, palms up and extended toward Aric.

"I'm one of the best doctors in Cantral. She'll be fine." His Adam's apple bobbed, and he placed the wand at the back of Regina's head. As he held it in position, he closed his eyes and said under his breath, "Come on, Reggie, wake up."

The computer beeped. Her body convulsed, and she fell against the mattress. Aric grabbed her shirt, reaching for the paddles with one hand.

Monica fumbled with them, but Aric grabbed the cord, yanking the paddles away.

Regina's eyes popped open, and she feebly pushed at Aric's hand. "Let me go."

As the defibrillator paddles clattered to the floor, Aric sat back in his seat. "It worked!"

Breathing a sigh of relief, Monica laid a hand over her heart. "You really scared us, Regina."

Regina propped herself up on her elbows. "What happened? I was mad about something, but now . . ." Shaking her head, she squinted. "What are you two doing in my room?" She shot up off the bed. "I'm going to be late for the—" Her face turned white, and she sat back down. "Aric?"

Aric held her hand. "Don't get excited. You're not going to be late. I'm here to take care of you."

She waved him away. "It's not that." Her face twisted, and she held a hand to her mouth. "I think I'm going to be sick."

He scooped her up into his arms and ran for the bathroom. They disappeared inside, and the sound of retching issued from within. The pungent smell of vomit wafted through the bedroom.

Monica grimaced. Poor Regina. Monica retrieved the defibrillator from the floor before sticking it back into Aric's bag. Her fingers brushed against folded papers. She glanced over her shoulder. How long would they stay in the bathroom?

Reaching back into the bag, she angled her head to the side, trying to get a better look at the pages. Regina never gave her a chance to ask about Aric's memory drug. He wouldn't keep papers about it in here, would he? But then again, she kept her mother's diary with her, close at hand, where no prying eyes could find it.

Curving letters spelled Amelia's name across the top of one page, followed by the words *Case Study #1*. As Monica pulled the papers from the bag, her hands shook.

"What are you doing?"

Monica whirled around.

A tall, brown-haired woman stood in the doorway. She glided into the room and shut the door. "What are you doing? Where's my daughter?"

"I was just—"

"Oh, Mother." Aric poked his head out of the bathroom. "You've arrived. I thought you weren't going to be here for another hour or more."

"I had a particularly enthusiastic transport driver." Aric's mother wrinkled her small nose. "Has someone been sick?"

Monica stuffed the pages back into the bag.

"Ah, yes." Aric inched out of the bathroom and closed the door. "But Regina will be fine in a minute."

His mother crossed her arms. "Let me see her, Aric."

"You know she wouldn't like that."

"I don't really care about her ego right now. She's sick and needs attention." She swept past him to the bathroom door. "She probably worked herself into this state by being over-emotional again." Turning the knob, she called, "Regina? I'm coming in."

"No!" Regina's voice sounded shrill, though muffled by the door. "I'll be out in a second. I'm fine."

Regina's mother turned to Aric. "How long has she been like this?"

"Only a few minutes. We just got back from our reviews. Aaron did something to her chip." Aric clenched his fist. "He could have killed her."

"What do you mean?" The woman narrowed her eyes. "You can't just 'do' something to someone's chip." She shook her head. "She's probably just upset about having to come home." Turning to the door again, she said, "Regina, if you don't come out here in five seconds, I'll . . ."

The door opened and Regina shuffled out of the bathroom, her eyes red. "Hello, Mother."

Monica shifted in her seat. Maybe she could slip out quietly and avoid any questions about the papers.

"You have a lot of explaining to do." The woman wrapped Regina in a hug, then held her at arm's length. "You look underfed and un-rested. From what I hear, you haven't kept up with your schoolwork. What have you been doing?"

Regina brushed her mother's hands away. "Nothing. I've been doing school; I just keep forgetting to log my hours in my tablet." She rubbed the back of her head, mussing her hair even more. "Besides, it's Aaron you should be mad at. He has no reason to send me home. I did my work."

"Your uncle has his reasons," the woman said. "And I would rather have you home anyway, away from all of . . ." She gestured to the room. "This."

"But I love it here." Tears filled Regina's eyes, highlighting her already-red lids.

Her mother's gaze slid to Monica. "And who is this young lady? Someone to fill your place so quickly?"

Her stare lingered. Monica squirmed under the scrutiny.

"No, Amelia was here before the reviews." Regina wiped her eyes. "She's from Cillineese. Gerald's her father."

Monica stood and inclined her head. "It's nice to meet you, ma'am."

"And you." The woman's brow creased. "I'm Veronica, but we've corresponded before during some of your studies. I'm sure you remember all those messenger tubes." She held Monica in an unwavering gaze. "You look different than I imagined. Less like your father than other people have indicated. I think . . ."

Monica gulped. Amelia was supposed to know Veronica? "But a lot of people say I look like my father."

Veronica wrapped an arm around Regina's shoulders. "You do. I met him when his brother, Joel, married my sister, but that's not who I . . ." She shook her head. "Never mind."

The blood drained from Monica's face. Veronica was her mother's sister? Was that the resemblance she was thinking about? What if she figured out Amelia wasn't who she said she was?

Regina wriggled from her mother's grip and stood by the bathroom door, her face still pale.

"Amelia is also a patient of mine," Aric spoke up, frowning at Regina. "I'm sure you heard, Mother, about my accomplishments."

A smile broke through Veronica's somber expression. "Yes, I received a messenger tube a day ago. I'm so proud of you, Aric." She clasped his hands in hers. "You're going to make a fine ruler."

He looked at the ground. "More importantly, Amelia is well."

Veronica shrugged. "Though a little worse for wear." She shot a look at Monica. "But why the crutches?"

Aric opened his mouth, but Monica spoke up first. "They operated on my leg, and the wound hasn't healed yet."

"I see." Veronica looked at her wristband. "And when will you be returning to Cillineese?"

"Mother, please," Regina groaned. "Stop interrogating her. You're here to drag me home. Can we go now? I'd rather not prolong all these good-byes."

"I'm glad you're feeling better." Smirking, Aric poked her in the shoulder. "Don't you want to say good-bye to Julienne?"

"I'd be happy if I never saw her again." Regina stuck her tongue out at him.

"Regina!" Veronica glared at her daughter. "Don't say such things. I thought you promised to be nicer to her. She is going to be higher ranked than you in just a year."

"Don't worry about that," Regina said in a sweet voice. "I'm sure by that time you'll have me parceled off in some distant city-state, bound to marry someone fifteen years older than I am, who'll die and leave me to rule by myself, just like Aunt Felicia."

Veronica tapped a button on her wristband.

"Ow!" Regina grabbed the back of her head.

"How dare you!" Veronica snapped. "I've let you run wild too long, Regina. I'm glad Aaron is sending you home. Uncle Trallen has more time to help discipline you than Aaron does. If your father—"

"Mother, please." Aric stepped between Veronica and Regina. "She's had a rough day. Aaron did something to her chip; I told you that. Don't be too hard on her."

Monica shrank from the bickering trio.

"I'm not too hard on her. That's the problem. She needs discipline. Letting her come here was a bad decision."

Regina continued rubbing the back of her head. "I haven't run wild. I've learned a lot. I know Aric's been keeping things from you."

"What?" Veronica set a hand on her hip. "That's probably just another one of your lies. Don't try to distract me, young lady."

Putting his hands on Veronica's shoulders, Aric looked her in the eye. "Mother, you're not listening. Aaron did something to

Regina's chip." He pointed at Regina. "He put her to sleep. She just dropped to the floor like a stone." Gesturing with his hand, he said, "Slammed her head on the table on the way down, and now she doesn't even remember going to the review."

"What do you want me to do?" Veronica sighed. "Ask him to step down because Regina fell asleep in class? Who would we report it to? And if he gets relieved of power, who takes his spot? You? You're not old enough yet."

"Besides." Regina glowered. "Aric tampers with chips, too." She crossed her arms over her chest and smirked at him. "Don't you, Aric?"

"Regina." Aric growled. "You promised."

She leaned against the wall. "Then get Aaron to let me stay."

"Aric." Veronica placed a hand on his shoulder. "What's she talking about?"

"We can discuss it later. Amelia and I have another meeting with Aaron to talk about her health and her future here." Aric crossed the room in three strides and grabbed his bag. "I hope you and Regina have a safe trip back to New Kale, Mother. Say hello to Uncle Trallen for me." He took Monica by the arm. "Aaron will be expecting us."

"We can't go!" Regina stamped her foot.

"We most certainly will discuss it later." Veronica pointed a finger at Aric. "You may be higher ranked than I, but I'm still your mother, and I won't have you breaking the law."

Aric released his hold on Monica's arm. "It was for Regina, Mother. I didn't know how to wake her up any other way. I admit it." He shrugged. "I reset her chip."

"You what?" Veronica rested a hand on the wall, her face white. "You could have killed her! You should have asked Aaron for help. If he did something to her chip, then he can fix it. You shouldn't have taken matters into your own hands." She tapped her forehead. "What were you thinking?"

"I was thinking my sister needed to be taken care of by someone other than that maniac." He pointed at Regina. "Besides, she's fine, and I think it's time you two headed home."

Veronica's scowl softened. "Yes, she is fine." Her eyes scanned his face, a look of worry growing on her brow. "I'm just afraid of what trouble it might get you in. Aaron would rather have his own son rule instead of you. His position was hard won. He won't let it go easily." She reached out and hugged her son close. "I pray you'll be safe."

"Mother, please." Aric patted her on the back. "I'll be fine."

Drawing away, she looked at Regina. "You're right. It's time to go."

"I haven't packed yet," Regina said.

"We'll have a Seen do it and send your things on another transport." Veronica put an arm around Regina's shoulder and steered her toward the door.

Monica breathed a long sigh of relief. They were finally leaving. Who knew that three people could have such a noisy conversation?

"It was nice to meet you, Amelia." Veronica turned to look back at her. "I'm sorry you had to witness such a breach of etiquette, but I'm sure you understand, don't you? Having a younger sister, you two must know all about . . . conversations like these."

"Oh. Yes. It was nice to meet you, too." Monica managed a weak smile. From what she had seen, Audrey and Amelia really cared for each other. Did Audrey miss her older sister? A pang of sorrow shot through Monica's heart. The poor girl didn't even know her sister was dead. She thought her sister was doing better. Who would tell her that Amelia had died and an imposter was wearing her chip?

Monica touched the chip under the dress. No one. At least not yet.

CHAPTER 19

"Good-bye, Regina," Monica whispered.

Regina looked away and said nothing. A grim expression on her face, her mother steered her out of the room.

"My mother's right." Aric fiddled with the handle of his doctor's bag. "I'm sorry we put on such a display. You must think us unseemly ruffians now, unable to control our tempers." He sighed and gestured to the exit. "Shall we go? I received a message from Aaron while Regina was . . . indisposed. We're to meet him back at the schoolroom."

"Do we have a choice?"

"No, not really." Aric shrugged and held open the door.

"And I don't think you're ruffians, just a little louder than I'm used to."

Aric laughed. "You're very kind."

Monica repositioned her crutches and headed down the hall, a deep feeling of dread growing in her stomach. "Do you know what

Aaron wants? He seems to get angry so easily. I'm not sure how to read him."

"I do." Aric followed Monica up the stairs. "But don't ever try to read Aaron yourself. He can tell, and he'll change his mind on issues just to confuse you."

Focusing her attention on the polished steps, Monica frowned. "Really?" How did someone like Aaron get to run the world?

"You're incredulous?"

Heat crept up Monica's neck and cheeks. Apparently Simon's vocabulary lessons weren't as thorough as he said they were. "I—I guess so. How did he get to rule if he's that way?"

"You're just trying to make conversation, aren't you?"

"No, I want to know." Monica climbed to the top step, then turned down the corridor toward the main schoolroom.

"You must have skipped out of a lot of history lessons, then." Aric walked beside her now, smiling. "How'd you manage it? I've done some research on you, and I know your tutor is pretty tough. It doesn't seem like he'd let you out of a line-of-succession lesson, especially since you'd be eligible to marry into a Cantral family line."

"What?" Monica's cheeks felt fiery now. Simon was going to have a lot of explaining to do next time she saw him. Of course Amelia could have married someone in the Cantral line, Cillineese being as important as it was, but what did that have to do with anything? "I'm not sure what you're talking about."

"You must have been sick during those lessons." Aric stopped in front of the classroom door. "Aaron wasn't originally supposed to be the ruler. Everyone knows that. Maybe your tutor isn't everything his records say."

"No! He's an excellent teacher. It's my fault for not paying attention."

"Then maybe you should find a tutor to help you with your lessons while you're in Cantral." He pushed the door open and held it in place. "Ladies first."

She brushed by him and entered the schoolroom once more.

Aaron sat at one end of the table, his feet propped up. He tapped at his tablet, murmuring to himself.

Closing the door, Aric said, "We've returned, as requested."

"Of course." Aaron swung his feet from the table. "Is your hysterical sister on her way to New Kale?"

Aric's jaw tensed, and his knuckles turned white where they clutched his medical bag.

"Regina is gone." Monica took a step forward, knocking the edge of Aric's shoe with her crutch. She couldn't let him do anything stupid, or she would never find out about the memory-enhancing drug. And if she lost her doctor, she would also lose her advocate in the Council.

Aric glared at her but kept his mouth shut.

"Excellent." Aaron gestured toward the nine empty chairs. "Please, have a seat. We have a lot to discuss and only a little time before my next appointment."

Monica selected the seat at the other end of the table, farthest away from Aaron Markus.

Broadening his stance, Aric shook his head. "I'd rather stand, sir."

"If you wish." Aaron held out a hand, palm up. "The papers, please. I'd rather have the hard copies at the moment. They'll be easier to show the subject."

Aric unclipped his bag and handed over the stack of pages Monica had seen earlier. "*Amelia* has a name, Uncle. She should already be feeling the effects of the Antrelix, but I wouldn't advise questioning her until it's been in her system at le—"

"Yes, yes." Taking the pages with one hand, Aaron waved him off with the other. "Some medical disclaimer. I've heard them all."

Monica shrank in her chair. So they *had* given her some kind of drug. In her tea? Or maybe in those pills. Did Tresa know all along?

"It's not just a disclaimer, Uncle." Aric took the pages back from him and flipped to the middle. "You can see the graph here with our rat subjects. They all performed better after they had been on Antrelix for three days. She's only had one dose."

Monica closed her eyes and listened to the voices debate her future. Why did they even bother bringing her into this discussion if they weren't going to include her? They spoke as if she were one of their lab rats, no different than Vinnie.

"Then give her the other two this evening." Aaron sounded frustrated now.

"It doesn't work that way. They need time to get into her system. If I just increased the amount, I could overdose her and fry her brain. Whatever information you want from her would be lost."

"I'm sure you'll think of some way to overcome this small difficulty. You've proven you're good at improvising."

Aric didn't answer right away. Monica opened her eyes. He stood with the papers in his hands, a stony expression on his face. "What do you mean?"

"Your sister is obviously awake now, or your mother would have come storming in here, demanding things of me, as usual. So." Aaron lifted his hands, palms again up. "You figured out my program. Innovation. It's a great gift for someone in your position."

"There's a difference between programming biochips and prescribing medication. There's only so much I can—" Aric stopped and stared at Monica. "Unless."

"Have an idea, do you?" Aaron leaned back in his seat. "I can see the lightbulb above your head."

Monica looked up, but no bulb shone above Aric's neatly combed hair. What idea did he have planned now? Whatever it was, it couldn't be good. Already the medicine had brought back painful memories. If only she had Amelia's thoughts for a day, she could tell the Council what they needed to know, and she would be off their leash and allowed to roam, to get to the computers.

Aric tapped his chin. "Still thinking, but it could work. Unless I make a gross miscalculation, and then we would just end up with the same results of overdosing her." He frowned. "If you could program a chip to put someone to sleep, I'm sure I could come up with a code that would enhance the brain function long enough to open her memory banks and force her to remember." As he began to pace, his speech accelerated. "Her chip is integrated into the brain stem well enough. I was even able to use hers for part of her diagnosis. It might be an older model, but it's surprisingly well built. It must be one of the last in its generation." He stopped his pacing. "But I still hate you for what you did to my sister. This idea doesn't change anything."

"Of course." Aaron smiled. "You can hate me as much as you want as long as you get me my information in a timely manner."

"And the fact that it's illegal doesn't bother you at all?"

"Should it?" Aaron shrugged. "If you don't write a report on it, no one will find out."

As the information flooded Monica's brain, her heart raced. Enter a code into her chip? They'd find out in a split second that she didn't have one.

"No!" She jumped to her feet. A jolt of pain shot through her leg, almost bringing her to her knees, but she stayed standing. "You can't! You said I had a week to remember. It's only been a day!"

Rushing to her side, Aric growled. "Sit down. You're going to hurt your leg even more." He grabbed her shoulders and thrust her back into her seat. "Don't you want to be pardoned? It would be much easier if you could remember it yourself, but you claim you can't. So this is the next best option."

She shrugged his hands off her shoulders. "I'm trying to remember. The Council gave me a week. It hasn't been a week yet." What did it matter how she spoke to them now? They would kill her if they found out she had no chip.

Aric turned to Aaron. "Did you give her a week? You never told me a timeline."

"Did I?" Aaron frowned. "Must have slipped my mind."

"I—I have it in writing." Monica stood, this time careful not to put any weight on her right leg. "I still have the note the Council sent me." She looked up at Aric. "Doesn't that mean they have to keep their promise? My tutor didn't go into law very much, but I remember that part."

"That is true." Aric's eyes narrowed. "If you have it in writing, then it's legally binding, but only if it's signed by all eight members. A contract determining the pardon or termination of a rebellious prisoner has to have all eight, not just Aaron's."

"Oh." Monica's stomach knotted. Did it have all the signatures? After reading it she had tucked it in the drawer beside her bed, so she couldn't even check.

"Did it?" Aric looked at Aaron again.

"It was just a hastily drawn-up decision to ease the girl's mind." Aaron picked up his tablet. "Felicia insisted."

Aric sighed. "Then that's a no?"

"I believe it has only Felicia's and my signatures." Aaron waved a hand dismissively. "It was not important enough to bother the others with."

"I'm sorry, Amelia, but they are allowed to do whatever they want. The computer considers you condemned and waiting termination as a traitor. Without an official pardon . . ." Aric slid back into his seat. "Uncle, it will likely take a day or two to even write the program for the chip. Then there're the test runs. It would be better just to go with the Antrelix. It's proven to work, given time."

Monica's hands shook as she rested them on the table. So the note meant nothing?

"Fine." Aaron kept his stare on his tablet. "Continue the Antrelix but work on the program just the same. I have a meeting to go to."

He walked to the door. "I want a progress report this afternoon." He yanked the door open and stormed through.

Monica groaned inwardly. More of that medicine? One dose had already given her too much to think about. It would only distract her from her studies. How would she concentrate on learning programming if painful memories kept resurfacing?

"Are you all right?" Aric laid a hand on her shoulder. "Is your leg hurting again? I warned you not to stand on it. It won't be well enough to walk on for at least another day, now that you've gone and hurt it again."

"It feels okay now." Monica twisted her leg so she could see the back of her calf. The clear stockings Tresa had insisted she wear revealed every ugly black stitch that pierced her skin, but no new blood flecked the material. "It's not bleeding. Do you think I'd be able to try walking tomorrow? I don't think it's worse."

Aric knelt and placed a finger next to the wound. "I'm not sure."

"What are you doing?" Monica hopped away from his hand, heat rising to her cheeks.

"I thought you wanted me to see if you could walk." He grabbed her crutches and handed them to her. "I can't just say, 'You can walk again' without seeing the injury first. It would be irresponsible."

She took the crutches and backed away another step. "You saw it. What do you think?"

He started packing his notes back into his bag. "I think you're a terribly paranoid girl who doesn't trust anyone and acts like every shadow frightens her, but your leg is suitably healed to walk on. At least for short periods of time. No running, jumping, or whatever it was your Seen said you did to rip it open."

"I'm not paranoid." Monica drew farther away until her back touched the wall. "But even if I am frightened, I think you would be too, if someone was giving you medicines without telling you, and the ruler of the world was threatening to terminate you at every turn." She drooped her shoulders. The fight seemed to drain with every word. "I'm sorry. Thank you for checking my leg."

"You're welcome." He snapped his bag closed. "I think I'm going to have to add 'mood swings' to my list of side effects."

Monica hung her head. Now Aric was upset with her. With him mad and Regina leaving, she had just rid herself of her last potential friend among the Nobles. This would be so much easier if she could be a wall slave again and disable the computers like she did in Cillineese. But there was no wall slaves' access to the computer room. The Cantral computers were too important to risk.

"Are you coming?" Aric stood by the door, one hand on the knob. "I need to give you your second dose in a few hours."

"I'm coming." Monica followed him out the door. "I need to study some more. I've been reading some programming textbooks, trying to jog my memory."

"That was an excellent idea. I should have prescribed it myself." Aric smiled, showing a row of perfect white teeth. "So have you noticed any memories returning? Possibly from early childhood? Antrelix affects long-term memory more quickly than it affects short-term memory."

"Some." Monica nodded. The image of the woman who invaded her thoughts last night came back, but this time she looked like Veronica. Monica wiped the memory away. Now her brain was just completely confused.

They walked in silence for a few yards.

"What if the program kills me?" Monica's words snapped the still atmosphere in two. "Regina got sick, and you expected something bad to happen. What if it happens to me?"

Aric missed a step in his rhythmic stride. "Ah." He tucked his bag under his arm. "That won't happen. Resetting a chip, while it uses a less complicated code, is also more dangerous, because the chip has to be off for a split second, which could kill someone. The program I suggested will only route more of your body's power

into the chip and enhance brain function. It's not nearly as dangerous, just a bit more complicated."

"I don't like this plan," Monica muttered.

"Then remember everything you're supposed to, and we won't
have to go through with it." Aric stopped at the top of the stairs
leading down to Monica's bedroom. "So where are you heading?
To your room, the library, or . . ."

"I'm not sure where else to go." She frowned. "Am I even
allowed to go other places?"

"Of course."

"I just figured they wouldn't want me wandering about, considering my status." Monica stepped down onto the first stair.

"You would have to be escorted, naturally." Aric joined her on
the stair. "You're not allowed to go anywhere alone."

Monica eased herself down to the next step and then the next,
widening the space between her and Aric. "I was alone in the
library and on my way there this morning."

"You were?" Aric asked. "Your Seen was given specific orders.
She'll have to be punished."

"No!" Monica whirled around to face him, staring up into his
glaring eyes. "Please don't punish her! I wanted to go by myself.
How could she disobey my orders?"

"I can't bend the rules just to please your whims. They're in
place for a reason. She should have known that her previous orders
are not overridden by yours." Aric brushed past her. "Let's go."

Monica sat down on the step. She couldn't let him hurt Tresa.
Not after all she had done to help with the plans. She had suffered
enough. "No."

"What do you mean, no?" Aric stopped and turned. "Staging
a sit-down protest?" He shook his head. "Are all sixteen-year-old
girls this unruly?"

"I'm not going to let you hurt Tresa. She has a name, you know.
She was only trying to help me." She hugged her crutches close.

These were dangerous waters to tread—maybe even more dangerous than the underground river in Cillineese. Aric might react in any way imaginable. "You treat your sister like a treasure, but your disdain for Seen and wall slaves is clear—yet they're no different than Nobles."

"You're one of those 'Free-the-Slaves' Nobles, aren't you?" Aric rested a hand on the wall. "You do realize you're talking to the person who's going to be running this whole show in a year, don't you?"

"I've been reminded of that many times today." Monica glared down at him. "But it doesn't change my opinion of you. You can terminate me if you want, but I won't let you hurt Tresa."

CHAPTER 20

"You remind me a lot of Regina." Aric climbed a step closer to Monica. "I could just carry you back to your room and lock you up until we're done with your doses. How would you like that?"

Monica scooted up the stairs until she sat on the landing. "I'd fight you. It'd be too difficult to hold me."

"Dropping you a few times won't hurt you too badly." Aric advanced another step. "I think I can manage a sickly girl who doesn't even weigh eighty pounds."

Firming her jaw, Monica stared at him, daring him to try it. "Just don't hurt her, and I'll come willingly."

"And say I was beaten by a little girl in a battle of wills?" Aric laughed. "I don't think so."

"No one has to know!" Monica grasped the crutches tightly.

"You and I will know. That's enough for me."

Monica narrowed her eyes. "You're going to be like Aaron, then?"

"What do you mean?"

"You're acting defiant when you don't get your way." Monica scrambled for something to say. She couldn't let Tresa down. "I won't tell anyone I traveled unescorted. I won't even walk these halls again by myself. I promise. Just don't hurt her."

"I am not like Aaron." Aric put his bag on the landing beside Monica. "Don't ever say that again, or I will make sure you regret it."

Monica tightened her grip on her crutches. "That just proves how much like him you are."

"Get up." Aric grabbed her by the arm and pulled her to her feet. "I was starting to like you earlier, but now you're being more annoying than even my sister. You're not as important as you think, Amelia. There are much bigger things going on in Cantral than your silly illegal computer programs."

Monica tipped forward and almost toppled down the stairs, but Aric's hand steadied her. "I'm just trying to keep Tresa from getting hurt. I will go along willingly and take the drugs and everything if you promise not to hurt her."

He released her arm. "All right, but if I find out from anyone you've been wandering by yourself again, I won't hesitate to demote her and send you packing." He pointed down the stairs. "Now get going."

She picked up her crutches and eased down the steps, keeping her head turned to the side so she could see him out of the corner of her eye.

After retrieving his bag, he followed, tapping on his wristband with one hand. "I'm having the Antrelix delivered to your room. It should be there soon after we arrive."

They continued the rest of the way in silence.

Aric opened Monica's bedroom door and ushered her inside. "Where's your Seen?"

Monica did a quick scan of the room, but there was no sign of Tresa anywhere. The bed and cot now stood neatly made, and the room looked as though no one had ever occupied it. "I'm not sure. She didn't tell me if she had anywhere else to be."

"So not only do you not discipline her, but you let her wander as she pleases?" Aric settled into a cushioned chair by the door, resting an ankle on one knee and leaning against the back. "You do have strange ideas. No wonder your family is in such trouble."

Monica sat on the edge of the cot and lifted her book bag strap from her shoulder. It would probably be best to ignore him until Tresa returned. Maybe he would get bored and leave. She sighed. No, of course he wouldn't. He would want to be there when the drug arrived and make sure she took it.

"Don't feel like being talkative?" Aric plucked his tablet from his medical bag. "Trust me—I don't enjoy being here any more than you do. I have some studies to attend to and no time to babysit a distant relation. That's your Seen's job." He tapped on his tablet. "Let's just find her, shall we?"

"You can do that?" Monica sat up straighter. It would probably go badly for Tresa if she had to be called back to the room, but what sort of device could track a slave anywhere in the palace? The Nobles' wristbands could see only people close by.

Nodding, Aric pulled his finger down the length of the gray tablet screen. "Anyone can, if they have the right program. I had to write this one myself." He tapped the screen again. "She's not in this section. Where did she wander off to?"

"She probably had to go get something. Someone might have sent her on an errand."

"I found her." Aric's eyes moved back and forth, roving the tablet screen. "It's hard to remember what number belongs to which Seen, especially with all the wall slaves' numbers cluttering the screen." He stood and crossed the room in a few quick strides. "I'll show you."

Monica scooted to the edge of the cot and grabbed her book

bag, hugging it close. "You don't have to do that. I'm sure it looks cluttered."

"You don't have to be so frightened all the time." Aric sat beside her and held the tablet out. "I'm sorry for my . . . outburst earlier." He placed the flat computer in her lap. "It was unkind of me, and I won't let it happen again. You were right; I was acting like Aaron."

Keeping one eye on Aric, Monica picked up the tablet, wrapping her scarred fingers around the smooth metal back. Black numbers and letters floated around in outlined passages on the blue-gray screen, indicating where every person in that area moved.

"This is amazing!" She studied the map for a few moments more. Getting hold of a map like this was just what she needed to find the computer rooms. She pointed at a hallway marked with red lines. "What's the difference between the hallways lined with red and ones in black?"

Aric put a finger on the screen, and the plastic rippled beneath his touch. "The red are the wall slaves' walkways. They're not usually on a tablet map, but"—he slid the computer from Monica's hands—"being the future ruler of the North has its privileges. That, and knowing a few choice hacking programs. Aaron's computer has even more details on it, including the computer rooms. I don't have access to those yet." He slid the map out of view and called up another screen. "I'll summon your Seen now. She's been gone a long time."

Standing, he pointed at Monica's bag. "Don't you have a tablet of your own? Every programming major I've ever met has had one. It's hard to code without it."

"Ah, no." Monica's hand flew to her bag, and she clutched the smooth material. "It was lost in a shipment of my things. I hope it will arrive soon, but it was supposed to come on a different transport—with my Seen nurse from Cillineese, and as you've said" —she laughed weakly—"Seen are kind of unreliable."

"You're right." Aric slid his tablet back into his bag. "Which reminds me, I should oversee the packing of Regina's things, but I can't leave until your Antrelix and your Seen arrive."

Monica suppressed a sigh. Where had Amelia hidden that tablet? Simon had searched her whole room while looking for her notes, and nothing like these handheld computers had turned up. If only she had a map like that. If she did, she wouldn't even need to wait until Amelia's chip was pardoned, she would know exactly where to go without having to search.

A knock sounded at the door.

"Perfect, that must be the Antrelix." Aric yanked the door open.

Shora waited outside, her whole body trembling and her hands clasped behind her back.

"Well?" Aric's voice dropped low. "What is it?"

"I'm . . . I." She looked up at him, her eyes wide. "I just brought the package that was requested." She held out a palm-sized brown plastic envelope. It slipped from her fingers and landed on the floor without a sound. Her lip quivered, as if she were expecting a harsh rebuke.

A frown furrowed Aric's brow, and his lips pursed, but he said nothing as Shora stooped and retrieved the envelope.

Shora handed the package to him. "I'm very sorry, sir."

"It's all right." He clutched the envelope and reached out to her with one hand.

She flinched but stayed put.

He patted her on the shoulder. "I'm not mad. Thank you for delivering this."

Her face paled. "You're welcome, Master Aric."

"That's enough." He smiled, though the corners of his mouth were tight. "You may go."

She dipped a shallow curtsy and darted away, her small shoes clattering on the wooden floors.

Aric shut the door and reclaimed his seat. "She probably got lost on the way here. This isn't her normal section."

Frowning, Monica gave a slight nod. But Shora had been in the room earlier, so she knew the way from before. Someone had sent her to Amelia's room on purpose.

"As soon as your Seen gets here, I'll give you the Antrelix and leave you alone." He twirled the brown packet between his fingers. "I bet you're sick of me by now."

Monica crossed the room to her bedside table where her stack of computer books lay. She pulled open the nightstand drawer and slid out the piece of paper from the Council. "I'm not sure about this drug and the program you're talking about. They don't seem safe."

"Antrelix is perfectly safe." Aric sat up straight. "I wouldn't blindly give a drug to a patient, no matter who that patient was. Antrelix has been tested and retested on animals and humans alike."

"Seen?" An angry fire churned in Monica's stomach. "You've only tested it on slaves, haven't you? I'm your first *Noble* test subject, aren't I? I saw the number on the papers you gave Aaron. You wouldn't risk the lives of Nobles to try your new memory drug, would you?" She brandished the page at him. "The Council only wants more power. They have too much already. Can't you see? They don't even value any life other than their own anymore."

Aric shot from his chair. "That's not true!" He strode across the room and grabbed her hand that clutched the note. "Yes, I've only tested on Seen, but the Council doesn't just want power. They want order." He stared down into her eyes. "They want order. It will save lives in the long run. You know how long it's been since we've had a war. Without your family causing trouble, rebellions would never happen. Only the old and sick die. The world runs in order—the air, water, and land are all balanced and used efficiently. The Council only works to keep the earth at peace."

"Peace?" She yanked her arm from his grip. "How can you think that? Wall slaves and Seen toil their entire lives only to be terminated in their old age, when they should have safety and comfort after all their labors. Is that peace?" She tossed the paper onto the bed. "And the peasants are told where they can go, who they can trade with, what they can grow. Yes, they're *safe*, but are they at peace with the threat of the Nobles hanging over them, threatening termination at every turn? The wall slave children cower in fear at every noise, every shadow, thinking it's a Noble come to end their lives."

"Enough!" Aric raised a hand. She flinched, but he only ran it through his hair. "You are just as rebellious as your father and uncle."

"I am not! I'm—"

"You see?" he said, pointing at her. "Maybe I should inform my uncle that the Antrelix won't work and you're more useful dead than alive. What do you think? Would you like that? You wouldn't have to worry about remembering anymore."

She glared at him. Saying anything would just keep proving his point, at least in his mind.

He nodded. "And we could finally be rid of your family."

Monica tried to maintain her glare, but tears welled in her eyes unbidden. Did he not listen to a word she said? Was he really so callous that her speech didn't affect him? How could someone have such compassion for one person and such loathing for another?

He snatched the paper from her bed. "What is this, anyway?"

"The note that Aaron sent. The one that doesn't have enough signatures to mean anything." She clenched her teeth until her jaw ached. "All of this just makes me so angry. I'm not sure what to think about anyone anymore."

Aric unfolded the paper and stared at it for a few seconds. "It does say you have a week, and you're right. There aren't any signatures other than Aaron's and Felicia's." He handed the page back. "But you knew that, I'm sure. You're just going to have to get used to the idea of taking this." Holding up the Antrelix package, he said, "None of this was my decision, and you keep acting like it is, blaming everything on me, as though I already have control." He clenched the package in a fist. "I don't, Amelia! I wish I did, but I don't."

"But you *will* have control, yet already you don't care about anyone outside your family."

The door swung open, and Tresa tiptoed in, a large metal tray balanced in her arms, brimming with covered plates and a steaming mug.

She stopped in the doorway, her eyes wide. "Miss Amelia?"

Monica's back stiffened. Aric stood only a few inches in front of her. What must it look like to Tresa? Monica edged away from him, almost dropping a crutch.

Aric turned on his heel and snatched the cup from the tray. "It's about time. What took you so long?"

Bowing her head, Tresa muttered, "I'm sorry, Master Aric, I have only excuses to offer."

"And I'm sure you have plenty." He ripped the package open and poured a fine white powder into the mug. "You'll want to drink it quickly." After selecting a spoon from the tray, he stirred the drink with a few short strokes, clinking the spoon on the blue stoneware.

Tresa set the tray on her cot and stood by the foot of the bed, her hands clasped behind her back. Her eyes met Monica's with a questioning look.

Monica broke the gaze and took the cup from Aric. Hands trembling, she held the cup close to her chest, the heat emanating through the stoneware, warming her already sweaty hands. "Thank you. Maybe it will taste better if I drink it while I eat."

"Drink it now." Aric crumpled the packet and slid it into his pocket. "I don't have time to stay that long, and I want to make sure you actually drink it. I can't have you dumping it down the drain."

After taking a deep breath, Monica closed her eyes and took a swig of the liquid. The bitter, filthy taste from the night before hit her tongue and rolled down her throat. She gagged but forced down another sip.

Aric stood beside her with his arms crossed until she had gulped down the rest of the vile tea.

Monica held the mug away from her lips as the taste slowly dissipated.

"Good." Aric pointed at Tresa. "And you had better not leave her alone again. Lucky for you, your charge is very persuasive, but from now on your chip signal and hers will be bound together within a thirty-foot area." He took the mug from Monica and shoved it into Tresa's hands. "If you get farther apart than that, you'll both be zapped. I'll be leaving now, and I'll send the order down to the computer room."

Monica glared at him. "What if my Seen is assigned elsewhere and another Seen has to watch me?"

"It will transfer to the new Seen, of course." Aric met her gaze then turned to Tresa. "Make sure she keeps taking her antibiotic."

Tresa bobbed her head. "Yes sir, Master Aric."

Grabbing his bag, he nodded to Monica. "I want to hear reports on any side effects or memories you have, and don't leave anything out. It's in your best interest to remember, you know." He swung the door open. "If you remember enough, maybe we won't have to use the program on you."

"Good-bye." Monica tried to say the word as flatly as possible, but it came out as a scared squeak.

He closed the door with a firm click, and the sound of his boots tromping down the hall issued into the room.

Monica rested her crutches against the wall and sank onto the cot. Letting out a deep sigh, she closed her eyes. He was finally gone. And she was probably in deep trouble. How could she let herself spout such a long tirade? She should have kept her mouth closed as always. She would be no use to the slaves dead, and there would be no escape if the Council decided to terminate her.

"What was that all about?" Tresa's voice sounded troubled. Something clinked on the tray beside Monica's head.

Monica opened her eyes and turned to see Tresa's hand still gripping the mug she had set down. "What was what?" She slid off the cot and hopped across the room.

"When I walked in, the tension was so thick I could have cut it with a knife." She picked up the tray. "Sit down, eat, and tell me what happened between you and Master Aric."

Monica climbed onto her bed and sat cross-legged, despite the ache in her calf. She untied her boots and shoved them off the bed. "We were arguing."

"You didn't look like you were arguing." Tresa settled the tray on Monica's lap. "It's considered highly improper for an unmarried young man and woman to be in a room alone together. Didn't you know that?"

Monica's cheeks flushed hot. "It's not like I had a choice. He wouldn't have left even if I asked him to. And we *were* arguing." She bit her lip. "But I'm afraid I spoke too boldly." Picking up a napkin from the tray, she concentrated on the metal's warmth on her knees as she tried to think of what to say. "He's just so arrogant and uncaring about everyone outside his immediate family. He thinks the slaves are worse than trash."

"Did he say that?" Tresa sat on the edge of the bed, and Vinnie poked his head out of Tresa's apron pocket.

"No, but he shows it in the way he treats them, and that's more telling than anything he says. You can't trust what Nobles say. You can only trust what they do, and sometimes even that is twisted."

"All Nobles?"

"All of them." Monica folded her napkin again. She couldn't eat their food and live in their rooms anymore. It was time to go back to the walls. "I'm not hungry."

"What about you?" Tresa plucked Vinnie from her pocket and handed him to Monica.

"What about me?" Monica cradled Vinnie in her hands. He scampered up her arm and perched on her shoulder.

"You're a Noble. Should I not trust what you say?"

Monica's back stiffened. "I'm not a Noble." She picked the tray up from her lap and plunked it down beside her. It landed more forcefully than she had intended, and the utensils clattered and the mug turned over, dripping the last dregs of tea onto the floral bedspread.

"Really?" Tresa grabbed the cup and righted it. "You can't change your identity as easily as you think. You were born a Noble, and therefore you are a Noble." She slid the tray out of Monica's reach. "I think you're making generalizations about the Nobles just as they make generalizations about the slaves. Both groups are at fault for that."

"I just want to get this over with." Monica brushed away Tresa's comments. They might be true to a point, but the wall slaves weren't the ones killing people. "I feel like I'm wasting my time. There are so many slaves suffering, and I'm sitting here, living like a Noble while they slave away the same as always. I should just . . ." Sighing, she glanced at the door and lowered her voice before continuing. "I should just find the computer room and demolish the whole thing. It worked in Cillineese. It'll work here, too. I want to end the slaves' suffering. I almost failed last time because I took too long. What if that happens again?"

"It won't." Tresa reached out a trembling hand and patted Monica's knee. "All of this is necessary. The Cantral computers are probably a lot more complex than the one in Cillineese, and besides, Cantral doesn't have a dome, so we can't get gassed."

Monica nodded. "I'm just so afraid I'm going to get sucked into this Noble world and lose sight of the bigger picture. This game I'm playing is too overwhelming. I almost got you in trouble today." She forced herself to look Tresa in the eye. "I told Aric I had gone places unescorted, and he threatened to punish you for it. I didn't know I wasn't supposed to go anywhere by myself."

Tresa looked away. "I had forgotten about it this morning as well." She clenched her hand into a fist. "It would have been my own fault if I had gotten punished. I was just so worried about Shora that it slipped my mind."

"I hope Aric doesn't mention our argument to anyone." Monica grimaced. If her words reached Aaron Markus's ears, she would be dead in a matter of hours. They could do without whatever knowledge they were trying to get from Amelia if they thought she was as rebellious as her father. "If he does, this won't end well for either of us."

"But we'll be ready for them." She held out the tray again. "Are you going to eat now?"

"I guess so." Monica stared at the food, not really noticing what was on the plate. Why had she let herself get so worked up like that? A few weeks ago, she would have cowered in front of Aric, and now … Heat rose to her cheeks. Now she was yelling at him, putting them both in an awkward situation. What if he did tell someone?

CHAPTER 21

"A ric thinks I can try to walk tomorrow." Monica scraped the last of the beef soup out of her bowl and set the dish down on the tray with finality. The dark, rich flavors churned her stomach like every other Noble meal.

Tresa sat beside the bed, mending a small black dress. "I know. I received your medical orders on my wristband earlier."

Ripping off a chunk from her bread roll, Monica said, "Do you think he'll take the sutures out soon?"

"It's likely." Tresa made another tiny mend in the dress hem. "I'm surprised you haven't ripped them out already, knowing how impatient you can be."

Monica held the chunk of bread above Vinnie's head. He jumped, snatched it, and turned the morsel around in his paws as he nibbled.

"Is that something Alfred taught him?" Tresa smiled.

"Yes. He'll pull a string to get a treat, too." Monica petted his head. "And no, of course I don't want my leg to get infected. I know what gangrene can do to someone. I've seen it happen too many times."

Tresa snipped the thread. "With the drugs you're on, it would be practically impossible for you to get an infection."

"Really?" Monica extended her leg and peeled away the knee-high stocking, revealing the long incision on her calf.

Tresa jumped up, scissors in hand. "That doesn't mean you can take the stitches out!"

Smiling, Monica nodded. "I know. I just wanted to get a better look at them." She pulled the stocking the rest of the way off. Turning her leg to one side, she grimaced. Though the wound didn't really hurt anymore, the pink puckered skin around the black stitches was enough to make anyone feel a little queasy. "It doesn't look very healthy to me." She ran a finger next to the thread, feeling the bumpy, slick skin beneath her fingertip. "But if my doctor thinks it's well enough to walk on, then I'm not going to argue."

Tresa settled back into her seat and retrieved her mending from the floor. "It looks remarkably well for a wound that's only a few days old." She folded the dress into a small bundle. "I suspect Master Aric will use some wound glue on the incision if he's going to let you walk on it tomorrow. Otherwise we'll risk ripping it open." She smirked. "Again."

As the memory of the initial incision came to mind, a quiver of pain ran through Monica's leg. "I don't think he said he'd take the stitches out—just that I could walk." She bit her lip. Now images of dragging Amelia through the messenger tunnels popped into her head, along with the journey to Cantral and the weeks spent in Cillineese memorizing protocol and vocabulary words.

Monica put a hand over her eyes. "I hate this Antrelix stuff. I don't want to remember these things."

"What things?" Tresa touched Monica's arm.

"Just everything." Monica lifted Vinnie from her shoulder and stroked his brown fur with one finger. "Everything keeps coming back to me at the worst moments. Right now I can't get Amelia out of my head. I met her in Cillineese, and I stole her spot here in Cantral. We cut her open and buried her in the tunnels without even a prayer." She blinked back tears. "The spot where I dug is ingrained in my mind now. I don't think I'll ever forget it."

Tresa squeezed Monica's arm. "I'm sorry. I wish we could have just dumped the drug, but with Master Aric standing there . . ."

"I know, I know." Monica sniffed. "I understand. It's just that I've tried to not remember any of this, and now I'm being forced to." She wiped her eyes. "I guess I'm being ridiculous. You've probably seen worse things than I have, but you don't complain."

"No, Monica." Tresa smiled and squeezed her arm again. "There are very few people who've worked as hard as you have to help us. And I thank you for that. I think you've earned the right to cry about difficult memories."

Monica managed a weak smile. "Tha—"

Someone knocked at the door.

Monica grabbed Vinnie from her lap. He squeaked loudly and nipped at her fingers. "Are we expecting someone?" She slid off the bed, careful not to put any weight on her right leg. "I wish my wristband would tell me what I have to do every day." She grabbed Vinnie's cage and stuffed him inside, despite his clawing protests, and shoved the cage back into its hiding place.

"I don't think we're expecting anyone." Tresa put away her mending and walked slowly to the door, calling out to whoever stood on the other side, "Just a moment, please."

Scrambling back onto the bed, Monica hissed, "Okay."

"May I help you?" Tresa said the words as she swung the door inward.

Brenna stood outside, her book bag in hand and her eyes red and brimming with tears. "I'm sorry to disturb you, Amelia, but can I come in?"

Monica sat up straighter and nodded to Tresa. "Of course you may, Brenna."

Brenna slipped inside and whispered, "Thank you. I don't know what to do. Regina's gone, I didn't get to say good-bye, and Julienne is teasing me mercilessly about my grades. I know I don't really know you, but you seem nice, so I thought you would listen."

"Of course." Monica patted the bed. "Do you want to sit down?"

Brenna nodded and dropped her book bag by the door. "Thanks." She scampered across the room and climbed onto the bed. With her bedraggled blonde hair and tear-stained face, she looked more like a little girl than the young adult she was.

She nestled into a reclining position at the foot of Monica's bed. "Oh." Sitting up straight again, she nodded at the tray. "I'm sorry! I didn't know you were eating."

Monica shook her head. "It's okay. I'm done."

Tresa appeared beside the bed in a split second. "Then may I take it for you, Miss Amelia?" She spoke in a flat tone, as if she had no feelings on the matter.

"Yes, thank you."

Tresa balanced the tray on one hand and exited the room.

"So." Monica turned back to Brenna. Tresa had better not go too far away or they'd both get zapped. "Do you know if you're being sent home?"

Wiping her eyes, Brenna shook her head. "I hear tomorrow. They found a slot for me in their schedule for a review." She sniffed. "I've never had to have one before. Everything was easy enough before this year. Julienne was always friendly to me, but now . . ."

Monica shifted in place. Should she ask more questions? It would probably be best to show interest, but what could she do? She was in more danger than Brenna would ever be. Brenna would just be sent home if her grades were bad—sent home to a palace no less.

"Graduation is so close now, and our projects are expected to be better than anyone else's," Brenna continued, "but how can we all be better? Especially me. They won't even let me do what I need to for my project. They say traveling off the continent is suspended for everyone, but there are delegates here from Eursia right now, so I don't think that's true."

Nodding, Monica only half-listened until the words *off the continent* reached her ears. "What?" She blinked. "Why would you go off the continent for studies? And what continent?" Cocking her head to one side, she frowned. What was a continent, anyway? And how would you go off of one?

"Ours, silly." Brenna smiled through her tears. "I want to go to Eursia to study archæology. There are practically no dig sites here. They've all been excavated too thoroughly. That's why I can't fulfill my project requirements as well as the Council expects." She blushed. "I know I don't look much like an archæologist type, but it's what I'm interested in. My father is stuck in the Eursia capital now, actually. I'd love to join him, but like I said . . ."

"Travel's suspended," Monica murmured. Another whole continent? What was Brenna talking about? Why hadn't Simon ever mentioned something like this before?

"Exactly." Sighing, Brenna lifted her hands. "If the Council sends me home tomorrow, I know I'll never get travel clearance. Only people living in Cantral are even considered, unless some marriage arrangement has been made." She reclined again. "So I'll probably never get to go."

Monica hugged one of the fluffy pillows from her bed. "Then how did your father end up there if he's not from Cantral?"

"He was assigned there to help upgrade their security. They're always having problems with the computer systems in Eursia." Brenna smiled, all traces of her tears gone. "He used to be head of security in Cantral. They assigned him here after he showed so much promise in Larnel." Her smile faded. "But Mother and I had to stay home until I got this school transfer, and Father wasn't even on the continent anymore at that point."

"I'm sorry." Monica barely squeezed the words out of her tightening throat. Brenna's father used to be head of security for Cantral? But that would mean . . . Monica gulped. "What's your father's name?"

"Foxlar, but he usually goes by Fox." Brenna slid off the bed and grabbed her book bag. "I'll show you a picture."

Dryness spread through Monica's mouth, cleaving her tongue to the roof. Fox? At the mention of the name, mental pictures sprang to life, pictures she wished more than ever she could shove away. Fox—the man who killed her father right in front of her—the man who, with his constant searching for her, forced the slave council to fake her death and shift her from one dorm to another for months. She had been so scared, eight years old and newly orphaned for the second time, sometimes having to hide in the wall slaves' curtained toilet rooms for hours before the slave council had time to come and take her to her new dorm.

"Are you okay?" Brenna held a computer tablet in her hands. "You look a little pale."

"I'll be fine." Monica wiped a hand across her brow. "Aric's my doctor, you know, and he has me on a new drug to . . . help. It's doing things to my head."

Brenna wrinkled her nose. "That's terrible. I keep forgetting you've been sick. You seem so well." She pointed at the crutches leaning against the wall. "Except for those, of course, and being a little thin."

Heat crept up Monica's neck and burned her cheeks. "I just haven't felt like eating lately."

"I'm sorry." Brenna put a hand to her lips. "I let my mouth run away again. It's always getting the better of me. I shouldn't have said anything."

"It's okay." Monica stared at her skinny arms that wrapped around the white pillow she clutched to her chest. It was true, anyway. She was too skinny. She had never had enough to eat until now, and whatever spice the Nobles put in their food still made her feel queasy every time she ate.

Brenna held out her tablet. "Here's a picture of my dad."

After dropping the pillow, Monica accepted the tablet, now aware how terrible her bony, scar-laced fingers looked as she wrapped them around the thin metal computer.

The portrait of a man took up the entire screen, and the sight of his face turned Monica's stomach. It was him. There could be no doubt. His cold eyes stared up at her, the same way they had stared at her father as he terminated him without emotion.

A stab of sorrow ran through Monica. There had to be something else to think about, but Brenna would expect some sort of comment on the picture. "I think I can see the resemblance."

"Everybody says I look more like mother, but I prefer to think I look more like my father." Brenna took the tablet back and stared down at the picture. "I miss him. I haven't seen him in five years."

"I'm sorry." Monica forced the words out. How could Brenna miss a man like him? But maybe she didn't know what he was really like or how many people he had killed. And if she did know, would she care? So far it seemed like all the Nobles cared little for the slaves.

Brenna rubbed a finger across the tablet screen. "If I convince the Council I should stay, maybe my transfer will finally be approved. Especially since the delegates are here. They might be trying to open the routes again." She laid the tablet in her lap. "One can always hope."

"Yes, there's always hope," Monica whispered. As the images of Fox's cold, killing expression returned, she superimposed it on Brenna's face. No, they really weren't the same. Brenna had a heart. She had a soul. Maybe a friendship with her could bring about the hope they both needed.

CHAPTER 22

Monica lounged on her bed reading one of the computer books again. The section on program cloning still seemed the most likely choice for Amelia's project, but the book had so little information on the codes and programs that were used in the process.

She sighed and closed the book. If only someone were around who could answer questions about the programs. Aric could probably tell her anything she wanted to know on the subject, but she had already risked enough by ranting at him earlier.

Brenna sat at the foot of Monica's bed. She held her tablet in one hand and a stylus in the other. "This plan isn't coming along very well. I can't think of what to say. They might ask any kind of questions. There's no way to prepare."

Monica crawled across the bed and peered down at the computer screen. "Where did you get your tablet?"

"I was issued my first when I turned five, right after I got my chip." Brenna tapped the stylus against the page and typed in a few words with its black pointed tip. "And I've gotten a new one every other year since then." She frowned but continued writing. "What do they use in Cillineese if you don't have tablets? I've never heard of a student not getting one before."

"I must have misplaced it." Monica sat down in front of Brenna. The Antrelix brought back the memories in a foggy haze. She had started her education when Cillineese was first terminated. She was only four, but Joel, her real father, provided her first tablet a year early to try to teach her to read.

Blinking, she put a finger to her temple. Where had she left it? Was it destroyed when the cleanup crews swept through after the termination? Once a termination was complete, the dead Noble family's belongings were destroyed or refurbished and redistributed to others. Of course, even if she had her first tablet, it would be outdated now, probably unusable.

She stared at Brenna's stylus as it flashed back and forth, up and down the screen, tapping in letters one by one. Amelia had to have had a tablet, but where had she hidden it?

"I have something typed up now." Brenna pushed a switch at the top of the computer. "At least it helps me gather my thoughts. But I'm sure I'll get stage fright and go blank when I'm in front of the Council." She stowed the tablet in her book bag.

"I bet you'll do fine." Monica rested her head on the headboard.

The weight on the other end of the mattress shifted. "Are you okay? You can tell me to leave any time you want, you know." Brenna sighed. "I know I can be bothersome. Julienne and Wren remind me all the time."

"You're fine." Monica opened her eyes and met Brenna's worried gaze. "They're the ones who have a problem."

"I know." Brenna crossed her arms. "I wish Julienne would leave. At least Wren is related to a Council member. Julienne's not at all, *and* her grades are terrible. You heard Aaron talking about them. Mine are better than hers. She was supposed to graduate two semesters ago."

Monica wrinkled her brow. "Why does she get away with every-thing, then, if she's not even related to anyone on the Council?"

"You mean you don't know?" Brenna leaned forward, her eyes gleaming. "She and Aric are engaged. It's not like Aaron can just throw out the future ruler's fiancée. I thought you knew that. Everyone does."

Monica scrunched her nose. "Engaged? Really? Julienne and Aric?"

Brenna nodded. "Unfortunately. Someone owed someone else a favor for something or other, so the marriage was decided as a pay-ment of debt." She sighed. "And it was planned so long ago he didn't even have a say. Just think, if he had had a choice, it could have been you. Cillineese is a major city-state, and your father is—"

"Brenna!" Monica gasped. "That's ridiculous." She shook her head. That would have been terrible—to have to pretend to be someone else and be betrothed to someone she didn't know at the same time. "I'm sure they'll be happy enough. Julienne seems well suited for the role."

Grinning, Brenna slid off the bed. "Well, he could always divorce her if they fight too much."

"They don't allow that anymore, and you know it." Monica shook her head. It was no laughing matter. How did Aric feel about the whole arrangement? "Don't you have a meeting to prepare for?"

Brenna's smile disappeared, and she scowled. "You had to bring that up again. You're no fun, Amelia. I would think a girl your age would be dying to get out of this room, get to know peo-ple, and talk about anything and everything. You know, catch up on gossip." She pouted. "And you just want to stay in your room doing nothing but reading your silly books."

"I'm still recovering." Monica picked her book up again. "And I keep feeling sick after all these drugs they're putting in me. I'm sorry you don't approve, but that's the way it is."

"All these drugs?" Brenna picked up her bag. "I did hear something about you being Aric's guinea pig." She sashayed to the door. "I guess you're going to have to give up on the relationship idea, then. He usually only experiments on Seen. So this must mean he really doesn't like you." Opening the door, she smiled. "Well, I guess it wasn't meant to be. I'll see you tomorrow." The door closed behind her.

"If you pass the review." Monica glared at the door. How could someone be like that? Was Brenna even upset about the review in the first place? Or did she just want to come in here and gather gossip?

Monica groaned. No, she shouldn't think that. Of course Brenna had been upset. She was crying earlier, wasn't she? Regina had been terrified at the thought of getting kicked out, too. Brenna's tears had to be genuine. But if they weren't, would she go spreading rumors around the palace? After all, Nobles couldn't be trusted.

Groaning, Monica leaned against her headboard. Why were things so complicated? There were too many people to keep track of in the Nobles' world—too many people to please.

Monica grabbed her book bag. But she was generalizing again, just what Tresa had warned about. Amelia and Audrey seemed nice enough—maybe there was hope for the other Nobles.

"Miss Amelia?" Tresa poked her head into the room.

"Oh, you're back." Monica tried to smile.

Tresa nodded. "Is Miss Brenna still here?" she whispered.

"No." Monica pulled her mother's diary from the book bag. "She left a few minutes ago."

Smiling, Tresa slipped into the room and closed the door. "Good. I hoped I had stayed away long enough, but I wasn't sure. Since I couldn't go very far, I waited just around the corner. I had someone else take the tray."

Monica smirked. "So you don't like her much?"

"I can't speak badly of my betters." Tresa covered her mouth with a hand, hiding a smile. "But I'd rather avoid Nobles altogether. My mother used to say that I would make a good wall slave."

Monica winced at the words. "No one makes a good wall slave. People aren't meant to creep around inside palace walls, fearing for their lives."

"Of course. I know. I shouldn't have mentioned it."

"I'm sorry." Monica flipped through the journal pages. "I think I'm too sensitive right now." She fingered the loose paper stuck inside the diary. "Brenna isn't who I thought she was."

"She finally showed her true face?" Tresa shrugged. "I should have warned you about her, but there was never an opportunity. The Noble children will fight for a place in Cantral like cats, claws extended and hackles raised. I don't trust any of them."

Monica put the journal to the side. "But you said not to generalize about the Nobles or anyone else, for that matter."

"There's a time and a place for it." Tresa glided across the room and slid into her chair beside the bed. "If a child is here in one of the sought-after learning positions, they probably cheated to get here. You might find some worthy Nobles outside of Cantral who are kind and good, but here." She sighed. "Here they're few and far between."

"And the Cantral Nobles are doing their best to kill any Noble who stands up." Monica stared at the wall. "Brenna's father is Fox."

"Fox?"

"Fox used to be head of security in Cantral. Over the whole palace, every wing." A lump formed in Monica's throat, but she worked past it. "He killed my father."

"Your father?" Tresa frowned. "But I thought he died in the Cillineese termination."

"My adoptive father." Monica closed her eyes, fighting back tears. "The only father I can remember. At least until I started taking this drug." Her hands trembled as she continued. "I don't want to remember my past, Tresa. It's too painful. Why should I have to see my parents' faces every night? They won't help me take down the computers."

Tresa took Monica's hand and squeezed it tightly. "I'm sorry. I wish I could help you avoid that drug, but I don't know how. Aric will make sure you take it tomorrow, too, and the day after, if he decides you need more."

"No." Monica pulled her hand away. "There won't be a day after. Aaron told him to write a program to stimulate more memories through my chip."

Tresa paled. "I see."

"So I only have tomorrow to get better, and then I don't know what we'll do."

"You'll have to figure out what Amelia was studying." Tresa tapped Monica's computer books. "There's nothing else to do. If you want to stop taking the drug and you want the memories to go away, then give them what they want."

"You sound like you're on their side." Monica glared at the books. "I have an idea of what she was studying, but it's a stab in the dark." Fingering the cover of her mother's diary, she sighed. "I wish I could talk to Simon."

"Maybe you should." Tresa plucked her bag of mending from the floor. "In fact, I think that's a fantastic idea." She fished another small black dress from her work bag and laid it across her lap.

"But there's no way. I can't walk, and even if I did get back to Cillineese, I couldn't get in. The Cantral security teams have been trying for weeks, and if they can't, there's no way I can. Simon and I had a hard time getting me *out* in the first place."

Tresa jabbed a piece of long black thread into the eye of her needle. "Getting in does pose a problem, but I don't think walking will."

"Why?" Monica narrowed her eyes. "Aric said I can't walk until at least tomorrow and only short distances even then."

"Have you ever heard of a tunnel bug?" Tresa rested her hands in her lap.

Wrinkling her nose, Monica nodded. "Slave transports. They're crowded and awful. People die on those things."

"Ah, yes." Tresa shook her head. "But I didn't mean those."

"Then what did you mean? Actual insects?"

"No, of course not. I meant the tunnel bugs the Nobles take from city to city. They're a bit more . . . accommodating than the slave transports."

Monica widened her eyes. There were rumors about such vehicles, but only the messengers spoke of them. They said the vehicles looked nothing like the slave transports and moved more slowly, often in hidden tunnels beneath the messengers' passages. "You've been on one?"

"Yes." Nodding, Tresa said, "The Nobles call the slave transports Tunnel Beetles or Roach Coaches, if they're annoyed."

"They would," Monica growled. "They have no—"

Tresa held up a hand. "Let's not go into that right now. I think if you really need to talk to Simon, you could take one to Cillineese—if you can figure out how to get inside the dome once you're there. Riding a bug would spare your leg the journey. Your wristband can tell you the routes and schedule for the regular transports. It would be simple to catch one. I'm sure they still go past the routes to Cillineese."

"I couldn't." Monica gestured at the door leading to the hallway. "I'm not even allowed out of my room unaccompanied. They wouldn't let me waltz onto a tunnel bug and catch a ride to Cillineese. I bet they wouldn't let me within a mile of the place."

"As if you can't sneak out of here. Your rat never seems to get tired of wearing your chip." Tresa bent over her sewing again, as if those words had closed the topic.

CHAPTER 23

Monica nudged the computer books lying on her bed. It would be nice to talk to Simon again. He would certainly have ideas on computer cloning, and maybe they could look for Amelia's notes and tablet again. But how would she get into Cillineese once she arrived? The gate could be forced open only from the inside. Then there was the problem of getting *into* one of the tunnel bugs. "Don't you need a chip?"

"For what?" Tresa looked up from her mending.

"To get on a tunnel bug. I thought for sure you had to have a chip to get onto one." Monica tugged her necklaces out from beneath her dress collar and let the chip and ripped medallion dangle from their cords. "So I couldn't sneak out *and* ride a bug."

Tresa sewed in silence for a few moments.

"Perhaps you could grab onto the outside of one of them?" Tresa looked up from her stitching. "Since the Nobles' tunnel bugs are considerably slower than the slave transports, I think it might be possible to grab the safety rails on the sides as one passes."

As Monica imagined flinging herself at a moving vehicle,

grabbing on, and clinging desperately to a flimsy metal bar, her heart skipped a beat. "I've never seen a tunnel bug before. I don't know if your idea is even possible."

"Then you're going to have to trust me. I have seen them. I think it's possible. I know I would try it if I could."

"You don't have to carry around those." Monica jabbed a finger at her crutches leaning against the wall. "I'll still need them, even if I'm allowed to walk tomorrow."

Groaning, Tresa laid her hands in her lap. "I'm trying to be helpful. You wished to talk to Simon, and I'm trying to figure out a way to make that happen. You don't have to take my advice. Let them find out that you don't have a chip, then, and see what happens."

Monica tucked her medallion back under her dress and pulled the chip's cord from around her neck. "I guess it's worth a try. Simon has guards posted at the tunnel entrances, so maybe if I knock they'll hear me." She clutched the chip in her fist, letting it dig into her palm's new skin. "I'll go then. Tomorrow night after Aric says I'm allowed to walk."

"Then you'll be trusting Master Aaron to not change his mind and use the program on you earlier than he originally said. He isn't known for his patience, you know." Tresa's nimble fingers deftly finished sewing up a hole in the skirt of the dress, though they trembled as she stitched.

"It doesn't matter if I trust him or not. I can't walk." Monica pulled her foot into her lap and ran a finger down the stitches criss-crossing her calf. They no longer hurt to the touch, and the redness around the black thread had almost disappeared. "I don't want to risk ripping this open."

"I didn't cut you very deeply. Just enough to convince Aric." Tresa folded the dress and selected a black shirt from the bag. "I think if I put some wound glue on it, you'd be safe enough. No running, of course."

Monica tied her chip's cord around her neck. "You're serious?" She looked at her leg again and flexed her toes. The soreness spiked in her muscle, but not as badly as the day before.

"Of course I'm serious." Tresa scowled at the shirt in her lap. "I think it will work, and I think it's important that you go tonight. As I said, you can't trust Master Aaron."

"I found that out this morning. He said I had a week to remember, and now it's just two more days . . . or less."

Tresa folded the shirt in her hands. "Would you like me to fix up your leg or not? I won't have any more dillydallying on the subject. It's your decision, but please make it soon. I have other things to worry about."

"I'm just not sure yet." Monica shrugged.

As Tresa clutched the wad of mending, her fingers turned white.

Monica studied the tight lines around Tresa's mouth and her clenched hands. She was definitely being grouchier than usual. Something besides the trip to Cillineese must be bothering her. "What's wrong?"

"It's nothing much." Tresa spread the small shirt out again, smoothing the wrinkles with her trembling hands. "I'm worried about Shora and my other nieces. I was so fortunate to be transferred here where I have family, but . . ." She shook her head. "You don't really want to hear about this, do you?"

"Yes, I do." Monica tried to sound reassuring. "What's wrong?"

Tresa nodded. "Shora's mother is being transferred to New Kale, but her children are all staying here. They only have me to look after them, and my schedule is nowhere near theirs. The youngest is only four—too old to be transferred with my sister." She held up the tiny black shirt. "I worry about them so much now. It's their first night without her. I wish I could be there to tuck them in and to sing them to sleep, but I know that's impossible."

"Oh!" Monica bit her lip. Those poor children. "I'm so sorry."

"Shora blames herself." Tresa sighed. "She thinks she's being punished for talking to me—that whoever sent her to spy on you found out."

"Is there anything I can do?" Monica tapped her wristband. "Maybe give you some kind of order that sends you near where they're working?"

Shaking her head, Tresa resumed her sewing. "I can't leave you alone, remember? I certainly couldn't take your chip with me. Nobles don't go into Seen dorms. It would raise too many questions. The only way I could spend time with them would be to file an official request, and the Seens' requests are always ignored by everyone but Madam Felicia, and she hasn't time to sort through every appeal that comes across her desk."

"Right." Monica rested her chin on her hand. "How about this? If I can figure out a way for you to go see your family, then I won't try to get to Cillineese tonight, but if you can't see your family, then I'll go. If I'm assigned another Seen, I have to stay put."

"But what about Aaron? If he decides to—"

"Let me worry about Aaron!" Monica shook a finger at her. "For once act like a Seen so I don't have to order you to listen to me." Lowering her hand, she sighed. "Besides, we know those children are alone tonight, and we don't know if tonight's my only chance to go to Cillineese."

"That's true." Tresa's shoulders drooped. "The mother in me is saying to listen to you."

"Good." Grabbing her stockings from under her pillow, Monica slid off the bed. "Do you know where Felicia would be? I want to talk to her."

Tresa glanced at her wristband. "She should be in her office. There are no more Council sessions after six, but I doubt she would see you. She'll be heading back to the southwest wing soon."

Monica slipped a knee-high stocking over each leg. "She seemed willing to hear my case in the Council room. You weren't there." She dropped to her hands and knees. "Where are my shoes?"

Tresa stuffed her mending into the bag. "Monica, please get up. I'll find them."

"I need to practice my walking, don't I?" Monica clambered to her feet, keeping her weight off her right leg. "Besides, no one's here. You don't really have to be my Seen when we're alone. I was just trying to—"

"I know what you were doing." Tresa walked to the other side of the room and opened the closet door. "But helping comes too naturally for me to ignore the impulses." She crouched just outside the closet and reached into the dark recess. "I suppose it won't hurt to try to talk to Madam Felicia. The children need me." Her voice came out muffled as she dug in the closet.

Monica gathered her book bag and her mother's journal while Tresa located a pair of shoes and a hairbrush. "I'm sure she'll listen to us."

"Then you have a lot more confidence than I do." Tresa tucked a pair of boots under her arm and extended a wooden hairbrush to Monica. "Here. Your hair is a mess. Again."

Monica grasped the hairbrush and ran it through her tangled locks. As the hard bristles caught on snags and knots, she winced. "I wish I could just cut it off short. Whenever my comb got stolen in the walls, I would just find someone to hack off my hair if it got too tangled." She tugged the brush through her hair again and grimaced.

"Let me do it, then." Tresa plunked the shoes on the floor and took the brush. "It's painful to watch." She grabbed the ends of Monica's hair and started brushing the shoulder-length tips before making her way up the strands.

Monica relaxed as Tresa's gentle hands worked the brush through her hair, never catching a knot too quickly or causing pain. "You're good at this."

Nodding, Tresa continued brushing without a pause. "Linna, one of Shora's little sisters, has a terribly sensitive head, so I've learned the best way to brush hair." Her fingers worked out the last knot. "There."

"Thank you." Monica slid her feet into her boots. "Appearance isn't on the top of wall slaves' lists. Simon did insist on cutting my hair for me a few days before I came, but other than that, he seemed to think my vocabulary and etiquette lessons were more important." She smiled. "And I'm pretty sure I've failed miserably in etiquette so far."

"Etiquette is often overlooked by most Nobles, especially when they're nervous. It used to be much more important to them than it is now." Tresa slid back two steps and looked Monica up and down. "I think you're acceptable. Under the circumstances, Madam Felicia should be forgiving about your lack of style."

"Lack of style?" Monica's cheeks burned hot. "What do you mean?" She looked down at her dress. The fabric was still brand-new, warm, and incredibly soft. What more would it need? "Cillineese is a major city, so I thought Amelia would have stylish clothes."

Tresa shook her head. "Amelia was sick for months and hadn't updated her wardrobe in quite some time." She placed the hairbrush on the bedside table. "And most people would have called Amelia a . . ." Looking up, she sighed. "A geek? I think that was it." She took Monica's book bag. "An outdated term, really, but the children still use it to describe someone who doesn't dress in the latest fashion and only cares about her studies."

"I've never heard that before." Monica pulled her feet onto the edge of the bed and buttoned her shoes. "But the Nobles seem good at making up expressions that I've never heard." She grabbed her crutches. "And I was always considered one of the best listeners when I was little. My mother always counted on me as her warning system. I heard the Nobles say hundreds of things I never understood."

"I'm sure you'll hear a hundred more in the next few days." Tresa waved at the door. "If we don't hurry, Madam Felicia will have returned to the southwest wing, and we'll have missed our chance."

Monica tucked her crutches under her arms and hopped to the door. "I wish I could start practicing my walking."

"That would never do." Tresa held the door open for Monica. "If a Noble saw you, Aric would be sure to hear about it, and then we would have a big problem on our hands."

"Right." Monica waited while Tresa closed the door behind them.

"Of course I'm right." She led the way down the hall and up the stairs. "Her office is near the main Council chamber." She stopped at the base of the stairs. "Do you need me to walk more slowly?"

Monica shook her head. "I think I'll be okay." She put a tiny amount of pressure on her injured leg with every step, and the pain lessened each time.

Following Tresa proved to be more difficult than it had been before. She kept hurrying ahead and waiting at the top of each flight of steps, and every time she came to a corner, she stopped for a moment and peeked down the side hall. She stood still until Monica caught up to her again. "I'm trying to be careful. I think it would be best that as few people as possible see us." She poked Monica's crutches. "These announce our presence well enough without people catching sight of us, but I want to be cautious. Master Aaron might not want you talking to Madam Felicia. She's a Seen sympathizer, and he's not overly fond of either of you."

She led Monica past the main schoolroom and down the hall to the foyer in front of the Council room. Pointing at the single door to the left, she whispered, "Her office should be down the hall through there."

"Okay." Monica hopped to the door and placed her hand on the knob. When Tresa didn't follow, she stopped and looked back over her shoulder. "You have to go with me, you know. I can't go anywhere by myself."

Gritting her teeth, Tresa sidled up to Monica. "Anybody on the Council makes me nervous, sympathizer or not."

Monica pushed the door inward. "Me too."

They entered an oval room, similar to the receiving hall for the main Council chamber. Four doors stood like compass points around the walls, two on either side of the entrance and two opposite them.

Monica scanned the palely lit area. All was silent and motionless, as if inviting them to come farther inside. "Which office is Felicia's?" she whispered.

"I don't know." Tresa's hands shook as she gripped Monica's book bag. "I've never been here before."

Glancing around the room again, Monica tried to find a sign that would indicate Felicia's office. There. A small golden *SW* marked the door directly to her left.

She breathed a sigh of relief. "I should have noticed it earlier." Pointing at the door, she nudged Tresa with her other hand. "See? Southwest. That's Felicia."

"I see it." Tresa edged away from Monica. "You can go in there without me. You'll be close enough even in the other room to satisfy the computers, and you won't be alone, since she's in there. Or you could give me your chip."

"I'm not bringing it out in the open! Besides we only think she's in there," Monica whispered. "We don't know for sure." She limped to the door, keeping her voice low. "I think it would be good for you to come in. It'll show her that you really want this."

Tresa crept up to Monica's side again, her hands clasped behind her and her face creased with worry lines, as if she were a child awaiting a promised punishment. "Maybe I'm not so sure anymore."

CHAPTER 24

"Here goes." Monica knocked on Felicia's office door.

Silence reigned on the other side. Monica shot a look at Tresa. What if no one was in there? They would have come all this way for nothing, and no decision would be reached.

"Come in." The soft words broke the quiet but did nothing to calm Monica's rapid pulse.

She grabbed the slick doorknob and pulled. The door swung open without a sound.

Felicia sat hunched over a desk in the middle of the small room. Her fingers skidded across a computer screen embedded in the desktop.

Monica stepped into the room and grabbed Tresa's arm, forcing her to follow.

Felicia looked up, and her gaze locked with Monica's. "Oh, Amelia, I didn't expect to see you, of all people." She glanced to the side, as if looking for someone lurking in the shadows. "Does Aaron know you're here?"

Shaking her head, Monica shut the door. "I thought you would be the most likely person to listen to my request."

Felicia tapped a thumb against her computer screen, and it went black. "That depends on what your request is." She pushed her fingers through her neatly brushed brown hair, combing it away from her narrow face. "According to the rules, I should call Aaron in here to discuss anything pertaining to your case."

"It's not anything to do with my case." Monica threw a look at Tresa, who had once again assumed the posture of a subservient Seen—head bowed and hands folded behind her back. "I was told that you handled Seen requests. Is that true?"

"Yes." Felicia nodded, drawing Monica's gaze to the dark circles under her eyes. "And if all the requests that came in could be stacked . . ." She held a hand a foot above her desk. "They would be at least this high. I never have time to read more than half a dozen before my other duties call me away."

"I don't doubt it." Monica took a step closer to the desk. How would Felicia react to this request? Her workday was almost done, so she might deny it, saying it would take too much time. Monica took a deep breath. Only one way to find out. "I have a request for my Seen. I came to ask you myself, since you have all of those others stacked up, and you wouldn't get to this one for a while. It's time-sensitive." As the words came tumbling out over each other, she winced. Simon's rules of protocol jumbled together in her head, at war with the butterflies in her stomach.

Felicia picked off a speck of fuzz from the shoulder of her light green sweater. "And you think it's more important than the other requests?"

"No." Monica widened her eyes. "I don't. It's just that I can do something to help in this case, and I thought you would hear my request."

Sinking back into her seat, Felicia's shoulders relaxed, and she folded her hands in her lap. "All right. I'll listen." She glanced at her gold wristband. "My children are waiting for me at home. They get anxious when I don't arrive on time, so I suggest you hurry."

Heat rushed to Monica's cheeks. Felicia was a mother? It would have been nice to know that earlier. "My Seen's case is similar, ma'am. Her . . ." Monica breathed a long sigh. "Her sister was transferred today, and her children are all alone now, and she—my Seen—would like to be with them this evening, but she has to stay with me, since I can't be unaccompanied."

"I see." Something shimmered in the corner of Felicia's eye, but she blinked, and it disappeared. Her face remained calm and rigid as she spoke. "I suppose I could find another Seen to stay with you."

"Thank you," Monica whispered, "but there's one other problem. Our chips' signals are tethered together, and—"

"It's no problem." Felicia looked at her wristband again and slid out of her chair. "A tether is easily transferred from one Seen to another. I'll switch it to whoever is assigned to stay with you and put the change of Seens through the computer. If that's what you really want, it makes no difference to me. I need to go now." She snatched a cloth bag from a hook near the door and slung the strap over her shoulder. "Tresa, I hope you can bring some comfort to those children."

Tresa stared at Felicia, her eyes wide. "Thank you, ma'am," she murmured.

"Amelia, I hope your situation improves. I heard about the invalidation of your seven-day grace period, but I'm afraid I can't do anything about it." Felicia clasped Monica's shoulder and slipped past her. "I trust you won't tell any of the other Council members about this meeting. The result would be worse for you than it would be for me, let me assure you."

"No, I won't, but—"

"Good. I really must go now." She swung the door open and

slid out, disappearing through the next door before Monica could say another word.

"She knew my name." Tresa's hands still trembled as she held the door open for Monica. "But now you can't—"

"I know." Monica stalked out of the room. "But that was the plan. If you got reassigned, then I wouldn't go."

"Right." Tresa opened the door to the foyer in front of the Council chamber.

They walked back to the hallway, Monica still pondering the events.

Tresa's voice stayed at a whisper as they crossed into the stairway leading back to Monica's room. "I'm sorry you can't go to Cillineese tonight, but I'm not sorry that she allowed me to go to the dorms. I'm so relieved." She patted Monica's shoulder. "Thank you."

"You're welcome." Monica followed her down the last flight of stairs. Felicia's unlined, yet somber face came to mind as Tresa opened the door.

Monica kicked off her shoes as she hopped through the doorway, flinging them to the side. "She seems rather young to be a Council member, don't you think?"

"Madam Felicia?" Tresa grabbed the boots. "Monica, it would be easier if you would not kick these off like that."

"Sorry." Monica leaned her crutches against the wall. "Yes, Felicia. She seems young to me." She ran a hand across the now-made bed. The wall slaves had been hard at work.

"I suppose she is rather young." Tresa tucked the boots into the closet.

"She looks barely older than Aric." Monica sniffed. A slight flavor of lemons and cleaning solution hung in the air, another indicator that a slave had labored in the room.

Tresa emerged from the closet. "I believe she is twenty-seven, but I'm not supposed to pay attention to such things, you know.

The ages of our masters doesn't matter to us Seen. We are to treat them all with equal respect."

"Like you treat me?" Monica knelt beside her bed, pulled Vinnie's cage out, and unlatched it.

"No." Tresa glared. "Besides, you're the one who keeps reminding me that you're not a Noble. Felicia might be a sympathizer, but she wouldn't hesitate to punish a Seen if one were to get out of line."

Monica's breath caught in her throat. Every time she formed an opinion of someone, something new came to light that changed her mind. Why couldn't people be clear about who they were and not lie? She bit her lip. But then, she was one to talk. What would Regina and the others think of her if they knew who she was?

"Why would she do that?" Monica asked. "If she sympathizes, why doesn't she work for better conditions for you?"

"She can't appear soft. She's the only woman on the Council." Tresa laid Monica's bag on the bed and gathered her mending. "We Seen talk about Felicia all the time. She's improved our living conditions and some of the rules we have to live by, but there's only so much she can accomplish with Aaron turning down most of her proposals. She's no programmer, so she has to petition for someone else to write any new laws for the slaves, if she does manage to get a rule passed by Aaron."

"And few will." Monica sighed. At least Felicia was trying. Monica lifted Vinnie from his cage and let him crawl up her arm. *I guess I'm not the only one who has to pretend.*

Tresa tucked her mending bag under her arm. "Few will is right." She walked around the room in a quick-march step, opening drawers and looking under the night table and bed.

"What are you doing?"

"Making sure I haven't forgotten or misplaced anything." Tresa's brow furrowed. "I know you don't like people speaking badly about the wall slaves, but some of them are thieves." She dug in her mending bag. "I think a pair of socks I needed to darn is gone."

"I know a lot of wall slaves are thieves. I've had my share of things stolen by them before." Monica stroked Vinnie's scruffy brown fur. "I guess whoever took it knew it was yours. Nobody dared take Nobles' things unless the Noble was sick or moving and not likely to miss—" She widened her eyes. "Tresa!"

Tresa almost dropped her bag. "What?" She turned to the door then put a hand to her chest. "Don't startle me like that. I thought someone had come in."

"You don't think a wall slave would steal a tablet, do you?" Monica grabbed Vinnie, and he nipped at her fingers.

"I don't know." Tresa shook her head. "I suppose it's possible, but it would have had to be turned off, or someone would have tracked it through the network. The slave would have been terminated if he carried it into the walls."

Monica slid Vinnie back into his cage. "What if it was turned off and stolen right before the computers were destroyed?"

"I think it's possible. Why?"

"Something that was said earlier." Monica clenched her teeth. "Now I really need to go to Cillineese. I think I might be able to find Amelia's tablet. Simon and I never thought to look in the wall slaves' dorms. We tore Amelia's room apart looking for any kind of notes or computer, but we didn't find anything. If I can find it, I'll need some time to—"

"I know. I know. You'll need the extra day to study it, so you have to go tonight." Tresa dropped her bag on the floor. "I suppose we'll have to cancel our request. You can't sneak out of here if another Seen is watching you. There's no one else we can trust."

"No." Monica pounded a fist on the bed. "You need to be with those children. I know what it's like to have your mother transferred. They need you."

"But this will be better for them long-term." Tresa's shoulders sagged, but her voice held firm. "This trip is much more important than it was a few minutes ago. You'll be a step closer to gaining the Council's trust and being allowed to roam free. Once that happens . . ."

"I can be free to find the computers," Monica whispered. This breakthrough was what she had been waiting for, but how could she let those children be without Tresa the very day their mother had been snatched from them?

Monica clenched her fist tighter, digging her fingernails into her palm. How could she not? If she went, then they would be free and would be able to see their mother again. Wouldn't that be better than one night of comfort? But how to explain freedom to a child who has never known it?

"I'll stay." Tresa's murmured words broke Monica's frantic thoughts into splinters.

"I said no." Monica tugged on a lock of her hair. "There has to be a way. If only I could think of it." She bowed her head and tried to bring back all the events of the past few days, but they jumbled into a tangled mess with all the memories from years ago. Pictures of people, places, sights, and sounds, all demanding immediate attention bombarded her from every side.

She put her hands over her ears, but it didn't slow the flood of images—her mother taken away when she was little, her real father handing her to Faye to be whisked out of Cillineese before its termination, standing before the Council and cowering under their questioning glares. Then the flood slowed to a trickle. A shrill noise filtered into the flow—the fire alarm going off in the library, Regina falling in the schoolroom, Aric showing her his tablet, then the talk with Felicia in her office.

In a moment, Monica's mind was her own again, and she forced her thoughts into a semblance of order.

"Are you all right?" Tresa now sat beside her on the bed, a hand on her shoulder. "You look rather pale. It'll be okay, you know. I can stay. Shora will take care of the other children."

"More memories are bothering me." Monica squeezed her eyes shut again. "It must be another side effect." She wiped a hand across her face, rubbing out the tears that had trickled down her cheeks unnoticed. "But I have an idea now." She plucked Vinnie from his cage once more. He would be a welcome distraction as she tried to explain her half-formed plan.

"Let's hear it." Tresa folded her arms in front of her. "But if I don't like it, I'm staying."

"In a way, Aric gave me the idea." Monica petted Vinnie's head as she tried to think of her next words. "Aric showed me his computer earlier, and he was able to see the whole palace on a map he had on the screen, even the wall slaves' passages, as well as who was in them. He told me Aaron's had even more details."

"Aaron's program?"

"No, Aaron's map. It shows everything, even the computer rooms, but . . ." Monica gritted her teeth and continued. At least she could get Tresa's opinion on the idea. "He probably keeps it with him."

Tresa nodded. "I'm sure he does." She pointed at the door. "As much as I hate to say it, Shora and the others will probably be fine without me. We'll get the orders changed. I should have considered this earlier." Rubbing her temples, she shook her head again. "They'll be fine."

"No, they probably won't be." As Monica's own experiences in the dorm came to mind, her stomach churned. Why did these decisions have to be so difficult? "Dorms can be terrible places. Sometimes people are really nice, but others . . . I know the Seen dorms are better than the wall slaves', but the people in them aren't much better." More memories surfaced—small children, barely old enough to work on their own, having their meager possessions ripped out of their bunks; clothes and simple decorations that no one cared about were carried away just for the thrill, leaving the owners cowering by their beds. Very rarely, one could be assigned to a dorm where people were like a family and got along well, like in Alyssa's, but those were few and far between. "When a child's parent is transferred, the other slaves usually consider them to be easy pickings. Anything they have is going to be stolen."

"That won't happen." Tresa crossed her arms again. "Their dorm is women and children only. No one would bother them."

"The women can be the worst offenders," Monica growled. "They steal for their own children and care nothing for others when the opportunity arises."

Tears misted Tresa's eyes. "They'll be fine," she murmured, as if to reassure herself more than Monica. "I know those women. They aren't the nicest, but I can't imagine them doing that. I've lived here for months now."

Monica let Vinnie crawl up to her shoulder. "If I can get Aaron's tablet, I'll figure it out somehow. I could take it to Cillineese and ask Simon to show me."

"And how do you propose getting the new Seen to sleep while you're gone? She might wake up."

Monica patted her bed. "I'll stuff some pillows under my quilts—she'll assume I'm still asleep."

Tresa shook her head slowly. "I admit a map would be helpful, but, like I said, Aaron probably keeps his tablet with him all the time, especially if he has an illegal program on it."

Monica pulled the chip's cord from around her neck and let it dangle in front of her. "I know. That will make taking it a little bit more difficult."

"A little bit?" Tresa scoffed. "You would have to sneak into his bedroom, look for his tablet, take it, and bring it back, all the while hoping he doesn't wake up."

Monica clutched her vial in a tight fist. "You're right." Closing her eyes, she sighed. "If only there was a way."

"Maybe there is." Tresa picked up her mending bag again. "If you think the map is important, then you need to get it."

"I've never sneaked into a Noble's room when one of them was in it."

"He would be asleep." Tresa shrugged. "Unless . . . unless we could get him out of his room."

"Get him out of his room?" Monica stopped Vinnie from playing with her hair.

"Yes, so it would be easier for you to sneak in." Tresa rubbed her chin. "Maybe if we can create a distraction just long enough for you to sneak in and get the computer and get out again."

"I don't know." Vinnie crawled up Monica's arm. Monica lifted him from her shoulder. "I can't create a distraction *and* sneak in at the same time."

"Then I'll do it. Once the children are asleep, and the others know I'm looking out for them, I'll be able to leave the dorm and be free to do what you need me to."

Monica widened her eyes. "You'd do that? But they'll punish you!"

"It would be worth it." Tresa smiled. "Even just to hear Aaron roar about being awoken in the middle of the night."

"Now we just need to think of a distraction." Monica let her gaze wander around the room. A distraction, something that would make Aaron leave his room for a few minutes in the middle of the night. A false call to a meeting? His wristband's beeping would wake him.

She shook her head. No. She didn't know how to fake a wristband call. Someone on the slave council would know, but there was no way to contact them. She touched her wristband, running a finger across the smooth surface. "What about a fire alarm?"

"A fire alarm?"

Monica tapped a button on her band. "A test of the alarm went off on Regina's band when I was in the library with her. What if we were able to create a real alarm? Regina said there were levers around the palace to trigger an alert."

Tresa looked at the door. "That would definitely get him out of his room. It would be easy enough. I could do it. Most of the alarms are on the wall near hallway exits. They're easy to find."

Monica shook her head. "But once they look into it and see your chip was at the spot when it was triggered, you'll be demoted!" Vinnie pawed at her fingers. She patted his head. "But maybe . . . Vinnie could do it! He does anything for food. If Alfred can teach him to pull a string to get some food, I'm sure he could pull a lever, too."

"I don't know." Tresa eyed the rodent. "I'm not sure we can trust a rat with something so important."

"You won't be trusting a rat." Monica slid him into his cage and latched it. "You'll be trusting your son. He's the one who taught Vinnie the tricks."

Tresa frowned. "I suppose it'll work, but what food will you give him?"

"Meal bars are his favorite, but I don't have one, so maybe you could get a snack for me from the kitchen?" Monica handed the cage to Tresa. "And you can take him with you."

"No." Tresa slid a hand into her pocket. "I haven't eaten my dinner yet. He can have it, and I think it'd be best if he stayed here. There'd be too many questions if I brought him with me. We'll meet somewhere near the bedrooms after your new Seen falls asleep." Tresa handed her meal bar to Monica. "If you can bait an alarm with the meal bar, I'll release Vinnie a few minutes later, once you've had time to get into position. There's some floss in the bathroom cupboard—its string Nobles use that to clean their teeth—you can use it to tie the bar to the lever."

"Thanks, Tresa. I'll leave the chip with the new Seen. I think I can put it into her pocket once she's asleep. If the tablet doesn't have the programs I need, then I'll have to figure out what to do from there." Monica placed the meal bar on her night table.

Nodding, Tresa dropped her bag onto her chair. "I'll go get the wound glue then, if you're sure this will work." She scuttled into the bathroom.

"I wonder how long it will be until everyone's asleep." Monica tapped her wristband and the backlight illumined the time— 7:50 p.m.

The screen turned red for a split second and vibrated. Monica flinched. It hadn't made a sound since the meeting with the Council.

The wristband lit up again, and small black letters marched across the screen. *Seen Assistant Temporarily Reassigned – New Assistant – Chip #3507290 – Arriving 8:00 p.m.*

She swung her legs off the bed and tickled the wood floor with her stocking-covered feet. Putting more pressure on her toes, she slowly rose from the bed, one hand clutching a bedpost. She added more weight to her right foot. The skin around the black stitches stretched and pulled beneath her stocking but held firm despite the whispers of pain shooting up her calf.

The bathroom door swung open, and Tresa slipped into the room. "I just got the reassignment order." She held out a thin white tube. "We'll have to hurry."

CHAPTER 25

With Monica sitting in the cushy chair, Tresa knelt in front and finished applying the wound glue. "The seal will last for many hours, but it'll start to wear off after that." She screwed the tube's cap back on and closed her eyes for a second. When she opened them again, the lines of tension around her mouth and eyes disappeared. "I'm going to bandage it as well, just in case." She withdrew a white piece of fabric from her pocket and secured it around Monica's leg, covering the stitches.

A knock sounded at the door.

"Your replacement?" Monica asked.

Tresa nodded. "Not changing your mind?"

Monica shook her head. The plan had to proceed. "Unless you changed yours."

"I'm in this until the end." Tresa picked up her bundle once more, crept to the door, and opened it. "Ahla?" She gasped. "What are you doing here?"

Monica craned her neck to try to see around Tresa, but she blocked the view completely.

"Is Miss Amelia here?" The words were spoken barely above a whisper. "I was assigned here, so I came."

"Yes, of course." Tresa glanced over her shoulder, meeting Monica's gaze with a wide-eyed stare. She sidled out of the doorway, allowing a pale woman with a protruding belly to step into the room.

The woman laid a hand on her stomach as she put her back to the wall and bowed her head.

Monica broke away from Tresa's stare. This Seen was pregnant? She looked ready to give birth any day. Why wasn't she on maternity leave? Even the wall slaves were allowed to stop working a week before delivery.

Clearing her throat, Monica assumed her role as a Noble. "That will be all, Tresa. You may go now."

"Yes, Miss." Tresa left the room, closing the door with a bang.

Monica tried to look the Seen woman in the eye, but she kept her head down. "Your name's Ahla?"

"Yes, Miss." Ahla nodded, and her braid of auburn hair fell over her shoulder.

Her heart melting, Monica got up from her chair. She couldn't keep up the pretense. This poor woman needed help. "Would you like to sit?"

Ahla raised her head, her eyes wide. "Miss?"

"Would you like to sit?" Monica pointed at the seat. "I know it's not conventional, but you look like you need to sit down."

"Miss Amelia, I'm not sure." Ahla stared at the floor, her ghostly pallor taking on a red tint.

Monica crawled onto her bed. "What if I ordered you to sit?"

Ahla stayed quiet.

"Sit down, Ahla." Monica tried to make her voice as firm and commanding as possible, but it felt so silly to be ordering around a woman who was obviously at least five years older than her, yet who cowered in her presence.

Ahla trudged to the seat and lowered herself onto the cushion. She let out a small sigh of relief that was cut off abruptly.

"Thank you." Monica settled against her pillows. A twinge of guilt tugged at her. Ahla would be more comfortable sitting on the bed, but she would probably tell the other Seen about Miss Amelia's strange ways as it was.

Ahla sat silently in her chair, looking all around the room, as if nervous about something.

"Are you all right?"

Ahla flinched. "All right, Miss?"

"Yes, all right." Monica sat up straighter. "You look nervous."

"I have no complaints, Miss Amelia."

Monica rolled her eyes. There was no need for Ahla to act like she didn't matter. It wouldn't help her do her job any better, so why did the Nobles have those rules? "That's just what you've been trained to say. You can say what you want. I won't get mad at you. We treat our Seen better in Cillineese than they do here in Cantral." She smiled. At least they were treated better now. No one ruled over them anymore.

Her eyes widening, Ahla stared at Monica. "If I may, Miss . . . I'm very confused by your behavior."

"I know. I'm sorry. I can be pretty confusing. It's just the way I am." Monica shook her head. "And please no more of those 'if I may's' and 'pardon me's.' They're a waste of time on me. I'm considered unrefined around here, anyway, so it won't hurt my reputation."

"I'll try to do as you request." Ahla grimaced and laid a hand on her stomach.

Monica slid off her bed. "Are you okay?" She put a hand on Ahla's shoulder, but she flinched away from her touch.

"I'll be fine, thank you, Miss."

Edging toward her closet, Monica lifted a hand. "All the same,

I don't want you doing anything for me. Just stay there, and I'll get you anything you need."

Ahla tried to rise but soon gave up the struggle and settled her hands back into her lap. "I'm not sure about this, Miss. If someone were to come in and see me sitting while you work, I would be demoted for certain."

"This is my room, and it's nighttime." Monica stared at the wall where the closet was hidden. How did this thing open? "No one should come in unless they knock first. It won't be a problem."

"Yes, Miss," Ahla whispered.

Monica's fingers pushed into a small crevice in the wall paneling, and the hidden closet door slid out of the way on its own, operated by some mechanism.

She selected a plain white nightgown from the rack of neatly arranged clothing. It seemed silly to get changed into different clothes to sleep in when her current dress wasn't even dirty.

Fingering the small pearl buttons at the back of the collar, she walked into the bathroom. Why did Nobles have so many outfits? They didn't do any tasks that stained or tore the garments, so they probably wouldn't need more than one change of clothes and a couple pairs of underwear. The wall slaves were lucky to get a spare shirt, and their clothes were getting dirty and torn all the time because of their chores.

After closing the door and changing clothes, she glanced around the room. Now would probably be the best chance to look at the tunnel bug routes. It would help pass the time until everyone was asleep. Tresa had said that the schedules should be on Amelia's wristband.

Monica perched on the toilet tank lid, resting her feet on the closed seat. If she kept looking at her wristband for a long time and pushed a lot of buttons while out in her room, it would probably make Ahla more nervous, and the poor woman was already as jumpy as a wall slave.

She tapped her wristband, and the small screen lit up with options and the time. *8:20 p.m.* One of the options caught her eye immediately. *Transport Routes & Times.*

"Perfect." When she pressed the glowing words, the screen flickered before revealing a list of times and tunnel bug stops. The names of the stops were unfamiliar, but small yellow words flashed in the screen's corner saying *Directions.*

Holding her fingers poised over the wristband, she frowned. This was almost too perfect, as if someone were making sure every step was there when she needed it.

She shook her head and touched the yellow words. But that couldn't be. Of course the Nobles put the buttons where they needed to be. There were programming upgrades in wristbands all the time, so the Nobles would have plenty of chances to improve easy access.

A map appeared on the screen, and a red dot blinked on one spot with words next to it that said *Current Location*, and according to other words on the screen, the red dot was in the bathroom.

She tangled her fingers in the thin leather cords that held her necklaces. The chip wouldn't be with her when she sneaked to Cillineese, but maybe she could use the map anyway. Her hands trembling, she touched the screen again, pulling her finger across the glass surface. Yes! The map traveled with her finger until it reached a glowing green dot labeled *North Wing Station.*

After giving her wristband the command to go to sleep again, Monica opened the cabinet door and selected a white container from a shelf. She pulled a long string from the container, broke it off, and held it up. Nobles used this to clean their teeth? She tucked the piece into her pocket and crept back into her room. Ahla still sat in her chair, staring at the wall, her hands folded on her pregnant belly.

Sighing, Monica hung her dress up in the closet. This might work. Just maybe. What if Vinnie didn't cooperate? Could she gather the nerve to sneak into Aaron's bedroom without the distraction of the alarm?

She let the closet door close once more and climbed back onto her bed. "Ahla?"

Ahla jerked to attention. "Yes, Miss?"

"You can go to sleep now. I won't need anything else for the night." Monica tunneled her legs under the covers and patted the blankets. "I'm going to bed."

"All right, Miss." Ahla struggled from her seat and shuffled to the metal cot by the door. "Thank you."

Monica nodded and lay down. The soft white pillows enveloped her head, and the satiny sheets caressed her arms and legs. Fingering the fine sheets, Monica peered over her covers to catch a glimpse of Ahla. She lowered herself onto the cot with a wince, the full black skirt of her Seen uniform spreading out around her as she reclined.

Ahla swung her feet, still in shoes, onto the cot and breathed a long sigh. After placing her hand on the wall for a second, the lights started to dim before going completely dark.

Monica bit her lip to keep it from trembling. She had to firm her resolve. The tablet needed to be found. The fire alarm, Vinnie, and Tresa were all vital parts of the plan. Would everything work out? What if it didn't? She had to find the tablet. There was no other option.

CHAPTER 26

Ahla's breathing steadied into an even rate at 10:14 p.m., according to Monica's wristband.

Monica's eyes stung from trying to stay awake for so long. If she hadn't kept pinching herself every few minutes for the past hour, she would have fallen asleep.

Her heart raced as she slid off the bed, untied her chip's cord, and crept to Ahla's bedside. It would have to stay behind with Ahla. If it was a newer model, it had to stay close to someone's skin, and if she took it with her, both she and Ahla would be zapped, and the Council would know who sneaked into Aaron's room.

She knelt beside Ahla's bed. Ahla lay on her side, her breathing still even. Monica gripped the glass vial. *Don't wake up.* She slid it and the cord into Ahla's pocket then shuffled away. Ahla remained motionless and quiet.

After letting out a long sigh, Monica scuttled to her bed and dropped to all fours. She snatched her old Seen dress from the floor, taking it from Vinnie as he chewed on the hem. He squeaked in protest.

After stuffing some of her pillows underneath her quilt to make it look like she was still in bed, she stripped off her nightgown and changed into the ragged dress. If anyone saw her in the tunnels, they would assume she was only a wall slave in cast-off Seen clothing.

The fabric that once felt so silky now seemed to chafe her arms, and the ragged, above-the-knee hem felt scanty, though her old wall slave dress covered even less skin.

After she pushed the last button into place, she transferred the string from her nightgown pocket to her Seen dress. She dropped to all fours again, slid Vinnie's cage out from beneath her bed, and unlatched the container. "Ready to go?" she whispered, slipping him out and then onto her shoulder. "You'd better be." He gripped her dress with his claws.

She grabbed Tresa's meal bar from the night table and stuffed it into her pocket along with the string before darting for the wall slaves' panel. Shoving it open, she glanced over her shoulder and caught a glimpse of Ahla's sleeping form. A lump rose in her throat. *Please stay asleep.*

After closing the panel, Monica skulked through the wall toward the Council meeting room. Her bare feet made almost no noise on the solid wood steps as she climbed as quickly as her injured leg would allow. The pressing walls of the passage felt like home, just as they once did, but now she didn't know where they led beyond general directions. They were unfamiliar mazes, just waiting to lead her astray.

She crouched at the top of the passage stairs and looked both ways down a hall stretching out in front of her. Which way? She had climbed enough stairs to reach the same level as the Council offices, but where was Aaron's room?

Squinting at her wristband, she shook her head. The wall slaves' passages weren't on a regular map. Aric had said he had to write a program so they would show up on his tablet, so Amelia's wristband probably didn't have them listed.

No numbered dots moved on her screen as they had on Aric's. Tracing a finger over the screen, she pursed her lips. Now where was she?

After surveying the map, she located the most likely spot—a corridor just a few yards away from the Council meeting room.

Everything remained quiet all around. Vinnie sniffed her ear, tickling her with his whiskers. A faint smell of cleaning solution wafted down the hall, an indicator that the wall slaves had started the night shift, cleaning the rooms that were inaccessible while the Nobles went in and out of them during the day.

The soft whisking noises from scrub brushes scuffled from beneath tightly closed access panels. Whispers that only a trained wall slave's ear could pick up danced through the passage.

As she placed a hand on a closed panel, her heart ached. The wall slaves were there, hard at work as always, their noises once so familiar, yet now so foreign. Everything seemed fruitless—from the making of friends with the Nobles to the mission for the tablet. Would she ever get to see the computers that held them all captive?

She inched open an access door.

The brushing noises stopped. "Who's there?" someone called from inside.

Monica ducked into the room.

A young boy crouched in the middle of the study, a scrub bucket at his side. Another child, a girl, stood beside a large bookshelf, a rag in one hand. They stared at her, unblinking.

"Hi." Monica raised a hand slowly. "I need some help."

"Help?" The boy raised one thin shoulder. "We have our own work to do. We can't help with yours, too."

"No, not help like that." Monica pointed to her wristband. "I need directions. I'm sure you know your way around this wing, right?"

The girl nodded and continued dusting.

"Can you tell me how to get to the main bedrooms? I'm new

to this wing, so I don't know where everything is yet." Monica rocked on her heels. It wasn't that unusual of a request, since wall slaves were transferred frequently, they often needed help finding their way around.

"Get your chip to tell you. We don't have time." The boy bent back to his work.

"Rhet!" the girl whispered. "We can help and work at the same time." She crouched beside the bookcase, still dusting, her voice barely audible. "Keep going right down the corridor you just came out of, go down a flight of stairs, go left, and you'll come to the hallway where most of the bedrooms are." She looked Monica in the eye. "But everyone's asleep by now, so whatever your assign—"

"Thank you." Monica ducked back into the passage. The master bedroom would probably be easy enough to find on her own, and she didn't want to raise even more suspicion by asking more specific questions.

"I haven't seen her around before," Rhet muttered.

The girl said something, but it was cut off as Monica closed the access panel.

Monica crept through the corridor on silent feet, following the girl's directions. As she trotted down the stairs, two women passed by. One kept her gaze on the ground, while the other looked at her, as if wondering the identity of this new girl.

They edged past without a word, and Monica continued down the steps, turning left into the corridor where the bedrooms were supposed to be. A wall panel interrupted the long passage every couple of dozen feet, stopping where the hall dead-ended.

She paused at every panel, checking each view port before creeping to the next. The bedrooms behind each access were too small to belong to Aaron Markus. Skipping the next few, she hurried to the end of the hall, stopping at the last door. She double-checked her bandage. Good. It had stayed in place.

Crouching outside the panel, she sucked in a long breath.

Soft breathing noises issued from within the room. She pressed an eye against the view port. A large bedroom with a vaulted ceiling loomed on the other side. Soft lamps glowed on a post in each corner, casting just enough light to reveal the outline of a giant bed in the middle of the room. Fabric hangings draped across the ceiling, reflecting the light off the white material.

Monica nodded. This had to be Aaron's room. She backed up and walked to the end of the passage. Now to get into the corridor and find the alarm.

She located an access leading into the hall and checked to make sure no one lingered on the other side. Pressing a hand on the wall panel, she frowned. *It was probably locked, but maybe—* the door swung open easily. She yanked her hand back, her breath catching in her throat. *Or maybe not.* This must be an older part of the palace.

Vinnie started to crawl from her shoulder, down her arm.

"Not yet." Monica caught him and held him in one hand as she ducked into the hall. He probably smelled the meal bar in her pocket and wanted it.

Softly glowing lights shimmered near the baseboards, barely illuminating five doors along the hallway. An end table stood near the passage exit. According to Tresa, that was a likely spot for an alarm. She let Vinnie perch on her shoulder again. Running a hand down the wall, she approached the table on silent feet.

A light glimmered on the wall a few feet above the table, illuminating a lever with the words *Fire Alarm* printed in bold white letters across its black surface. She gripped the string in her pocket. This was it.

She tied the string around the lever, careful not to tug on the metal. After stripping the meal bar from its wrapper, she held it close to her face and sniffed the dry, grainy hunk. Vinnie touched his nose to her neck.

Monica smiled at him. At least someone would enjoy the meal.

She secured the other end of the string to the meal bar, adjusting the knot so the bar hung a few inches from the table top.

"Monica?" a whisper floated down the hall.

Monica jerked, and Vinnie squeaked, sliding down the front of her dress. She snatched him up. "Sorry."

"Monica?" The voice hissed. "Are you there?"

"Tresa?"

"Yes."

"Shh. Just a second." Monica held Vinnie up to the meal bar, letting him sniff it. He reached for it, but she held him just out of reach. "You can have it in a few minutes." Cradling him in her hands, she crept to the hallway entrance.

Tresa peeked around the corner. "There you are." She glanced over her shoulder. "I was starting to worry you couldn't come."

"It took a while for Ahla to fall asleep." Monica held Vinnie out to Tresa. "You sure you want to do this?"

Tresa picked up Vinnie. "Yes. I just wish it didn't have to involve the rat. Are you ready?"

"I think so. Thanks for doing this." Monica crept back to the panel and ducked inside. After hurrying back to Aaron's room and crouching outside its access panel, Monica let out a long sigh. Now to wait for the alarm. Would Aaron and Melody leave like they were supposed to?

Closing her eyes, she counted the seconds. When would Tresa release Vinnie? Would he reach the lever like he was supposed to? He knew the meal bar was there, so he would probably go for it, but what if he just ran away?

She pressed an eye to the view port. Aaron lay on the bed still resting peacefully. Seconds later, a loud beeping sounded from inside the room, and a wail echoed through the walls. Monica's wristband stayed silent, though beeping came from all around, echoing in the hallway, issuing from the panels lining the passage—the call for Nobles to rise from their beds and flee the flames.

"Aaron, wake up," a soft whisper sounded in the bedroom. "The fire alarm is going off."

Monica peered into the view port. A woman sat up in bed, one hand on Aaron's shoulder. *Melody*—her father's sister—Aaron's wife.

Aaron turned over. "The Seen will take care of it." The siren grew louder, almost drowning out the words.

"We have to go—the rules—" Melody shook his shoulder.

"The rules?" Aaron sat up. "Are you serious? I'm not going anywhere."

"Well, I am." Melody grabbed a silky robe from a bedside table, threw it over her shoulders, and headed for the door.

Monica hugged herself. Why didn't he just leave?

"Melody, get back here."

Melody opened the door and slipped out.

Monica bit her lip. *Get out of there, Aaron.* The siren continued its bloodcurdling scream.

"Melody!" Aaron leaped out of bed and strode from the room. The door slammed shut again. It was now or never.

Monica crawled into the room, the siren never ceasing its wail. She scurried across the room and licked her dry lips. If the tablet was here, Aaron would keep it close by, probably on a bedside table.

She turned her head slowly. A narrow, waist-high table stood next to the bed, so close, the edge touched the mattress. Could it be there? Creeping closer, Monica held a hand out to the night table. Nothing but a small book lay on top of it, but maybe the tablet was in one of the drawers?

She gripped the cold, metal pull and slid the drawer out. Pens, a few pieces of paper, and some other items she couldn't identify rolled around the bottom. After sliding the drawer shut, she sneaked to the other side of the bed, where another night table stood.

A thin handheld computer lay on the smooth wood surface. A

black cord protruded from one end of the tablet and led toward the wall. Monica gave a tug on the cord where it entered the computer. It didn't have anything like this when Aaron held it in the schoolroom. It had to be detachable.

With another tug, the cord popped out of the tablet. She pushed the freed cord behind the nightstand and started to rise.

The siren stopped. Monica breathed in sharply.

Voices sounded outside. "Some prank, no doubt. I told you to ignore it."

"And if it was a fire?" The voices grew closer.

Monica pressed the tablet to her chest and scrambled through the opening. Her whole body shaking, she turned and eased the panel closed.

"Then the Seen and safety sprinklers would have taken care of it." The bedroom door opened and shut.

Monica scurried back up the corridor toward her room. That was a close call. She took the stairs two at a time, though her leg ached. Time was of the essence now. If she didn't make it back from Cillineese before Aaron got up in the morning, there was no telling what would ensue when he discovered his tablet missing.

CHAPTER 27

onica slipped back into her bedroom without a sound. She eased the access panel shut and sneaked across the floor.

Ahla lay asleep on the cot, her breathing steady.

Holding the tablet close, Monica crept by the sleeping Seen, sidled into the bathroom, and resumed her perch on the toilet tank. The tablet could take a while to decipher, and the extra light it emitted might wake Ahla.

Pressing the top of the tablet, just as Aric had done to turn on his, Monica tapped her toes on the toilet lid. Would it work? Aric said that Aaron had maps just like Aric's, but what if he was wrong?

The tablet blinked to life, and four columns of small images appeared on the screen with a short label under each. The pictures looked like the file folders Simon kept in his desk drawers.

She scanned the selection. *Schedules* and *Checked* were some of the files, but there it was! A folder labeled *Maps* hovered in the lower right corner.

Tapping it with her thumb, she smiled. Good. A map of the north wing popped onto the screen—long corridors, large rooms, some with black numbers above them, some without any sign of life. Numbers in a small red font flickered on and off, moving around the narrow passages between the halls and rooms.

Monica sighed. Wall slaves. So Aaron's computer had the same program that Aric's did. She pulled her thumb across the screen, and the map traveled beneath her touch, rooms zipping by under her finger.

Her eyes raced to keep up with the moving labels attached to each room—Council Meeting Room, N Office, Main School-room—they all moved by in a split second. Finally she came upon a label that read *N Tunnel Transport Station*.

She traced a path from the station back to the familiar territory around Amelia's room. With only two or three turns, it wasn't hard to memorize, especially with the aid of Simon's drills and the Antrelix.

With a tap of a finger, she closed the map, and the tablet's start screen appeared. Just as she reached for the off button, she caught sight of a folder she hadn't noticed before. *BetaPrograms*. Aric had mentioned a beta something or other when he was ranting about Aaron's sleep program.

She selected the image. The four columns disappeared, and ten more folders took their places, larger than the previous rows. Some had labels with names she couldn't begin to decipher, but the folder in the lower right corner bore the name *SleeperBeta2.3* and to its left, a second folder said *SleeperBetaAwake4*.

Poising a finger over *SleeperBeta2.3,* she bit her lip. This would ensure Ahla stayed asleep. Monica tapped the words. Another screen appeared—this one with three images, one labeled *Edit,* another *Run,* and the third *Transfer*.

When she pressed the Run option, it pulsed under her fingertip, and another screen of options appeared. A map took shape with three different numbers, two in Amelia's room and another in the walls nearby.

Monica mouthed the numbers as she looked at the map. Which one was Ahla's? It must be one of the numbers in the room, and it had to be the one that wasn't Amelia's. Simon had made Monica repeat the number so many times she would never forget it.

She selected Ahla's number, and yet another new screen appeared. Words with a countdown next to them floated in the middle of the screen. *Are you sure you would like to execute this program? If no answer is selected, program will commence in 00:10 . . . 00:09 . . .*

Monica gritted her teeth. Yes, the program would keep Ahla asleep, but . . . She glanced at the closed bathroom door. The Seen already lay sleeping peacefully.

The counter continued to tick down. *00:04 . . . 00:03.*

Monica sighed. Would the program hurt Ahla or her baby? She couldn't risk two lives.

00:02 . . . 00:01.

Monica punched the No button.

Program terminated. The words flashed once, and the tablet displayed the screen of options once more.

She turned off the tablet and crept out of the bathroom. Glancing at Ahla's sleeping form, Monica nodded as she sneaked to her bedside. Every life was too important to risk.

Monica tucked the tablet beneath her pillow. It would wait until she returned.

After ducking back into the wall slaves' passage, she took a deep breath and followed the map's directions. She stepped over a pipe protruding from the wall near the floor and bent under a ladder that allowed slaves to access the level above. Musty smells of dust, sweat, and age assaulted her nose—reminders of her past life in these halls she once called home.

The passage ended abruptly at a solid wall. Monica doubled

back a step. Two hallways jutted off, one to the left and one to the right, but, if she remembered correctly, she needed to continue straight on.

Her wristband's screen shone bright in the darkened passages. She crept back to the dead end and ran a hand down the wall. Her fingers drummed against the crevices as she slid them across the paneling. Maybe there was a sealed access here. Not many of the slaves' passages were dead ends. If they seemed to end abruptly, it was usually because of a doorway in the Nobles' rooms, and then there would be a ladder to climb up and over the door to where the slaves' passage continued on the other side.

Looking up, she squinted at the darkness. No ladder. Nothing but blackness and the faint outline of the ceiling.

Kneeling by the wall, she shone her wristband along the surface. The small blue light revealed a rusted metal view port that barely showed through a layer of plaster and whitewash.

She braced her bare feet against the rough floorboards and pulled on the edges of the flaking plaster. The white chalky material crumbled beneath her tugging, and soon a flickering light shone through the metal bars.

She pressed her face to the rough surface. Flecks of plaster dug into her cheeks, and the smell of coppery metal tickled her nose. On the other side of the view port, a doorway stood immediately to her left at the top of a long flight of stairs, descending into darkness.

She glanced around the narrow wall-slave hall. There had to be some way to access the stairs. Wall slaves obviously weren't meant to go there anymore; otherwise the view port wouldn't have been covered over. More searching revealed a knee-high door just below the view port. After her hands proved useless to pry it open, she shoved a bare foot at the stubborn panel.

The wood shuddered, and more plaster and dirt rained to the ground. Another kick and the door swung out, scattering debris down the stairs. Pebbles danced down the wooden steps, echoing in the silence.

She wormed her way through the door and tumbled onto the stairs, sliding down three steps before coming to a stop.

Scrambling to her feet, she glanced around the stairway. Dust motes floated in the air, drifting up the stairs and catching the light from her wristband. Her hands stinging, she turned her palms up. Small abrasions crisscrossed her skin, and drops of blood oozed from some of the deeper cuts.

Monica shoved the access door closed again and swept her foot along the stairs, scattering some of the dirt farther down the steps. It would have to do. No time to cover her tracks.

She tiptoed down the stairs and through a concrete-walled tunnel, white lights shining overhead. Her feet smacked against the cold gray floor, and the fresh scent of flowers like the ones in the Cillineese gardens hung in the air. The walls felt much like the comfort and closeness of the messengers' passages, but the odd flooring and rich perfume kept her mind firmly in the Nobles' world of luxury.

The hallway ended abruptly in an unlit, oval-shaped cavern. A tunnel lay at the other end, extending from left to right and disappearing into the walls. She skulked across a raised concrete platform on one side of the oval toward the tunnel.

Creeping nearer to the edge of the platform, Monica tensed her muscles. Now the hard part. Tresa said these bugs came by slowly, but she had ridden one only a couple of times. There was no telling how difficult it would be to catch the outside of a moving vehicle.

Monica peered over the platform edge. It stood about five feet off the tunnel floor where two grooves ran through the tunnel's concrete bottom, extending from one side of the oval to the other, fading into darkness to the right and left.

Sitting cross-legged, she tapped her wristband and brought up the bug schedule. At least the Nobles had regular routes planned from city to city.

Her wristband dimmed as she sat in the stillness. The train would arrive soon. Her heart thumped, as if counting the waiting seconds. When the wristband went into hibernation mode, everything turned black.

She pulled her knees up to her chin and closed her eyes. The bandage on her leg rubbed against her other calf, reminding her of the injury. It hadn't hurt at all during the trip to the station, but now it stung, as if thinking about it made the wound worse.

A faint rumbling shook the room. Monica opened her eyes. A row of gold-colored lights embedded in the floor lining the edge of the platform flashed to life, illuminating a few feet of concrete floor and the tracks below.

Monica scrambled to her feet and backed against the wall. As the rumblings grew louder, she hid in the shadows, crouching in a corner away from the lights.

Short shrill whistles filled the air, echoing and bouncing around the room. Monica slapped her hands over her ears.

A red box-shaped vehicle the length of a Noble's banquet table and twice Monica's height raced into the cavern on clacking wheels, billows of steam flooding in its wake. Lights mounted on its front nearly blinded her, and she held up a hand to shield her eyes.

White letters on the box's front read *Slave Transport*. Within a second the box zipped through the room, speeding down the tunnel and disappearing from sight.

The lights in the floor flickered and shut off.

Monica crouched in the darkness once more, her stomach twisting in knots. A slave transport. As many as seventy-five people would be crammed in that pit of a car, traveling for hundreds of miles at high speeds. If a slave couldn't stand the entire time, he would fall and be suffocated by the pressing weight of the other passengers.

Blinking rapidly, she tried to rid herself of the horror stories so many slaves had told in the dorms. Transfers were bad enough because a slave would be taken from his family, but he or she also might not survive the journey.

More rumblings echoed through the cavernous station.

Monica straightened and shuffled near the edge of the platform, placing her toes by one of the lights.

As the rumblings grew louder, the lights turned on, shining up into her face. She stepped forward, past the lights until she stood at the very end of the platform. The slave transport had been traveling too quickly for her to catch hold of. At least a Noble transport would probably stop.

She peered down the tunnel. A pair of bright flashing lights careened toward her, riding the wave of rumblings. She jumped back from the tunnel opening and landed hard on her right foot, sending jolts of pain through her calf.

The sleek black transport the same size as the slaves' bug pulled to a stop in front of the platform. Lines of silver streaked across its sides, lighting up the metal in short pulses of dazzling color.

Monica ran to the bug's side and glanced all around its slick surface for something to grasp. The bug was traveling to the left— East—according to Aaron's map. Perfect.

Five evenly spaced metal bars protruded from the transport's back, as if they were meant to be a ladder. Another row of identical bars jutted from the transport's top.

The bug's headlights flashed once and then twice, and a bell sounded before it started to slowly pull away from the platform.

Monica jumped onto the bottom ladder rung and hooked her arms under a higher bar as the transport started to gather speed. She wasn't going to let it leave without her. No one got on or off so maybe it stopped at every station, regardless of need to pick up or drop off passengers.

Wind whipped around the sides of the bug, snatching at Monica's hair and slapping her in the face.

She bowed her head, but the wind still grabbed at her clothing. As the bug traveled on and on, her arms started to ache. Sliding her elbow under the bar, she risked a glance at her wristband. The map was still positioned at the transport station, and with the turns and curves going by so quickly, it was impossible to use her finger to keep the map on track.

As she readjusted her grip on the ladder, the transport took a sharp turn to the right. She swung to the left, and her feet flew from the bottom rung. The momentum wrenched her elbow, still jammed behind the rung.

She swayed, suspended over the tunnel floor. Tracks and rails rushed past in a dark gray blur.

A crunching noise popped in her joint. Pain shot through her arm. Gasping, she grabbed the rung again with her other hand, pulled her body back to the bug, and planted her feet firmly on the lowest ladder step.

Gritting her teeth, she tried to even out her breathing and ignore the throbbing pain coursing through her arm. Had she broken it? The dim light barely revealed the outline of her limb, so there was no way to check for swelling or bruising.

The bug kept going, heedless of her pain, and the endless jostling made her head ache. They swept by one station without a pause, but finally the swaying and rumbling slowed.

As the transport pulled up to another station, Monica breathed a sigh of relief. Blue lights shone in the floor in the same places the gold lights had glowed in the north station.

She scanned the entire area as the train hummed with vibrations, waiting for potential passengers. A steel sign with blue lettering hung on the wall—*East Wing.*

Monica re-gripped the bars on the transport. East wing? But why didn't it stop in the north east? She was almost to Cillineese. She reached out and brushed a toe against the tiled edge of the platform. Should she get off here and walk the rest of the way? Or would it be better to wait until the transport was closer to Cillineese? The east station was probably still a few miles from the Cillineese border. She had walked the messenger route between the two enough times to know the distance.

The bug's lights flashed twice, and the bell chimed before the transport started to move forward. As it made its way out of the station, she craned her neck to look over her shoulder. It was too late to stay now.

The lights in the station's platform winked out, and darkness engulfed the tunnel once more. As the bug regained speed, Monica cringed, anticipating every jolt and bump that sent more waves of pain through her arm.

Minutes later, the train whizzed past a junction in the tunnels. The headlights illumined a sign in the offshoot tunnel—*To Cillineese*. A bold red line ran through the words, cutting them in half with the streak of color.

Monica glanced frantically from one side to the other. She had to get back there, but was it safe to jump? The bug was going too fast. Gritting her teeth, she growled. Of course it wasn't safe, but what other choice did she have?

She released the transport and fell toward the tracks.

CHAPTER 28

Monica tumbled between the tracks, her momentum tossing her into somersaults before she skidded to a stop. Her head rested on a metal rail, and her legs lay across another. Ribs aching, her lungs seemed to be collapsing. She coughed and tried to get to her knees, but her arms and legs wouldn't respond.

A buzzing sounded near her head. An electric current? Her head seemed to vibrate in time with the noise. She drew her arms to her sides. If there were electricity nearby, she didn't want to get shocked. On top of her other injuries, it would probably stop this mission for good.

She struggled to her knees, coughing until it felt like her chest would explode. Rumbling sounded again. Another train?

As she tried to rise, stabbing pain rushed through her limbs and abdomen. She pushed herself up on her left arm and tucked her right arm to her chest, protecting her injured elbow. If a train were coming, no pain would be able to keep her on the tracks. Anything would be better than getting crushed under a tunnel bug.

She shuffled back toward the passage marked *Cillineese*. Every joint and muscle ached, but she trudged on. The rumbling increased. She had to retrieve the tablet and get to the north wing before morning.

Headlights appeared in the distance. She groaned and broke into a run. The junction. She had to make it to the junction. Moments later, she arrived at the side tunnel and ducked under a shoulder-high crossbar she hadn't seen earlier.

A train rushed by whipping her hair into her face and blowing dust through the tunnel. Monica coughed and covered her face. The train passed in seconds and she was able to see again. A sign on the front of the crossbar that blocked the tunnel read *Danger – Quarantine – Do Not Enter.*

Monica laughed though it made her chest ache. Quarantine? Who did the Nobles think they were tricking with a sign like that? Didn't everyone know what happened to Cillineese? The Council loved to broadcast the news whenever a rebellion was squelched by the domes. It showed their power and control. A quarantine couldn't serve that purpose.

Tapping her wristband, she brought the screen to life and held her left arm above her head, shining the light on the bug tracks. A quarantine would temporarily hide the rebellion. It also explained to the other cities why Cantral hadn't sent in any security teams to Cillineese—a temporary measure to conceal their failure.

The blue light from her band shone a few feet ahead. Insects scurried out of its path, and a brown rat stared at the beam for a moment before waddling into the shadows.

As her leg made its complaints heard over all of her other aches, Monica limped into the offshoot tunnel, trying to relieve the stress on her wounded leg. At least the bandage and glue offered support and protection.

She alternated between walking, limping, and jogging slowly the rest of the way to Cillineese, finally coming to a stop at a huge metal barrier. Tapping a knuckle against the cold metal, she looked the barrier up and down. This was so solid it had to be part of the dome. There probably weren't any Cillineese guards down here watching to make sure no Nobles found a way in. Simon had never even mentioned the Cillineese station when they were setting up the guards' shifts, but he had to know about it, didn't he?

She held her wristband high, letting the light sweep across the tunnel's ceiling and walls. A set of four stairs on the right led to a door halfway up the tunnel wall. She scrambled up the concrete steps and tugged on the dented steel knob.

The door swung easily on its rusty hinges and banged against the tunnel wall. Beyond the doorway a flight of stairs ascended into darkness. If this door opened so easily, there must be another at the top of the stairs blocking the way. The security team would have left no stone unturned in the effort to get into the city. She scrambled to her feet and climbed the stairs. The sooner she found Simon, the better.

More than fifty steps went by under her aching feet and legs before the stairs ended at another sliding steel door. Monica looked behind her down the chasm to where darkness shrouded the transport tunnel. She tapped on the metal door. Would anyone be standing guard? Maybe. The Cantral security team must have tried to get in this way.

She knocked again and waited for what felt like an hour, but according to her wristband only a few minutes passed. When five more minutes came and went, she knocked a third time, rapping on the metal until her knuckles hurt.

"Who's there?" a muffled voice called. "You security team people won't fool me this time."

"My name's Monica." She put her face close to the door. Finally! Someone was answering. "I need to talk to Simon. It's urgent."

When no one replied, she raised her hand to knock again.

"Simon?" The voice sounded incredulous. "He's not to be disturbed."

"He'll want to talk to me, really!" Monica rested her palm on the door. How could she make this person understand? "I shut down the computers. I'm the reason this door is closed in the first place!"

"Ahh." The voice breathed a long sigh. "I think I remember your name now. Repeat it again please."

"Monica." She rolled her eyes. It was good for the guards to be thorough, but this was taking too much time.

"If I get in trouble for letting you in, it's going to go badly for you," the voice muttered. "I'll open the door, but just enough for you to crawl through."

There was silence for a moment, followed by a scraping noise, and the door slowly lifted from the floor.

Monica dropped to her stomach and wriggled through the opening. Her shoulders rubbed against the bottom of the door. Just as she reached the halfway point, someone grabbed her, dragged her to a standing position, and pinned her arms to her sides.

"Hey!" She kicked at her captor but didn't connect with flesh.

"Stop struggling." Her captor released her and pushed her back.

Monica planted a hand on the wall to steady herself. Her head swam from being dragged up so quickly. "I'm not going to cause any trouble! Will you take me to Simon now? He'll want to see me."

The man spun a wheel on the wall, and the door banged shut. "I suppose I can take you to him. My shift is almost done anyway."

Monica nodded. "Thanks."

He led her down the long, winding messenger tunnel, passing other metal access doors and guards standing at their posts.

Monica trudged behind the man, limping every few steps. He seemed familiar. The sound of his voice triggered a memory she couldn't quite place, but he probably wasn't anyone she knew.

When they reached a flight of stairs leading into the wall slaves' passages, Monica struggled up every step. Her knees ached almost too much to move, but she forced herself to keep climbing, even as the distance between her and the man grew with every step.

He stopped at a landing and looked back. "Are you coming? I need to return to my post."

"I'm trying." She lifted herself up two more stairs. "But my leg is injured, so climbing stairs isn't very easy right now."

The man studied her for a moment. "I suppose I could carry you, but only to the main level. I'm too big to fit in the narrower passages."

As Monica took a few more steps, she grimaced. "If you're worried about your post, I'm sure I can find my own way to the library. I've been through these passages a hundred times." She tripped on a step and continued climbing on all fours. The passages would be easy to remember, especially with the Antrelix still bringing fresh memories to mind.

"I'd be in trouble for sure if I did that. I can't leave you alone here. Not until someone says you are who you say." He jogged down the rest of the steps and scooped her into his arms.

She squirmed. "Let me down! You don't need to carry me."

He tightened his grip around her knees and shoulders until she couldn't move. "This is much faster. Settle down. We'll be there in a minute." He took the stairs two at a time, bouncing Monica until her head ached.

She gripped her hands into fists and tried to ignore his fingers digging into her arms. It would be over soon. She would talk to Simon, they would find the tablet, and she would go back to Cantral, ready with information for Aaron.

In a few moments the man stopped and set her on the ground. Monica sank to the floor and looked around. The stairway continued up another dozen steps before ending at a bare wall with a door on the right—the wall slaves' dormitory.

The man tapped three knuckles against the wall beside a hall-way that branched off to the left. "I hope someone is awake and close enough to hear that." He stuffed his large hands into his pock-ets. "Now that I think about it, you do look familiar."

"Really?" Monica rested her head on her knees. If only the throbbing would stop. "You seem familiar to me, too." Her voice probably sounded muffled, but at the moment she didn't care.

"Yes, but it doesn't make any sense. You can't have come to the border without getting shocked unless you're part of the security team. I doubt they would ever choose someone . . ."

"Someone as scrawny as me?" Monica lifted her head.

"I was going to say young." The man shrugged. "But yes. You aren't the security-team type. I've seen plenty of them in my days as a messenger."

"I don't have a chip. That's why I can get through the border. I'm not on the security team. I avoid them as much as possible. If they found me, they would kill me."

The man knocked on the wall again. "If someone doesn't come soon, I'll have to take you back to the border."

Monica shot to her feet, and a wave of pain rocked her back-ward. "You can't do that!" She pressed her injured arm to her chest. If only she could run, she would dive into the wall slaves' passages and evade him in minutes. "I've worked so hard to get here. Isn't there another option? If we go outside we can get into the palace through the main gate."

"I've never been outside in my life." The man stared at the ceil-ing. "I don't know the way to the outer exit." Knocking on the wall again, he sighed. "Third try. I won't try again."

After a few moments, the sound of pattering feet echoed in the hall, the access panel swung open, and a small towheaded girl appeared, a battered messenger bag at her side. She stared at Mon-ica and the man with wide brown eyes.

She pulled the frayed leather strap over her head, and corkscrew curls fell across her face. Pushing them away with one hand, she extended the bag to the man. "The cook sent rations." She still stared at Monica. "Who're you?"

"Thank you, Krin." The man slung the bag over his shoulder. "I'll distribute them for you."

"I'm Monica." She nodded at the little girl.

"Oh." Krin eyed her for another second. "I don't know you." She turned to the man. "Why are you up here? You're supposed to be at your station."

"Factual as usual." The man reached out and patted her on the head, but Krin ducked away. "I'm here because she"—he pointed at Monica—"wants to see Simon. Can you take her to him for me?"

Krin looked Monica up and down. "I don't know where he is, and she could get away from me."

"I'm sure you'll find him." The man started down the stairs. "And she's injured. She wouldn't be able to escape your watchful eye." He thundered down the steps and disappeared in moments.

"Don't worry. I'm not going to try anything." Monica shuffled to the passage Krin had come from. "Let's go. I need to find him as soon as possible."

"I'll go first." Krin hopped in front of Monica and led the way through the dark passage. A few lights flickered on and off here and there, dotting the corridor like glowworms feebly hanging on to life. "He might be in the receiving room."

Monica ducked under a pipe that jutted across the walkway. "What receiving room? I was here just a few days ago, and there wasn't any receiving room."

"It was set up just two days ago." Krin pushed on a wall panel, and an access door swung open. "We'll go there first."

"If you say so." Monica slipped through the opening behind Krin and emerged into a long hallway with large dust-covered chandeliers overhead. A receiving room? What had Simon been up to these past few days?

Krin walked on, passing under the balcony leading to the library, circling around the steps where Monica had fallen and hit her head trying to escape from Gerald after he discovered her identity so many weeks ago.

They turned left and entered another hall. A boy sat in front of a door a dozen yards ahead.

"Alfred?" Monica called. The boy certainly looked like him with the same dark hair and angular face, but from so far away it was difficult to tell.

The boy jumped to his feet. "Krin? Who's this?"

Monica sighed. Definitely not Alfred.

"She says she's Monica." Krin skipped ahead and hugged the boy, her shoulders coming only to his waist. "You said you were leaving."

He patted her on the head but kept his gaze on Monica. "Plans change, kiddo."

Monica limped up to the pair. "I need to speak to Simon."

"He's asleep." The boy pried Krin's arms from around his waist. "Why did you call me Alfred? Do you know him?"

"Yes, he's a friend of mine." Monica pointed at the door. "If Simon's in there, I really need to talk to him. He won't mind being disturbed for this. Trust me."

"I don't have any reason to trust you." The boy looked her in the eye. "But Alfred and Simon have talked about you before. Not to me, of course. I'm not privileged to know such information." He laughed. "My little brother knows more about this whole situation than I do, and he won't tell me anything."

"You're Alfred's brother?" Monica gasped. "Then you're Jonas? I know your mother, Tresa! I just saw her a few hours ago."

The boy narrowed his dark eyes. "I haven't seen my mother in months. How could you know her?"

Monica put a hand on her hip. "I was just in Cantral. Tresa's very worried about you two—"

"What's all this yammering?" The door opened, and Simon poked his head out. A pair of glasses perched on the end of his nose. "Can't an old man study in peace?" His gaze wandered from Krin, to Jonas, to Monica. "Oh, Monica. What are you doing here?" He opened the door wider and shuffled out. "Quite unexpected. Have you shut down the computers already? Exemplary performance, my girl. I thought you would take at least another week to return. If you made it back alive at all, that is."

CHAPTER 29

imon looked down at Monica, his eyebrows raised. "Well? Did you succeed? Can we open the barricades now?"

"No." Monica looked at her dirty bare feet. What happened to the pessimistic Simon she knew just a few days ago?

"No?" Simon took his glasses off, wiped them on the hem of his uniform, and shoved them back into place. "What do you mean *no*? Then why are you back?"

She sighed. "I haven't done it yet. I came to get your help. Aaron Markus is hounding me for information on Amelia's project, Aric is giving me drugs that make my head spin, and I'm sick of it. I need help."

Simon opened the door wider again. "Come along." He pointed at Jonas and Krin. "You two shoo!"

"I thought you wanted me to guard the door," Jonas said.

"I can change my mind can't I?" Simon waved a hand. "Get out of here."

Krin ducked behind Jonas while the boy glared at Simon. "I'm only sticking around for my brother, but if you keep treating me like this, I'm going to go back to the city. I'd find work in the fields easily enough."

"Maybe so, but you wouldn't last more than a day before you came crawling back." Simon laughed. "Now come, Monica. It seems we have a lot to discuss—particularly my disappointment."

Monica limped past him into the receiving room. There was the old Simon again. Things were never good enough for him.

"Before you go, Jonas, please find the nurse and send her here straightaway. Monica seems to have injured herself yet again."

Jonas muttered something under his breath.

"I don't even care if she's asleep." Simon slammed the door and ushered Monica to a padded leather armchair in front of a well-worn desk, apparently the same one that used to stand in the library. A dozen lamps all pointing at Simon's work space emitted light in the otherwise dark room.

She sank into the chair and closed her eyes. Pain pulsed through her injuries. If only she could just go to sleep.

The sounds of Simon's footfalls rounded the desk, and his chair creaked. "Don't go to sleep just yet. Tell me what all this fuss is about. I have one hundred or more things to do, and I haven't time for your usual roundabout way of getting to the point."

Forcing her eyes open, she tried to concentrate. "Amelia was working on something that the Council really—"

"Yes, yes." Simon waved a hand. "I know all that. We've been over it a dozen times. We didn't find anything. You were supposed to study computers and make something up."

"That's the problem. I don't know what to make up. I don't know anything about computers. I have an idea, but I need help." She leaned her head against the back of her seat. "Amelia must have had a tablet computer. We didn't find one when we searched her room. I think a wall slave might have taken it when she was so sick. Sometimes the children dare each other to do stupid things like that."

Simon stroked his chin. "It was rather odd that we couldn't find one. I know she used to have a tablet, but it's been a few years since I worked with her as her tutor. I thought perhaps she had transitioned back to pencil and parchment just like Audrey; those two are quite alike you know. Well. They were alike—since Amelia is dead and Audrey isn't—they're not so alike anymore."

Monica glared at him.

He shrugged. "It's true. But you could be right about the tablet. As much as I hate to admit it." He shuffled some papers on his desk. "It will be easy enough to search the dorms. Almost all the wall slaves are living in the city now. A few stayed behind along with a handful of Seen, but they've taken residence in the Nobles' old rooms." Grinning, he handed her the papers. "You might like to see these."

"What are they?" She thumbed through the five pages of Simon's spidery handwriting with her left hand, still holding her right to her chest.

"More of your mother's journal entries, of course." Simon leaned back in his seat, obviously pleased with himself. "I worked on them in the late hours of the evening, so you'd best be grateful. I've had other more important things to work on, that's for sure."

"Oh!" Monica hugged the papers close. "Thank you! But how did you manage it? I had the journal."

"I copied the originals before you left while you were busy studying. It took quite some time to write them all out by hand."

A shaft of light appeared at Monica's left. She turned in her seat. A tall, thin woman wearing a blue dress stood in the doorway.

"What's so urgent that can't wait until tomorrow, Simon?" The woman marched into the room. "If your head is hurting again, I already told you to stop reading this late at night. We need to save the painkillers for—"

"It's not for me, you silly woman." Simon bristled. "It's for Monica. I want you to look at her. She's acting strangely. Even for her."

"I see." The woman walked to the desk and stood in front of Monica, her features shadowed in the dim lighting. "You've injured yourself again? I'm beginning to think you like being bandaged."

"Jasmine?" Monica widened her eyes.

"Of course it's me." Jasmine put her hands on her hips. "What have you gotten yourself into this time?"

"I have so many aches and pains. I don't know where to begin." Monica managed a smile.

Jasmine's stance relaxed, and she pointed at Simon. "Go turn on the overhead lights. These lamps are no good for examining my patient."

"It drains the power supply," Simon grumbled, but he shuffled to the wall and swiped his hand across the white marble surface. "The waterwheels still aren't functioning at full capacity."

The lights flickered on, making Monica blink.

"You look terrible." Jasmine crouched beside the chair. "Try to tell me what happened."

"Thanks." Monica laughed softly. Where to begin?

She closed her eyes against the bright lights and told her story, beginning with trading places with Amelia, having her leg cut and stitched, playing a role as a Noble—all the way to the transport journey, hurting her elbow, and coming into the receiving room.

Jasmine made tsking noises at the appropriate places in the story while she examined Monica's leg wound, and then her elbow.

Sucking in a deep breath, Monica moaned. "That hurts."

Jasmine stepped away and nodded. "I don't think your elbow is broken, but I still don't know how to use the X-ray machine. The Noble doctor won't teach me, so I can't check it to be sure." She sighed. "As for your leg . . . You're going to have a horrific scar if you keep tearing it open. It's bleeding again in spite of the glue." She rewrapped the bandage around Monica's leg. "I can get you some medication to help with the pain."

"If my elbow isn't broken, then what's wrong with it?" Monica glared at the throbbing limb.

"It might be dislocated." Jasmine shook her head. "I'm sorry, but I'm not comfortable putting it back in place. I can see if the doctor will help us, but he's less than cooperative right now. Especially after—"

Simon shooed Jasmine away with a wave of his hand. "If you can't do it, be off with you. Monica and I have things to discuss. I'll fix her arm myself."

"No!" Jasmine pushed Simon's hand away. "You'll do no such thing. I'm going to go get the doctor." She hurried to the door. "Don't you dare touch her while I'm gone."

Simon nodded as the door closed with a bang. "That certainly made her run."

"You wouldn't really have tried to put it back, would you?" Monica edged to one side of her seat, away from Simon.

"Only in an emergency." He circled around to his seat and, letting out a long sigh, lowered himself into the high-backed chair. "Late nights aren't good for old men such as myself, but there wouldn't be enough time to get everything done without them."

Monica nodded. "What's been going on here anyway? Why are you in this place?" She gestured to the now brightly lit room. "And how did you get some of the Seen and wall slaves to come back?"

"One question at a time, please." He wiped his glasses on the hem of his shirt again, though they didn't look dirty. "That's another little project I worked on while you were so absorbed in your studies. It didn't come to fruition until after you left." Putting his glasses back on, he smiled, wrinkles forming around his mouth and eyes, more than usual. "I'm the temporary leader of Cillineese. Can you believe it? We held an election of sorts, based on my readings in the ancient history books, to decide what kind of government we wanted. It took three days to organize the affair.

Of course, afterward, some of the citizens also wanted to lynch Gerald, but I put a stop to that. He's tucked safely away in a secure location."

Blinking, Monica tried to keep a straight face. "*You* are the new leader? Why do we even need a leader? Can't people decide what to do for themselves?" She frowned. "And what's lynch?"

"Is it so hard to believe I'd make a good leader?" Simon raised his eyebrows. "And yes, they can decide for themselves to an extent, but things were rather hectic around here for a time. I'm sure you remember." He pointed a finger at her nose. "And lynching isn't something a nice girl like you needs to add to her vocabulary. So you'd best forget it."

She wrinkled her nose at him. "Fine. You're the new leader. What do you *do* exactly?"

"I make sure everyone still does his or her job, but with fair rules and regulations. The slaves are now free citizens here and have to be integrated into society. A few of the older ones had quite a difficult time adapting." He straightened. "Unlike myself."

"At least you can't use their chips anymore." Monica sighed. "But I suppose a leader is necessary."

"Stop it!" A yell echoed outside the door.

Monica jerked around in her seat.

The door opened, revealing Jasmine and two men. A large man shoved a shorter man into the room and followed him in.

The shorter man held a black medical bag in one hand and pushed back his bedraggled, shoulder-length hair with the other. "I can walk perfectly well on my own, you brute. I won't have you shoving me. Do you want me to treat the riffraff or not?"

The larger man backed up two steps, and after Jasmine entered, he closed the door and stood in front, his arms crossed.

Jogging forward, Jasmine called, "I'm sorry sir. It's just a precaution. We're trying to keep you safe."

"Safe!" The short man thrust her away. "Bah. You're keeping me locked up is what you're doing."

Jasmine stumbled back. The guard took a step forward, but she shook her head. "I'm fine," she mouthed.

The doctor strode to Monica's chair and looked her up and down before glaring at Jasmine. "She can't possibly be a Noble. You won't trick me into treating a wall slave at this hour. She can wait until morning like the others."

"She is a Noble," Jasmine snapped. "Ask Simon."

The doctor shook his head and turned his attention to Monica. "So you hurt your elbow, did you? Let me look at it."

Monica shrank from his piercing gray eyes. He didn't want to help her. What if he did something wrong on purpose just to make her worse? "I'm fine."

"No, you're not!" Simon barked. "Doctor, as her guardian, I give you permission to treat her as you deem necessary."

"You're not my—" A look from Simon cut off Monica's protests. It was three against one, and she was the smallest person in the room and in no shape to run.

The doctor prodded Monica's arm while she kept her gaze on the far wall.

After a few moments, he said, "It's definitely not a break, just a partial dislocation. Not bad at all. Anyone with an ounce of sense could see that."

Jasmine's lips were now set in a thin white line, but she stayed quiet.

The doctor handed Monica a small red pill. "Take this; it will help with the pain."

Monica glanced at Jasmine, who gave her a quick nod. Monica eyed the pill before swallowing it.

Pointing at Jasmine, the doctor rolled up his white shirtsleeves and buttoned them in place. "Come hold the patient. I need to work the arm back into its socket, and I don't want her to squirm." He turned to Monica. "This will hurt quite a bit."

"Yes sir," Jasmine whispered. She helped Monica to her feet and then stood behind her, arms wrapped around her shoulders.

Monica gritted her teeth as the doctor gripped her forearm in one hand and upper arm in the other.

"Ready?" The doctor tugged on her arm without waiting for an answer.

A pop sounded from her elbow, and pain exploded across her arm, erasing almost all memory of the throbbing in her head. She tried to jerk away from the doctor's cold, tight fingers, but Jasmine held her steady.

"Hold still." He unclipped his black bag and withdrew a canister and white gauze. "I'll have to cast it now."

Jasmine's taut, thin arms still wrapped Monica in a crushing embrace. "Shouldn't we X-ray it just to make sure everything's okay?"

"Who's the doctor here?" He tore the lid from the fist-sized container and stuffed the gauze inside.

"I agree with Jasmine." Simon stood from his seat where he had been watching in silence. "It seems to me we should make sure her arm is not permanently damaged."

The doctor shook the gauze around inside the canister. "It's not possible."

Monica tried to break free of Jasmine's grip. Her arm felt like it was on fire. A large purple and green bruise started to appear around her elbow where the doctor's fingers had pressed into her skin. "I can't have a cast!"

"No X-ray or cast?" Simon shook his head. "Very foolhardy, I say. I think you should have both. What if surgery is required?"

The doctor continued working with the bandages. "There can be no X-ray because I'm out of film. There's none left, thanks to you forcing me to treat those peasants. We can't get any more unless traders are allowed through the dome."

"That's impossible." Simon sighed. "Unless you want to die. Which I'm not opposed to at the moment. You're starting to annoy me."

"You can't give me a cast!" Monica shouted. "Why won't you listen to me?"

CHAPTER 30

Monica kicked the doctor in the shins, unable to reach any higher with her short legs, but he ignored the blows. "Simon, I thought you were on my side! Don't betray me again!"

"Stop!" Simon barked and circled around the desk. "Of course I wouldn't betray you. I never have." He shooed the doctor away. "Let's hear what she has to say."

Monica wriggled free of Jasmine's grip. "If I have a cast, my doctor will notice right away. He's checked on me every day since I took Amelia's place. Do *you* want to come up with an explanation on how I suddenly got a cast without his approval?"

"I see." Simon looked down at the doctor. "Are there any other options that would work as effectively as the cast?"

The doctor snatched his bag from the desk. "Riffraff. That's what you all are. I wish the termination had gone through. Then at least I wouldn't have to stand for this insubordination. Once Gerald is rest—"

"That's quite enough." Simon poked the doctor's shoulder with a long, bony finger. "Now tell us if there's an alternative, or you will find your situation here becoming much more unpleasant."

"There's a type of bandage that helps keep a joint immobile. It so happens I have some." He stared at Monica. "But what's all this about another doctor?" His eyes narrowed. "What aren't you telling me?"

"Nothing that you need to know." Simon waved a dismissive hand. "Jasmine, please look in his office for one of these bandages. Monica and I have some searching to do. Meet back here in . . ." He looked at a pale spot on his arm that marked where his wristband used to be. "Soon. We'll be back shortly."

Monica turned her wristband around, but its screen was a vibrant, blank blue. "What's wrong with the wristbands?"

"You can explain, Simon." Jasmine jogged to the door. "I'll meet you back here later."

"Don't think you can get away with bossing me around!" When the door closed, Simon turned to Monica. "Jasmine thinks because she's taken care of you and Alfred she actually has a say in matters." He muttered something more under his breath, too low for Monica to make out.

"What's going on with the wristbands?" Monica held hers out for him to see.

"They all stopped working once the computers were shut down. You should have noticed that." Simon marched toward the door. "But you were busy studying. Now let's go look for that tablet." He held the door open. "We won't be gone long."

Monica limped after him. Of course she hadn't noticed. She had no wristband while waiting to leave for Cantral, and Simon had had her nose pressed in a book almost every minute of the day. She followed him out the door and waited while he closed and locked it. "I don't think this leadership position is good for you. It's making you even more sour than before."

"Nonsense." Simon withdrew the heavy brass key from the

lock. "I'm just as sour as ever. No more. No less." He slipped the key into his pants pocket. "Now what's the fastest way to the wall slaves' dorm? This is exciting. I've never been in one before. By the time I was transferred here, all the Seen had their own dorms."

"They're not exciting at all." Monica limped ahead of Simon, retracing the steps she and Krin had taken just a few minutes ago. "They're terrible. I never want to have to live in one again."

"Yet a fascinating part of our history. You haven't read the books by the ancient architects who thought up the system and the walls. It's quite an amazing study. I've read dozens of descriptions, but since I haven't had time to explore them yet, it will be interesting to see if they're accurate."

Monica stopped in the middle of the long hallway of chandeliers. "Interesting to see if they're accurate?" She laughed. They wrote about the wall slaves yet wouldn't let them be seen out in the open? "I'm sure no writer could ever accurately describe how horrible the dorms are. They're stifling hot in the summer, freezing cold in the winter, overcrowded, and a breeding ground for germs. You're with your family one day and the next they're gone, and you have no idea where or if you'll ever see them again."

Simon turned in a circle in the middle of the hallway. "This corridor is getting rather dusty, don't you think? I should get someone to clean it. And before you say I should do it myself, I'll remind you that I am much too old to be climbing up there."

"What does it matter?" Monica resisted the urge to stamp her foot. It would hurt too much, and he probably wouldn't notice anyway. "Didn't you hear a word I said?"

"Of course I did. I'm old, not deaf." Simon continued his slow rotation. "Now how do we get into the walls? The panels are too well hidden for me to spot."

Monica pried open the disguised access panel. The electronic lock had been disengaged since the computers were shut down, so it was easy enough to get smaller doors open. It was useless to try to convince Simon of the wretchedness of the slave dorms anyway. He would see for himself.

Simon crouched outside the opening. "This won't be pleasant."

Monica crawled through the opening into the dark slaves' passage. "I could search by myself, but it'd take twice as long. Besides, you said you wanted to see a wall slaves' dorm."

Grumbling, Simon followed on hands and knees, leaving the access door open behind him. "I should have come on an exploratory mission a week ago, but—"

"You were too busy running Cillineese." Monica scrambled up the steps in front of him. The pain in her arm and leg had already dissipated to a dull throb. "Come on. It's just up this flight and to the right." She stopped at the top landing and turned to wait for him.

Simon's body seemed unnaturally large in the narrow passage, and he squinted in the dim light. "I didn't imagine them being this tight of a fit."

"No. I guess you didn't." Monica smiled. Now that Simon was in the stairway, it was easy to tell how much wider his build was than that of an average wall slave. Natural selection along with malnutrition forced their bodies to become smaller and lither than those of the Nobles or even the Seen.

He joined her at the top of the stairs a moment later, breathing heavily. He cleaned his glasses and cleared his throat. "Well, what are we waiting for? Don't have all day, you know. Get in there and start looking."

Monica pushed the dorm door open. A musty, dirty smell greeted her as the door pulled a draft from the middle of the room. She palmed the wall, and fluorescent lights along the ceiling buzzed to life. Drops of water splashed from a drippy faucet to her right. A rusty bucket caught each drop, but with every addition, some spilled onto the blackened wood beneath.

She took a step into the room. The floorboards creaked beneath her bare foot. A row of bunk beds stood in a line on either side of the long, hall-like room. Light gray curtains lay on the floor, torn from where they once hung on the bunks.

"Oh." Monica crept up to the first bed and fingered the tangled paper decorations hanging from the upper bed's slats. Pieces of ripped stars and crescent moons lay on the board beneath where a mattress and thin blanket once lay. "It's been ransacked."

She turned on her heel, surveying the rest of the beds. All the mattresses, pillows, and blankets were missing, as well as most of the curtains, though the more holey pieces still hung from their hooks or lay on the floor.

"Not exactly what I was expecting." Simon's voice sounded subdued.

Monica crouched and picked up a flattened rag doll. The same materials as the curtains made up its face and arms, but brown stains dotted its down-turned mouth, and moth holes marred the fabric, like pockmarks on skin. "What were you expecting?"

"A neat and orderly habitation, of course." Simon tapped a well-worn post of one of the bunks. "Most of the wall slaves left in such a hurry I thought they didn't take much, but it seems they did. The refugee camp set up for them had furnishings, so they really didn't need to take their bedding."

Monica laid the doll on the bed with the paper hangings. Did the little girl who owned it survive the termination? Or was she in the lower levels, suffocated by the gas? "I hope she's okay."

"Who?" Simon looked up from where he had ducked down to search under a bed.

Shaking her head, Monica joined him in the search. "Never mind." She crouched beside the bed at the head of the row on the left and slid underneath. "I hope whoever stole the tablet didn't take it with them when they left."

"It's unlikely. A child probably took it on a dare and doesn't even know what it contains." Simon shuffled across the room and picked up some of the strewn bed curtains.

As an army of dust bunnies assaulted Monica's nose, she sneezed. The dirt and grime certainly gathered quickly with no one to tend to them. At least someone had cleared out all the storage boxes that were usually stowed beneath the beds. "There's still another dorm to search after this one if we don't find it here."

He tossed the curtains onto one of the bunks. "If I've read the palace blueprints correctly, which I did, then this dorm is closer to Amelia's room, and it's unlikely the tablet was taken by a slave in the other dorm."

Stifling a yawn, Monica nodded. What time was it anyway? She should head back to Cantral the minute the tablet was found. There was no telling if she would be able to catch a transport again, especially with her arm throbbing.

"I really should have made Alfred do this," Simon muttered.

Monica crawled out. If someone had hidden the tablet under a bed, it wasn't on the floor, but maybe . . . She dropped to her hands and knees again, rolled onto her back, and slid under the bed once more.

A row of bowed wooden slats crossed from one side of the bunk's frame to the other, a bed-sized board covering them. Pieces of rumpled meal bar paper, torn and dusty, stuck out from between the slats and the board. Monica yanked a piece, and a cloud of dirt fell in her face. She screwed her eyes shut and slid out from under the bed.

Coughing, she flattened the paper on the floor and glanced over the shaky writing. Words with unusual spellings and misshapen letters filled the page, but each word was written straight across the paper, as if trying to conserve space. The same words repeated themselves over and over—words like *chip*, *meal*, *bunk*, and *bath*.

Monica folded the paper and tucked it back under the bed.

Some writings of a wall slave trying to teach herself how to read? Where was she now? Was she dead and disposed of in the city furnaces? Or was she struggling to adapt to city life, trying to find someone among the thousands of residents to take her in?

"No time for dawdling!" Simon called from across the room. "Staring at a bit of paper isn't going to get us anywhere. If that's what you think a computer tablet looks like, you've been neglecting your lessons more than I ever expected."

"Of course I don't think it's a tablet." Monica ducked beneath the next bed and examined its underside. Nothing. "This is going to take a while." She slid across the narrow aisle to the third bed in the row.

"Obviously. Perhaps I should fetch Alfred."

The bunk's legs blocked her view of everything but Simon's shiny boots and the hem of his pants.

A search beneath four more beds proved fruitless. Monica rolled to the next one down the row. Staring up at the underside, she heaved a long sigh. Seven down, forty-three to go.

Simon's shoes clomped near her head. "Found anything yet?"

"Trust me, if I find something, you'll hear about it."

"Then I'm going to go get Alfred. I'm sure he's better at scrambling under these beds than I am. It's not dignified for the ruler of Cillineese to partake in such activities, not to mention that—"

"You're too old?" Monica scooted to the next bed. "I know all your excuses, but that's a new one. Being 'ruler of Cillineese' shouldn't stop you from helping me." Something gritty and rough stuck in the bed slats stopped her search.

"But age certainly does." Simon walked to the door. "I'll be back in a few minutes."

"Fine, but it's not going to take much longer." She yanked the gritty substance free from beneath the bed and held it close to her face. An ancient meal bar? She tossed it to the ground.

She crawled out from under the bed and glanced around the

room. There was no sign of Simon anywhere. He must have left in a hurry. Sighing, she eased herself under the next bed.

Uncountable minutes slipped by as she finished searching under each lower bunk on the left side of the room. As she stood from examining the last bed, she sneezed.

Wiping her eyes, she sneezed again. She roughed her hair with a hand, releasing the rest of the dust to the floor. Thirteen lower bunks searched. That left just the thirteen upper bunks and the twelve bunks on the other side of the room.

She heaved a sigh. This was taking too long. If the tablet wasn't even here, she would still have to get to the other dorm and search those beds too. That wouldn't leave much time to return to Cantral and clean up by morning. If she wasn't back to her room before Tresa, there would be a lecture waiting.

Leaning against one of the bunks, she pushed the worn wood. The bunk didn't budge an inch. She knelt and ran a finger around a large piece of metal embedded in the leg. Were they bolted to the floor?

She pushed the bed again, but it didn't move. So knocking them all over wouldn't work. Anything lodged beneath the slats would fall out if the beds could be toppled. She crouched beside the bed, lifted the board off the slats, and pushed it over the side.

The board fell to the floor with a clatter, revealing the slats and bed beneath. She shuffled from bunk to bunk, shoving the boards away. Dust flew with every board, and bits of paper, crumbs, and even a wristband fell to the floor.

As she finished searching half the beds on the right side of the room, doubts began to worm their way in. What if the tablet hadn't been stolen and Amelia didn't have one? Monica threw another board to the floor. She needed to stop this doubting and focus or she might miss something.

When she turned over a board on one of the top bunks, something gray thumped against the bed slats. Her heart racing, she pounced on the object, snatched it up, and held it close. The slick metal surface felt cool beneath her fingertips. She caressed the computer's plastic screen with a scarred thumb. Finally! Amelia's tablet. What else could it be? No wall slave ever had anything like this.

A fingernail-sized piece of plastic fell from the lower left corner of the tablet and dropped to the floor. Monica stooped and picked it up between thumb and forefinger. Had it broken when it fell?

"What's the banging about?" Simon marched into the room.

Alfred stumbled in after him, stifling a yawn.

"I found it!" Monica held the tablet close. "I found the tablet."

Alfred leaned against one of the beds and yawned. "You mean I didn't have to get up?"

Simon hurried over and grabbed the tablet. "Excellent!" He looked over his shoulder. "Though you really made a mess of things."

"Hey!" Monica stopped herself from reaching for the tablet. "I need that back, Simon. I have to return to Cantral as soon as possible so I have time to clean up."

Not looking up from the tablet, Simon nodded. "You certainly are filthy, but I must examine this first. I know more about computers than you do so I need to help you figure out what to tell the Council. Then we can finally get moving on our plans."

"I'd appreciate the help, but I might be able to do it by myself. I have been reading, you know."

"Yes, yes." Simon waved her away. "Let's go back to the receiving room. I want to have my materials close at hand as I study this." Turning the tablet over, he muttered, "If it works at all. It looks as though it's been dropped." He glared at Monica. "There's a piece missing from the corner."

She held the gray bit of plastic out to him in an open palm, tensing her muscles, anticipating the raging dialogue that was sure to come. "I accidentally let it drop when I was searching, and that broke off."

Simon snatched the piece and stuffed it into his shirt pocket. "Another reason I should keep the tablet for now."

As he retreated toward the door, Monica stared at him. Where was the lecture? His old personality still reared its head, but maybe responsibility was good for him. Maybe it would calm him even more over time.

Simon tromped out of the room and down the stairs. "Come along. We don't have all night!"

Groaning, Alfred opened his eyes and followed him. "Can I go back to bed now?"

"No!" Simon's voice carried back up the stairs.

Monica trotted after the two. If the tablet still worked, she could be heading home in minutes. She shook her head. No. She had no home—but Cantral was the closest thing at the moment.

CHAPTER 31

"The tablet definitely works. In spite of your carelessness." Blue shadows danced across Simon's face as he scrolled through Amelia's computer's information. "She has an interesting filing system." He frowned, the darkness exaggerating the crease in his brow. "Or lack thereof."

Monica sat in the armchair in front of Simon's desk, examining the tight wrap that encased her elbow, holding the joint stiffly in place. He had been poring over the small computer for thirty minutes, enough time for the doctor to set the fabric wrap around her arm and tell her to restrict her joint's movement. As if that was even an option.

She fiddled with the strap of the bag Simon had given her to carry the tablet. Turning in her seat, she caught sight of Alfred, who had given up the fight against sleep a few minutes ago. He lay spread out on the dark floral rug, snoring gently, one arm over his eyes.

"Most of her items," Simon muttered, "require her chip to access them, and I'm certain you weren't foolish enough to bring that with you, but she has notes in some files that don't require it. Something about cloning and chips and lots of scraps of code that she seemed to be in the middle of writing." He scratched his head with a long black stylus that he had been using. "Cloning was banned years ago, before even I was born. Too many messy outcomes and much too expensive." He shrugged. "In theory, of course, it's brilliant. Who wouldn't want to have two of me?"

"I can think of some people." Monica rested her chin on her hand. "I don't think she's talking about cloning in that sense. She's talking about chips. I read a section about it in a book on computers. It said that chip cloning was banned in some year or other. I don't remember which."

"Do you remember the name of this book?" Simon laid the tablet on the table. "I'm sure I have whatever it is in the library. Thanks to me, our library is almost as well stocked as the north wing's."

"I . . ." Monica tried to bring up the image of the book's cover in her mind, but it wouldn't come. Why couldn't the Antrelix work now when she needed it? Of course, she hadn't really looked at the cover, just what was inside it. "I don't know."

Simon picked up the tablet again and shut it off. "Then I can't help you anymore. You're going to have to figure out this coding and encryption on your own. We know Amelia called her language Anagram, but she never taught it to me."

Monica shook her head. "I thought you were Amelia's teacher. How could she write in a computer code you don't even know?"

Standing, he handed her the computer. "I taught her what I knew and recommended a different teacher for her once she had surpassed me in computer knowledge. He worked with her a few years before being transferred to Cantral for some other student who was apparently more important. She was self-taught after that. She made the language up around the time her tutor left." He circled around the desk and stood beside Alfred. "Don't you remember *anything* from all our lessons?" He nudged Alfred with a foot. "I thought we went over that."

"You just said you taught her everything she knew." Monica picked up the papers Simon had translated, folded them, and pushed them into the bag with the tablet.

"I . . . might have exaggerated a bit." He tapped Alfred again with a boot. "Come on, boy, get up. You can go to bed once you show Monica back to the border."

Shaking her head, she stood. "I don't need to be shown, Simon. I've walked that route a thousand times. Probably more than Alfred ever has."

Simon prodded Alfred a third time. "If you don't get up, I'll get a bucket of cold water and dump it on your face. How would you like that?" He turned to Monica. "Perhaps, but the guards don't know you. They wouldn't be happy about a ragged Seen girl wandering around their tunnels. They're restless as it is."

Letting out a moan, Alfred rolled onto his stomach and climbed to his feet. "I agree with Monica."

"Don't be lazy. It's only around two in the morning. There's plenty of time left for sleeping." Simon ushered them out of the room. "And Monica, I don't expect to see you back here until the computers are destroyed. Is that clear?"

Monica stumbled out of the receiving room and had barely regained her balance when the door closed behind them. "That's really encouraging." She marched down the hall. "Let's go, Alfred."

He trotted after her, his bare feet making slapping noises on the tile floor. "I'm glad you're okay. Simon was really worried about you for a day or two, you know."

Stopping outside the wall access panel, Monica pressed on the wood. "Really? He doesn't act like it, but . . ." She swung the door in and let Alfred go first. "He never has before."

"He's different." Alfred shut the panel behind them. "He keeps acting all nice and then getting grumpy again, especially when working on those pages from your mother's journal."

Monica tiptoed down the stairs. "Speaking of mothers." She turned and descended the stairs backward so she could see Alfred's face. "I met yours. Tresa, right? She's my—I mean Amelia's—nurse in the north wing."

His eyes widening, Alfred shook his head. "I was told she was transferred to the south wing, not the north."

They entered a dimmer section of stairs, where over half of the lights flickered or didn't work at all.

Monica turned so she could walk more easily. "Well, is her name Tresa?"

"Yes. That's her name." Alfred's voice sounded wistful.

"She said she had sons named Alfred and Jonas. Maybe she was just transferred again once she was in the south wing. Transfers between wings happen all the time in Cantral."

Continuing in silence, they reached the messenger tunnels in moments. Alfred charged into the lead now, his head bowed, as if in concentration.

Monica trotted after him, her leg giving off only a dull ache. Maybe she shouldn't have brought up the subject. Jonas had acted strangely when she had mentioned Tresa to him, too. Maybe they wanted to forget her so the separation wouldn't be so painful. Alfred had been carefree before the Cillineese termination, as if he didn't have a worry in the world, and everything was right. Had he forgotten Tresa so easily?

"Are you coming?" Alfred called from farther up the tunnel, his outline barely visible in the dimness.

Monica picked up her pace. She must have slowed to a walk as she mulled over her thoughts. Moments later, they arrived at the passage leading to the door she and Simon had taken to go out into the messenger tunnels on her first journey to the north wing.

"I can't go this way." Monica fingered the strap of her bag. Her leg was doing well at the moment, thanks to the medicine from the doctor, but there was no telling when it would wear off.

"Why not?" Alfred pointed at the dark passage. "It's the way you went the first time. Simon showed me."

"There's a faster way to go." Monica brushed past him, heading down the passage that led to the tunnel bug station. "It's a more direct route."

Alfred ran beside her. "If you say so."

They continued jogging side by side until they arrived at the door leading to the bug station. A burly, brown-haired man stood at attention, his arms crossed over his large chest.

He looked down his long, pointed nose at them. "What are you children doing here this late at night?"

Monica retreated two steps. The first guard had said his shift was almost complete. This must be his replacement.

"Aren't you going to say anything?" Alfred hissed.

"Oh." Monica nodded. "Sorry. I need to get through that door." She pointed at the steel plate behind the man.

The man raised an eyebrow. "It's too late for pranks. Whoever dared you to come bother me is just going to have to be disappointed. Now scram."

"I'm serious!" Monica sighed. Of course she should have said it differently, but there probably wasn't anything she could say to convince him on the first try. "I need to get to Cantral tonight, and the fastest way is through the bug station. So if you'd kindly open the door, I'd like to leave."

The man let out a short, barking laugh. "You're kidding, right? If you step outside that door, you'll be killed in an instant. A few people have tried it, and it wasn't pretty."

"Well, if people have been allowed to try it, you should let me, too." Monica stepped closer to the door.

The man blocked the exit with his body. "Not a chance. I'd lose my job."

"Just tell him Simon sent you already," Alfred groaned. "I want to go back to bed."

"Simon sent you?" The man stood taller and widened his stance. "What did he say?"

Monica shrugged. "Just to let me through."

"If you know Simon," Alfred said, "you should know me, too. I'm usually with him, and I can confirm that he wants her to go to Cantral."

Leaning forward, the man squinted and looked Alfred up and down. "You do seem familiar. You're his little page boy, aren't you? Always running errands for him?"

Alfred nodded. "That's me. Now can you let her through?"

"Simon must hate her if he wants her dead." The man shrugged.

"I won't die. I don't have a chip." Monica gritted her teeth. "We're wasting time. Just let me through. If I die, I die. Alfred's here, he'll tell everyone it was my fault."

The man started to turn a wheel on the wall, shaking his head. "If Simon says you have to go, I guess you have to. But this is really going to hurt. Don't say I didn't warn you."

The door slowly rose, creaking and groaning. The bottom lifted a foot from the ground and stopped. The man pushed and tugged on the wheel until sweat beaded on his forehead, but it squealed and wouldn't move an inch.

Finally, he stuck a stick through the wheel's metal spokes and jammed it against the wall. "That's as high as it'll go. Sorry."

"It's fine. Thank you." Monica dropped to her hands and knees and shoved her bag through the opening. "Bye, Alfred." She wiggled through and began tumbling down the stairs on the other side.

She threw her arms out and caught herself on the narrow walls, slowing her descent.

"Bye! Thank you . . . for telling me about my mother." Alfred's voice came through clearly, as though he were bent down, calling through the opening.

Monica righted herself, dusted off, and grabbed her bag. The familiar burning sensation coursed across her arms. She grimaced and shook off the pain.

After clicking her wristband's screen on, she ran down the stairs. The steep steps flew by under her pattering bare feet, and the declining slope rushed her forward.

The stairs ended abruptly. She stretched her hands out and banged into the door leading to the transport. It gave under the pressure, swinging out over the steps leading into the tunnel. She scampered down the stairs and took off at a trot along the abandoned Cillineese bug passage, her bag flopping at her side. As she ran, memories of dozens of other journeys in messenger paths came back to mind. So many messengers had helped her, risking their lives to do so, and she hadn't freed them yet.

She glanced at the smooth dirt ceiling with only thick beams interrupting its seemingly never-ending path through the earth. There were probably messengers up there now, in the passages overhead, running on swift, quiet feet in the middle of the night, delivering some message that a Noble thought important enough that it couldn't wait until morning. How often had she been awakened in the early hours of the day by her father stumbling out of bed to a beeping wristband, hastily putting on his boots, and dashing out of the dorm? Now she was a messenger herself, running in the waning hours of the day, carrying a message to the Nobles that would bring her freedom and their destruction.

CHAPTER 32

The boards blocking the way to the Cillineese tunnel track came into view in minutes. Monica ducked under them just as she had before and glanced both ways down the main tunnel. She needed to go to the left, the way she had come, but when would the next bug run? And in which direction would it be traveling?

Breaking into a run, she bolted down the transport tunnel to the left, in the middle of the bugs' path. At least she could get to the east station and wait for a transport there. There was no way she could catch a bug if it was going full speed, especially not with her hurt arm.

A rumble filled the tunnel. Monica's heart beat even faster as she sprinted, bowing her head and pumping her arms and legs with all her might. Her leg and arm ached furiously despite the pain medication, but she couldn't stop. If a bug was coming, it would squash her flat.

Twin lights appeared ahead, beacons in the tunnel darkness, coming closer with every second. Monica skittered to a halt and looked frantically behind her. It was too far to run back, and there was no telling how much farther it was to the east station.

The tunnel bug barreled onward, rattling the ground beneath her feet. She pressed herself against the wall and tucked her bag behind her. Squeezing her eyes shut, she turned her head to the side, pushing her cheek into the tunnel's dirt wall.

A roaring wind swept by, drawing her hair away from her face and whipping it around. The sound of metal grinding on metal squealed in her ears. As she lifted her eyelids for a second, the red body of a slave transport pelted by.

Dust flew into her eyes, and she scrunched them closed again. The gritty particles stung, but she forced her lids shut for a few moments more.

As the rumblings diminished, she blinked rapidly, clearing her vision of spots and grit. Her legs shaking, she started to run again. The station wouldn't be much farther away. If a slave transport just passed, then a Noble bug should be coming soon, if the schedules were consistent.

The light from her wristband blinked and shut off, enveloping her in darkness. She pressed the screen. The wristband came to life, revealing once again the time and options it displayed before entering Cillineese.

Monica breathed a sigh of relief. Going out of the computer's reach for a few hours didn't hurt the wristband. If it hadn't come back to life, she would have had to come up with some kind of explanation to get it fixed. Wristbands didn't just break.

She shone the meager blue light across the tunnel's expanse. The beams reflected off something to the left. The east wing station? She let her arm fall to her side and ran to the spot.

A raised platform loomed almost a foot above her head. She pushed her toes against the platform's solid concrete wall. The grit clung to her toes, but the surface was too sheer to grip.

Lifting her hands above her head, she touched the platform's cold tiles with her palms. She tensed her shoulders and pressed the surface, dragging herself halfway up the wall. Her feet scraped the concrete as she scrambled for a foothold. Arms quaking, she forced her elbows onto the platform and wrenched herself up the rest of the way. Her elbow screamed in pain, and she bit back a squeal.

She rolled onto her back and lay panting. Tiny stabs ran through her elbow and upper arm except where the cloth wrap protected her joint.

Crawling to her feet, she shook her head. Another injury to hide from Aric. The bruise on her elbow would be the hardest to explain.

The station filled with rumbling noises, and lights in the floor turned on, flooding the cavern in a misty blue tint.

Monica ducked into the shadows by the wall and crouched low. Moments later, a rushing wind filled the station. As the breeze diminished, a sleek Noble transport glided in. Steam billowed into the room, wafting around Monica in a hot embrace.

The transport rested silently in front of the platform, the silver lights pulsing on its sides. She crept up to it on all fours and grabbed the ladder on its back end. It continued waiting as she hooked one arm under a rung and hugged the bag to her chest, making sure the strap was securely over her head and shoulder.

A whooshing noise came from the transport. Monica craned her neck to see around the side. Was it about to move?

The right side of the bug trembled and rose in the air in an arc, curving over the top of the transport and resting on the roof, cutting away one wall and revealing the plush interior.

Monica inched farther away from the platform until the interior of the bug disappeared from view.

Low voices emanated from inside, and two shadowed figures walked out of the bug and across the platform. The blue lights illumined their faces for a split second, two Noble men she had never seen before. They quick-marched up the stairs leading into the east wing and disappeared in the dark stairway.

As the bug door slid back into place, Monica rested her head on a rung. If they had turned even for a second, they would have noticed her for sure.

The bell clanging, the transport's lights flashed twice before it pulled out. It picked up speed as it trundled along, passing station after station. The bug stopped at every other wing, first south with its lights and sign letters in a dull bronze, then west with its colors a fiery red.

Monica clung tightly to the ladder with every turn and jerk, hoping and praying that no one else would be on the platforms, that no one would see her holding on to the bug for dear life.

The bug turned another corner, curving to the left. Finally, the north station came into view. The gold lights flared bright, and its plaque glimmered as the bug pulled to a stop.

Monica stumbled off the ladder onto the platform and almost fell to the floor, her knees quaking. She forced herself to stay upright.

Her eyesight blurry and her head hurting, she trotted up the stairs. A quick glance at her wristband revealed the time—3:39 a.m.

Shaking her head, she located the wall slaves' panel she had come through. Just a little farther to go, and a soft bed would be waiting.

After sliding into the wall passage, she jerked the panel closed again and brushed the broken, crumbling plaster into a corner. Even if someone did wonder at the mess, there would be no one to blame it on. She smiled past the pain and sleepiness. Anyone who investigated would decide no one could have come down this hall without the computers knowing and give it up as a mystery.

She scuttled down the wall slaves' passage, keeping her book bag and injured arm pressed close to her chest. With one final hop over a pipe jutting across the path, she arrived at her bedroom.

Pushing the door open with her book bag, she shoved it through first, then crawled in. She glanced all around and jumped to her feet. As she closed the panel with a foot, Ahla's gentle breathing hummed in a natural rhythm. Her leg aching, Monica gazed longingly at her bed but stopped there only for a moment to lay her bag on the covers before creeping to the bathroom. Sleep would have to wait until she was clean. If she went back to Aaron's room now, the smell of the sweat and grime would probably wake him.

A quick shower washed away all the dirt from her fall, the dust from the dormitory, and the sweat from her run. She reveled in the hot, pinpoint droplets of water that pummeled her, but only for a few minutes.

The scent of perfumed flowers filled the room as she toweled off. She slipped her Seen dress on once more. There was still a trip through the wall passage and wall slaves to fool.

Her hair stuck to her through the dress's thin material. After tying her locks back with a black stretchy cord taken from the bathroom cupboard, she switched off the light with her uninjured elbow and sneaked into her room.

Monica grabbed Aaron's tablet from beneath her pillow and powered it on with one hand while fishing in her bag for Amelia's computer with the other. The bandage clinging to her elbow chafed her scraped skin, but the security it offered her sore joint was worth the minor abrasions.

The screen on Aaron's tablet brightened and flooded the room with light. Monica flinched and stuffed it under her pillow while she turned Amelia's tablet on.

As she started up the computer, she glanced from the screen to Ahla's motionless form. *Don't wake up.* The bright light from Aaron's computer, although exposed for only a short time, might be enough to rouse her.

Monica tugged Aaron's computer out from under the pillow and held the two tablets close together. Aric had connected a handheld computer to his tablet somehow. There might be a way to connect these two as well.

She turned Amelia's computer over to look at the bottom end. A plastic flap covered part of the side, barely visible in the light from Aaron's tablet. Simon had given her a hurried course on transferring computer files and connecting tablets while he tried to decipher Amelia's notes. It wouldn't be too hard to figure it out.

Picking at the flap with a nail, she flipped it open, revealing a short metal prong and a row of different shaped openings, some square, some rectangular, and one circular.

She turned Aaron's computer over and located an identical flap that hid the same circular prong and openings. Placing the two tablets on the bed, Monica eyed the opening in Amelia's computer and the prong on Aaron's. Just like Simon said.

A quick, gentle push connected the two, and the tablet screens changed. One word flashed across their otherwise-blank faces. *Syncing* . . .

Monica let her tense muscles relax. Syncing was normal, wasn't it? She had read something about it in one of her computer books. The tablets were talking to each other or something.

After a moment, the word disappeared, and the two screens lit up again. A line split each across the middle, half of each screen showing the original images from one tablet and the other half showing the other tablet's.

She scrolled through Aaron's tablet screen on the half assigned to it on Amelia's tablet until she found the map. After selecting it with a finger, she dragged it onto the half of Amelia's tablet assigned to Amelia's programs.

When the program hovered over an empty space on Amelia's half, Monica drew her finger away, and the file fell into place. A copy stayed behind on Aaron's screen, and a new version glimmered on Amelia's.

Monica's heart raced as she eyed the rest of the programs.

What else would be useful? The sleeper program? But would she be able to force herself to use it? There was probably information even more valuable on the tablet, but there was no time to look for it now.

She unplugged the tablets from each other and snapped the flaps closed. At least it had worked.

She shoved Amelia's tablet into her bag and tucked Aaron's computer under her arm. Now the hard part. Returning it to his room, and this time he would be there.

Feeling awake and refreshed, Monica tiptoed back into the wall passage and raced down the stairs toward Aaron's room, her footfalls soft and silent as she darted down the hall.

Panting, she turned into the corridor of bedrooms. As she rested in the pitch black of the wall slaves' passage she caught her breath. She peered through the view port. Everything lay silent on the other side.

Crawling on hands and knees, she eased through the opening. The soft breathing continued at a steady rhythm.

Monica rose to her feet and glanced around. Two indistinct forms lay on the bed, looking like shadowy lumps in the dim light. She edged to the bed, sliding one bare foot across the thick dark carpet a few inches at a time before pulling the other foot to join it.

One of the figures on the bed turned, revealing her face—Melody. Monica jumped back a step.

Melody breathed in deeply, and her eyes remained closed.

Monica clamped a hand over her mouth. Melody was still asleep. She had to be.

Letting out a short sigh, Monica crawled to the side of the bed where a nightstand stood. She gritted her teeth until her jaw hurt. If either of them made another noise she would jump out of her skin.

She groped behind the night table. Where was the cord? Her hand connected with a piece of rubber. There! As she forced the cord back into the hole it had come out of earlier, her fingers ached. She set the tablet on the night table in the same place it had rested before.

Someone groaned and let out a long sigh.

Monica dropped to her stomach, gritting her teeth.

The bed squeaked as someone shifted position.

Monica ducked and rolled under the bed. The ruffle along the bedside brushed against her feet as she scooted farther in. Dust unreached by cleaning wall slaves tickled her nose.

The bed groaned again and a pair of feet hit the floor somewhere near Monica's head. She flinched but pressed her lips firmly together. Had Aaron or Melody heard her? Was one of them waking to investigate? They had already been disturbed once tonight. Would they be easier to awaken now?

Soft footfalls walked away from the bed. A light clicked on somewhere in another room, sending some stray rays beneath the bed, shining on Monica. She turned to the side just in time to see a figure disappear into a side room.

Monica bit her lower lip. Melody going to the bathroom? Whoever it was hadn't used the door out to the main hall. There was no telling when she would be back. Would it be safe to move now? What if there was no other opportunity?

After sliding out from under the bed, she darted across the room and dove for the access panel.

Breathing a sigh of relief, she closed the panel then laid a hand on her chest and instinctively felt for Alyssa's medallion, but there was nothing at her throat. A sharp cry escaped her lips. Where had it gone?

Gulping, she shook her head. It must have slipped off somewhere. How could she have lost something so precious?

Monica wrapped her arms around herself. Another reminder of her failures. The loss of Alyssa's medallion. Poor Alyssa had died. Her husband was a furnace worker, so he had probably perished in the gas that had taken most of the slaves who worked the tunnels and furnace.

Monica wiped her eyes, then peered into the view port again. No sign of the medallion anywhere, but maybe it was under the bed.

A door on the left opened and closed. Melody shuffled out of the bathroom. She stood beside the bed, looking around. Her gaze seemed to meet Monica's, staring right into her eyes.

Shaking her head, Monica clenched her fists. Nobles didn't usually know where access panels were, and even if they did, the view ports were disguised. Melody couldn't see her.

Melody frowned and climbed back into bed.

Monica rose and shuffled down the eerily quiet corridors. With every turn her leg grew number, and drops of warm blood oozed down her skin.

She reached her bedroom in minutes and crawled inside. Sighing, she crept across the room and retrieved a spare nightdress folded in one of the bathroom cupboards. She changed quickly and shoved her Seen dress down the laundry chute. After unwrapping the bandage from around her leg, she pushed that down the chute as well. Dried blood flecked her cut, but no new droplets appeared, so it was probably safe to leave it open to the air. She scurried to Ahla's bedside. Kneeling beside it, she slipped her hand into Ahla's pocket and fished her vial out. Ahla's breathing remained even.

Monica crawled back to her bed and started to climb in, but a squeak stopped her. Vinnie stared at her from where he sat on her pillow. "Vinnie!" she hissed. "You came back!" He sniffed her hand as she stroked him with the other. "I didn't think you would." She retrieved his cage from beneath the bed and put him back inside.

"Goodnight." After snapping the cage closed, she slid it back into place and climbed into bed. Finally. The mattress welcomed her weight, cushioning her weary muscles.

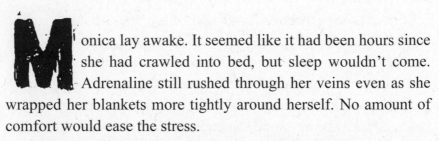

CHAPTER 33

Monica lay awake. It seemed like it had been hours since she had crawled into bed, but sleep wouldn't come. Adrenaline still rushed through her veins even as she wrapped her blankets more tightly around herself. No amount of comfort would ease the stress.

Ahla's breathing changed from a steady, deep rumble to a ragged, gasping cough.

Monica sat up. What was going on? She slid off the bed. "Ahla? Are you okay?"

Ahla moaned, but her eyes remained closed.

Fear gripped Monica as she stood by. What should she do? Was something wrong with Ahla's baby? Kneeling beside the cot, she shook Ahla's shoulder. "Ahla, wake up, please, wake up!"

Ahla scrunched her eyelids more tightly closed. She drew in another deep breath and opened her eyes.

Monica jumped away from the bed.

"Miss Amelia?" Ahla sat up and swung her feet to the floor.

"I'm sorry. I didn't mean to make any noise." Wincing, she put a hand to her bulging stomach.

Monica shook her head. "I'm fine. It's okay. I was just worried about you." The words tumbled out over each other, and Monica backed up against her own bed. "Your breathing wasn't normal. Are you all right now?"

Ahla's face turned pale. "I—I was?" Using her hands to push herself, she rose from her cot. "I apologize again. I didn't realize." Closing her eyes for a second, she shook her head. "It seems like I was only asleep for a few minutes."

Monica crept forward and palmed the wall. The lights flickered, then turned on. Blinking, Monica edged back to her bed. "Are you sure you're all right?"

"Yes, Miss I'm fin—" Ahla's face contorted in a grimace. She put a hand to her stomach. "I—I think." She winced again. "I think I might need to go to the infirmary." The words came out in gasps. "Please forgive me, Miss Amelia, but I think I should call in a replacement."

"Don't apologize!" Monica took Ahla's other hand. "Let me help you." She slipped off Ahla's wristband and tapped in a command to call the Seen infirmary nurse.

Sweat beaded on Ahla's forehead as she gasped. "Please, Miss, I'll be all right."

"No." Monica entered the last command and pushed the band back onto Ahla's arm. "Don't worry. You haven't done anything wrong. I'll make sure you're taken care of."

Shaking her head, Ahla let out a low moan.

Monica gritted her teeth. This was all her fault. She made the decision for Tresa to go back to the dorm. The children had needed her, and getting Aaron's tablet would have been more difficult, yes, but what if Ahla's baby was hurt? Tresa's nieces and nephews would have been tormented, but at least they would have lived through it.

"You'll be okay." Monica took Ahla's hand and squeezed it. The words seemed to fall flat in the midst of Ahla's quiet moans. They wouldn't be any comfort in this storm of pain.

Monica crouched by the cot. Why was this happening? "Is—is it time for the baby to come?" Monica wrinkled her brow. It was a personal question, but the nurse would need to know, if she didn't already.

"I have over a week to go." Ahla hissed the words through clenched teeth. "But I've wondered if the nurse is wrong about the date." Tears welled in her eyes and streamed down her cheeks as her muscles tensed. "My last child wasn't nearly so large." She shook her head. "Why am I saying this? I'm sorry. I shouldn't. You must be so angry."

"I'm not angry." Monica sighed. Was the Seen training so ingrained in this poor woman that she thought of the rules even over intense pain? "I haven't ever been angry or upset in any way at you. You're fine."

Someone knocked at the door.

"Come in!" Monica pushed herself to her feet and edged away from Ahla.

The door inched open, and a young man peered in. His bushy eyebrows turned down, and a grimace puckered his thin lips. "I'm sorry to disturb you at this hour, Miss Amelia, but I received a call to come here."

"Yes, please come in!" Monica beckoned to him. "Can't you see she's in labor?"

The man hurried in, followed by a little girl about six years old.

"Of course, of course." The man crouched down and pulled Ahla to her feet. "Put an arm over my shoulder, Ahla, and we'll be to the infirmary before you know it."

Ahla did as he said, her eyes clenched tightly shut. "Thank you, Jacks."

Jacks shuffled to the door. "Please excuse us, Miss Amelia. I'm so sorry to trouble you at this early hour." He shoved the door open farther with a foot. "I'll be sure to see that—"

"I don't want her punished!" Monica scurried for the door. "Say I didn't wake up. I was asleep when this happened, okay? Whatever it takes, just make sure she isn't punished for disturbing me. It's not her fault."

Jacks's brown eyes widened, and he edged out of the room. "Oh, no, Miss. There's no danger of her being punished." He nodded at the little girl who stood like a statue nearby. "Trella will stay with you, if that's acceptable. I've had your tether connected to her chip. She might not look like much, but she can handle any task you request."

Ahla moaned again.

"Of course." Monica sighed. There was no time for these formalities. "Just get Ahla to the infirmary!"

"Yes, Miss. Right away." The two shuffled from the room. Jacks swung the door closed, shutting out Ahla's quiet groans.

Monica sighed. She turned to the little girl standing beside the cot. "So you're Trella, huh?"

The girl stared at her with wide blue eyes. After a moment, she nodded slowly, and her black hair fell in front of her narrow face. "Yes, Miss."

"You remind me of someone I know." Monica smiled. Maybe if she displayed friendliness, Trella would feel more at ease. She looked too young to be working on her own, but appearances could be deceiving. Receiving an unusual assignment so early in the morning would be frightening for any child.

Trella stared at her for a long second before looking at the ground.

Monica climbed onto her bed and sat a few feet away from where Trella stood. "Do you know Shora?"

"Yes, Miss." Trella continued staring at the ground, as if it were the most interesting thing in Central.

Monica's eyelids drooped, weighed down by lack of sleep. This was going to be tougher than she thought, but if this girl knew Shora, maybe she knew why Shora was sneaking around. Though if Shora wouldn't even tell Tresa why, it was unlikely. But it was worth a try. "Is she . . . your cousin?"

Trella clasped her hands behind her back. "No, Miss."

"Your sister?"

Trella's eyes widened. "Yes, Miss."

Monica's heart sank. No wonder Trella was so quiet, then. Her mother had just been sent away with almost no chance of ever seeing her again. Why had the computer picked Trella to come sit with the prisoner? Was she the most readily available? She should be with her siblings and Tresa. Maybe she had the lightest workload of the Seen. "I'm sorry about your mother."

"You—" Trella's voice squeaked. "You know about that, Miss?"

"Yes, and I'm sorry." Monica slid off her bed again and inched toward Trella. If only she could give Trella some kind of comfort, but the little Seen would probably panic if she were touched by a Noble. "I wish there was something I could do, but I don't know . . ."

Trella's lower lip trembled.

Monica clenched a fist. How could the Nobles be so cruel? They—

She slowly unclenched her fist. There would be time to deal with them tomorrow. Once she was given her freedom, she would find a way to break into the computer room and end their reign. The Seen and wall slaves wouldn't have to suffer anymore.

Trella's sniffling broke into her thoughts. Silent tears rolled down her pale face as she stood at attention in front of Monica, shaking like a young tree in the breeze.

"I know what it's like," Monica whispered. "I lost my mother when I was young. People will say it gets easier . . . And it does, for the most part, but then there are times when you'll wish so badly that she was with you that your heart will ache until you think you can't stand it anymore." Monica shook her head. This wasn't helping. But how could she comfort someone when there was no comfort to be had? "But then you have Tresa. I'm sure she'll be like a mother to you. Even if she can't replace your mother, she'll be a comfort."

More tears streamed down Trella's cheeks. "I miss her already. I wish she didn't have to go away."

Monica reached out and hugged the trembling little girl close. Would she jerk away and cower in fear?

Trella melted into sobs and threw her arms around Monica's neck, burying her head on her shoulder. "We'll never see her again! Rhea isn't even old enough to remember her."

Monica drew Trella to the floor and sat cross-legged, hugging the sobbing girl close. "I'm so sorry," Monica whispered. "I'm going to try to fix it. We'll find a way to bring her back."

Trella's sobs continued for another few minutes until they started to ease. Her breathing steadied, and she stopped shaking.

Her arms aching, Monica patted Trella's head. Tears dampened her shoulder from Trella's crying, and her cheeks were wet from her own tears. Memories of her mothers returned as she sat rocking back and forth. There was Emmilah, who had taken care of her like she was her own, and Rose, her birth mother whom she could barely conjure an image of a few days ago, whose likeness flooded her mind now—Rose, combing Monica's hair late at night, sitting with her when she was sick and too ill to go anywhere, crying when she told her daughter she had to go away for a while and might not see her again.

Monica blinked at these images. When did all this happen? Before the Cillineese termination? Was her mother saying goodbye? Did she know what was going to take place?

Keeping her eyes closed, Monica rolled the thoughts over in her mind until she fell asleep, hugging Trella tightly.

CHAPTER 34

An ache spread through Monica's limbs and joints. She blinked open her eyes. Soft strands of hair tickled her nose. Holding back a sneeze, she sat up and looked around.

Trella lay on the floor next to Monica, her hair spread out behind her, thumb in her mouth. Redness rimmed her lids, the only indicator that she had been crying a few hours before.

Monica brushed a strand of hair from Trella's face and stood. Her eyes burned from last night's tears, and a pounding pulsed in her head.

She glanced at her wristband—7:17 a.m. Did Ahla have her baby yet? If it wasn't her first child, the labor shouldn't take long. Most wall slaves had their children quickly and were back to work within two or three days.

A thick bandage on Monica's arm caught her eye. She unwrapped the cloth to reveal a bruise that spread five inches across her right elbow. Wincing, she limped to her closet. That wouldn't go unnoticed. She wound the cloth around her arm again. Maybe if she wore long sleeves she could hide the bandage for a while.

She shoved the closet door open and searched the hanging garments for something suitable. A dark green dress caught her eye. Darker piping emphasized its seams and neckline and the cuffs of the long sleeves.

Monica ripped it off its hanger and changed quickly. The sooner she got dressed, the sooner she could contact the Council and give them Amelia's tablet. As she buttoned up the back of her dress her elbow ached, but she fastened the last button without much trouble.

She crept back to her bed, stepping over Trella's motionless form. Amelia's tablet still lay on the comforter where Monica had left it the night before. The tablet's gray screen looked like a sleeping face that could be awakened with the touch of a button.

Pressing the corner of the tablet, Monica sighed. How would she ever decipher the coding if not even Simon knew what it meant? She had so little knowledge of computers—just a few key words that allowed her to stumble through her interrogations.

Tapping a file folder labeled *School Projects*, she glanced down at Trella who lay fast asleep. Monica shook her head. The poor girl was probably exhausted after being awakened so early in the morning.

A beep from the tablet brought Monica's attention back to the task at hand. Text appeared on the screen. *Chip Identification Needed to Proceed*.

She frowned. Why would Amelia make her tablet require a chip just to view some school files? Shrugging, she withdrew her necklace and held the glass vial over the tablet's surface. Another beep sounded from the computer, and the text vanished. More images appeared on the screen, some with names like *CodeTest1* and *Test7Good*. Among the jumble of files, one stood out with the simplest name: *Notes*.

Monica tapped that file and waited for it to open. The same text as before flashed on the screen again. *Chip Identification Needed to Proceed*.

Rolling her eyes, she held the chip to the screen. Amelia must have been really worried about who looked at her files. More text appeared on the screen in short, choppy lines.

Test 6.4 partial success, but chip #2 held new coding for only 10 minutes before shutting down. Chip #1 had successful transfer.

I don't understand how Joel accomplished what he did. In every one of my trials, the second chip has died. Even with the notes I found I haven't come close to replicating his conclusions. I'm beginning to believe a clone transfer really is impossible and that the information Veronica provided me with is false. Could she be holding some information back? I have a few more ideas to try before starting a new approach. If only my head didn't hurt so much I could concentrate better.

Monica scrolled through some text containing scraps of partial code and notes on program technicalities. Veronica? Regina's mother? Regina's mother had said she had corresponded with Amelia, so maybe it was her.

The text changed to another journal entry, leaving the technical jargon behind, and Monica continued reading.

Test 7 was a complete success. I now have two chips sending the same signal to the computer with no adverse effects to the chips' circuitry. Veronica wasn't lying as far as I can see. I will have to show her if we ever get a chance to meet. There's no telling if the chips would harm a person if they were implanted, but I am not willing to test it on a human subject. Perhaps if I could find an animal test subject.

I've heard scientists of old used rats in some of their experiments. I could petition for one to be implanted with a chip, but it would most likely be too risky. Someone would wonder why and ask too many questions. I will just have to be content with these findings. The mystery of Brenna and Rose is solved. My only question now would be why?—but of course Joel is no longer here to ask. I wish I could study these findings further. Maybe a Seen would volunteer to take a chance. Laney might be willing enough, and she would never betray me. It would only benefit her if it succeeded.

Monica gulped. Joel? Brenna Rose? This was about her parents! What was Amelia trying to solve? When it came to what was really important, the text was vague. Who cared about the applications for the project? What was the program exactly, and what mystery was she talking about? Monica tugged a strand of her hair. Her father left other notes behind? Why didn't she know about them before?

She reached into her book bag again. The edges of Simon's translated papers brushed against her fingertips. Drawing them out, she sighed. Her parents had such high hopes for their daughter, yet they died, and if she failed, she would soon join them. She flipped through the few pages of translated papers. One was dated soon after the first that Simon had completed last month, but the other had a date almost five years later. Had Simon skipped to the end of the journal, or had her mother written only a few entries until the last year of her life?

Monica held the first entry close and began to read.

May 1, 2852

My little Sierra,

It is still a few weeks before you are scheduled to enter this world. I ache to hold you in my arms, little one, but at the same time I dread your coming.

I know your father and I have laid a terrible burden upon you, bringing you into this world, and I pray I will be able to comfort you and hold you in the coming days.

Your father has plans that he has yet to set in motion, but if discovered, the plans alone will condemn this whole city to death. It will be a few years before he has all the information he needs, but his investigations have caused a stir. He recently left us to travel to Central and has yet to return home.

I pray every night that he will return safely and unquestioned.

I have heard the Cantral security teams can be brutal in their inter-rogations, especially since Foxlar has been assigned. I know of his techniques firsthand. I hope that you never have to fear such things. Nightmares torment me often, and I can feel you stirring inside me, as if you can see the violent images in my head.

Do not worry. The Lord protects us, and your father is a genius with computer chips. Even if the plans are found and Cillineese is terminated, he has a way to whisk us from this place. I have faith in the Lord's protection and the abilities He has given Joel. Without them I would never be who I am, and you would never have existed.

These matters are too weighty for the moment. My life before is not something I wish to burden you with, though I know I will have to tell you eventually. Perhaps when you're much older, if things turn out well, I will divulge them to you, but I feel our world will change and never be the same before that time ever comes.

I just felt you kick! Are you protesting my conclusion? Don't worry, Sierra, the knowledge you need for the times ahead will be supplied in full.

Monica folded the page. Sierra. A name she would probably never be called again. Before Gerald had reminded her of her name a month ago, she hadn't known any other than Monica, but when she was whisked off to Cantral, her new parents changed it for her safety. What would it have been like to be raised as a Noble? Of course, with Joel's and Rose's political views, even if they hadn't been terminated so many years ago, they would certainly have been executed by now. Would they have taught her more about this God her mother spoke of so frequently? Only the songs whispered by some of the more religious wall slaves gave Him any mention, so there was little to go on.

She turned to the next page. And why had Simon skipped to the last page? The date read *May 15, 2857*. That was just a week before Cillineese was terminated.

Today will be my last day in Cillineese, my last day to see you.

You're sitting on the floor in front of me with Faye, playing with your new tablet. I wish I could see you write your first words, see you learn to read, and grow into a fine young lady. I've begged your father to think of another plan, for another way, but—

Footsteps sounded in the hallway outside. Monica stuffed the papers back in her bag, tied her necklace around her neck, bolted to the door, and opened it before the person could knock.

Tresa stood outside, fist poised in front of the door. "Oh. You're up already." She smiled and looked over her shoulder. "Your plan worked! I was so scared we'd be found out, but I've heard people are saying the alarm was a malfunction. They don't know we had anything to do with it. But." She lowered her voice. "I'm supposed to take you to Aric. Aaron has decided he wants to try the program early, just like I thought he would. I wonder if the fire alarm upset him."

Monica staggered back from the door. "What? But I just—"

"Did you get it?" Tresa darted into the room and shut the door. "If you were successful, then it's not an issue." She glanced around the room. "Where's Ahla?"

"She went into labor last night." Monica bit her lip. Ahla! She had forgotten all about her while reading Amelia's tablet. "A few hours after I got back, I had to call the infirmary nurse. He brought Trella as a replacement."

"Trella's here?" Tresa glanced around the room until she spotted Trella. She swooped over to where the girl lay. "Trella! I was so worried."

Trella rubbed her eyes. "Aunt Tresa?" She lifted her arms to her aunt, and Tresa scooped her up.

"You should have woken me last night," Tresa hissed. "I was frantic when you were gone this morning,"

"I'm sorry." Trella's eyes locked with Monica's, and she stiffened. "Miss Amelia is still here," she whispered, though her words carried across the room as clearly as if she had spoken normally.

Tresa stood Trella in front of her and put a hand on her niece's head. "You're right, of course. That was no way for me to behave in front of our mistress."

"It's all right." Heat rose to Monica's cheeks. There was no need for this acting anymore, not after spilling her guts to Trella last night. The little girl knew she wasn't a well-behaved Noble already. "We need to get going, Tresa. I have to talk to the Council before Aric—"

"*Miss* Amelia . . ." Tresa said the name slowly. "I don't believe this is the best time for this topic."

Monica shook her head. "There's no time for word games. Trella won't tell anyone, and we need to go to the Council now."

"Aunt Tresa?" Trella whimpered. "What's wrong?"

"Don't worry, Trella. It's nothing." Tresa laid a hand on Trella's head. "You know the Nobles are worried with all these different things going on—our guests from Eursia and Miss Amelia being sick."

Trella gazed at the floor, frowning. "Rhea and my assignments aren't near any talk like that, but Shora talks—" She broke off and shrugged.

Tresa turned and knelt in front of Trella. "What does Shora talk about?"

Turning to the side, Trella shrugged again. "Nothing much. Just in her sleep."

"It's okay, honey." Tresa put her hands on Trella's shoulders. "You can tell me. We'll make sure Shora doesn't get in trouble, okay? Miss Amelia's a sympathizer. You can trust her."

Her eyes widening, Trella stuck her thumb in her mouth again and nodded.

Tresa gently tugged on her niece's hand, forcing the thumb from her mouth. "Please, we don't have much time. Miss Amelia could be punished if we don't hurry. Tell me what Shora said."

"Something about the people from Eursia." Trella once again shrugged her thin shoulders. "And errands. She kicked me, so I woke up. I asked her what she meant, and she just turned over." She brought her thumb up to her mouth, then dropped her hand to her side and squeezed a fistful of her dress. "She started talking like that a few nights ago."

Monica gulped. Three nights ago was when Shora had first sneaked into her room, snooping around.

"Is that all you remember?" Tresa stared hard at Trella who squirmed and turned her head, avoiding her aunt's penetrating gaze.

"Yes." Trella gazed at the exit longingly. "Can I go now? I'm hungry, and I have to work with Rhea this morning. She's slow, and I don't want to get behind."

"Yes, you may go. I had the chip tether transferred already." Tresa sighed and released Trella's shoulders. "Just find a way to send me a message if you remember anything else, okay?"

Trella nodded and darted out of the room.

When the door clicked shut, Tresa whirled around. "Are you insane?" she hissed.

Monica stumbled back. "What? I thought we could trust her. She just . . . last night . . ." She rubbed her forehead. How to explain her thoughts? Amelia's notes and her mother's words were still swirling in her head, tangling the past and the present into a foggy web of confusion. "We're so close, there's no way she could spread any rumors, and we need to move quickly."

"Yes, we're close, so we have to be even more careful now!" Tresa put her hands on her hips. "Come on, we need to go. There's no time for breakfast." She picked up a brush from the dresser and tossed it to Monica. "Just brush your hair on the way. Let's go talk to Aric."

Monica caught the brush and gripped the handle until her knuckles turned white. "I'm sorry, okay? But I still think we'll be fine. We didn't tell her anything. She can't spread rumors if she doesn't know anything." She grabbed her boots from her closet and shoved her feet into them.

Tugging her mother's journal out from under her pillow, Monica glanced around the room for the bag from Cillineese. There on the floor. She grabbed the bag and stowed the journal and Amelia's tablet with Simon's translated papers. "Is there any way we can check on Ahla, find out how she's doing?"

"Not on our schedule. Maybe after our meeting. But I'm sure she'll be fine; this is her third child." Tresa held the door open for her. "Is your leg all right?"

Monica trudged into the hall. "Yes. It stopped hurting last night. The glue held after the second application. Even when I jumped off the bug."

The door banged shut. "You *jumped* off the bug?" Tresa hurried to Monica's side. "What happened? Should I take a look at your leg to make sure it's okay?"

"Yes, I did, and no, I'm fine." Monica waved off the questions. "I had to jump because it wasn't stopping at Cillineese. It swept right past the tunnel I needed to take, so I jumped." As she walked, she tugged the black bristle brush through the stubborn knots tangling her hair. "It's not a big deal." Pain flared in her elbow with every stroke, and she forced herself not to wince. Tresa would have another reason to be mad if she saw the bruise. The elbow really wasn't that badly injured, especially since the doctor popped it back into place.

Tresa heaved a long sigh, then led the way up the stairs. "Fine. Let's hurry up. Aaron's message said Aric and another doctor would be in the infirmary to oversee the program, but Aaron won't be attending."

"What?" Monica stopped dead in her tracks. "But then I can't show Aaron the tablet! They'll find out about the chip."

"Miss Amelia!" Tresa turned and glared. "Lower your voice, please. We are *not* in your room anymore. I think this trip wasn't good for you. It's made you too bold in your choice of words. We have to go to this meeting; there's no time to reschedule. We'll explain when we get there. Aric is sure to understand and take us to Aaron."

"I'm sorry." Sighing, Monica yanked the brush though her hair one last time. "I'm being stupid. I think the lack of sleep is affecting me." She stowed the brush in her bag. "I won't say anything else until we get there."

Tresa nodded and walked up the stairs in front, pausing at the top of every landing until Monica joined her.

When they entered the main hall, they turned to the left, going down a flight of stairs Monica had never been on before. A few unfamiliar Nobles and Seen brushed past without a word, but one man with blond hair and piercing blue eyes stared at her as she passed.

Monica looked down at her unlaced boots and scrunched her shoulders. Maybe if she didn't look at the others, they wouldn't take notice of her. They probably knew who she was, the condemned prisoner from Cillineese. Perhaps they knew more about her fate than she did. How much did the Nobles living in the north wing know about the Council meetings?

She shook off the ideas. She was being paranoid again. The man probably didn't even know he had looked at her and was thinking about something else. Placing a hand on her chest, she felt the glass vial beneath her dress. If Aric insisted on running the program, would it affect the chip even though it wasn't in her head? Or would he know something was wrong and demand an X-ray or some other kind of scan?

"Miss Amelia," Tresa whispered in her ear, "please hurry along. We haven't time to dawdle."

Monica blinked and quickened her pace, following Tresa down another flight of stairs, through a hall with white, sterile-looking walls, and into a square room lined with white chairs.

Gripping the handle of her bag, Monica gulped. "This is their infirmary?"

"Yes." Tresa tiptoed to a white door on the other side of the room, rapped the wood with a knuckle, then took a step back. "Just remember to stay calm and try to talk them out of it," she whispered.

Monica gulped. "No problem." The words came out in a squeaky rasp. This was it. She would either convince them and gain her freedom or be found out and meet her death.

When the door opened, Aric peered out. His gaze stopped on Tresa. "Ah. You're here. Excellent." He looked Monica in the eye. "I'm sorry about all this, Amelia. I don't agree with Aaron changing his mind about these things. A ruler should keep his word." He opened the door wider. "But come on. Let's get this over with."

"Wait!" Monica fumbled with her bag. "But I found, ah—I . . ." She jerked the tablet from the bag. "My tablet was found and returned to me. The transport with my things finally arrived, and the Antrelix really helped my memory a lot." She held the computer up. "Can't we talk this over with Aaron?"

Aric's eyes widened. "The Antrelix worked? Excellent." He rubbed his hands together. "You were supposed to send me reports on side effects and such, remember?" He grinned. "Of course you remember, your memory will be excellent from now on. At least . . ." He frowned. "None of the Seen I've tested so far have had it wear off. Long-term trials are still under way." Tapping frantically on his wristband, he nodded. "Aaron is available, unless something has come up on his schedule since last night. I haven't downloaded the newest version from the network yet."

"Okay . . ." Monica tried to smile. Network? Downloaded? The words were familiar because of reading those computer books, but their definitions remained elusive. Did this mean she could show Aaron the tablet and be on her way?

"Let's pay him a visit, shall we?" Aric poked his head into the other room and called, "Change of plans, Yortha. I'm taking Amelia to see Aaron."

"What?" an older woman screeched. "You've wasted my whole morning, young man. I hope you're happy!"

Aric shuddered and closed the door. "Let's go meet Aaron. I'm curious to see what your project is, too." He peered at her blank tablet screen. "How about letting me take a look first?"

"I think I'd better not show it to anyone but Aaron, if that's okay." She ducked out of the infirmary and into the hallway. There was no way she would trust Aric with her tablet, at least not before Aaron saw it.

He shrugged. "Aaron's on a thirty-minute break to review various documents in his office before the next Council session. If we hurry, we can catch him." He stopped midstride on the stairs leading back toward the Council chambers. Turning slowly on his heel, he frowned. "Where are your crutches? I never cleared you to walk."

Monica bit back a gasp. Her crutches! Since her leg had stopped hurting she had forgotten about needing them. "I . . ."

He thundered back down the steps, pushing past a middle-aged man on his way. The man muttered something about bratty children but continued upward.

Aric dismounted the last step and stood beside her. "Well? Let me guess—you 'forgot' them." He shook his head. "Impossible. What were you thinking?"

"My leg stopped hurting." Monica backed into Tresa who had been following close behind. "Tresa put some wound glue on it last night . . . in . . ." She searched for a good excuse. "Preparation for today." She grimaced. It was in preparation, just not in preparation for what he would think.

"Have you been taking the antibiotics?" Aric glared at her, as if she had done something horribly wrong.

She nodded. "Yes. Mostly."

Shaking his head, he sighed. "I'd better check on the wound to make sure it's not infected. I thought you said the Antrelix was working. How can you keep forgetting all these things?" He knelt and prodded her calf around the laceration.

Heat rose to her cheeks. Getting touched by a Noble was bad enough, but out in the open where everyone could see was even worse. She slid her foot away from his hand. "It's fine. Really."

"It looks red to me. After this meeting, I want to examine it more thoroughly." He nodded at Tresa. "At least your Seen did a good job with the wound glue."

Monica looked back at Tresa. Though her head was bowed, her cheeks were obviously pale. "Can we go now?" Monica edged away from Aric again.

"Very well." Aric climbed the stairs after her, Tresa following at his heels.

Monica hurried up the steps. That was a close call. If Aric had decided not to listen to her and try the program anyway, then everything would already be over and this march to Aaron's office wouldn't be a hearing about her tablet. It would be a death march.

CHAPTER 35

"**A**aron?" Aric tapped on the north wing office door. "I'm here with Amelia. She would like an audience with you."

Monica stood behind Aric, Tresa at her side. She fiddled with the strap of her bag. Would Aaron be willing to listen?

Knocking again, Aric whispered, "He might not have heard me."

Tresa grasped Monica's hand and squeezed it.

"All right, all right," Aaron called from inside the room. "Come in, come in. I heard you the first time."

Monica returned the squeeze and followed Aric into the room.

He turned as he crossed the threshold. "Your Seen can stay out here."

Monica tensed. "I'd rather she come in if that's okay."

"There's no need. She wouldn't understand what's going on. Don't worry about the chip tether. We'll just be in the next room." Aric grabbed Monica's shoulder and guided her into the office. "Aaron's waiting."

"It's okay," Tresa mouthed.

Aric shut the door with a firm click and stood only a few inches from Monica, facing Aaron. "I'm sorry to disturb you, Uncle, but something has come up."

"I bet I can guess." Aaron leaned back in his plush office chair, twirling a round metal object between his thumb and forefinger, a bored expression on his face. "Our dear Amelia isn't pleased with my decision to go ahead with the program. What she isn't aware of is that this is in the best interests of our city." He leaned forward and placed a half circle medallion on his desk. "And we all want what's best for Cantral, don't we?"

Monica's heart seemed to leap into her throat. Alyssa's necklace! So it had come off in his room. She nodded; she had to think clearly, or she'd never get through this. "Ah, yes. Of course I want what's best for Cantral, but I don't think the program is necessary anymore." She withdrew her tablet and held it up. "The lost shipment with my tablet arrived. The tablet has all my notes on my project. I still don't know them well, but you have the information, so we don't need Aric's program."

Aaron folded his hands on his desk just behind the necklace. "I wonder why I didn't hear about this shipment. It's interesting that you should have just found your tablet." He twirled the necklace's cord around with his forefinger. "It so happens that a fire alarm was pulled last night, and computer records indicate that no one was close enough to have done so. And someone was in my room last night fiddling with my tablet. Some of my files are not exactly where I left them."

Aric stiffened beside Monica. "Your room? That's awful, Uncle. But certainly you've already found out who it was and punished him."

"Yes . . ." Aaron glared at his nephew, seeming to forget Monica's presence for a second. "The computers reported nothing unusual."

"Then how—how would you know that someone was there?"

Monica's thoughts flew at a thousand miles per hour. How could she have been so careless?

Raising an eyebrow, Aaron held Alyssa's necklace up. "Because this doesn't belong to my wife or myself, and it wasn't there when I went to bed last night." Dropping the necklace, he sighed as it clattered against the wood. "And now I have the two best programmers in Cantral, and possibly this continent, before me, and I'm forced to wonder what projects you two have been working on during your . . . doctor visits."

Monica felt the blood drain from her face. "We're not working on any project!"

"Uncle, you've said before, I'm just a doctor." Aric held up his hands in a defensive gesture. "I'm no programmer."

"Aric, my dear boy." Aaron opened his desk drawer and pulled out his tablet. "You proved me wrong when you woke your sister early from that sleeper program. No novice could come up with a counter code for that application in mere minutes."

Aric's cheeks flushed. "Of course. I tried to write counter code, but it was too complicated, so I just reset Regina's chip to default settings. And rest assured, my visits with Amelia are strictly medical. I have yet to see her complete even the simplest task on a tablet or even a wristband. I've even seen beginner computer history books on her nightstand. I think her sickness addled her more than I originally thought."

"I'm not addled!" Monica longed to bolt out of the room, but she had to stand her ground. "But Aric's right about one thing. He's only ever come to my room for medical reasons. Just ask Tresa— my Seen! She'll tell you."

"Uncle, you know I would never program something to compromise the computer's ability to detect chip location and movement. I have as much faith in our system as you do. My first thought is to assume everything works. If the computer showed no one at the fire alarm switch, it must have just malfunctioned.

And maybe a wall slave left that necklace during a cleaning and you didn't notice it earlier." Aric pointed a finger at Monica. "But if the system is failing, this girl is a more likely culprit than I am. She is proven to be involved in some way with the downfall of the Cillineese computers. Perhaps she even programmed the virus that took them out."

Monica shook her head. "I didn't write any virus!" This was going all wrong. They were supposed to give her time to explain. "And I couldn't have written a program to stop the computers from detecting chips. I was too sick to do anything for so long."

"Yes, she was." Aaron stood, shoving back his chair. "And I seem to recall it was you, Aric, who wished to bring her here in the first place. Don't try to twist history with me. It will never work."

Aric swallowed but said nothing.

"I admit that I could have missed noticing the necklace, but we checked the fire alarm. It is not malfunctioning. Someone must have masked a chip's presence near that alarm." Aaron turned on his tablet with a touch of his thumb. "Now Amelia, if you have nothing to hide, you'll hand your tablet over. I'll examine the files myself." He then tapped his computer and set it on his desk. "Aric, I'm having a Seen bring your tablet here. I will be examining it as well. And if I find anything . . . you will be going to court before the Council for high treason."

Aric's face turned a ghostly white. "You can't do that. It must be examined in front of a panel of witnesses."

"Do you dare suggest that I might tamper with evidence?" Aaron's eyes narrowed. "Don't forget that I am still the ruler of the north wing. To even suggest such a thing is a serious offense."

Muscles twitched in Aric's jaw. "No sir. I was merely stating the laws."

Monica looked from Aric to Aaron and back again. Did Aaron need to examine her tablet in front of witnesses as well?

"As a good citizen of Cantral?" Sarcasm laced Aaron's words.

"I see. Don't worry. The appropriate panel will be assembled for your review. I'll make sure of it."

"And Amelia's tablet will be reviewed then as well?"

Monica glanced at Aric. So he was wondering the same thing.

"No. I will be reviewing it now. She is still considered a prisoner here and has no rights. If she has a program that can stop the computers from communicating with the chips, then it must be destroyed immediately." Aaron held his hand out to Monica again. "If you would please give it to me, I will attend to it in a few moments."

"But . . ." Monica felt ready to jump out of her skin. Her heart beat so loudly that the wall slaves could probably hear it.

"I suggest you do as he says, Amelia," Aric whispered. "He is within the law."

"But I never wrote anything like the program he's talking about! Something like that isn't possible, not without killing the person." Monica held her tablet close. This was her last chance. She had to just tell them what Amelia wrote about. "I remember that the programs I have are for chip cloning, that's all!"

"Chip cloning?" Aaron snatched the tablet from her before she could react. "That was outlawed years ago."

Monica jumped forward, but Aric stretched out a hand and held her back. "Don't," he whispered. "It'll only make it worse."

"Why do you care?" she hissed. Turning to Aaron, she said, "Please, I haven't used it on anybody. I was trying to solve a mystery in Aric's mother's family tree. It could be . . ." She stopped. What was she thinking? She was talking as if Amelia's projects were her own—as if she were really Amelia.

"If there's a discrepancy on one of the family trees, it is merely a calligrapher's error, and you should have had a history major look into it." Aaron waved the tablet. "If I find one line of code that has to do with cloning, I will see you terminated. You've caused enough trouble here. We have many other things to be worrying about than one girl and a rebellious city. I should have had Cillineese demolished weeks ago."

Monica shook her head. He couldn't get in, but Amelia didn't know. He had to be bluffing. "No. You wouldn't!"

Aaron placed his and Amelia's tablets on the desk. "Aric, I know you carry a chip scanner with you—don't bother to deny it. I want you to scan this girl. If she's been disguising herself from the computers, remnant coding might remain behind in her chip. It will take less time than deciphering the protective locks she's probably plastered over the programs in her tablet."

Aric shook his head. "And give you another infraction to show the panel? As it stands, you have no evidence against me, and I would rather leave it that way."

Backing toward the door, Monica shook her head. They couldn't do this!

Someone knocked softly on the wood behind Monica. She jumped.

"Come in, come in." Aaron sighed. "And don't even think about going anywhere, Amelia. From now on, you are under lockdown. You're not to leave your room unless accompanied by a security team member."

The door opened, and a young Seen man entered. He bowed and extended a sleek tablet computer to Aaron.

Aaron plucked it from him. "You may go back to your regular duties."

The man bowed again and backed out of the room.

Monica peered around the door before it swung closed. Tresa stood outside, her hands folded behind her back and her head bowed, like that of a proper Seen, but her shoulders were tense. The door closed. Monica trained her eyes on Aaron again. Had Tresa heard everything?

"You have a protection code on your tablet." Aaron held up

Aric's gray computer. "That's an infraction of the rules. Do you have something to hide?"

"No sir." Aric's voice held firm, though his hands trembled as he reached for the tablet. "I will unlock it for you. I only kept it sealed because of Regina. She often stole my things to spy on me."

Aaron handed Aric the tablet. "Then I will let the infraction pass this time. I know how your sister can be, but I will remove it permanently when I examine your tablet, seeing as she is no longer here."

Nodding as he typed in the password, Aric sighed. "Yes sir. The rules are present for good reason, of course."

"Indeed they are." Aaron's gaze followed Aric's fingers like a rat stalking its prey.

Aric tapped the screen once more then handed it over, his shoulders sagging.

Tucking it into his desk drawer, Aaron smiled. "That's settled then." He turned his cold gaze on Monica, and a shiver coursed through her. "Now, young lady, if Aric won't scan you, I'll do it myself." He tapped his wristband, and a green light pulsed on the screen.

Monica flinched. "I don't have any remnant coding, sir! I never changed anyone's chip."

"Then you shouldn't mind being checked." Aaron picked up his tablet and held it in one hand. "While this can see your number from here, it has to be brought close to be able to read the program coding the chip carries."

Panic rose in her chest, but she pushed it down. Maybe, just maybe, his scanner would pick up Amelia's chip's code from where the chip hung on its string. There wouldn't be any remnant coding to find, and she'd be safe.

He grasped her shoulder with a firm hand, his fingers squeezing so hard prickles ran through her skin. "Don't worry, you won't feel a thing, and since you say you're innocent . . ." He held the tablet above the back of her neck. ". . . then you're perfectly fine."

As the seconds ticked by, Monica clenched her fists. It had to pick up the chip's signal. It just had to.

"It's not detecting anything other than the number—perhaps your hair is in the way." Aaron pushed her hair to the side. A cold fingertip pressed against the nape of her neck. "Odd."

"What's wrong?" Aric smirked. "Is your scanner program not working, Uncle? Perhaps you should have a technician look at it."

Aaron glared at him. "We won't discuss the legality of this at the moment. Get over here. I want you to look at this."

Panic glued Monica in place. Her breathing came fast and heavy as Aaron bent her chin down and ran a finger across her neck again.

Aric shuffled over. "What is it?"

"She has no scar." Aaron pressed on the nape of her neck.

"Maybe she had a better surgeon than most. Regina's scar is also barely visible. It's not uncommon—the younger generations' scars are almost nonexistent."

Monica tried to step away from Aaron, but he gripped a fistful of her hair. "You're not going anywhere until I get a reading on your chip."

"You're hurting me!" she squeaked. "Maybe your scanner is bad, like Aric said. The Council won't let you get away with this. Readers are illegal!"

"They can do nothing to me." Aaron touched the edge of his tablet to her neck. "If it doesn't pick up the signal this time . . ."

"Uncle?" Aric placed a hand on Monica's shoulder, next to Aaron's. "What's this?"

"What?" Aaron drew his computer back.

"This." Aric grasped the knotted end of the leather cord around Monica's neck.

Monica jerked away and whirled to face them. "It's just a necklace!" If they found her chip . . .

Aric frowned. "Then you won't mind if we see it."

She shook her head. "It's nothing special."

"I don't care about any necklace." Aaron waved a hand as if to dismiss it. "I want to know why my scanner isn't reading your chip's encoding. Perhaps the program you say you never wrote is the reason. I'm detecting the chip number, but that might not be enough for the central computer to log your presence, and I suspect you would know how to block it." He turned to Aric. "Call the security team. I believe we found our mole. Our guests from Eursia were right after all, and I was ready to send them home."

"Mole?" Monica gulped. "I don't know what you're talking about. Aric made it so I've always had to have an escort—just ask him! I wasn't allowed to go anywhere by myself without getting shocked."

"Aric told me about the binding order he had issued to your chip, but your whereabouts is something we cannot confirm." Aaron held up his tablet. "Thanks to your chip-masking program, I have no idea where you've been. You could have gone to Cillineese a dozen times since your stay here. I wouldn't wonder if your sickness was faked."

Aric stepped between the two. "Uncle, excuse me, but I think you're being a little hasty. Amelia hasn't been able to walk except on crutches for the past few days, and the other doctors will confirm that we removed a tumor from her lower right leg. We even have it stored for study."

"Why are you defending her?" Aaron furrowed his brow and looked from Monica to Aric. "You're still under suspicion. It does not help your case to—"

"I don't care about my case," Aric muttered. "You'll never convince the Council to terminate me. Besides, she's been through a lot, and she was kind to Regina. I know for a fact she hasn't been lying about her sickness. No one could fake a tumor."

"No, but I will not be satisfied until I get a reading on her chip." Aaron grabbed Monica's arm and pulled her from behind

Aric. "Since she's well again, she's no longer your patient, or your concern."

"I believe whether she's my patient or not is up to me. I've yet to discharge her from my care." Aric glared at Aaron but didn't move.

"Just to leave no stone unturned." Aaron pushed Monica's hair away from her neck again and grabbed the cord. "She protested about touching this a bit too much for my liking."

"No!" Monica jerked away.

The cord snapped and stayed behind in Aaron's hand.

"Just a necklace?" Aaron held up the leather string, the vial dangling close to his clenched fist.

Dizziness washed over her. "No," she whispered. This couldn't be happening. He was supposed to look at her tablet, and she would go free. How could everything go so wrong?

Aaron held the vial up to the light, squinting at the glittering cylinder. "Aric? Could it be?"

"Fox's chip-less girl?" His face turning pale, Aric looked at Monica. "And I defended you! All the while you've been lying, trying to tear our world apart?"

"No!" Monica clenched her hands into fists. She was dead. They would have the security team come and terminate her. "I'm not trying to tear it apart. You Nobles don't understand!"

Aaron's hand tightened around the vial. "Who are you, then? Amelia had a chip in her brain when she entered Cantral, and now you have it around your neck. Did you kill her to take her place? Another scheme of the 'slave council'? Now you're murdering children to avoid a little work?"

"No, no, that's not it." Monica stared past him at the wooden door blocking her escape. They would never listen to any explanation she tried to give. "She was dead when I took the chip. I would never kill anyone!"

"Tell that to the security team." Aaron set his tablet on the desk and punched a command into his wristband. "They'll get more information out of you."

Aaron's fingers on his wristband brought back memories of Regina in the schoolroom the day before. Monica blinked rapidly, focusing on Aaron's band. There had to be a way to escape.

She jumped and yanked the wristband from his arm. The metal links scraped across his skin.

Aric grabbed her around the waist and pulled her away from Aaron. "What are you doing?"

Kicking and squirming, Monica tried to escape from Aric's tight grip, but she was barely half his size, and he didn't seem to notice her heels pounding his shins. "Let me go!"

Aaron reached for his wristband, but she bit at his hand and kicked him in the stomach. "Can't you control the little viper?" he hissed.

"I'm trying!" Aric whirled her around and pressed her against the wall, pinning her by her shoulders.

"Let me go!" Monica kicked at him, but she didn't make contact.

Red-faced, Aric turned to Aaron. "Take it!"

Monica wrenched free for a second and scooted away with the wristband. She frantically searched through the options as she ran to the other side of the desk.

"What do you think you're doing?" Aaron growled.

Aric rounded the desk after her.

Monica dove beneath the desk and pulled the chair in front of her. Where was the sleeper program? Aaron had activated it for Regina from his wristband. It had to be there. She scrolled through another screen of options.

Aric tugged at the desk chair, but she wrapped a leg around one of its feet, holding it in place. "If you don't struggle anymore, it'll go easier for you."

"Get my wristband back, boy!" Aaron yelled.

Monica's leg throbbed where she held the chair in place. The sleeper program! She punched in the command to activate it for the chips in the room.

Aric shook his head as if confused and stared at her before dropping to his knees. His eyes rolled back, and he slumped to the floor. A thump sounded behind her.

She breathed a sigh of relief and climbed out from under the desk, rolling the chair past Aric's unconscious body. Scrambling to her feet, she glanced around the room. Aaron lay flat on his back in front of the desk, his breathing heavy.

Monica snatched the vial from where it lay on the floor, turned to Aric, and whispered, "Sorry, but this system has got to stop. I can't let you or anyone else rule the world. The computers have to be brought down."

CHAPTER 36

"**M**iss Amelia!" Tresa hissed from behind the door.

Monica slipped the vial into her pocket before grabbing Alyssa's necklace from the desk. She picked up Amelia's tablet and shoved it into her bag. After jumping over Aaron's sleeping body, she yanked open the office door.

Tresa stood on the other side, her face white, clutching a fistful of her skirt in one hand. "What happened? Where are Master Aric and Master Aaron?"

"They know, Tresa! They know." Monica held up Aaron's wristband. Her heart raced. Thoughts whirled so fast she could barely think. The words came tumbling out of her mouth in a jumble as she tied Alyssa's medallion back in place. "He thought I sneaked into his bedroom by writing some kind of program to disguise my chip, but then he found Amelia's around my neck. He knows I'm not her. The security team is coming!"

"Who found Amelia's chip? Aaron?"

"Yes, Aaron!"

Tresa released her skirt and clenched her empty fist. "How'd you get away? What happened?"

"I put them to sleep with Aaron's program." Monica strapped Aaron's wristband to her arm and tugged Amelia's off over her hand. "I got his wristband."

Tresa tugged Monica down the hall toward the Council meeting room's waiting area. "Calm down. If the security team is coming, we need to keep our wits about us if we're going to get out of here." She yanked open the door and glanced each way.

Trembling, Monica followed her silently. What to do now? She couldn't go to the computers. The plans were ruined. She had failed.

"Come on." Tresa pulled her into the waiting room. "What do you think we should do? Do you need to go back to Cillineese? Did Simon say what he wanted you to do if this happened?"

"I don't know!" Monica looked at the exit. Would someone come bursting in at any moment? "He said I shouldn't come back until the mission was complete. I have nowhere to go!"

Tresa caught Monica's hands and flipped her palms up, revealing scars and pink skin around her arms where the wounds had been deepest. "Monica, these scars tell me you've been in situations much worse than this. You faced the Council and helped me stay with my family. You can figure this out." Firming her chin, Tresa looked Monica in the eye. "You brought down the Cillineese computers—you can do the same in Cantral."

Nodding slowly, Monica closed her eyes and tried to calm her breathing. "Thank you, Tresa." She opened her eyes. The plan had to proceed—even if she died trying. "I'm going to the computer room. I'll put the guards to sleep. There has to be some way to get in without a chip."

Tresa hugged her close. "Then let's go."

Monica returned the hug, then pushed away. "I have to do this myself. I don't want you to get in any more trouble." She pulled her mother's journal from the bag at her side but left the translated papers. "Will you keep this safe for me?"

"Of course, but—"

Monica plucked the vial from her pocket and handed it to Tresa. "Here. Keep this with you. Our chips are probably still tethered. And check on Ahla for me, too, won't you? Make sure her baby is okay."

"But, Monica!" Tresa closed her hand around the vial.

"Don't follow me, or I'll put you to sleep, too!" Monica yanked open the door to the hallway. "Enough people have died, Tresa. Thank you for everything."

"All right." Tresa hugged the journal to her chest. "I'll go, and the moment you succeed, I'll have a messenger run to Cillineese to tell Simon and bring him here."

Monica smiled. "I'll do my best, but I'm not promising anything."

She slipped out of the room and closed the door. Aaron's band beeped on her wrist. *Security Team Arrival 00:00:30.* She breathed a long sigh. He must not have sent them a high-priority alert, or they would have arrived already, but thirty seconds was still too little time.

She trotted to the schoolroom and ducked inside. Where was the computer room? Simon had provided an overview, but he had never been there himself.

Crouching in the darkness, she dug into her bag and drew out Amelia's tablet. She pulled up the map program she had transferred there last night and the palace map popped into view. Dots appeared on the screen with chip numbers next to them, indicating where various Nobles roamed the halls.

Marching footsteps echoed past the schoolroom. Monica stiffened and scrolled across the map more quickly. The security team would find Aaron and Aric in moments, and then the hunt for her would begin in earnest. There would be no escape, not with a dozen or more people looking for her.

She located the computer room entrance. The label appeared

on the other side of the wing near most of the meeting rooms—a section of the north wing she hadn't yet seen.

Opening the door an inch, she peered out. Voices rumbled nearby, the deep voices of men in discussion. Had they discovered Aric and Aaron?

She yanked her shoes off, set them on the floor, and jogged from the room, her bare feet falling silently on the carpet. The rooms rushed by. As she quickened her pace and circled around a corner and down the hall toward the meeting rooms, a twinge pinched her calf muscle. The pain medication the doctor in Cillineese had provided must have started to wear off.

At each intersection, she glanced at her tablet, double-checking the directions. When she sprinted into an unfamiliar hall, her wristband beeped. Words flashed red across the screen. *Security Code Green . . . Immediate Action Necessary . . . Security Code Green.*

She pounded into a wide-open, circular room. They must have found Aaron.

A man stood next to a tall, narrow, black door at the other end of the room. He stared at his wristband. His face pale, he looked around until their gazes met.

"Who are you? What're you doing here?" The man's hand hovered over his wristband, as if to enter a command. His arms rippled with muscles that bulged beneath his white shirt. He could probably break her arm in a second. "Haven't you seen the green alert? No one should be down here. I'm going to have to detain you." An edge of frustration crept into his voice. "This had better be a drill."

Tucking the tablet under an arm, Monica touched her own wristband. There was no use explaining. No Noble could be trusted. She drew a finger across her screen, pulled up the sleeper program, and found the man's number on the map.

He narrowed his eyes. "What are you doing?" As his fingers tapped his own wristband screen, he shook his head. "I can't find you here. What's going—"

Monica pressed the sleep command. He collapsed to the floor in a heap in front of the black door. With his eyes rolled back in his head, he stared at the ceiling.

She winced as she stepped over the man's body and pressed a hand on the door. "Sorry."

No matter how hard she pushed, the door stayed shut. She gritted her teeth. The green alert message still flashed across her stolen wristband. There was no time to lose. The security team would be searching everywhere for her. If they figured out how to wake Aaron he'd tell them everything and find her in moments.

Crouching beside the man, she glanced around. The door needed a chip to be opened, but maybe the guard's wristband would work. She set the tablet and book bag on the floor, gripped his thick, hairy forearm and unclasped the silver links. As she held it and pressed it against the door, the same message flashed across his screen. Nothing happened. The words continued to pulse, and the door remained shut.

She tossed the man's wristband to the side. He was way too big to move by herself, but what else could she try?

Hooking her hands under his arms, she braced herself and tugged. His shoulders lifted an inch. She shuffled to the side, trying to bring him around to face the door, but no matter how much she strained, he wouldn't budge. His head lolled back; his mouth fell open. The odor of past meals and unbrushed teeth assaulted her senses.

She scrunched her nose and turned away. And Nobles thought wall slaves smelled bad? As she tried to move him again, sweat trickled down her forehead. Letting out a gasp, she let him rest on the floor again. There was no way. He was too big to move. He probably weighed three times as much as she did.

As she slid to the ground and put her head on her knees, her elbow throbbed. She clutched the medallion hanging at her neck. "I'm sorry, Alyssa. I've failed everyone. I messed up everything.

There aren't any wall passages to the computers. I can't lift this man." The words poured forth, tearing at her tired mind and soul.

Memories of crowded slaves in the dorms trampled her conscience. She laid a hand to her forehead. Why did Aric have to give her that drug? Those years of the crowding with everyone so close were too much to bear a second time—too much to feel again as she bore this failure. But what did it matter? Soon the security team would come, and they would kill her. They didn't need a chip to terminate someone. They had other ways to torture people.

Footsteps sounded in the hallway. Monica flinched and shot to her feet. "Who's there?"

"Just me," a voice squeaked. Shora peeked her head around the corner of a hall. "What're you doing here, Miss Amelia?"

"I'm wondering the same thing about you." Monica tucked her tablet into the bag and slung the strap over her head. "You appear everywhere. Who are you working for, anyway?"

Shora pointed at the Noble. "What happened to him, Miss? Should I call the nurse?"

Monica set her hands on her hips. "You came in here and startled me out of my skin, and I want you to answer my question."

"I'm sorry, Miss, but I'm not allowed. You're not even supposed to be here alone." Shora stared at her, her blue eyes wide. "I'll have to report that you're here."

"Aric won't get your message." Monica returned her stare. "I think you've been spying for him, so you can give up the act now."

Shora cocked her head. "Spying for Master Aric? Why would I do that? He gets informed of most everything already. He doesn't need me."

"You're a good actress, just like Tresa said." Monica glanced around the room. Maybe she still had time to leave and get away. But could she return to Cillineese as a failure? Where else would she go?

"I'm not acting." Shora raised her thin wrist and started typing on her band's screen. "It's true. Master Aric doesn't make me spy on anyone."

Monica dashed across the room and grabbed Shora's hand. "Don't!"

Her eyes widening, Shora stood stock still, her fingers poised over the screen. "I'm sorry, but I have to! I'll—"

"Get in trouble, I know." Monica stripped the wristband from Shora's arm. "If you help me, and I succeed, you'll never get in trouble with the Nobles again. They won't be able to hurt you or terminate you ever."

Shora made a short squeaking noise. "Please give that back—I need it! I can't do any of my chores or know where I'm supposed to go or—"

"Shh!" Monica raised a finger to her lips. "You won't need it in a few minutes. Just help me get this Noble to the door, and I'll go into the computer room and free you. You'll see."

"You can't—"

"Just help me, okay?" Monica said the words louder than she meant to, and Shora flinched. "I'm sorry, but this needs to happen now if either of us is going to live through this. They'll kill me if they find me, and I can't let anyone else down. And once you're done, you can go report to whoever you're spying for, and you might not get into any trouble, even if I fail."

Shora set her hands on her small waist, copying Monica's earlier stance. "Fine, Miss Amelia, but I think Trella is right about you. You're strange, and the least Noble-like Noble I've ever met." She dropped her gaze for a second. "If you were a regular Noble, you'd punish me for saying that."

Smiling grimly, Monica shook her head. "No time for punishments. I need to get in here before the security team arrives. Help me get this guy's hand on the door. I think it'll open if he touches it."

CHAPTER 37

hora's small, pale hands joined Monica's, grabbing the sleeping Noble under the arms. They yanked on him, dragging him a foot closer to the door.

Panting, Monica stepped over him and tugged a hand toward the door, but his fingers didn't even brush the black wood. "A little farther and I think that'll do it."

"Good, because I'm late for my next assignment." Shora grabbed the man's other forearm. "I don't want Linna to have to work by herself. She won't finish in time, and we'll both get hurt."

"Right. We don't want that." Monica widened her stance to brace herself and counted aloud. "One. Two. Three."

On three, they heaved the man toward the door again, Monica's elbow aching in protest. He moved a few more inches. Monica slapped his hand against the door. A green light blinked on.

Monica jumped as the door rose into the ceiling. She pressed Shora's wristband into her palm and pushed her toward the exit, away from the computer room. "Go! Get out of here! Don't let them see you."

Shora nodded and scampered away.

When the door started to slide closed again, Monica ducked beneath it. Inside, darkness shrouded the entire room. She caught her breath. This was it. This was the way to the computers.

Shouts sounded outside the door. She touched her wristband, letting its pale light shine on a downward staircase. Of course. The computers would be deep in the earth near an underground river so they could have a constant power supply. The Cillineese computers had been in a similar location.

As she trotted down the stairs, the voices grew thinner, more distant. She glanced over her shoulder every dozen steps or so. Only the soft paper-thin scraping of her bare feet on the wooden steps and her bag thumping against her side made any noise.

After the first hundred stairs pounded by, her leg started to ache, and warm liquid oozed down her leg. She knelt and shone the light from her wristband on the area. Only a trickle of blood streamed from around the wound glue, but if she kept running, it would get worse.

Thundering footsteps echoed from higher on the narrow staircase.

Fear leaped into Monica's chest, forcing her heart into her throat. The security team! As she fumbled with her wristband, the footsteps seemed to get louder with every second. Her fingers wouldn't respond to her commands. She abandoned trying to find the sleep program and ran down the stairs even faster than before, making sure her feet hit the boards without a sound. The computers had to be nearby—she had to have gone down 150 stairs—yet there was no sign of them.

After she galloped down a dozen more steps, a small, glimmering green orb appeared in the distance, struggling through the darkness to blend with the light from Monica's wristband. As the stairs grew steeper, her pace increased until her legs moved almost on their own with the momentum of her flight.

An opening appeared just ahead with light streaming through. The sound of rushing water flooded her senses. A roaring river flowed through a square concrete room, swirling in a large whirlpool at the room's center.

Monica pulled her bag from over her head, laid it to the side, and crouched by the entrance. If she needed to run, it would be best if the bag wasn't encumbering her. A few paces away, two men and a woman walked quickly back and forth between eight large boxes that formed a ring around the swirling pool. A glass screen taller than anyone in the room stood between the pool and the boxes, protecting them from the spray.

The woman held a tablet in her hand and spoke to one of the men. She turned around and faced Monica. When their gazes met, the woman's mouth dropped open.

Monica widened her eyes. *Felicia?* What was she doing down here?

The man stopped speaking and turned, following Felicia's line of sight. "What is it?" His words barely sounded over the roar of the river.

Monica slapped her wristband, pulling up Aaron's program. Three numbers appeared, and she hurried to select them.

The man dashed over and grabbed her by the arm. "Who are you, and what are you doing? I should terminate you on the spot! You're not authorized to be here."

"Varick!" Felicia rushed to join them, her face pale and drawn. "You're scaring her. She must have been sent down here for some reason, maybe because of the alert. We haven't heard anything from above yet."

Monica stared. Why was Felicia defending her?

"Maybe she *is* the reason for the alert." Varick glared down at Monica.

"What's the problem?" The second man scurried over, his pointed noise and small eyes reminding Monica of Vinnie's features. "Who is this? You promised the review would go smoothly, Felicia. I cannot delay getting these patches and repairs back to Eursia."

Monica tried to reach for her wristband again, but Varick gripped her arm so tightly it went numb.

"We're trying to figure this out, Tyrell." Felicia held up a hand, as if to appease him. "I understand the urgency. The Council assigned me to this task with haste in mind. We will finish on time."

"Well, girl?" Varick shook Monica by the shoulders until it felt like her eyes were going to roll out of her head.

Felicia grabbed Monica's arm and yanked her away from him. "What are you doing?" She pointed to the band on Monica's wrist. "Can't you see the color? She's obviously someone important. I know you don't bother to know everyone in the north wing, Varick, but I know her. She's related to Aaron. What would he say if he found out you were shaking her to death?"

Varick glanced away. "She needs to be made to talk. Aaron can't let just anyone in here. You know the rules."

"What about my programs?" Tyrell's whiny voice seemed childish in the midst of Felicia's and Varick's strong tones.

Monica's thoughts spun, but she tried to concentrate.

The sound of voices and footsteps echoed into the room above the roaring water.

Felicia's fingers dug into Monica's shoulder, the skin beneath her polished fingernails turning white.

A group of three men burst into the room. The leader strode ahead of the other two, a tall man with blond hair and piercing gray eyes.

Monica stifled a yelp. It couldn't be! He was supposed to be in Eursia. Brenna had said her father was there, stuck until further notice.

The man smiled. "Ah, there she is."

Monica whispered, "Fox." The man from her nightmares stood

before her, a smirk on his perfect face. The man who had killed her adoptive father. How could he have returned to haunt her?

One of the guards strode over and stood beside Monica, as if ready to grab her.

Varick stepped up to Fox and looked him in the eye. "What is the meaning of this green alert? We haven't ever had a green alert. Here you go putting us into a frenzy to follow procedure to fix this problem, and now this!"

"Please." Fox pushed him to the side with the palm of his hand. "Be silent. It makes you appear less foolish." He pointed at Monica. "I've searched for you for over eight years, and it's been quite perturbing, but now that I've found you, I mean to see you join the rest of your family. As soon as your m—"

"What are you talking about?" Felicia stepped in front of Monica. "This is Amelia, Aaron's niece. She has computer knowledge valuable to the state and won't be going anywhere. You don't have jurisdiction here anymore, Fox. You're only an escort."

Monica tried to bring up the sleeper program, but her fingers shook almost too badly to type. Five numbers appeared on the map, but how could that be? There were six other people in the room! Three numbers showed up clustered close together, while two others appeared right next to each other, overlapping. She glanced from person to person. The program would probably work on all of them, but who was who?

"This is not Amelia." Fox let a leather string slide out of his hand. A glass vial dangled at the end of the cord. "Thanks to some information I've gathered with the help of a Seen, I believe her to be Sierra, daughter of Joel, past ruler of Cillineese."

Monica widened her eyes. So Shora had been spying on her for Fox. She gulped and looked down at her screen again. The two numbers together must be the guard and Felicia, but it was impossible to tell them apart. And if Felicia fell asleep, she wouldn't be able to help.

Fox continued, "She's been assumed dead with her father when Cillineese was terminated twelve years ago, but she escaped, and much to my chagrin, it's taken me this long to track her down. I've kept this chip with me since I found it as evidence so many years ago, as a reminder." He pointed a finger at Monica. "You thought you had me fooled with that, didn't you? Did you kill that little girl? Perhaps I should add that to your list of offenses."

"I've never killed anyone." Monica selected the three clustered numbers from the screen. At least some of them would be knocked out. "Unlike you. M—murderer." She meant the words to come out in an accusing tone, but they trembled and squeaked despite her efforts.

She selected the Run option for the program. Varick, Tyrell, and one of the security men fell to the floor in an instant.

Fox jumped away from them.

Felicia ran to Varick and dropped to her knees. "What happened? Varick? Can you hear me?" The man lay still, though he snored softly.

"You little . . ." Fox stepped over Tyrell's crumpled form toward Monica. "What did you do?"

The guard edged toward Monica. "What do you want me to do?"

"She's just a little girl," Fox snapped. "I can handle this. Go wake up Aaron and Aric if you can. Tell them what's going on. We can't have anyone else fainting on us. They need to figure this out."

"Yes sir." The man disappeared up the stairway.

His number vanished from Monica's wristband screen. Only one remained. *3507491*. That had to be Felicia's, didn't it? Felicia couldn't write programs, so there was no way she could hide her chip from the computer.

"You have no one to protect you, Sierra." Fox stared down at her. "I don't know what you did to the others, but let me assure you—you won't be able to do the same to me."

Monica backed against the glass wall surrounding the pool in the room's center. "This—this system has to end." Her throat went dry. "You can't just go around killing people." The glass felt cool behind her, and beads of condensation dripped down the back of her dress, dampening her skin. She poised a finger over her wristband. There was no way to put him to sleep, but maybe if she bluffed . . .

Fox took a step. "I told you it won't work."

"Maybe not." Felicia crept up behind him and slammed her tablet down on his head, smashing the computer to bits. "But this will!"

Fox fell to the floor with a thump, blood streaming from a gash in his head.

Felicia ripped a piece of fabric from the hem of her skirt and began bandaging the wound. "I didn't mean to cut him—just knock him out."

Staring at her, Monica shook her head. "I don't understand. Why are you helping me? You're part of the Council."

"Because I want my daughter to grow up to be like you, Sierra." She tied a knot in the bandage, securing it to Fox's head. "If that's really your name. I want her to know real freedom, not this façade that's forced upon her on the backs of others. I just wish my children never had to have chips in the first place." She reached back and touched her neck, parting her dark brown hair. "What must it be like . . . to not have a constant buzzing and urging of a fleck of metal in your brain, telling you where to go and what to do, as if it's your lord and master? You're the only one who knows what true freedom is like, and we need to bring that freedom to others."

CHAPTER 38

So what's your plan?" Felicia crossed her arms. "Now that I'm sure to be terminated for what I just did, I hope you have a good one." She pointed at a lever at the other side of the room. "There's a way to flood this place in case everything overheats or we have a surge of pressure in the underground dam. It shuts down the computers temporarily to protect them, but it would wash us away, too, and the computers would only be offline for a few hours at most. It's a last-resort measure. You don't want to use it unless you're ready to die."

"There's another way." Monica yanked the leather string from around her neck and held up Alyssa's medallion. "I'm going to cut the computer wires just like I did in Cillineese. It'll stop all the other cities from being terminated and free everyone in Cantral."

Felicia nodded slowly. "So that's how you did it. You certainly had us baffled. Aaron thought maybe someone had figured out how to penetrate the firewalls with a virus. No one has ever done it before, but if her reputation reflects reality, then Amelia could."

Shaking her head, Monica stepped over the fallen guard and

crouched by one of the large boxes. "Unfortunately, Amelia's dead. Whatever was making her sick killed her a few days ago, and I've been pretending to be her ever since."

"Amazing." Felicia shook her head. "I never met Amelia, so I wouldn't have guessed."

Monica ran a hand along the box's metallic side. The smooth gray sheet felt cool beneath her fingertips, though it thrummed with the activity of the computer's workings housed within. "Can you help me get these panels off?"

"No." Felicia sighed. "I can only do programming on some of the less important computers. If I touch the servers I'll be knocked out immediately. I'm not allowed to know much about the computer's workings. I'm the least important Council member."

"Then I'll have to do it myself." Monica located a circular black notch with a red light in its center by the panel's corner. "It's locked." She turned to Felicia. "The guard might come back any minute. If you really want freedom for your children, then you'll help me get this open."

"I don't want them to have the same fate I did." Felicia pointed at Varick. "If he were awake, he could open the door—he has the clearance—but he's out cold."

Monica scampered to his side. "We don't need him to be awake. He just needs to touch it." She grabbed one of Varick's limp arms. He was much smaller than the guard upstairs, but it'd be better to add Felicia's weight to the effort. "Can you help me drag him over there?"

"Of course." Felicia gripped his other arm just above the elbow. "On the count of three?"

"Yes." When Monica counted to three, they dragged him toward the computer's box step-by-step. When they pulled him over Tyrell's body, Varick's head thumped against the floor.

Monica yanked him forward and pressed his hand to the metal. "I hope this works. I don't know what else to do."

After a few seconds, the light flashed green. Monica exhaled. Had she been holding her breath all this time? She dropped Varick's hand, and it landed on the floor with a thump.

Felicia backed away, a bead of sweat on her forehead. "I'm supposed to transfer some programming for Tyrell and package it for him to take back to Eursia. The computer thinks I'm tampering with other things, since I'm on this half of the room. It's starting to send me warnings."

Nodding, Monica yanked open the computer's access door, revealing a tangled mess of whirring fans and wires of various colors. "Then do what you need to do to make them stop. I'll keep working." She looked over her shoulder at the room's entrance. Just watch for any guards, okay?"

"Of course." Felicia shuffled to the other side of the room, her brow creased and her eyes darting from side to side. "But I don't think this plan will work. There are emergency backup systems beneath the floor. The computers up here were built to take a beating in case of flooding, but even if these are destroyed, the sublevel computers will still function. The ones below are nearly impenetrable, unless the right access doors are open."

"Then I'll take care of those, too. We can use Varick to get to them as well." Monica gripped the medallion. This was what she had been trained for her entire life. She selected a thick green wire and poised the medallion's jagged edge over the wire's plastic-coated surface. "This is for everyone who's ever suffered and died because of you." She brought the metal disk down on the wire. It sliced clean through. A short burst of electricity traveled up Monica's hand from the severed wire, making her shudder, but the feeling soon passed.

A scream filled the air, rolling over the hissing, thundering whirlpool. Monica turned around. What was that?

Felicia lay on the floor on the other side of the room. She curled into a ball and clutched the back of her head, yelling incoherently.

The medallion fell from Monica's hand. "What's wrong?" She jumped to her feet. "What happened?"

Felicia gritted her teeth and ground out a few words. "The wire. The computer's retaliating. Shut it off! Quick! Cut another before—" As a convulsion rocked her body, her limbs twitched.

"Felicia!" Monica snatched the medallion from the floor and sawed another wire, tears welling in her eyes. This couldn't be happening. She was supposed to save people by terminating the computers. How could another person be dying?

A bundle of wires fell to the computer box floor. As Monica sawed through wire after wire, purple, green, blue, and red bits of plastic flew. With each severing, shocks ran up her arm.

She shot a look back at Felicia. The Noble woman lay motionless, her eyes closed, her arms and legs folded in a fetal position. Her dark hair spread out around her head, wet with sweat and the dampness of the concrete floor.

Monica groaned and cut another wire. This wasn't good enough. Which wire to cut? What if more people upstairs were dying? In Cillineese she had hesitated and people had died because of her cowardice. Had she now killed someone because she had acted too quickly?

The wires pricked her fingers, drawing blood from the pink scars lacing her hands. She dragged Varick's limp body an inch so he could reach the next computer box. When she dropped his hand, she left a bloody print on his sleeve.

She gritted her teeth and set to work on the second computer box. A dozen wires fell to the floor, followed by another dozen and another until the computer stood as an empty shell, the gutted body of a mindless tormentor. As the medallion's edge dulled with every cut, each wire became more difficult to sever.

She slid to the next computer and the next, tugging and dragging Varick along inch by inch. There was no time to check on Felicia, no telling what programs each computer was running, what havoc they were wreaking on the people of Cantral. Maybe, just maybe, she could save everyone else.

Blood dripped from her hands to the concrete floor, mixing with drops of sweat. Her sleeves stuck to her arms despite the cool air in the room.

Her arms trembling, she dragged Varick to the eighth box. When she pressed his hand against the metal, a green light blinked on. She pushed open the computer's door, the last one on this level, but even more lay below. Her hands and elbow ached, but there was no time to waste. The security team could come down at any moment.

Breathing heavily, she fumbled with the medallion. Now her people, the slaves, and everyone else would be free. Just two bundles of wire stood in her way. She raised the medallion and forced its now-blunt edge through the first bundle. She sawed the edge back and forth, sending more shocks up her arm, but finally it cut the last wire. Just one bundle to go.

Footsteps thundered on the stairs above. Shouts echoed all around.

Monica sawed on the last bundle, but the medallion's edge barely bit into the plastic and wires. With each stroke, her elbow screamed with pain, and blood dripped from her fingers onto the medallion's smooth surface.

Two security guards burst into the room, Aaron following at their heels, red-faced and growling.

"You!" Aaron charged at Monica. "How dare you use my own program against me!"

Monica sliced through a few wires, but half a dozen remained.

Aaron dove at her, but a security guard held him back. "Sir, I can deal with her. This little mouse isn't worth your trouble."

Monica summoned the will to slice through the last few wires just as the guard grabbed her and crushed her arms to her sides in a death grip. She gasped.

"Little mouse? Too much damage?" Aaron gestured to the boxes around the room. "This 'little mouse' gutted every terminal." He turned toward Felicia lying motionless on the floor. "Felicia!" He ran to her side and rolled her to her back. Brushing her hair from her closed eyes, he shook his head and turned to Monica. "You killed her!"

"Your computer killed her!" Monica growled. "She wanted to help—I didn't know what would happen."

"She would never help you." Aaron glared at Monica, rising to his feet again. "She would be loyal to the end." He pointed at the guard. "Take her away."

Monica ducked out of his grip, but the guard grabbed her again and pressed her arms against her sides. Struggling to reach her wristband, she gasped. "Let me go!" The sleeper program was only a hair's breadth away, but her fingers scraped the band's outer casing, not quite reaching the screen.

"Not a chance," the guard hissed. "You'll be executed in front of everyone as an example. This will take years to repair." He tightened his grip until it felt like her arms would break beneath the pressure.

Aaron crossed the room to where a second guard knelt by a large open panel in the floor. "What's the damage report?"

The guard held a foot-long computer tablet attached to wires below that ran to a lower level. He shook his head. "Not good. We've lost contact with all city-state domes, but the central hub is still functioning on emergency power." He tapped the tablet screen. "The slaves are under control, but the link to the general populace is weakening. We need a repair team in here immediately. I'll get some emergency supplies from the storage room." He laid the tablet on the floor and headed up the stairs.

"No," Monica whispered. The slaves were still in bondage. She hung her head and stopped her struggles. The Nobles had won.

"A repair team will be sent down immediately." Aaron poised

a finger over his bare wrist then stopped. "Of course." He marched to Monica and snatched the wristband from her arm, scraping the gold links across her torn hand and fingers.

She whimpered and tried to pull away, but the guard held her fast.

Aaron slid his band back onto his own wrist. "Assault on the ruler of Cantral and the heir of Cantral. Destroying the surface computers. Killing a Council member." He shook his head. "I don't think death is enough. We've never installed a computer chip in someone as old as you. Perhaps we should try it to see how it affects the brain. It could have interesting results, and it would be a good subject of study. Aric could be the overseeing doctor."

"No!" Monica clawed at the guard to no avail.

A subtle movement on the other side of the room caught Monica's gaze. Felicia's fingers twitched, and her head moved. Could she still be alive? Or were they just reflexes, electric pulses left over from the chip's energy?

The guard nodded. "I think inserting a chip is an excellent idea."

Aaron pointed at the stairwell. "Lock her in my office. The slaves' panels there are only accessible with a chip. She won't be able to get out."

CHAPTER 39

The guard dragged Monica toward the stairs. She kicked him hard. This couldn't be happening! How could she have failed? Tears poured down her cheeks as she caught the corner of the stairwell wall. She hung on with all her might. The guard tugged on her until her arm muscles felt ready to tear.

"Just get her out of here!" Aaron growled.

Felicia moved again. Her eyes fluttered open, and she slowly crawled to her feet, her arms shaking and her face pale. She inched toward the other side of the room.

Monica glanced in that direction. Of course! The lever! "Aaron!" she yelled, barely keeping hold of the wall. "You can't continue this society any longer!" Her fingers slipped, and the guard jerked her backward, the momentum forcing him to the ground with a thump.

Monica's head knocked against the guard's. Stars exploded in her vision. She scrambled to her feet and rushed forward, barely able to see. She dashed by Aaron toward the other side of the room. As she passed Felicia, their gazes locked for a split second, and the Noble woman gave her a short nod.

"Can't you do anything right?" Aaron yelled. "I'll get her myself!" He charged after her.

Monica stooped by the open panel in the floor and ripped the tablet from its wires. Sparks flew in every direction, some singeing her skirt. She turned and grabbed the lever on the wall, but it didn't budge. It had to move!

She turned, wide-eyed. Aaron was only a few feet away. This would be her last chance.

He grabbed her arm and started to pull her away. She jerked around, forcing his hand against the lever. A green light flashed. Monica yanked the lever down, and a roaring siren filled the room.

Aaron dropped his hold on her arm and backed away, his eyes wide. He turned and raced toward the door but tripped on Fox's body. He tumbled head-long, and landed face first with a sickening thud. The guard ran forward and tried to help Aaron to his feet.

Monica rushed to Felicia. "Felicia!" She stooped, grabbed her wrists, and hoisted her to her feet.

As the two staggered toward the door, Monica with her shoulder under Felicia's arm, the glass walls around the swirling whirlpool descended, and the water began to rise. In moments, the walls sank into the floor, and more water gushed into the room. Sparks flew from the open hatch, and the ceiling lights flickered, plunging them into darkness before the bulbs spluttered back to life.

Seconds later, water washed over the limp bodies of Fox and the other men, covering them completely. Aaron rose to all fours, shaking water from his dripping hair. He shot to his feet, shoved the guard away and dashed for the door, but the powerful flow kept him away from the stairs.

Monica lurched forward, still supporting Felicia with one arm.

The lukewarm water rose to their knees, but the door was still across the room. They had to pass the growing central vortex that threatened to suck them into the nothingness below.

Aaron waded closer to the exit. The guard stumbled after him but fell beneath the churning froth.

As Felicia strained to take another step, her eyes glazed over. "I don't think I can make it," she whispered.

"Yes, you can! We have to fight this, Felicia. You said your children are worried when you don't come home on time. Think of them now." Monica battled the strengthening current, forcing Felicia forward another two steps. "Think how they would feel if they lost you forever. I know what it's like. I won't let them experience the same pain. We have to keep moving."

The water rose to their hips, drenching their clothes and weighing them down. They fought for each step. The current brushed at the glue on Monica's leg wound, swirling it from her skin, and soon a pink hue tinged the water around her calf.

The guard emerged from beneath the foam a few feet in front of Monica, struggling against the current.

As Monica and Felicia edged close to the halfway point, the whirlpool tugged on their bodies, dragging them toward the spinning, endless loop.

"Come on, Felicia!" Monica yelled. "We can make it. It's only a little farther."

Felicia squared her shoulders and stood straighter. "We can make it," she murmured.

"Oh, my dear little sister." Aaron stood in the stairwell, drenched from head to toe, holding on to the door. "I never thought this day would come, that you would betray me."

Felicia froze halfway across the room.

Monica pulled on her arm. "Don't listen to him; we need to keep moving."

"Aaron, I haven't betrayed anyone." Felicia shook her head.

"I'm securing a better future for my children. One that will be better for us all."

"We don't have time for this!" Monica forced the Noble woman forward three more steps.

The security guard lumbered closer to the exit, his movement creating waves that almost knocked Monica off her feet. "Aaron, don't lock us in!" He knelt in the water and pulled Fox's limp form from beneath the current. "We're on your side. We've never done anything to stop the reign of your empire. We have only helped stabilize it."

"Yes, but I cannot have any witnesses to this. I'll have to make up a suitable story to cover the system's errors. We can't have people losing faith in our ways. Now I will bid you all farewell." He started to close the door. "And don't worry, Felicia, I will make sure your family is well taken care of. If my son can't have control of the north wing when I resign, then the southwest will do."

"No!" Monica screamed. "The computers are dead. The ones below ground, too! The access doors were open. The flood had to have shorted them out!"

Aaron shook his head. "They will be repaired. Once the water has drained and your bodies are carried away and incinerated, we will bring the computers back to life."

"Aaron, you're my brother. How can you do this?" Felicia's wail rose above the rushing water.

Aaron closed the door against the raging tide.

The guard dropped Fox's body back into the pool and rushed forward just as the door clicked into place. He pounded on the wood, but it didn't budge.

"No, no!" Felicia covered her face with her hands. "He'll have Elaine and Emerson killed for my crimes. What have I done?"

Monica glanced around the room. The water rose to her chest. Sizzling foam erupted from the computer boxes, and wire strippings floated in the midst of pieces of plastic. She tied her necklace tightly. There had to be a way out. There was always a way out. No matter how dark it was, there would always be a light. Her mother had promised that the God she believed in would come through, but where was the escape?

Monica tugged on Felicia's arm. "Where does the water flow? The whirlpool must go somewhere! Where does it drain?"

The guard continued to pound on the door, his fists and the roar of water drowning out Felicia's muttered reply.

"Where?" Monica allowed the flow to drag them closer to the gurgling pit.

"To some cavern below the palace. I don't know." Felicia stared at the door. Her hair stuck to her face, accenting her thin, angular features. "There's a turbine below that gathers power from the water. It would chop to bits anything that falls down there."

"Not if it's shut off." Monica pointed where the computer access panel had been, though water now rushed over the opening. "Water got inside the lower computers. They'll have shorted out. The turbine will have slowed down, if not shut off completely. It's our only chance."

"I don't understand." Tears streamed down Felicia's face. "I've never been good at being strong and decisive. It's all an act because of Aaron, and now . . ."

"That doesn't matter." Monica dragged the trembling Noble woman toward the pool. "You're just going to have to trust me. You've helped me, and now I'm going to help you. We're going to get through this."

The water rose to their necks.

Treading with one hand, Monica clutched Felicia's fingers with the other. "We're going down the whirlpool!" she shouted.

"What?" Shaking her head, Felicia tried to pull away. "We can't! It's not safe."

"And neither is drowning!" Monica stopped swimming. "Hold your breath!"

The water sucked them downward. They spun in circles, banging against a concrete wall. Something sharp scraped Monica's forearm. She held Felicia's hand as tightly as she could and prayed with all her might.

Water filled Monica's throat and trickled into her lungs. The tearing force of the whirlpool whipped her into a vortex of wet darkness. She held tightly to Felicia's fingers, but the surge tried to rip them from her grasp.

In moments the river swept them to the surface. Monica coughed, and water spewed from her lungs. She forced her aching muscles to tread water while still holding Felicia's hand.

Only a single row of buzzing lights illumined the cavernous ceiling and reflected on the dark water. They flickered on and off, like fireflies blinking in the distance.

The Noble woman's head listed to the side, her mouth and nose still under water.

"Felicia!" Monica drew her limp body closer. "You need to wake up! We made it!"

Felicia remained motionless, floating like a cadaver.

Monica grabbed Felicia under the shoulders and lifted her head above water. "Come on, wake up!" She glanced around. Where was the shore? The water stretched in all directions in a seemingly endless ocean. A sulfurous smell filled the air, and a whirring, splashing noise echoed around the walls.

Monica gulped. Was that the turbine? She paddled with the current, allowing its gentle swirling to guide her battered body along. As she kept Felicia's head above water, her arms ached.

Soon, Monica's feet struck the pool's rocky bottom. She readjusted her grip on Felicia and dragged her forward, fighting the strengthening current. With every step, the splashing noise grew louder, the swishing sound of paddles striking water—an unforgettable sound. A waterwheel spun nearby, hidden by the room's dark shroud.

Monica crawled out of the pool onto a smooth floor. She laid Felicia on the damp tiles. Placing one hand over the other, she pressed on Felicia's chest. The water had to be forced out. Once when a child had wandered too far into a bathing pool, her mother had to press on the girl's chest in the same way until she spat the water out, and she had awakened crying and shaking.

"Come on, Felicia, you can do it." Monica pushed down rhythmically on Felicia's chest. What if she was too late and the water had been in Felicia's lungs too long?

"Breathe!"

Felicia remained motionless, her face deathly pale.

As Monica continued her frantic compressions, words from her mother's journal came to mind. *Do not worry. The Lord protects us.* Monica shook her head. Did that include Felicia?

She sat back on her heels. It was no use. She wrapped her arms around herself, rocking back and forth. Felicia was dead, another victim of a certain wall slave's incompetence. Monica looked up at the dark cavern ceiling. Why did so many people have to die because of her? Had she done something wrong?

Closing her eyes, she let the sounds of the waterwheel and the waves washing against the shore envelop her. If only she knew more about the world, and of this God her mother spoke of. Simon tried to teach her much in a little amount of time, but huge gaps perforated her knowledge. There was so much she didn't know.

A sharp cough cut into her thoughts. She opened her eyes. Could it be?

Felicia coughed again, and water poured from her mouth. Monica turned Felicia onto her side, letting the liquid spill onto the floor.

"Felicia!" Monica whispered a short prayer of thanks.

Felicia opened her eyes and breathed heavily, her gasps scraping in her chest as if she couldn't get enough air.

"Hold on." Monica helped her to a sitting position and slapped her on the back, forcing more water out.

Coughing, Felicia nodded and wiped her mouth with the back of her hand. Her breath rattled less and less as the moments passed. She climbed to her feet, her arms and legs shaking.

Monica caught her hand. "Wait. You should rest. You just drowned!" As she rose, a stab pierced her calf. She hissed in pain. Why did her leg choose now to act up?

"There's no time to wait," Felicia said. "I'm fine, thanks to you. Aaron will have issued emergency protocol already. He'll have total control over the Council. He's already threatened my children. I need to make sure they're safe." She peeled her sweater away and dropped the sodden garment to the floor. "Where are we? I've never seen this room before."

Monica ran a toe over the slick tiles and let her gaze wander from the water to the exit door and over the rocky walls. This room was familiar—the wet tiles, the bars of soap lying around the floor, and the waterwheel. It had to be! "It's the west wing's bathing cavern for the wall slaves." Fiddling with the string at her neck, she nodded. This was where she had left to go to Cillineese. A place she wondered if she would ever see again. "I know how to get back to the palace."

"How do you know this is the wall slaves' cavern? You—" Felicia shook her head. "Of course. You've probably wandered all over the palace without a chip." She pointed at the flashing light above the exit door. "Is that the way we go?"

"Yes. We'll have to hurry. The computers are shut down, but it'll take a while for the wall slaves to realize it, and once they do, there's no way to tell how they'll react. If they see a Noble here . . ." Monica shrugged as she led the way to the door. "Some of them might want revenge."

"What kind of revenge?" Felicia shuffled beside Monica. "And they wouldn't be able to tell I'm a Noble, would they?" She gestured to her bedraggled hair. "I'm sure I look terrible."

Monica hooked her sore fingers under the door, forced it up into the ceiling, and held it there with no trouble. "You don't look terrible. Not by wall slaves' standards. But trust me, they can tell." She nodded to Felicia's dress as she passed through the doorway. "Your clothes, your face, your build. You're a Noble." After stepping out from under the door, she let it slide to the floor again. "A lot of people in the west wing know me, and I don't look quite as much like a Noble as you do." She jogged up a flight of wooden steps, trying to ignore the pain in her leg.

"I've never even seen a wall slave," Felicia murmured. Her shoes made squishing noises on the steps, and they continued climbing another flight of stairs without another word.

When Monica turned down a narrow side passage leading into the wall slaves' halls through the palace, Felicia stopped. "Where are you going? That crack in the wall can't possibly go anywhere."

Monica turned to look at her. "We have to."

"You *lived* here?" Felicia's pale, wet face glimmered in the overhead lights. She hugged herself. "The halls are so narrow and dark. It's hard to imagine that just outside—"

"We don't have time for this." Monica grabbed Felicia's arm and pulled her down the side corridor. "Do you want to save your children or not? And the wall slaves do live here." She turned down another passage, heading deeper into the palace. "I've always wanted to make a Noble come here to see what it's like, but right now it's too inconvenient to give you a full tour."

"I'm sorry. It's a lot to take in."

"It's okay. I felt the same way coming into your world." Monica stopped by an access panel. Swinging the door open, she beckoned for Felicia to go first.

Felicia grimaced and shuffled through on hands and knees. "I never thought I'd do anything like this."

"Me either." Monica crawled after her. As soon as she cleared the entryway, she sprang to her feet and glanced around. A simple parlor spread out in front of them. A few couches and tables stood here and there.

"I recognize this place." Felicia grasped Monica's hand, pressing on the scrapes from the computer wires. "I'll lead now."

Monica winced, but kept herself from pulling away. "Okay."

They passed through another vacant room and continued walking down a hall.

Felicia rubbed the back of her neck as they hurried through the corridor.

"Are you sure you're all right?" Monica placed a hand on Felicia's shoulder. "The computer must have hurt you really badly when I cut those wires. I'm sorry."

"I'm fine." Felicia dropped her hand to her side again. "The computer must have thought I was the one cutting wires. It probably zapped every chip in the room, but the others were still . . . asleep?" She shook her head. "What did you do to them, anyway?"

"Aaron had a program that could put people to sleep through their chips. I just used it. They would have been okay, but." Monica gulped. "The water . . ."

Felicia looked down at Monica. "You did what was necessary to end the system. Without the flood you wouldn't have been able to shut down the lower computers. It was the only way."

"Yes, but . . ." Tears filled Monica's eyes despite Felicia's words. Why did things always have to end in death? "I wonder why it didn't work on Fox."

"He might have changed the coding on his chip to block programs from affecting it, but we'll never know for sure, since his body was probably washed away with the flood."

They hurried down a few empty hallways until they came to a large double door where a sign above the exit read *Southwest Wing*.

Felicia pushed the door open. "Welcome to my home, Sierra."

She guided Monica into the dark corridor. As soon as Felicia's shoes touched the polished marble floors, chandeliers lit up above their heads, illuminating the gleaming paintings and curtains. The lights shone brightly for a few seconds before flickering on and off, just like the lights had done in every other room.

"It's not much farther to my rooms," Felicia whispered. "I just hope Aaron hasn't gotten there first. The computer malfunction will have distracted him."

As the pain in her leg grew with every step, Monica struggled to keep up. She had to continue. This journey would end soon enough, and she would be free. Thanks to the flood, no one else would ever have to worry about the computers or Aaron's threats ever again.

"Here we are." Felicia threw open another set of double doors into a wide living area.

Monica stepped onto the white carpet and ran a hand along the back of one of the four couches in the room's center. "Where are your children?"

Shaking her head, Felicia ran to one of the three doors off of the living room. "I don't know. They should be close by." She turned the doorknob. "Elaine?" Her face pale, she reentered the room and rushed to a second door, flinging it open. "Emerson?"

Monica hurried to her side as fast as her injured leg would allow. "They're gone?"

"They're not in their rooms." Felicia opened a third door, revealing a room with stark white walls and a large four-poster bed in the center but no children anywhere in sight. "Or mine, either."

"We should head back to the north wing, then." Monica clasped Felicia's shoulder. "The computers are down. Remember that. He can't terminate them."

"Of course." Felicia whirled around and charged back toward the door they had entered. "If he harms them in any way . . ." Clenching her teeth, she held the door open. "Let's go."

CHAPTER 40

Monica trotted behind Felicia's firm, determined steps. They passed through a central corridor in the north wing. Nobles of all ages ran through the halls, bundles in their arms, as if preparing to flee somewhere.

One man almost ran into Monica, but she ducked out of the way at the last second. As they crossed through the corridors, she pressed close to Felicia, using her as a shield. Where did these Nobles think they would go? If they ran into the city, the peasants might kill them, intoxicated by their freedom.

Felicia took Monica's hand. "It'll be all right. Humanity has gotten through a lot worse than this." She met Monica's gaze for a second, a worried look in her eyes. "At least Aaron will have more to think about than my children. After seeing this . . ." She pulled Monica out of the way of a man carrying a large bundle of canned foods. "I know he has a lot more on his mind than punishing me."

"Monica!" Tresa's voice issued through the crowd.

Monica craned her neck to see over the bustling people, but everyone was too tall. "Tresa!"

Frowning, Felicia looked down at her. "Monica? But I thought your name—"

"No time to explain." Monica rushed ahead, pulling Felicia along by one hand. "Tresa! Over here!"

Tresa appeared in the middle of a sea of scurrying people. "You're alive!" She engulfed Monica in a hug. "When the computers went down and the ground floor flooded, I feared the worst." Pushing Monica away, she frowned. "You've got blood all over you." She froze, her eyes wide. "Madam Felicia!"

"Don't worry." Monica pulled Felicia forward and joined the Noble woman's and the Seen's hands together, her fingers leaving red prints on their knuckles. "You two are equals now whether you like it or not."

Felicia smiled. "Tresa, are your sister's children alright?"

Nodding slowly, Tresa smiled. "Yes . . . Madam—"

Monica glared at her.

"Yes"—Tresa shuddered—"Felicia. I left them in the Seen dorms. It's too dangerous down here for children."

"I know." Felicia's shoulders drooped. "And I have no idea where my own are. Aaron—"

"A girl and a little boy?" Tresa pointed down the hall. "Aaron was taking them to the Council chamber, but . . ." She grinned. "Garth and Siren, two Seen men, detained him. He's tied up in the schoolroom now."

Felicia let out a long sigh. "Thank you. Where are my children? Are they all right?"

"They're fine. They're in the schoolroom as well." Tresa grabbed Monica's wrist. "And I see you need your hands bandaged again." She guided them down the hall. "A messenger says Simon is on his way with Jonas and Alfred. They'll be here any minute."

Monica allowed Tresa to steer them through the mass of people. Simon was coming? So soon? Tresa must have managed to get a message to him quickly. The tunnel bugs were probably still running.

They pushed through the crowd into the empty hallway leading to the Council chambers. Tresa opened the main schoolroom door and beckoned for them to enter. "Come. The children are waiting."

After Tresa stepped into the room, Monica followed and glanced around. Aaron and Aric sat gagged and tied to chairs. A large man sat at the table, staring at them as if daring them to move. Two children huddled in the corner. One, a little boy, lay asleep on the floor, but the second, a girl about seven years old, sat beside him, frowning and looking around, as if trying to ward off any danger with her glare.

"Elaine!" Felicia called.

The girl jumped to her feet and held her arms out. "Momma!"

Hugging her close, Felicia murmured, "Are you all right?"

Tears welled in Monica's eyes. This was a scene she would never experience, at least not from a welcome party that included Simon.

"Are you okay?" Tresa wrapped an arm around Monica's shoulders. "Simon will be here soon. I believe he has some things to talk about with you."

"I'm fine." Monica shrugged. "Has anyone gone down to the computer room?"

"Yes, Trig—a Seen—went down there soon after all the wristbands stopped working and the locks on the doors went crazy, flashing all different colors." Tresa smiled. "He was the only one brave enough to investigate. Everything is shut down. He found empty metal boxes and some sort of hatch leading beneath the floor, but nothing was running."

Monica exhaled, a wave of relief washing over her. Then the water did shut off the lower computers. "Good."

Tresa tapped the back of her neck. "We're finally free, thanks to you. There's no more buzzing, no more signals telling us where to go."

Felicia walked over, carrying the little boy on her hip. His head rested on her shoulder, his thumb in his mouth. The girl clung to the hem of her skirt, staring wide-eyed. "You never explained why you have three names now—Amelia, Sierra, Monica."

Monica grimaced. "It's a long story."

"We have time." Tresa motioned to the extra seats around the table. "It will be at least a few minutes before Simon arrives."

Aaron glared at Monica, and she backed up a step. "I'll stand, thanks." As her foot hit the ground her leg ached, forcing her to wince.

Tresa grabbed Monica's elbow. "Are you sure you're all right? Is it your leg?"

"Yes." Monica glanced down at her calf. Drops of blood issued from around the black stitches keeping the incision together. "It's holding out okay, though. We can take care of it after Simon gets here."

"If you're sure." Tresa put her hands on her hips. "Then I'll respect your wishes."

Monica nodded. "I'm sure."

Felicia sank into one of the chairs and shifted her son to her lap. Elaine leaned against her mother's side. Felicia glanced at her brother and turned back to Monica. "Who is Simon? I'm rather confused about some things."

"Simon is my teacher in Cillineese. He helped get me ready for my role as Amelia. I'm actually her cousin. My parents, Joel and Rose, the last rulers of Cillineese, named me Sierra, but when—" Monica bit her lip. "When the city was terminated, my father managed to arrange for my escape, and a wall slave couple in Cantral took me in as their own. My name was changed to Monica to try to keep me safe."

Tresa wrapped an arm around Monica's shoulders again.

"You've been very brave, and we can't ever thank you enough for what you've done for us."

Felicia shook her head. "No, we can't."

Shrugging, Monica looked down at her scraped hands. "What else could I do? Simon—"

"Did I hear my name?" The door banged open, and Simon strode into the room. "Well, Monica." He looked her up and down, a hint of a suppressed grin on his face. "Looking bloodied and bedraggled as usual."

Tresa edged to the open door. "I'll be back in a moment. I need to see Jonas and Alfred." She stepped outside and shut the door behind her.

"Well, then." Simon turned to Aric and Aaron. "It seems you all have everything well in hand."

"I did what you asked. I shut down the computers." Monica held out her bloodied arms and hands. "It's finished, right? I can go and live in Cillineese?"

"Hmm." Simon shook his head slowly. "You didn't read those journal pages I sent, did you?"

Monica drooped her shoulders. This was it. Another assignment, but what could be left? The computers were gone. With the help of the freed slaves, it would be easy to make sure the computers weren't put back into working order. "I read one, but I didn't have time to read but a little bit of the other, and I . . . I lost the pages in the flood."

"Always losing things, aren't you?" Simon shook his head. "It's a good thing I know you so well, my dear." He pulled some folded pages from his pants pocket and handed them to her. "The last few pages, all translated for your perusal."

"Thank you." She started to tuck them into her pocket, but when her fingers met her dress's wet fabric, she stopped. The pages would get ruined if she put them there.

"When I said for your perusal," Simon said, "I meant now. It's rather urgent."

"How can something my mother wrote twelve years ago be urgent?" Monica unfolded the papers.

"The importance hinges on recent events." Simon waved a hand. "Feel free to read them in private. I expect that you will react with your typical emotional response."

Monica walked to the corner of the room and sat cross-legged on the floor, aware of Aaron's glare following her. He couldn't do anything to her now. She smoothed the papers out and started to read where she had left off.

May 15, 2857

Today will be my last day in Cillineese, my last day to see you. You're sitting on the floor in front of me with Faye, playing with your new tablet. I wish I could see you write your first words, see you learn to read, and grow into a fine young lady. I've begged your father to think of another plan, for another way, but he's insisted that there is no other.

He says we should be thankful Veronica was able to make these arrangements, especially considering our relationship. I am thankful she's not reported us. She's been kinder to me than I could ever expect, treating me like a real sister instead of what I am.

I will board the boat today, leaving you in the capable hands of your father and your loyal nurse. This diary will be tucked away for you to find at a later date, just as I arranged years ago. I pray that sometime we will meet again, and that you will forgive me for any suffering I've caused you.

Your father is calling, so I will turn this journal over to him to hide where Simon will be able to find it once we are all gone. I shower you with hugs and kisses and pray the Lord spares you as He is sparing me. Perhaps the virus won't be discovered until after your father has completed it and none of this will have been necessary. If that is so we will be together again soon.

Monica reached the end of the page. As she folded it, a lump formed in her throat. She climbed to her feet, her legs shaking. "Simon?"

Simon reclined in the chair across from Aaron and Aric, his hands folded on his chest. "So you've finished reading?"

"I have." She extended the pages to him. "So my mother . . ." She shook her head. It was too much to take in. How could this be? Her mother died twelve years ago.

"Rose is alive." Simon stood and pointed at Aaron. "Don't try to go anywhere." He put a hand on Monica's shoulder and guided her toward the exit. "As I've just recently learned, alive and well."

Monica stopped in the doorway. "How? Why?"

"She's living in Eursia. Your father and Veronica made the arrangement years ago to save her life. There was no way for her to return once she left, but your father preferred she leave and never come back than to die because of his decision. He saved you both, the only way he could." Simon patted her shoulder. "He would be proud of you. You've accomplished everything he ever dreamed of, my dear. Your mother will be proud as well. You've fought long and hard and have finished the race." He took her hands in his. "You deserve a rest, but . . ."

"But . . ." Monica pulled away and caressed the translated pages. "I need to find my mother."

"Correct. I see that your emotions are working in tandem with sound logic."

"And all this time I thought she was dead." She tried to steady her voice. "How do you know she's in Eursia?"

Simon tapped the side of his head. "We Seen are good spies, my dear. You might have heard of Tyrell?"

"Yes." Monica flinched, remembering the flood of water gushing into the room, streaming over the unconscious Nobles, Nobles she had knocked out. "I think he drowned in the computer room. It . . . I . . ." She shook her head. How to explain the terror of those moments, the hopelessness of the situation?

"Ah. That's unfortunate." Simon nodded. "He was an emissary from Eursia. They've been trying to split away from Cantral's grasp, to replace its authority with their own. He came here with a security member named Fox under the guise of problems in their system, but they were here to retrieve some codes to break free of Cantral." He shook his head. "Eursia's computers have indeed had trouble with viruses tormenting their functions. Some of their cities are in ruins. They suspected Cantral of the deed, and Cantral suspected them. Messy business, politics. I, for one, suspect someone else entirely. The Eursians forced Seen to spy for them here in the palace, even reprogramming their work schedules, but I doubt they found much to prove Cantral's guilt. In any case, the only way to set all this nonsense to rest is to destroy the remaining computers in Eursia."

"But . . ." Monica's heart skipped a beat.

"I know." Simon held up a hand. "It is too much to ask. You've done your duty to the people. Now that the networks are down, others may travel freely from city to city, and the task of disabling each individual city's computer can be passed on to another. I understand."

"No. I'm going to finish this once and for all, and I'm going to find my mother." Monica firmed her jaw. "I will go to Eursia."

Simon grinned, showing his crooked teeth. "That's exactly what I wanted to hear."

"Monica!" Alfred ran down the hall, followed by Jonas and Tresa. He held up Vinnie in his open palms. "I found Vinnie in your room. He was really thirsty."

Monica let the rat crawl onto her shoulder. "Thanks, Alfred."

Tresa made a tsking noise with her tongue. "No more adventures for you, young lady, not for another week at least. Let's get those hands bandaged. And your other needs tended." She pointed at the giant bruise on Monica's elbow, revealed by a long tear in her sleeve. The bandage holding the joint steady must have ripped away in the torrent of water. "And what happened to your arm?"

"It's nothing, Tresa—just a bruise." Monica shook her head. "Do you still have my mother's diary? I think I might need it in the next few weeks. She might like to have it back."

Fishing the small book out of her pocket, Tresa nodded. "It's here." She held it out. "You might also like to know that Ahla's baby was born fine and healthy. She decided to name her Amelia. I suggested a more suitable name, but it's her child, so it's her decision."

"I'm so glad she's all right." Monica caressed the diary with trembling hands. "I think it's the perfect name for her. Amelia deserves a memorial of some kind."

Tresa nodded. "We can arrange to have her reburied back in Cillineese so her father and sister can know where she is."

"We'll have a proper ceremony!" Simon raised a finger. "I could officiate. I've read up on dozens of different types. I would know just what to do."

Monica smiled and shook her head. "We'll do whatever her family wants. It's up to them."

Felicia emerged from the schoolroom, still holding her son on her hip. She guided Elaine forward with her free hand. "Thank you, Sierra. I don't know if we can ever repay the debt we owe you, but I will do my best. If there's anything you need . . ."

Tresa stepped forward and took Monica's hand. "What she needs is the infirmary and to stop hurting herself."

"I might take you up on that anything-you-need offer." Simon pointed at himself. "After all, I was the mastermind behind this whole plan. At the very least, I think my own computer tablet is in order. A man like me will be able to find ways to use it for the good of all."

Smiling, Monica shook her head. "Thank you, Felicia, but seeing the slaves' freedom is enough payment. I need no other."

After arranging another meeting with Simon and saying good-bye to him and the others, she allowed Tresa, the Seen—no, the free woman, to lead her to the infirmary. There was still work to do, but she would be happy to do it, to find her mother, and to make sure the Nobles never took power again, no matter how long it took.